may be kept

CONSIDER THE SEASON

CONSIDER
THE SEASON

Reuben Merliss

DOUBLEDAY & COMPANY, INC.

GARDEN CITY, NEW YORK

1968

All of the characters in this book
are fictitious, and any resemblance
to actual persons, living or dead,
is purely coincidental.

Library of Congress Catalog Card Number 68-22610
Copyright © 1968 by Reuben Merliss
All Rights Reserved
Printed in the United States of America

29.998

For Leslie and Melissa

CONSIDER THE SEASON

Whoever wishes to investigate
medicine properly, let him first
consider the season of the year.

Hippocrates Prognostics

One

DAN FOUND Wolfe's Pharmacy on a corner next to a market. The plate-glass windows needed washing, and the displays were dusty. He went in and the druggist looked up from a newspaper. "Yes?"

"I'm McDermott. I called you about the job."

"So soon? I barely hung up the phone." He had a Jewish intonation.

"I came right from the bus station."

Wolfe was small and had a nervous trick of chewing on his mustache. He tore a piece of wrapping paper from the roll. "What's your name again?"

"Daniel McDermott."

"Mic? Mac? I always get mixed up."

"Mc. M–C. It doesn't make any difference."

"I'm Max Wolfe." They shook hands. "Are you registered?"

Dan handed him the letter from the Pharmacy Board. Wolfe read it. "So what did you come down here for?"

"I'm going to medical school."

Wolfe waved a sad hand, and walked to the soda fountain and filled a glass with carbonated water. "I wanted to go there too, when I was your age, but my father was sick and I had to work."

Dan sat down at one of the fountain stools.

"It's for a night job," Wolfe said. "To tell you the truth there's not much doing here at night. I'd close up at six, but

I don't want to lose prescription customers." He leaned back. "Do you mind working alone at night?"

"Why should I mind?"

"Maybe you're afraid of holdups."

Dan looked at the shabby store. "Do you get held up very often?"

"Once. I just handed them the money. No arguing. You do the same thing if you're working for me."

"You close the lunch counter at night?"

Wolfe nodded. "We got a girl to take care of it days, but she goes home at five-thirty and locks it up. All you'll have to do is take care of trade."

"No problem then."

A customer came in. Wolfe said, "Go make yourself something. Go ahead," and he walked away.

Dan suddenly remembered that he had not eaten since the bus left San Francisco early that morning. He put a milk shake on the machine, and was distressed by the old, dried rings on the Formica. He found a wet rag and wiped the counter clean. He drank the cold sweet drink slowly. His stomach was still tight and uneasy, and he didn't want to throw it up. Across from him in the mirror his own reflection, a blond, quiet-faced young man, sipped thoughtfully at a straw.

Wolfe came back. "I have a rheumatic heart. A couple of months ago I had pericarditis. You know what that is?"

Dan shook his head.

"I thought you might, you going to medical school. I was in the hospital for six weeks. I had to get some help in a hurry for the store so I had this fellow working for me part of the time, my wife part of the time. It's a lucky thing the Pharmacy Board didn't check up." He rubbed his hands together. "Well? What did you make up north?"

"Five dollars an hour. If you don't care about my studying I'll work for less."

"How much less?"

"Depends on how many hours."

They bargained and settled on four dollars an hour, Wolfe

deciding with the concession in salary he could afford to take off every evening and Sunday. He seemed pleased, and he said, "If it's okay with my wife, you start tomorrow."

They waited and about eight o'clock a very pretty young woman walked in. She was slim-faced, with high cheekbones, her dark hair combed straight back. Dan had seen ancient Cretan vases in the Golden Gate Museum on which were painted faces that looked like hers.

Max said, "Hello, honey," and kissed her on the cheek. "We're waiting for you. This is a fellow who answered the ad. He's from up north."

The girl shrugged her small shoulders. "I'm doing the hiring now too?"

"All right. You're hired," Max said. "It's a good thing too. You're the only one that showed up." He turned to his wife. "He's starting medical school."

The girl looked up with interest. "Where?"

Dan told her.

"I've got a cousin who's a psychiatrist in San Diego."

A customer came in and Max left to wait on him.

"What made you decide to study to be a doctor?" she asked.

He was hunting in his pocket for a dime. "I liked science," he said.

"Would you like to come to dinner? You'll be lonely down here."

"I don't get lonely," he said, still searching.

"Do you have any friends in Los Angeles?"

He shook his head. "Can I use the phone?"

"There's just the booth. Max doesn't believe in prescription-room phones."

He went to the booth and looked up the only Edward McDermott listed. He had called the number from the bus station several hours before when he first came in to Los Angeles but there had been no answer. He dialed it again, his hand trembling foolishly. At about the fourth ring a woman's voice answered.

"Is Mr. Edward McDermott there?" he said.

"Eddie? Sure. Just a minute. . . . Eddie."

Perhaps his father had remarried. Perhaps the woman who was answering was his stepmother. She sounded young, a suggestion of Kentucky or Missouri in her accent.

He heard the receiver being set down. After a minute a man's voice came on. "Yes?"

"Hello? Mr. Edward McDermott?"

"Yes?"

"This is Dan."

"Who?"

"Dan."

"Dan who?"

It was worse than he thought it would be. He finally said, "Dan McDermott."

There was a pause on the other end. "I don't know any Dan McDermott. Are we supposed to be relatives or something?"

He was beginning to realize that this voice was too young to be his father's. "I was looking for an Edward McDermott," he said. "I'm his son."

"Wrong Eddie McDermott," the voice said cheerfully. "There's another Eddie McDermott around. He works for Fidelity Insurance. I get his mail once in a while. Maybe that's the one you want."

"He works for Fidelity?"

"Last I heard," the man said. "Over on Wilshire. I get his mail every so often, and I bet he gets some of mine too."

"Sure," Dan said. "Sorry to bother you."

"Forget it. Good-bye," the man said and hung up.

Dan felt cheerful when he got out of the booth. There had been a man here all these years, and not a tombstone.

His mother had hated Eddie. Most of the time she wouldn't talk about him, but sometimes when she raged at Dan she would shout at him that he was just like his father. No feelings. No heart. Just a stone in his chest. When Dan got older he tried several times to talk to her about Eddie. "He ruined my life," she had said once, "but I'm sorry for him. He'll die alone. Nobody'll care. You'll see."

Max was writing in the order book. Sharon sat at the counter reading a magazine.

"What time tomorrow, boss?"

Max looked up and grinned. "He hasn't even been paid yet and he's already calling me boss. Six o'clock?"

"Fine."

"Sharp. Sharon always complains if I'm late for dinner."

"Where's a good place around here to look for an apartment?"

"Depends on what you want to spend."

"Not very much."

"Try Orchid or Wentworth. The next two streets down. Lots of older buildings there."

"Thanks. Good night," Dan said. "Good night, Mrs. Wolfe."

Sharon looked up from her magazine. "Good night," she said.

He took a five-dollar room in one of the hotels close to the bus station. All night long he heard the floorboards groaning and the noise of men coughing and spitting. He finally fell asleep when it was light, but even then he slept poorly, and awoke many times, not knowing for sure what had awakened him.

In the morning while it was still gray he gathered his shaving utensils and walked to the bathroom at the end of the hall. He thought if he could wash and get out quickly he might escape, but the morning sadness came on him with his face lathered. His heart began pounding and he sweated in panic. He waited, the razor in his hand, the lather drying on his face. Someone rattled the door knob and then irrationally the despondency lightened and he was able to scrape his face clean and escape.

He looked for a room near the store as Max Wolfe had suggested. On Orchid Street, two blocks off Melrose, he found an old brick apartment house. It looked shabby and inexpensive. The carpeting in the hall was stained and had bald patches. He rang the bell at the manager's apartment. The man who came to the door was middle-aged, with curly gray-blond hair.

"You have a vacancy sign," Dan said.

"An early bird, aren't you?" His voice was high-pitched and feminine.

"I have to be at school in an hour."

"Are you looking for a single or a bachelor?"

"How much?"

"We can talk better inside." He opened the door wider and Dan went in.

"I'm Goldie Lechinski," he said and held out his hand. "You got me right in the middle of breakfast." Dan was surprised at the luxury of the manager's apartment. It had white-wool carpeting and a curved modern sofa.

Lechinski sat down to a plate of ham and eggs. "Have you eaten yet? How about some coffee?"

"No time."

Lechinski started eating. "That single has a little kitchen, stove, and a small refrigerator," he said.

"How much?"

"Week or month?"

"Month."

"Then it's sixty dollars."

"For a single?"

The manager shrugged. "In the apartment house up the street they're getting ninety. We just haven't raised our rents yet."

After a moment Dan said, "Is it all right if I pay you just for the first week now?"

"Do you have a job?"

Dan gave him Max Wolfe's name, and the store address, and he wrote it down. "You have any blankets?"

Dan shook his head.

"I can let you have a few."

Dan put fifteen dollars down on the table.

"You want to see it?"

"Later," Dan said.

"Married?"

Dan shook his head.

"Free and easy," the manager said. He went to a board that was nailed to the kitchen wall and picked out a key. "There you are. Seventeen, on the second floor. Don't be a stranger."

The first class of the day was anatomy. The elevator was out of order and Dan climbed four floors to the laboratory and found himself among sixty other students waiting in the hall. They were to work in pairs for the year. Almost all the students had already chosen their partners and at eight they simply lined up to register their names. The remaining handful of boys stood in the hall uneasily, looking each other over. They began talking quietly among themselves until finally pair by pair they also joined together and went out to file their names.

It occurred to Dan there might be an uneven number in the class, and the last student would then be assigned a cadaver to himself. A very dark Negro boy had been watching him a few minutes. He finally walked up. "You teamed up?"

"No."

"Me neither," he said and waited. He was plump and wore old-fashioned spectacles with round lenses and gold rims.

Dan walked away and sat down in a chair. The Negro student hesitated and then went into the instructor's office. In a few minutes he came back out and said, "We're partners. Tank thirty-two."

"How many students are there?"

"Tough luck, friend. It's an even number."

Dan went into the office and signed his name. "Your partner's Oney Noble," the instructor said and made an entry into the book.

The dissecting room smelled of carbolic acid and formaldehyde. Dan found Noble waiting at the tank numbered thirty-two. He was thumbing through a manual. Dan set his books on the rack and took one of the stools.

As the organization of the class proceeded, Dan asked, "You from around here?"

"From Chicago," Noble said. He reached over and took the

anatomy text Dan had just purchased at the bookstore, and started reading it. Dan noticed he didn't have one of his own.

The laboratory was long and narrow, with twenty double rows of tanks. Dan wondered how the school got the cadavers. Most likely unclaimed bodies, he decided. In this particular large and unfriendly town unclaimed bodies were probably fairly plentiful, he thought.

At nine they got their instructions from the professor. Dan and Noble opened the lid of the tank, pressed the levers at the ends, and their cadaver rose dripping out of the formaldehyde.

Apart from his mother this was the first dead body Dan had ever seen. He didn't look at the face. He set up the manual on the rack and took out his dissecting instruments. He opened the skin on the arm and started searching for its veins, referring back to the manual from time to time so he could identify each vein by its proper Latin name.

Dan finally got a full look at the cadaver. It was the body of a strong young man. "What do you think he died of?" he asked.

Noble shook his head.

Dan turned and looked over the other thirty-one cadavers. Almost all were in the final stages of emaciation, the ribs standing out boldly on the chests, but their own cadaver seemed to have died in the midst of good health.

A buzzer sounded suddenly, signaling noon, and Dan wiped his instruments and folded the skin over his dissection. Noble took off his glasses and carefully wiped away small flecks of fat.

Dan phoned Fidelity Insurance from a booth on the first floor. The call went right through.

"Edward McDermott?" he asked.

"Yes," said the voice. It was hard to make much out of that voice.

"I'm Dan."

"Dan?"

"Yes." He was anxious to get it over with. "I've just come down from San Francisco. I'm going to school here."

"Just came in?"

"I couldn't get your home phone number."

"Wait a minute. There's too much racket in this room," the voice said. "I'll get this on another line." The line clicked off and then on again. "Who is this again?"

"Dan," Dan said. "Daniel McDermott." It was exquisite torture and he wished he hadn't called. Just knowing his father was still alive might have been enough.

"Let's get this straight," McDermott said. "Is this Helen's boy?"

He was angry by then, and he said, "You do remember her, don't you?"

McDermott was quiet for a while. Then he said, "I live at the St. Regis Hotel. That's why you couldn't find my number. How's your mother?"

Dan didn't answer.

"Are you still there?" McDermott said.

"Do you want to get together for lunch? I have an hour."

"You know where this place is?"

"I'll get it from the phone book."

"Be here about five. I'm done then."

"Five?" He had to start work at six. Finally he said, "I think I can leave a little early. I'll see you then." When he hung up the sweat was running in tickling streams under his shirt. He dialed the drugstore and told Max he'd be late to work.

The Fidelity Insurance Building was a modern one-story glass and brick structure. He got there a few minutes after five and waited, the knot of uneasiness back in his stomach. He knew he would be able to handle himself if his father was cold or nasty. His fear was that his father might be friendly or even show affection or regret, and then he might not handle himself at all well.

He stood in front of the building wondering what his father would look like and worrying that he wouldn't recognize him.

People were beginning to come out. First two young girls talking together, one of them searching in her purse for something. Likely car keys. Then several men, all much too young, followed by an older man, looking tired and hot. Dan's heart started beating strongly, but the older man stopped only long enough to find his car key in his pocket, and then went on up the street. By then people were walking out five or six abreast. Dan became fearful that his father might think that he had left, and he stood in the street squarely in front of the doorway.

About half-past five a slight man in a neat gray suit walked out of the building, and Dan thought, Jesus, this is my father. He started to tremble again, and walked up to him.

"Eddie McDermott," the older man said. He made no effort to say anything further and Dan awkwardly held out his hand.

McDermott said, "There's a place down the street where we can cool off." He started walking briskly down Wilshire, and Dan fell in beside him. They passed a bar on the corner, and went on a half block farther to a second bar, which advertised charcoal-broiled steaks. Inside there were booths along the wall. McDermott sat down and Dan slipped in across from him.

"How long have you been here?" McDermott asked.

"Since yesterday."

"Any particular reason for coming down?"

"I started medical school today."

The bartender came up. "A double shot of Old Crow," McDermott said.

"On the rocks?"

"That's it."

The bartender looked at Dan. "Just beer," Dan said.

"Bring him some Budweiser." The bartender left and McDermott asked, "Which school?"

Dan told him.

"I've got a nephew that went to medical school at Berkeley."

"I didn't apply there."

Eddie McDermott's hair was thin and gray and carefully

combed across a bald spot. He said, "It's a hell of an expensive course. How are you going to make it?"

"I have a job at Wolfe's drugstore."

"You look like your mother. How is she?"

"She died last year."

"Died?" He thought a moment. "Let's see. She would be about fifty or so."

"Forty-seven."

The bartender brought the beer and the whiskey and set them down.

"What happened to her?"

"Change of life, I suppose. She took an overdose of pills."

He shook his head. After a while he said, "Where's she buried?"

"What difference does that make? She was cremated. She always wanted to be cremated."

"She leave anything?"

"Enough to pay for my first semester's tuition."

"Committed suicide, eh?"

"On Christmas Eve."

"I guess you think in some way I'm responsible."

"No," Dan said. "I am."

They were quiet a few moments. Water gurgled as the bartender rinsed glasses.

"Who found her?"

"I did. A day too late."

McDermott shook his head again.

"I was the only one at the funeral. No flowers. No rabbi. She didn't believe in it."

"How do you figure you're responsible?"

"I know what happened."

"She never had what you'd call a stable life."

"You didn't help."

McDermott looked at him without answering.

"It doesn't make a woman stable when you get her pregnant and run off and leave her."

"Why did you come down here? There are good schools up north."

"I got the idea I wanted to find my father."

"That might be a little harder than you figured. You first have to find out who your father is."

It was icy cold, and Dan felt relieved. His mother was right. He got up and put a dollar on the table. "My end of the drinks," he said and left.

Dan got to his job only about fifteen minutes late. Max was waiting with his hat and jacket on.

"Sharon made some plans for dinner," he said. "Don't forget to put the grill on the door before you leave. You know how to set the burglar alarm?"

Dan shook his head, and Max showed him the spot behind the front door where the connection had to be made. "Sharon'll be in later if you need some help." He hesitated. "You short of money?"

"I've got enough until payday anyway."

"Don't close before midnight. You always get a few late customers." He waved and went out the door.

Dan went into the tiny prescription room, took off his street jacket and put on the tan pharmacist's jacket.

Prescription rooms had always fascinated him. They were filled with bottles of drugs that bore odd English and strange Latin names, old drugs that had also been used by Egyptian and Greek physicians and new drugs with intricate chemical formulas on their labels. Some smelled antiseptic, some musty, some piercing, and some pleasant and clean. A small bottle of tincture of myrrh was standing too close to the edge of the shelf and he pushed it back. He saw tincture of belladonna, fluid extract of cotton root bark, extract of licorice and oil of mustard. The bottles were crowded one against the other. He started to empty the overcrowded shelf when the gleam of silver caught his eye. On the corner of the prescription table was a twenty-dollar bill on which were pyramided two quarters and a dime. He pushed the money back so that no one could reach it from the outside. Then he took a towel, dampened it with warm water, and set about scrubbing the stained and dusty bottles. Later he wiped the shelves and served an occasional customer.

About eight Sharon came in. "For the first couple of days Max wanted me to help out," she explained.

"I could use some scouring powder," Dan said. She showed him where it was kept, and then stood watching as he worked.

"Max coming back later?" he asked.

She shook her head. "I put him to bed. He's sort of a hypochondriac." She watched him a while longer. "Do you mind if I ask you a question?"

"Go ahead," he said uneasily.

"Did Max say anything to you about me?"

"No. Nothing."

"He's always talking about me. Even with strangers sometimes."

"He just showed me how to close up."

"It's embarrassing," she said.

He was wiping the prescription counter top and she followed him. "If he knew I was talking to you, he'd have it all figured out we were going to bed together. That's the kind of a mind he's got."

A customer came into the store and tapped his quarter on the glass of the cigarette counter.

When Dan came back Sharon was sitting on one of the stools, eating ice cream. "I need to put on some weight," she said. "I only weigh a hundred and one. I can eat and eat and I don't gain. My girl friend says I'm lucky. I can eat all I want. But I get tired if I get too thin. I take vitamins most of the time." She kept talking and Dan listened sometimes and didn't at other times and finally after about an hour she went home. The store was empty for the moment and he went to the bathroom. He was surprised to see another twenty-dollar bill and a stack of change on the window sill. He remembered the pile of money in the prescription room and he realized that Max had set those small caches about to test his honesty. He carefully counted the money. Then he reached into his pocket, found a loose half dollar there, and added it to the pile.

The phone in the booth rang, and he answered it. "Yes?" he said.

"Wolfe's Pharmacy?"

"Yes."

"Who's this?"

"The pharmacist."

"Dan?" The voice was Eddie McDermott's.

"How did you get my number?"

"You told me where you're working. How's it going?" His voice sounded thick, as though he had been drinking.

"I just started."

"What did you run off for?"

"I had to get to work by six."

"You're a hard kid to talk to," Eddie said. "When you flipped off like that I thought I was talking to your mother again." He was quiet a moment. "Why did she kill herself?"

"I don't want to tell it again."

"You didn't tell it in the first place," Eddie said. Then, after a moment, "I'm good for a dinner once in a while. Just call me."

"Thanks," Dan said. Eddie waited and Dan hung up the live receiver.

He locked the store and walked home. The sea breeze was back, chilled with the ocean cold. He became uneasy before he got to the room. He opened the door and flicked on the light. The room was a musty box, with embossed green wallpaper and stained carpeting. He switched the light off quickly. He was prepared for the other things but he wasn't prepared for that dismal room. He walked to the window and looked at the backyard of an identical apartment house. Finally he turned on the light again, and opened the Cunningham *Anatomy* text. But the room, even from the periphery of his vision, was still too dismal, and his mind wandered and he was distraught and unhappy. He remembered seeing a restaurant on the corner of Orchid and Melrose, and he put the book under his arm and went out. The restaurant was called Hoagy's, the name in bright neon tubing.

He sat down at the end of a long counter.

"How late are you open?" he asked the waitress.

"Two on weekdays," she said. "All night Saturday." She was red-headed and pretty.

He nodded and ordered a hamburger and started reading the text, beginning the section on bones. He stopped occasionally to munch on the cold hamburger or to sip on his coffee. He ordered a fresh cup whenever the waitress came, and after a while she left him alone. He read until two, excited with the remarkable things he was learning. When he got back to his room he slipped into bed without turning on the light.

Even then he couldn't sleep. First one leg started itching and then the other. He got up and flicked on the single yellow bulb. A flea jumped from his ankle, leaving a red welt behind. He found more fleas in the mattress, hopping away from the light. He pulled his pants on angrily and shoved his feet into his shoes. He tugged the mattress off the bed and carried it on his back down the stairs. He dumped it in the hall before Goldie Lechinski's apartment and pushed the doorbell hard, holding it down. Goldie came to the door in a flowered bathrobe. His teeth were out, and his mouth looked strange. He covered it with his hand and mumbled, "What's wrong?"

"My mattress is lousy with fleas."

"Why did you bring it down here? Put some kerosene on it."

"You can put some kerosene on it," Dan said. He picked the mattress up, pushed past Goldie, and dropped it on his living-room floor. "Don't forget to get the parts where the springs come out."

"Wait a minute," Goldie said.

"Wait, hell," Dan said. He saw twin beds in Goldie's bedroom and went in, lifted the heavy brocaded spread from one, dropped it on the floor, and picked up the mattress. "You can have this one back when you delouse the other one." He carried it upstairs. He tossed it on his bed, and lay down on it. He fell asleep, still in his pants.

During the next few days Dan was busy beating a path for himself in the unfamiliar town. In the morning he was up by six-thirty and was at school before eight. By six he was at the store, closing at midnight, reading for several hours at Hoagy's, and finally going to bed in his room without turning the lights on. The morning sadness continued to trouble him. It eased off somewhat once school was well started, but still each morning when he shaved his hand trembled and he sweated until he was done. Yet he wasn't disappointed. Apart from the room it was going the way he thought it would go, and he needed nothing more except perhaps a girl and even that could wait.

After he had been in Los Angeles about a week he came home at night to find a tightly wrapped package outside his door. Eddie McDermott's name and address were in the upper right corner. He carried it into the room and after a moment's hesitation decided to turn on the light. The package held a white-wool sweater, and the card with it said *Best of luck down here, Eddie.*

It was a good sweater and the first gift he had had in several years. He examined it and the card with the small precise handwriting and suddenly for no reason he knew he started crying. He became furious, and threw the sweater aside. Later after he washed his face he picked it up, folded it, and put it away in a drawer.

A week later Eddie called. "I just want to know if you got that sweater."

Dan was embarrassed. "Yes," he said. "I was going to call."

"All I wanted to know is if it was delivered," Eddie said angrily and hung up.

The job worked out fairly well. Sharon visited the store from time to time. Sometimes she talked to Dan, following him about as he worked. Other times she would take a magazine from the racks and read it in the back, eating a dish of ice cream.

Max had odd kindly streaks. Dan came in one day and found a silver fountain pen in a case on the ledge. He started to put it away when Max said, "Hey, wait. That's for you."

Dan examined the pen.

"Give me that old pen you've got."

Dan took his green pen out and Max threw it into a waste-paper basket. "It leaks so bad I can't read what you write on the order book." He waited. "Go ahead. Try it out."

Dan tried it.

"I got it from a salesman. Less than wholesale," Max said. "Use it in good health."

Several times a week Max would put something aside for Dan to eat. "They've got such good corn beef at Marten's, I got Sharon to get one for you," he would say and stand about and take care of trade until Dan had finished. Sometimes he would save a sweet roll and sometimes hard-boiled eggs left over from his lunch. He watched enviously while Dan salted the white dome of the shelled egg. "Do you know what it tastes like to eat eggs without salt? You're going to be a doctor someday. You should know what your diets taste like. Why don't you eat it without salt?"

Dan came to work on time and stayed to the last moment. When he wanted a pack of cigarettes he made a note on a slip of paper that was kept in the register, and each week when he was paid he put into the register what he owed. About three days after he had started working for Max, he had said, "You owe me fifty cents, boss."

"Fifty cents?"

"The fifty cents I put on that pile of money in the back room."

Max had looked guilty. "Sharon's always leaving money around. I've got to talk to her," he muttered. Then he shrugged and took fifty cents out of the register and laid it down on the counter. "You know the way help is these days," he finally said.

Dan put the coin in his pocket.

"You're not offended?"

"Try a thousand dollars next time."

Max grinned and said, "It made me feel like such a sneak.

And you drove me crazy trying to figure out that half buck. What did you do that for?"

Dan had laughed with satisfaction and that was the end of that. He soon realized that Max was no longer bothering to check the cash register readings against its contents. It was a comfortable way to work and he was pleased with the trust. He invented his own system for keeping accounts, entering the figures in a little notebook that Max might see whenever he wanted.

His schoolwork was going well, but he remained uneasy about the cadaver and he was distressed each morning when he and Noble pushed down the levers at the ends of the tank and the perfect, strongly built body was lifted from its pool of formaldehyde.

Noble was a silent and sometimes unfriendly partner. Through his thick round glasses he struggled to see the anatomic structures he was obliged to dissect. His work was slow and he often came unprepared. He always seemed tired and sometimes Dan found him nodding in sleep instead of working. There was one odd thing about Noble that puzzled Dan: he bore an odor of fish that Dan could recognize through the pungent carbolic acid and formaldehyde fumes from the tank.

After about a month in school Dan was startled when one of the students, Wyndham, tapped him on the shoulder. "Can we see you a minute?" Wyndham said formally.

Dan put his scalpel down. "Sure," he said.

"Outside in the instructor's office."

Dan followed him into the small office. Two men were waiting there.

"You know O'Donnell," Wyndham said. "This other fellow in the sea-gull outfit is Howie Payne. He's our president. Shake hands with Dan, Howie." Howie was sitting on the corner of the desk. He reached out and shook Dan's hand and then offered him a cigarette.

"Don't worry about the time," Howie said. "We're allowed five minutes."

O'Donnell was smoking a cigar. He knocked the ashes into

a small tray. "Have you thought about pledging yet?" he said.

"To a fraternity?"

"Not a sorority."

"I couldn't pay the initiation fee."

"Listen," Howie said leaning forward, "I've heard some pretty good things about your work. Your spot examination grades are the top in the class. We can get the money from the alumni."

"Which fraternity?"

O'Donnell shrugged in humorous despair.

"Sigma Sig," Wyndham said.

"I'm Jewish," Dan said.

Howie stared at him and the room was quiet. Then O'Donnell finally said, "Jewish, with a name like McDermott?"

"That's my father's name."

"Is he Jewish?"

"I never asked him."

"Christ," O'Donnell said.

The four of them were silent again. Then Howie said, "I don't know how this happened." He shook hands with Dan again.

Wyndham walked out with him. "Jesus, I'm sorry," he said.

"It happens when you have a name like McDermott."

When he came back to the table Noble looked up. "Well?"

"Well, what?"

"Did they pledge you?"

"I'm Jewish."

Noble put his lower lip out. "How come—"

"My father's name is McDermott. My mother's name was Abrams."

Noble grunted. Then he said, "Let me get something real straight. Are you prejudiced against Negroes?"

Dan was amazed. "What the hell ever gave you that idea?"

"All right," Noble said. "All right. Maybe you're just prejudiced against people."

Later that week the students were given a black metal box of human bones to study. The bones Dan was given had seen more than one generation of medical students. They were polished and old and smelled of preservative. In the evening at the drugstore he took them out of their box, set them on the prescription counter, and marveled at their intricate shapes. Each small groove and protuberance had been given a name. He found the foramen of Morgagni, and the tubercle of Santorini, and the sinus of Valsalva. He wondered about the ancient doctors with the strange names and what they had done so that a part of a bone bore their name. He became so engrossed in studying the bones that sometimes he didn't hear when customers came into the store until they had walked up to the prescription counter. He would hastily hide the bones, serve the customer, and go back to his work as soon as they left.

He began bringing his box to Hoagy's each night, eating his hamburger, and surreptitiously studying the bones when no one was close-by. One night the pretty waitress leaned over the counter and said, "What's in the black box?"

It was the first time she had spoken to him about anything except his food. He closed the box and said, "Nothing much. Let me have some more coffee."

She looked at the big text on the counter. "Cunningham's *Anatomy*. We used that book in art school."

"An anatomy book?"

"I had to study it for a year." She poured two cups of coffee and walked around the counter and sat next to him. She smelled pleasantly of perfume with just a hint of sweat.

"Where?"

"Art Student's League."

"Is the painting business that bad?"

"It isn't real good, now that you ask. But I'm doing a penance here."

He was puzzled, but she arose to wait on a new customer. When she came back he was in the middle of a page. "Why do you come here every night? I don't think it's because of our hamburgers," she said.

He looked up, his finger marking his place. "I need a place to study."

"Why not at home?"

Dan couldn't avoid answering her without open rudeness, and he told her about the room.

The cook called her and she was busy until just before two. Then she came back with a piece of whipped cream pie. "You're too thin," she said. "Besides it's wholesome. They bake it themselves."

He put a half dollar down for the pie, but she pushed it back. "Do you know where Simon's Art Supply Store is?"

"Down the street?"

She nodded. "There's a clown face in the window. Go look at it."

"I'm color blind."

"Look at it anyway," she said. "It's important to me."

When he got to school the next morning he found a large notice tacked to the anatomy laboratory door. It said LEAVE ALL TEXTS AND NOTES OUTSIDE. AN EXAMINATION WILL BE HELD TODAY. He left his books on a shelf in the instructor's office. The students were unusually quiet, and Dan hastily scanned his dissection. Noble came in a few minutes later, looking worried. He leaned forward and whispered, "What are the wrist bones again? I forgot the second M."

"Second M?"

"Yes, you know. Never lift Tillie's pants, mother might come home."

"The multangulum?"

"Navicular, lunate, triquetrum, pisiform, multangulum major and minor, capitate. Home. What's the H?"

"Hamate. Where did you get that line about Tillie?"

"The fraternities have them," Noble said. "Wiggins got into the Jewish fraternity and I heard him reciting this. It helps."

"You know any more?"

"On old Olympus towering top a fat-assed German vaulted a hop."

"What's that for?"

"The cranial nerves. Olfactory, oculomotor—"

"Optic," Dan said. "Let's hear that again." And Noble repeated it. "I wonder who wrote these in the first place," Dan finally said.

"Probably jerks like us," Noble said and went back to his dissection.

About ten-thirty Dan was called into the office. All three instructors were there. "Sit down," the chief instructor said. "Don't be nervous. Your whole grade doesn't depend on this single quiz. What's the origin of the radial artery?"

"The brachial artery below the level of the condyles."

"What's the origin of the *teres minor* muscle?"

"The scapula and the *infraspinate fascia*."

They continued asking questions, and he answered them quickly and nervously, the pages and the diagrams in the Cunningham flashing in his mind. After a while he was aware they were no longer marking his answers down, but were leaning forward, interested, shooting question after question at him, barely giving him time to answer before a new one was asked. He kept turning in his chair, answering one instructor and then another.

After about ten minutes one of the instructors said, "Whew," and sat down, and then the other two stopped. The chief instructor pushed himself back in his swivel chair and looked at Dan. "How many hours do you put in on this a night?"

"Six."

"How much on weekends?"

"All weekend."

"All of Saturday and Sunday?"

"Till about two." He hesitated. "I lose a little time by working."

"You don't spend any time with your family? Go out?"

"No."

"I suppose this is what we're asking for," he said, "but when I see somebody really do it, it worries me a little." He lit a cigarette. "How do you think you're going to like taking care of sick patients, not knowing what's the matter with them half the time, not having a book that will give you the answers you need?"

"I don't know," Dan said.

"That's an honest answer. But we'll be finding out in a few years, won't we?" He nodded and Dan was dismissed, not knowing whether he had been praised or for some obscure reason found wanting.

The next day a failing list was posted in the anatomy laboratory. The moment the instructor walked out of the room the students crowded around the bulletin board anxiously.

Noble had remained at the tank, ignoring the list. Dan came back and said, "They've got your name up there."

"Don't let it break you up." Noble was apparently not surprised.

"I'm not broken up. I'm just telling you."

Noble had been searching for the antecrural nerve of the thigh for two days. Dan stopped his work and watched him. He could make out a fibrous band in just about the right spot. "Just a minute," he said and reached over and hooked the tip of his probe in the band. With a quick motion he split it open, exposing the gray, glistening nerve in its bed.

Noble looked silently at the nerve. "If you knew where it was, why didn't you tell me?"

"Because you're a surly son of a bitch."

Noble looked at him through the top of his glasses. "Me?"

"Anyway I just saw it now."

Noble shifted his dissection and began freeing the nerve. About a half hour later he touched Dan's hand with the back of his scalpel. "Do you think I cut the obturator?"

Dan leaned over and studied his partner's dissection. Then he picked up a tuft of fat in his forceps and shredded it with the tip of his probe. "Here's one end. Better grab hold of it." Noble took it in his forceps. Dan searched a little longer and found the other end. "Now all you need is a little needle job." He handed the roll of black silk and the thin needle to Noble. Working slowly because of his poor eyesight, Noble joined the two ends of the artery. Later in the morning he succeeded in having one of the instructors approve his dissection, and he was able to move on to the leg, where most of the class was already working.

That night when Dan came into Hoagy's the red-headed girl was waiting for him. She left two taxicab drivers and walked to where he sat and wiped the counter. "Did you see that painting?"

"I don't know anything about art. All I like are pictures of soldiers."

"I'll paint a helmet on that clown's head if that's what it takes."

"How about a hamburger?"

"Don't you get tired of them?"

"I have to eat something or you'll throw me out."

She laughed, and went back to the kitchen. When she set his food down she said, "Wait with the coffee."

He read and ate and in about fifteen minutes she came bearing hot coffee and sat down next to him. She chatted cheerfully about her house and how over the weekend she had tried to lay a tile floor in her bathroom. He had to put aside his book and listen. He was provoked by the loss of time, and the next night he sought another place to study. He walked up and down Melrose, but all he found was a noisy little bar where it was too dark to read. He had to go back to his room. When he closed the door he felt as though a cheap bare coffin had been nailed shut over his head.

He finally went out into the hall. For some reason that he didn't understand he was more comfortable there. He pulled a chair out and set it under the single light and started reading. He was uneasy that someone would see him and think him odd for sitting in the hall by himself, and he listened carefully, ready at the sound of footsteps to escape with his chair back into his room. No one came, and he was able to finish the entire chapter on the bones of the skull. When he was done he was tired and drowsy, and he fell asleep without turning on the light.

Yom Kippur came late that year. Most Yom Kippurs fell on hot days in September, but this one came in October. Max closed the store early, and Dan had the afternoon free. After school, while it was still light, he went up to the library and chose several books to read. He got off the bus downtown and found a second-hand clothing store where he bought a stained brown fedora. By then it was after sundown and he walked home. The fasting didn't bother him, but he was tortured by the desire for a cigarette.

He lay down in his room, still wearing his hat, and tried to read. After a while he gave up and managed to fall asleep. He awoke before it was light and shaved and washed and put on clean clothes.

It was the second Yom Kippur since his mother died. The first one he had stayed away from the synagogue. However he was miserable and he felt that in some way he had betrayed her. This year he meant to go. He started walking westward, toward the ocean, knowing that he would find a synagogue near Fairfax. It was farther than he thought, and it was well into the morning before he found one, a red-brick building on a corner opposite a small park. It was called Beth-Ami, the house of my people. The heavy doors were open and a number of people, the men with hats or skull caps, the women in bright clothes, were going in. Dan followed them. A man with a list in his hand caught up with him in the anteroom. "What's your name?" he asked.

Dan told him.

"Are you one of the congregation?"

"No."

"Do you have a guest ticket?"

"No."

"I'm sorry," the ticket taker said. "The seats for the services today are only by reservation." He hurried back to his place at the door.

Dan went outside again. There was no point in anger. It had been the same way in San Francisco, and probably it had been the same when Jerusalem was the capital of a nation, and old David sunned himself on the palace roof.

Across the street on the benches in the park sat a group of old men. He crossed the street and sat down with them. They all wore hats and were dressed in new clothes. One of the old men was praying in Hebrew, striking his chest at the end of each strophe. He stopped when he saw Dan. "No guest ticket?"

"I'm new in Los Angeles."

"Ha, you make them a twenty-five dollar donation, they give you a guest ticket no matter where you're from."

"I haven't got twenty-five dollars."

"So sit down, Jew," the old man said in Yiddish. "Here's the congregation of the no twenty-five dollarser's. Put your hat on straight. It's Yom Kippur."

Dan moved the fedora so that it sat straight on his head, the brim up.

"Good," the old man said and went back to his praying. "And for the sin of violence," and he struck his chest.

Across the street the doors to the synagogue closed.

"And for the sin of ensnaring my neighbor," the old man said and struck himself.

The buses and cars hurried along Beverly Boulevard, and except for the old men in the park with their new clothes, the day looked like any other day. Every so often one of them got up and made his way to the public lavatory, coming back later and taking up the prayer. Finally when the morning was over the synagogue doors opened and the people started coming out. Dan began the long walk back to Orchid Street. Long before he was there the sun set, and the streetlights went on. With great relief he lit a cigarette. When he got to his room he put the hat away carefully so that it would be wearable for the next Yom Kippur.

He was ravenously hungry when he came to Hoagy's. The waitress looked at him curiously. "Why so early?"

"The feasting after the fast," he said. "Let me have the menu." He ordered a full dinner and the odor of the cooking food delighted him. He was feeling gay and cheerful, and ahead of him lay a full evening to read if he could only find a place for it.

She set the salad and the warm meat-smelling soup before him and she said, "What is it? Your birthday." She seemed sad.

"I'm celebrating."

"Oh," she said, "it's Yom something or other. So that's why business is so slow. You sound like you enjoy that soup."

"Got your hair done differently?"

"No."

"Maybe you lost weight?"

She shook her head. "You finally looked at me. That's all."

The cook rang and she went back and brought him a plate of steaming beef. She watched him eat, and after a while she said, "It's hard to work tonight. It's been getting harder and harder for me this month. That generally means my penance is almost done." She looked down the counter at the other waitress. "Lorraine is supposed to work every Saturday but she takes half of them off. She gets migraines exactly at ten." She wiped the counter in front of Dan. "I'm thinking of getting a migraine myself tonight. There's no reason she can't work one Saturday by herself." She waited.

Dan was torn by indecision. Perhaps he could do both, he finally decided, and said, "I live right around here. I'll show you the ugliest room in Los Angeles if you come up."

"I don't need ugly rooms tonight," she said. "But I would like to spend the evening with you."

He wrote the address down and she put the slip in her apron pocket. "If it slows down I'll make it about eight-thirty. Why don't you put some coffee on?"

He walked to the art store and found the clown-face painting in the window. The eyes were askew and the forehead peaked, but with all the deformations it was gentle and tender and he liked it. He studied it a long time, feeling its sadness and wondering if the red-headed girl had painted it.

He stopped at Goldie's apartment to borrow a coffee pot. Goldie was sitting under a hair dryer that looked like a German helmet from the First World War. "Sit down," he said. "I'm just about ready to come out of this contraption."

"Can you lend me a coffee pot?"

"What?" Goldie reached up and turned off a switch. "These things make you deaf. What are you up to?"

"Nothing. Just want to make some coffee."

"On a Saturday night? You'll get old before your time."

It was Saturday night, the night for going out and maybe going to bed. He wondered what Goldie did on a Saturday night. "What kind of plans do you have?"

"I'll make the rounds. I'll stop in at Johnny's and the Candle Light. You want to come?"

Dan shook his head.

"Too bad," Goldie said. "I could show you a part of L.A. that you'll never hear about." He fluffed his hair, and went into the bedroom to brush it. He came back smelling of perfume. He opened his wallet and carefully took out all the cards and papers and put them into a drawer. "Precautions," he said. "Anything you want before I leave?"

"A coffee pot."

"One coffee pot coming up," Goldie said. He brought one out of his kitchen. "It's mine. It's not the building's."

"I may not even use it."

"Just get it back." He straightened his jacket and said, "Happy hunting," and went out the hall looking like a plump woman in a man's clothing.

The girl came about nine. She looked about the room and said, "What's the matter with it? You should see some of the holes I've lived in."

He took her coat.

"Lorraine was planning to get her migraine on time tonight.

You never saw anybody get so mad. Did you put some coffee on?"

"I have the pot anyway."

She went into the small kitchen and came promptly out. "We can have some hot water and peanut butter. That's all you have." She sat down and took off her shoes. "Did you see that clown face?"

"I liked it. Did you do it?"

"Anything familiar about it?"

"Why was it so sad?"

"It was a sad month in a sad year. Everything I did came out sad that month."

He looked at the clock. It need not take too much time and he would still have three hours left for studying. He walked to the couch and kissed her. She pulled him down and he became excited. It had been a very long time, and he made love quickly and eagerly.

Later he said, "I have a bed. It's softer than this couch."

With the light off and the girl beside him he felt almost comfortable in the room. It was hot and they were both sweating. She wiped his face gently with her palm. "I didn't really think I could feel this way again," she said. She kissed him on his lips and cheeks, and he caressed her and started making love again. An illustration from his anatomy text suddenly flashed in his mind, and he stopped moving, wondering whether the usual position for sex had any anatomic basis or whether it was simply traditional, imposed on one generation by the prejudices of the last generation. He pictured the sloping tube of the vagina pointing downward, and he thought the traditional position would favor the loss of the sperm. It would depend, he decided, on what the great apes did. They were so like men in their anatomy that their habits could serve as a model for uncivilized man.

He remembered vaguely seeing in Cunningham in an unread chapter a section on the genitalia of the primates. Perhaps their sexual positions were also discussed.

"Honey," she was saying, and kissing him repeatedly. He

put his arms around her and moved strongly until they were done. He waited until she was breathing evenly, and then he said, "Just a minute. I'll be right back."

He carried the Cunningham into the little kitchen, and turned on the light and started searching the pages.

She was talking to him from the bed. "Do you know why I'm here?"

"What?"

"Why I'm in your lumpy bed. Do you want me to shout it?"

He didn't answer.

"Can you hear me?"

"Sure."

"Where are you? In the bathroom?"

"I'll be right back."

"A funny thing. That clown has sad Irish eyes just like yours."

"Jewish," he said.

"It's one of the best things I ever did. Mr. Simon loves it."

He had found a small paragraph on the genitalia of the marsupials, and was searching beyond it for the primates.

She came up behind him suddenly and put her arms around him.

"Just a minute," he said.

She saw the book and let go of him. "Oh brother," she said.

"Go back to bed," he said, holding his place with his finger. "I'll be right there."

"I've planned this for two weeks, ever since I got a good look at your eyes, and you climb out of bed still dripping and read a book." She read aloud over his shoulder, "The vaginal tubes of the right and the left side in the diprotodons kink sharply as they pass the ureter." She stopped. "What's a diprotodon?"

"A kind of kangaroo, I think. Let's go back to bed."

He turned to the chapter on cervical vertebrae and started

studying it. The pressure of the girl's body next to him in bed helped, and he was able to read comfortably and happily. She moved sharply and he heard her strike a match and light a cigarette.

"Lie down," he said. "I'm glad you're here. You don't have to go, do you?"

She got up from the bed silently and started dressing.

He was still comfortable and he read as she dressed. When she was ready to leave he closed the book and sat up.

"You don't need a girl," she said. "All you need is a second volume." She shook her head. "I must be losing whatever I used to have"—and she put her coat on and went out the door.

He got back to the restaurant about eleven-thirty. Lorraine was there by herself, and she silently served him his food. He studied until the restaurant closed at two, and he completed the chapter on the neck vertebrae.

That week it turned cold, and Dan took Eddie's sweater out of the drawer and started wearing it in the evenings. It had been several months since he had spoken to Eddie, and as he thought about him he began to get uneasy. Perhaps Eddie had left Los Angeles, or had become ill. He was sixty or so and sickness can come quickly at that age. Dan finally phoned the St. Regis Hotel one evening at nine. "Is Eddie McDermott in?"

"I'll check." The clerk came back in a moment. "He went out an hour ago. He left a number he can be reached at."

"Thanks," Dan said. "I won't need it," and hung up.

The next day was Armistice Day and Max closed the store. Dan stayed late at the school library studying. He waited vainly for a bus and then in exasperation started walking the four miles to his room. About midnight he was trudging up Wilshire. In an alley coming off the street he saw a busboy emptying buckets into a garbage can behind Berman's Fish Shanty. The busboy glanced up, and Dan recognized Noble, looking old and strangely feminine in his stained apron and round glasses. They stared at each other for a few moments. Then Noble turned his back and went on emptying the buckets, with lobster claws and clam shells, into the big cans. After hesitating a moment Dan continued walking toward Orchid Street.

While the professor of anatomy had been content to let the students choose their own partners, the professor of physiology preferred to group them alphabetically. Dan's group, the M's through the O's, contained Noble, O'Donnell, and a slight boy named Norcross.

At first they studied the physiology of frogs. However, the frogs had tiny arteries, their veins were hard to cannulate, and their structure too distant and too cold to provide much information about men. Consequently in the latter part of the course they began working on dogs.

O'Donnell had appointed himself chief of the group. "I've had some experience in surgery," he said. "I've worked in first aid and done some suturing. Anybody mind?" He looked about for a challenger and, finding none, brought out his cigar stub and lit it. "McDermott can set up the experiment and call the shots. Noble can be my assistant. Dave, why don't you give the anesthetic?"

Norcross was barely nineteen, and looked sixteen. He shook his head and said, "How do you give an anesthetic to a dog?"

"Instructions are McDermott's department."

"Just follow the manual," Dan said.

The professor of physiology gave them instructions himself, and later O'Donnell sent Noble downstairs for the dog. He brought up an old Airedale, wheezing, short of breath, and blind in one eye.

"How many dogs they got down there?" Norcross asked.

Noble shrugged. "Maybe fifteen. Mostly mongrels. There's one German shepherd. Awfully big. I left him alone."

Norcross reached down to pet the Airedale, but the dog snapped at him, barely missing his hand.

"Let's get started," Dan said. "You give him one cc of Nembutal." He pushed the ampule toward Norcross.

O'Donnell did a good job of surgery, skillfully inserting the tubes into the dog's pancreatic ducts. They tested the effects of various drugs on the flow of the secretion, and later the instructor came and approved their results.

"Do we have to sacrifice the dog?" Norcross asked him.

"What else would you do?"

"Sew him up. Maybe we could suture the ends of the ducts together."

The instructor shook his head. "Mighty small chance. You'd be torturing the animal unnecessarily."

He went to the next table, and O'Donnell stripped his gloves off and started washing his hands. Noble was busy taking the graph off the drum.

Norcross hesitated, the syringe of anesthetic solution in his hand. Dan was watching him. "Never mind, Dave," he finally said. "I'll do it." But when he held the syringe in his own hand he also found it hard to push the barrel down. He remembered how the Germans had given intravenous injections of this same drug or carbolic acid or formaldehyde to Jews during the war. "Let me have a look at that duct. Maybe I can sew it up," he said finally and handed the syringe back to Norcross. He picked up O'Donnell's dirty gloves, and washed them in the sink, and dipped them in sterilizing solution, and pulled them on. He took a curved needle and managed to get a few sutures into the duct. The animal started writhing, and he said, quickly, "He's coming out, Dave. Give him some more." Norcross pushed on the syringe and the dog was quieter. Dan worked another ten minutes, but the duct was twisted and he couldn't reopen it. He put the instruments down. "We couldn't do anything with this dog anyway, even if I could get the duct together."

"We'd steal him," Norcross said. "They're not watching."

"I can't get another stitch into it," Dan said. "It won't work. You better give him the shot." He waited a moment. "Go ahead."

Norcross quickly pressed on the barrel of the syringe. The rest of the liquid went in and the dog stopped breathing.

Norcross was upset when he came in the next day. "I had nightmares about dogs. I was sweating all night," he told Dan. "I dreamed my own setter, Tinkle, came running up to me and I started to scratch her stomach and it was all cut open."

O'Donnell was listening. "Forget it," he said. "They're two-dollar dogs from the pound."

"What the hell's money got to do with it?" Norcross said angrily. A little later he said, "When I first learned to drive I was coming out of Big Bear. It was nighttime and I was passing some cabins and this little poodle, cute as a bug, all clipped with a bow around its neck, comes prancing right up to my front wheels." He grimaced. "I couldn't stop in time. I went back after it, but it dragged itself off in the bushes and it took me an hour's hunting before I finally found it. I dreamed about that, too."

"Just keep track of the experiment," Dan said. "You don't have to do anything. I'll manage the anesthetic today."

Norcross shook his head. "I know the way I feel isn't reasonable. It's kind of stupid as a matter of fact."

Noble nodded. "If it costs a couple of dogs for us to learn physiology it's worth it."

"I know," Norcross said. "I'm being stupid."

Dan started outlining the experiment, and Noble went downstairs to the kennel. He came up panting fifteen minutes later leading a husky half-grown shepherd. "I had to climb all five flights by shoe leather," he gasped. "The lousy elevators are being fixed and this mutt was trying to pull me down the stairs every chance he got."

"It's a German shepherd," Norcross said.

"Here we go again," O'Donnell said.

Norcross held out his hand, and the dog came nuzzling to it and put its head under Norcross's palm. Norcross scratched his head, and the dog licked his hand. "That does it," Norcross said. "We're not working on this dog."

O'Donnell said, "Oh Christ."

Noble said, "I'm not taking him back. If you want another dog you go yourself. I had to climb five flights with that crazy mutt and I almost broke my leg three times."

"A dog is a dog," Dan said. "If it's not this one it'll be another one."

"Not a shepherd," Norcross said. "I'll put up the money he cost the school and I'm taking him home." Norcross took the rope and tried to lead the dog out of the room. The shepherd, however, was excited and tugged hard, struggling to break away.

"He's smelling the bitches," O'Donnell said.

They watched Norcross dragging the animal across the room.

"They ought to have a minimal age in this school. Twenty-one at least," O'Donnell said. "We're going to get started late. Come on, McDermott, brief me."

Dan started reading the steps he had outlined, O'Donnell listening and nodding.

Suddenly there was a swirl of excitement at the door. A boy ran across the laboratory and said something to the instructor. The instructor sprang up and ran toward the door, his white coat flying behind him.

"What's that?" O'Donnell said.

Noble was watching too. "I just bet Dave broke a leg. That lousy mutt gets the rope tangled around your legs and then he pulls like hell." He hurried toward the hall.

"Probably somebody got nipped in the butt," O'Donnell said. "What do we do next?"

"We're going to attach electrodes to the ventricles and record direct electrocardiographic patterns."

O'Donnell was interested. "Are we? Let me see that." He looked at the laboratory manual, and the sketch, and he nodded and said, "I'll bet I get this open and the attachments on in ten minutes." Dan looked about the room. Only half the students were working. The others crowded anxiously about the doorway into the hall.

Dan took his sheet of paper and started outlining the later

steps in the study. He had been working for a few minutes when O'Donnell said, "Something really has happened." Dan looked up and saw Noble, his glasses off, pushing through the crowd at the door. He hurried to the desk. "Somebody fell down the elevator shaft. I think it was Dave."

Dan sprang up. "You can't fall down an elevator shaft. It's got safeties on it." He squeezed through the confused students, O'Donnell and Noble behind him.

"They were fixing it," Noble shouted over the noise. "Bernstein saw somebody go down the shaft. He thinks it was Norcross."

They got into the hall but the elevator door was closed and the instructor gone.

"He was dragging this mutt," Noble said, "pulling on him as hard as he could and he backed up to the elevator door and opened it, and fell down the shaft." They tried to go downstairs, but they were stopped at the second floor by one of the school custodians. Dan heard a siren screaming and through the hall window saw an ambulance skid to a stop before the building. The orderlies ran in with a stretcher.

The students in the hall were distraught and very angry. They argued among themselves as to how a modern elevator in a new building could lack such elemental safety features that a door could be opened into an empty shaft.

Dan went back upstairs and put away the instruments. He found the German shepherd, wandering about the laboratory, sniffing amiably at table legs. He put the rope back around the dog's collar and dragged him down the five flights, putting him back in the cage with the other reprieved animals.

None of the students were allowed to visit Norcross. He lay in the County Hospital under the care of the staff, and special nurses. He died on the third day without having regained consciousness.

Many of the instructors and almost all the students attended Norcross' funeral. Dan sat beside Noble, and when it was done they walked out together.

"I wish they had asked me to preach that sermon," Noble said. "I would have done a better job of it." He looked at Dan. "Do you know I went through divinity school? I have my degree in religion."

"You don't talk like it."

Noble grunted. "That was the one hard thing in that school. I had to watch my language. It damn near gave me an ulcer." Then he said, "I never practiced. In my last year I applied for medical school."

They were walking along Hollywood Boulevard, and it was starting to get dark.

"This fellow missed the point," Noble said. "He didn't understand partial choices. This wasn't really an accident."

"What do you mean? Dave was still too much of a kid. It upset him to kill a dog to learn physiology."

"That's an accident?"

"Falling down an elevator shaft is."

"A certain percentage of soldiers in a war are going to get killed. Now everybody that chooses to become a soldier takes his share of that per cent. See?"

"No." Dan was looking for Orchid Street.

"It doesn't matter," Noble said. "The young ones can get hurt. Do you remember what that anatomy instructor said about two of us getting TB? That's what really worries me. My mother and father both died of it, and my father sure took a long time dying."

"You haven't got that straight either. This instructor said there would be two cases of clinically recognizable tuberculosis in our class before we were done. To be clinically recognizable you don't have to be sick. All you have to have is a little shadow on an x-ray that goes away in a month or so, or maybe your skin test gets positive."

"You know damn well every so often a student ends up in a sanitarium. You're taking that risk and so am I. How's that any different from Norcross falling down the elevator shaft?"

Dan pointed to a dark street. "I live about eight blocks down there."

"I'll walk along. I took the evening off."

It was quite dark by then and they walked south across Sunset Boulevard. Dan was thinking about divinity school. "What made you change?" he said.

"I was beginning to have trouble," Noble said. "I kept changing what I believed in. Besides, a minister doesn't have much bait to offer. But a minister who's a doctor is something else. When I'm done school I'm going down to Mississippi and practice."

"You don't seem that religious."

"I'm not any more," Noble said. "But I'll put some guts into them about voting and registering and going to school. They need more guts." He walked along quietly for a few moments. "My brother-in-law called me a traitor last week. When I decided to go into medical school he nearly threw me out. Last week he was at it again, about me not recognizing my black heritage. What do you think a black heritage is?"

"Jungles and roast leopard," Dan said.

"It's more than that," Noble said, "but anyhow I got mad and asked him if he wanted me to study knuckle-bone rolling and that's when he called me a traitor. He's quieted down though. He and my sister went to visit their minister and he told them the black men will need doctors when they return to their heritage." He glanced into a shop window. "It's eight o'clock. Where do you study?"

Dan didn't want to tell him about the restaurant, and he said only, "At my place."

"I brought my notes."

Dan was trapped and after a moment he said, "Sure, come on up."

They walked to Melrose and then down Orchid Street. When Dan flicked on the light Noble looked around and said, "Nice place. Do you have it all to yourself?"

"I can't stand it."

Noble looked at him oddly. Then he sat on the bed. "Good bed," he said. "Why don't you make it once in a while?"

Dan shrugged and Noble got up and looked into the bathroom. "Most of the nights I have to study in the bathroom. It's the only place I can turn on a light and not wake somebody up." He sat down at the table and stretched his legs out luxuriously and took a folded notebook out of his pocket. Dan got the Cunningham from the kitchen and carried it to the bed and lay down. He wasn't sure how it would go, but for some reason, with Noble squinting at his notes at the table, he felt at peace and able to study. He started reading rapidly and from time to time when he looked up he was comforted to see Noble, book open before him, tediously underlining passages and making additional notes in a tiny hand on small scraps of paper. About midnight Noble fell asleep and Dan read happily until about two, selfishly letting Noble sleep in the uncomfortable chair so that he might read longer. At two he woke him up. "You can sleep on the couch," he said.

Without a word Noble got up, took off his glasses, and lay down on the couch. Dan covered him with one of the blankets, and Noble grunted and fell asleep again. The next morning they awoke together and walked to the bus stop, stopping at the small market for doughnuts and cartons of milk.

Thereafter whenever Noble had a night off he studied with Dan. It was a delicate friendship. Noble was easily angered by small and unintentional slights, and Dan had to speak cautiously. Yet when Noble was with him he studied well, and the morning sadness, always unpredictable, disappeared completely.

In the last few weeks of the anatomy course the students dissected the interior organs of the body, usually finding there the disease that had caused the death of the cadaver. Wyndham and his partners worked on the body of a thin colored girl. They found her lungs studded with holes, some no bigger than the head of a match and others large enough to contain an orange. The instructor had glanced at the lungs. "Tuberculosis cavities," he had said. Dan came to see for himself the marks of the ancient enemy of men. "I suppose there's nothing you can do for it once it's this far gone," he finally said.

Wyndham looked down at the numerous cavities and shook his head. "I don't know what she was breathing with," he said, and Dan tried to imagine how it would have felt to have such terrible holes in one's lungs.

Later that morning two other students found a lake of hardened old blood engulfing one lung of their cadaver. The instructor ran his fingers along the ribs and said, "Yes, here are the fractures. It's a hemothorax." He waited and let the students consider the long word. "Remember your Latin. *Hemo* is blood. *Thorax* the chest. Hemothorax, bleeding into the chest. Medical terminology isn't difficult if you remember your Latin. Hemothorax. Bleeding into the chest. Hematuria?" He looked about.

"Bloody urine," a student said.

"Good. Hemoptysis?"

"Bloody expectoration," Dan said. He reached into the open chest and felt the jagged knife edges of the broken ribs that had cut into the lung and caused the hemorrhage. He puzzled over why this man had been permitted to die. A doctor ought to have been able to suck out the blood with a hollow needle and a syringe, and free the lung, and make up the blood loss by transfusions.

He told Noble about it when he came back to the tank. "Maybe they just didn't know he was bleeding," Noble said.

"There's a couple of gallons in there. Go take a look."

Noble looked and came back and said, "It looks like a lot, but maybe the embalming fluid got mixed in."

When the instructor came by Dan stopped him. "Can you recognize a hemothorax while the patient's alive?"

"Sure. X-rays. Physical examination."

"What do you do for it?"

"Just drawing the blood out of the chest is usually enough. Sometimes you have to give transfusions and sometimes you have to go right in and find the bleeder and tie it off."

Dan looked down the aisle of tanks to where the two students were busily scooping handfuls of caked blood from the opened chest. "Why did he die then?"

The instructor followed his glance. "Probably he didn't get to a doctor in time."

It was a comforting explanation and, Dan thought, probably true. He was grateful to the instructor, and after he left he said, "Nice fellow," to Noble.

"The further you stay away from them the better off you are," Noble said.

Each day more of the students found the causes of death of their cadavers. One pair found a cancer in the lungs. A single look at that gray invading mass was enough to satisfy Dan. Another cadaver had died of hardening of the arteries of the heart and here, too, the deterioration of years was so well marked that it was easy to see that nothing could have turned back that disease either.

But he could find no cause of death in his own cadaver. When each new organ was exposed he studied it with care. A few times he thought he found something wrong, and he stopped the instructor and showed it to him. Each time, however, the instructor said it was a minor alteration that many men had, and it could not cause death.

Day after day went by without an answer being found and Dan developed the troublesome suspicion that the cadaver had been murdered. He wondered in what dreadful way a murder could be perpetrated so that no marks show on the skin or in the great organs.

When the heart failed to show any disease he looked up in desperation and said, "What the hell do you think killed this guy?"

"Looks to me like he just dropped dead," Noble said.

"What happens when you drop dead?"

"Your heart stops."

Dan picked it up. "Why would it stop?"

Noble looked at the intact organ. "I guess you're right," he said and went untroubled back to work.

Later, seeing Dan poring over the organs, he stopped his work and said, "He's dead, isn't he?"

"He'd better be."

"So what are you getting yourself all pushed out of shape for? He's dead, and it's legal or he wouldn't be here."

"What happens when a man gets electrocuted?"

Noble thought a moment. "I suppose it stops the heart."

"I don't know," Dan finally said. "Maybe it gives burns." He looked at the ankles and wrists. There were no burn marks.

Later that week a pair of students working on the far side of the room discovered that the large artery from the heart of their cadaver had torn, filling the chest with blood. The other students came up to look at it, and were amazed.

"One of the most dramatic occurrences in medicine," one of the instructors, a young man with a mustache, said. "It's a ruptured aneurysm. The spirochete of syphilis weakens the wall of the aorta. Then the aorta slowly balloons out till it's stretched too thin. Then it goes all of a sudden and the patient dies in a few minutes. Watch for it when you dissect arteries. We always have a few cases each year. Most of the cadavers are colored and the colored race has better than double the incidence of syphilis."

Noble immediately raised his hand. When the instructor failed to see him, he stood up. "Those are white man's statistics, aren't they?" he said.

The whole noisy room fell silent.

"Board of Health statistics," the instructor said.

"Who runs the Board of Health?"

"Jesus, Oney, sit down," Dan whispered. "You're not making sense."

"Those are white men's statistics," Noble said again loudly. His hand that rested on the tank was trembling. Across the room Dan saw the rigid backs of the other two colored students as they paused in their work.

The instructor turned coolly away without answering and Noble sat down. He did not speak to Dan again that morning and he left before the class was done. When Dan came out he was waiting in the hall.

"You're supposed to be my friend," Noble said. "Why didn't you say something?"

"Say what?" Dan said angrily. "I don't know how the hell you got this far in school. You're a dumb shit. You don't know—"

Noble hit him high on the face and then, as he stumbled back, hit him again in the chest and then in the face. Dan struck out once by reflex and missed, brushing Noble's glasses off.

O'Donnell, who was also coming out of the anatomy laboratory, said, "Whoa there! What's this?"

Noble picked his glasses up from the floor and walked away.

Dan's lip was wet with blood, and he wiped it dry with his hand.

"Let's see this," O'Donnell said, and bent Dan's head back. He took a handkerchief out of his pocket and held it against Dan's nose. "How do you feel?"

"Great."

"Wait a minute." He disappeared and came back with the young instructor. The physician removed the handkerchief, looked at Dan's face, and then put two fingers on the bridge of his nose and gently pressed. "I don't think it's broken," he finally said. "Just a bloody nose. What happened?"

Dan didn't answer.

"A little altercation," O'Donnell said.

"Keep your nostrils pinched together," the instructor said and showed Dan how.

The next morning Noble came about an hour late. He sat down silently and started work without looking at Dan. The instructor tapped Dan on the shoulder and said, "The dean's waiting for you in his office."

Dan went down the four stories and knocked at the door. The dean was a large-boned elderly man who had written several books on the history of medicine. "Sit down, Mr. Mc-Dermott," he said.

Dan sat down in the chair beside the desk.

"How's your nose?"

"It's all right now."

"Looks a little swollen." The dean also put two fingers on the bridge of Dan's nose and pressed. "Not broken though. You can get it x-rayed at the student health office if you want, but it doesn't look as though it needs it. There's no deformity."

"It's not bothering me."

The dean returned to his chair and looked out the window. "Mr. Noble told me you attacked him verbally. Used obscene language."

Dan hesitated, and finally said, "Yes."

The room was quiet while the dean waited.

"I wanted to explain to him about statistics. How they get weighed by other facts," Dan said.

"But you did use obscene language?"

"Yes."

"All right," the old man said. "I won't ask you what words you used." After a while he added, "There's more here than I know about." He waited a little longer. "If you've got something I should know about Mr. Noble, go ahead and tell me. It's important. A doctor's problems can hurt a lot of people." He waited a while longer. "You provoked him with offensive language. Is that all you're going to tell me?"

"That's all there was to it," Dan said.

"All right," the dean said, "I suppose the real problem is that we're coming to the end of a year and everybody's getting a little short-tempered and tired." He paused. "We'll leave it there. You ought to watch your language, and you look like you could use a little more rest."

Dan had a sore swollen nose for several days. An unfriendly silence lay between him and Noble, which grew worse as Dan worried more about the death of the cadaver. He frequently thought about the seemingly perfect body during the day, and his already troubled sleep was further disturbed by dreams of men dead without a mark on their bodies. He lost weight and the lines on his face deepened. The morning sadness increased so that he would come to his shower still foggy with sleep, and would awake in the hot water, his mouth dry and his heart pounding in fear.

On a warm May morning what he had been fearing finally happened. He found himself trapped in the dim bathroom of his apartment. He stood razor in hand, unable or unwilling to finish his shaving. The last bad attack after his mother died had started the same way. It was a year and a half before. He had been shaving in his small apartment in Berkeley and he had sweated and trembled and finally put the razor down. He had gone back to bed, not because he was comfortable there, but rather because there was nothing else that he could think of to do. He got thirsty from time to time and he got up to drink. He didn't eat, and the days were oppressively long. He didn't sleep either, but lay instead all night long looking at the ceiling. He waited for it to get better like a child might wait to get over the measles, but instead it grew worse. Later when he had seen his face in the mirror and saw how the flesh had fallen away he forced himself to eat some bread and drink milk. When that was gone he called a market and had more bread and milk sent up. Even so he ate only several days a week and he became so weak that often when he walked about he'd have to hold onto the wall or a chair.

He couldn't read. He couldn't watch television. He could barely talk. The manager of the chain drugstore where he had been working called to find out when he would return. He gave vague answers, not sure himself. The only visitor during the three months was a girl, several years older than he, whom he had taken out and gone to bed with several times. She came to see him after he had been home a month or so. He wouldn't talk to her though, and she left in annoyance after a half hour.

He had developed other symptoms after a while, probably, he thought, due to starvation. He sweated a great deal, his heart beat painfully, and his breathing was difficult. Finally one day in bed he started thinking of going down to see his father and starting again in school and everything got a little better. He forced himself to eat more and that helped. Later on, Phyllis, the landlady, started bothering him about the rent, and he went out and walked slowly to the bank and drew out some money and paid her. That helped too. Then he found he could watch television. For weeks it was all he could do. Later on he was able to go out and talk to people. Even later he was able to return to work and earn money. The very last thing was reading. That was the hardest thing of all, and when that came back, just before he left San Francisco, he knew he was safe again.

Standing in the bathroom in Los Angeles he felt just as he had in that other bathroom in Berkeley and he wondered wearily if he had the same three months to go through again. He went back to bed, badly frightened.

About eleven o'clock there was a knock on the door. He didn't answer. The knock was repeated and Goldie poked his head in. "I was worried about you," he said. "I didn't hear you moving around this morning. You got some kind of bug?"

Dan didn't answer.

"Usually I hear you splashing like a porpoise, and then clumping around and slamming the door. No door slamming today. I know everything that goes on in this building. All I've got to do is listen. Some guy up on the top floor can be screwing and I hear the bed springs squeak." He closed the door behind him. "What's the matter?"

"Tired, I guess," Dan said.

"Since when did you ever get tired? Up with the dawn and never to bed. It's some kind of a bug." Goldie sat down. "It's nice outside. Real sunny. Why don't you go out and get some sunshine?"

"I don't feel like it."

"It's good for you. The landlord prescribing for the doctor.

Get some sunshine." He waited, his brittle gaiety slowly crack-
ing. After a while he said, "You have a bug." He walked
to the bed and put his moist hand on Dan's head. "No fever.
How are your bowels?"

Dan didn't answer.

"Where does your father work?"

"Fidelity Insurance."

"Oh yes, let's see, that's over on Wilshire isn't it?" Goldie
stood hands in pockets watching him for a few moments. Then
he went out of the door leaving it open.

About an hour later there was another knock, and Eddie
walked in, crisp and clean. "What's up?"

Dan was surprised to see him. "Did Goldie call you?"

"What are you doing in bed?"

"Maybe I'm just tired," he said, almost believing it.

"Tired? At your age?" Eddie sat down on the edge of the
bed. "What's the matter with you?"

"I don't know. I've had it before, whatever it is."

"Did you call a doctor?"

"I don't think one would help."

"What's the matter with you?"

"I don't think it's physical."

"You having some trouble with a girl?"

"No."

Eddie looked at him then for a long time. "I don't know
what's eating you, but, Jesus, you got it made. This pharmacy
racket to pay your way through school, and then the best racket
of all, being a doctor."

Dan sat up on the edge of the bed. Eddie watched him.
"If you don't feel good, why don't you just stay in bed for
the rest of the day?"

"It won't be for just a day. It goes on for months. And
I'll quit school," Dan said.

"So what? There are a million jobs a kid your age can get.
What's the matter with the pharmacy business? Get a drugstore of your own. What's wrong with that?"

Dan shook his head.

"I don't think there's a thing the matter with you that a good stiff kick in the ass wouldn't straighten out," Eddie said. "You're probably in a decline right now over some piss-ass broad. It's one thing to play around but another thing to get involved. You know what I mean?"

"I guess so," Dan said. He was thinking of shaving.

"You don't get involved," Eddie said. "You can get away with a box of candy sometimes. If they keep on bitching you give them something more, that's all."

"You said it already."

"I'm saying it again," Eddie said. "You should know it at your age." He stopped. "Can't you even listen to somebody when they talk to you?"

"You say the same damn thing over and over again."

"Jesus," Eddie said. "I haven't heard from you all year and you call me up—"

"I didn't."

"All right, your buddy, that queer downstairs, called me. You'd think you were dying from the way he was talking."

"I'm not seeing anybody. I haven't time."

"Not at all?"

"Just once, maybe six months ago. It didn't amount to anything."

Eddie shook his head. "You can build up frustrations."

"I'm not frustrated."

"Once in six months and you're not frustrated?" Eddie grunted. "If I went six months I'd be dragging my butt too."

"That's not it." He hesitated a long time, the irrational, suffocating despondency making it hard to talk. Finally he said, "I can't figure out what killed my cadaver."

Eddie looked at him strangely.

"I got into a fight with my partner at school. We used to study together."

Eddie continued to stare. "What difference does that make?"

"I don't know what difference it makes," Dan said angrily. "I'm just telling you what happened. You asked me."

Eddie took off his jacket, rolled up his sleeves, and settled

back on the couch with a newspaper he had brought. Dan
lay silently, eyes open, hearing occasionally the rustle of the
pages as Eddie turned them.

Goldie knocked and came in. "Your office called," he said to
Eddie. "They're on the phone."

"That's Rose," Eddie said. "I wonder if you mind giving
her a message."

"No trouble."

"Tell her I won't be in today. Okay?"

"Okay," Goldie said.

A little later Dan got up and slipped into his underwear.
"I'm going to shave," he said. "Stay around until I shave."

Eddie stared at him again. "Can't you shave by yourself?"

"Just sit down," Dan said. "It won't take me long." He
was afraid to go into the bathroom, and instead he went into
the kitchen and let the hot water run. He had no mirror
there, but he soaked his face and then shaved by touch. And
when it was done he felt triumphant, and he washed his face
and searched for the remaining little tufts of beard, and cleaned
those off with his razor.

He put his shirt on. He saw Eddie sitting on the edge
of the sofa watching him and he said, "Thanks."

"For what?"

"I don't know," Dan said. "I'll walk downstairs with you."

"You going to school?"

"Yes."

"You'll be late."

"A few hours."

Eddie watched Dan walk toward the door, and then he
stepped ahead and opened it, and they walked down the hall
together.

"I don't understand you," Eddie said. "You're a funny kid."

Two

DAN GOT THROUGH that morning with difficulty, not knowing
when the despondency would return with such fresh vigor that
it would overwhelm him. But later on, just before noon, he
finally found the cause of death. He opened the stubby pouch
of the stomach and on its lining he found a pearly gray
splotch. He felt it, and scraped it with the back of his knife.
He finally tapped Noble's finger with the blunt end of his
forceps. "Take a look," he said. They were the first words they
had exchanged for two weeks.

Noble looked briefly. "What's that?"

"I don't know. It's hard." He held up the organ.

"I'll bet it's syphilis," Noble said.

"How do you know?"

"I took a couple of books on syphilis out of the library."

"Anything about statistics in them?"

"Yes."

"Oh?"

"The statistics are weighted," Noble said. "You can't properly
compare Negroes and whites since Negroes live only—"

"I know," Dan said. He felt the apology coming and he didn't
want to hear it. He had no intention of trusting Noble's
friendship again. "I'm glad you finally learned about statistics.
Why syphilis?"

"It's the great imitator."

"What's it supposed to imitate?"

"Anything. A cold. The clap. Heart trouble." He went back to work.

Later when Dan had a chance he visited the tank of the two students whose cadaver had died of syphilis of the aorta. "How does the stomach look?" he asked.

"Here," the student said and showed him. It had no hard pearly patch on its lining.

Noble looked up when he returned. "Well?"

"Nothing like it."

Dan waited until the chief instructor was free, and then called him over. The little man peered through the lower portion of his bifocal lenses and then felt the stomach with his fingertips. "You've found it," he said. "It's from a corrosive of some kind. Have you seen the kidneys?" Dan showed him one. "It looks pretty good. So it must be Lysol. Or maybe carbolic acid. Most likely Lysol. You can get it in any market. Mercury or arsenic would have affected the kidneys too."

"What do you think happened?"

"It's not homicide," the instructor said. "You can't poison somebody with Lysol. It smells too strong."

"What if he were drunk when they poisoned him?"

The instructor shook his head. "We couldn't get the body then. The coroners wouldn't release a homicide body. It's a suicide." He wiped his hands on the towel hanging at the end of the tank and went on to the next pair of students.

The buzzer rang then and it was time to quit. Dan put his instruments away and closed the tank and washed his hands. He was still troubled, however, and when he got to work that night he opened a bottle of Lysol and smelled it. It was tarry and made him cough. Max was busy in the back of the store, and Dan put a few drops into a glass, filled it with water, and tasted it. It was nauseating and bitter.

When Max came out, he began distantly, "We're almost done with anatomy," he said.

Max liked to hear about school. He paused and said, "How do you like it?"

"Some parts fine."

"The dissecting would get me," Max said. "I got a sensitive stomach."

"Did you ever hear of a person taking Lysol to commit suicide?"

Max wrinkled his face. "Lysol? How would they ever swallow it?"

"My cadaver did."

"What a lousy way to die. He would have to be crazy to do that. Maybe they got him from Camarillo. They got people there that have been in ten or twenty years. Who's going to claim a body when somebody's locked up for twenty years? Who cares?"

"What's Camarillo?"

"It's on the way to Ventura. It's where they keep all the chronic mental cases. Take care," he said, and went out the door.

The next morning after they settled down to work Dan asked Noble, "Is Camarillo county or state?"

"It's in the county . . ." He stopped. "I'm not sure. Maybe it's the state insane asylum. One or the other."

"What do they do with the bodies there?"

"Someone would think he was your brother," Noble said and went on with his work. Dan copied down the number on the metal tag attached to the great toe. At noon he went to the basement, where the caretaker worked. It was an abandoned dissecting room. The ancient wooden tables were draped in cloth. The walls were taken up by lockers, and he realized that young men in long, odd-cut trousers and white coats similar to the one he wore had worked at these tables while Cleveland worried in Washington and while Dewey was fighting in the bay at Manila. He found a side door and went through it. This second room was even darker. It had a square tank like a small swimming pool in its center. Someone smelling of cigars came up behind him and said, "What is it, young man?"

"Are you Mack?"

"That's what they call me."

Dan explained what he wanted. The caretaker took the slip with the number on it and searched a large book that had many ink entries. "All we have is the name and the date of death. You want that?"

Dan nodded, and the attendant said, "Jesse Davis. October 12, 1959."

Dan wrote it down. "Did he come from Camarillo?" he asked.

"All we get are city bodies. Camarillo is out in the county."

By the time he got to the street he was angry with himself. He had gone further than he should. He had found the cadaver had a name, and that likely he wasn't crazy and that he had taken the Lysol in a sudden and incomprehensible act, and that perhaps someone coming by could have put a hand on his shoulder and stopped him. Dan wondered where he had been on October 12, 1959. Columbus Day, 1959. He didn't remember. Either playing down at Stinson Beach, or reading, or sleeping, while this man drank a glassful of Lysol. His thoughts distressed him and he crumpled up the slip of paper and threw it away.

That afternoon he got sick. First his throat started aching and later in the chemistry laboratory he had a chill and began shivering. In a little while his hands were too unsteady to hold a tube or pour the reagent. When class was out he stopped at the phone booth and called Max. "I think I have the flu," he said.

"Go home. Go to bed," Max said. "Drink something hot. Do you have any Empirin?"

"I'll be all right once I get to bed."

He took a bus home, but by the time he reached the apartment house he was feverish and nauseated. Goldie's door was open and he was sitting on the couch talking to a young man. He watched Dan plod up the stairs. "You sick again?"

"It's just the flu this time," Dan said. Once in his room he dropped his clothes to the floor, pulled down the door bed, and climbed into it. He was dozing when someone rapped on the door.

"Yes?"

"Hello," said the voice on the other side. "Dan?"

"It's open," Dan said. Max came in, a small package in his hand. "I brought you some Empirin," he said apologetically, his head awry.

"Thanks," Dan said.

Max rubbed his hands together. "Well? How do you feel?"

"Lousy. How did you find out where I lived?"

"I called the number you left at the store. Some fellow answered. A pansy?"

"I don't know."

"He's a pansy. I can tell."

"Who's in the store?"

"Sharon. It smells stuffy in here. Do you want me to make you something to eat?"

Dan shook his head.

"You should have something hot. It opens the pores."

"I'd throw up."

"All right. Take the Empirin."

He went into the kitchen and brought out a cup of water and gave it to Dan with two white pills. Dan swallowed them.

"That'll help." Max sat down on the edge of the bed. "How's school?"

"All right. Not too hard."

"You learned a lot already. I can tell by the way you talk. Did you study anything about sex yet?"

"Just anatomy."

"What does it mean when a woman's cold?"

He was nauseated. His legs hurt. The thin blanket failed to warm him, and he was imprisoned in that terrible green room. It was hard for him to talk. But most of all he didn't want to share Max's misery. He looked away. "I don't know any more about it than you do."

"She doesn't reach a climax."

Dan didn't answer.

Max shook his head. "And she won't even do it at all for months. Two months since the last time. Is that normal?"

"It's probably psychological."

"You think so?"

"I guess so."

"Well, you should know. The customers tell me every night you're studying in the store. Maybe I'm too old for her."

The pills Max had given him were starting to work. He began sweating and his legs felt better.

"There could be something the matter with her. It doesn't have to be you," Dan said.

"She had experience before we got married. Sex satisfied her then."

Dan didn't say anything.

"The fellows she had before we were married were all bigger than me."

"She told you this kind of stuff?"

"Lots of times." He chewed nervously on his small mustache. The only sound in the room was the ticking of the cheap alarm clock.

"Anything wrong with you there?" Dan finally asked.

"How does a man know if he's too small? His wife tells him. That's how."

"She's not very big herself."

Max looked up quickly, suspicion in his eyes.

"I mean she's not a big girl."

"Oh." A little later he said, "I was lucky to get a girl like that."

Dan rolled over to see him better. Max was serious. "Haven't you ever wondered why she married me?" he went on. "I don't make a lot of money. I'm older than her. I'm kind of a slob the way I dress."

"She is very pretty," Dan said after a while.

Max nodded. "She was starting to get into trouble before we got married. She was running around a lot, and she comes from a good family. It scared her. She wasn't happy with any-body, and kept trying one after another and getting in deeper and deeper with all kinds of boy friends, and she got frightened and she married me. She thinks I don't know why, but I do."

"I don't know what to tell you," Dan finally said. He raised up on one elbow. "Listen. If you knew somebody's name and when they died, how would you find out what happened to them?"

"The police probably. Are you still nauseous?"

Dan nodded.

"Ginger ale. That'll settle your stomach." He got up.

"I'll be able to go down myself after a while."

"You stay in bed," Max said.

Dan fell asleep. When he awoke it was quite dark outside. The drummer across the hall was tapping his drums. By his bed was a moist paper bag with a note on top. "Stay in bed. I'll call you tomorrow." In the bag were three bottles of ginger ale surrounded by half-melted ice cubes wrapped in plastic. He drank a bottle. It tasted good, and, as Max had promised, it quieted his stomach, and he went to sleep.

In the morning he got up and tried to shave, but he was weak and he stopped with only half his face shaved. He was fearful at first but the symptoms were different and when he took his temperature he found it 103 degrees. He went back to bed and tried to sleep, but several radios played loudly and he heard phones ring and doors slam. From the floor below a man sang in a pleasing tenor voice a song in which the phrase "Cry me a river of tears" was repeated frequently. It sounded like Goldie. The stuffiness of the room grew worse as the day got warmer, and finally he couldn't stand it any longer. By then his legs felt a little firmer and he dressed and walked downstairs.

He knocked and Goldie came gaily around the door still singing. "How are we this morning? We looked kind of peaked yesterday."

"I was wondering if you'd let me use your phone," Dan said. "I must owe you five bucks for all the times I've used it." He took five dollars from his wallet and handed it to Goldie.

"I wouldn't think of it," Goldie said, grinning, and took

the money. "Come on in. I want you to meet somebody."
Dan followed him into the apartment. A blond young man
was sitting on the couch. Tee shirt, tight white-denim trousers.
"He's from San Francisco too. You might know each other."

The boy on the couch got up and shook hands with Dan.
"Nice to meet you," he said. He picked up a suede jacket
from the table. "I have to be going," he said to Goldie.

"Come in here," Goldie said and the two went into the
bedroom. Dan could hear them negotiating. He sat down and
dialed the operator. When she answered he said, "I think I
want to speak to the police."

"Just a moment," she said. The blond boy came out buttoning
his jacket. "So long," he said.

A policeman's voice came in on the phone.

"I know the name of a man and when he died. How do I
find out what happened to him?"

"In the county or the city?"

"The city."

"The Hall of Records." The policeman gave him the address.
"They'll have a certificate on file."

"Will they show it to me? I'm not a relative or anything."

"It's a public document," he said and hung up.

"Wasn't he something?" Goldie said.

"Do you have a pencil?"

Goldie gave him the stub of a pencil. "Why are you always
so unfriendly?"

"I'm friendly. How do you get to Broadway?"

Goldie told him, and he went out and took the bus to the
Hall of Records. A clerk with an eyeshade over his eyes and
a pencil tucked behind one ear copied down the name Dan
gave. He returned a few minutes later with a slip of paper.
"Jesse Davis," he said. "Died October 12, 1959. Is that the
one?"

"That's it."

"You can have a copy for two dollars."

"I don't need a copy."

"All right," the clerk said. "He lived at 4933 Hoover. He

was thirty-three. He died of suicide with Lysol. He was born in Covesville. That's in West Virginia." The clerk looked up from the slip. "That's it."

"It doesn't say why?"

"It's only a death certificate." He handed Dan the penciled slip and went back to his work.

Dan found a phone booth in the hall and looked up the address of the *Times* and the *Herald*. The *Times* was closer and he went there first. A girl led him into a small room and brought him a volume of bound newspapers for the month of October 1959. He read the four-year-old news. The Supreme Court gave an opinion rejecting any further delay on school integration in Arkansas. Tunisia and Morocco joined the Arab League. An amusement park in Oxnard burned down and three children died. Jesse Davis, however, was not mentioned.

His fever was still high and he found it hard to lift the heavy book. He left it lying on the table and went downstairs and drank a cup of coffee at a hamburger stand. Afterward he walked to the *Herald*. He had better luck there. In a paper dated October 15 he found a paragraph on the third page with the heading: UNEMPLOYED AIRCRAFT WORKER POISONS SELF.

The body of Jesse Davis, 33, a former employee of the Canoga Park Division of the North American Aircraft Company, was found in his room on Hoover Street by the landlady, Mrs. Rose Nello. Davis apparently died by self-administered poison taken during the night. Mrs. Nello told police that Davis had been brooding a great deal, and was undergoing treatment at the psychiatric unit of General Hospital. Mrs. Nello did not know of any local relatives.

He read it twice. It was exactly what he had feared.

He went outside and stood on the corner. A cold wind moved up the street bearing the smell of motor oil and car exhaust. He put his collar up and jammed his hands into his pockets. He waited and caught a bus that took him to the General Hospital. The record room was downstairs, off an ancient stone-floored hall. He explained what he wanted to the girl at the counter. He signed her book and she brought him the chart.

Some of the notes were hard to read, written in the fast script of men who write a great deal. Other notes were type-written and were probably dictated. Davis had been anxious to talk, and he talked a great deal. Much of what he told was about his childhood. A picture of a boy came out of the typed sheets and cramped doctor's notes—a twelve-year-old West Virginia kid, levis and wool shirt, living in a town that broadened out of a pocked two-lane highway over the mountains. He had fought with one of his teachers. *He was trying to push me around,* Davis had said during one of the interviews, *and I was tired of school. I had enough school. I wanted out.*

When he spoke of his jobs, he said *I didn't like the work* or *The boss was always ordering me around.* And when he was seventeen: *I got mad at my father. He was always raising hell and yelling that I wasn't bringing in enough money, and once he got me real mad, and I shoved him. Then I got my stuff and I got on a bus to Wheeling.* He had jobs in Wheeling, sometimes in gas stations, once in a meat-packing plant, but always after a month or two months or six months he left. The same thing happened with his girls. *I was going with a pretty nice girl but she started to talk about getting married, and I ran.* He had finally gotten a girl pregnant. She was a filing clerk in the meat-packing plant. He married her, and stayed with her only two months at first. *There wasn't anybody else,* he said. *I just got fed up. I got this room over on Randolph Street and I moved there.* Later he came back. He didn't explain why. He probably didn't know why. Neither did the doctors. The disease, or whatever it was, grew more malignant as he grew older. Finally he left his family for good, and went to Detroit, and from Detroit to Seattle, and lastly to Los Angeles, where in October he drank a bottle of Lysol.

When Dan got home he was even more grim and despondent than when he left. Jesse Davis, the cadaver he knew more intimately than he had ever known a living man, had lived a miserable prewritten role, and there was no sense either in his life or his death.

Dan was heartily tired of his own persistent despondency. He sat down on his bed and thought of ways to lighten it. Eddie might have been right. He had gone a long time without a girl. He tried to remember the name of the red-headed waitress, but he couldn't. He wasn't sure he ever knew it.

He went out and walked to the art store, and strained to see the signature on the clown's face in the dimly lit window. Joan Means. Then he went to Hoagy's. Lorraine was behind the counter.

"What happened to that girl that used to work here?" he asked.

"Joan?"

"Yes."

"She quit."

"Where does she live?"

"We don't give out that information to customers," Lorraine said, and went back to stacking dishes.

The only one left was Sharon. He changed a quarter and phoned the store. "Max?"

"How are you feeling?"

"I still have a little fever."

"Maybe you ought to see a doctor. Sharon's doctor is Dr. Witus. Maybe he won't even charge you, you being a medical student."

"I don't think I can work today."

"It always takes three days for the flu. You need anything?"

"I got those pills you left. Thanks for the ginger ale." He hesitated. "Is Sharon coming down to help you?"

"What for? Business is slow."

"I'll see you tomorrow," Dan said. He hung up and dialed Max's home number. He had often called it before to ask where certain items in the store were kept.

The receiver was lifted and his heart began pounding. "Sharon?" he asked.

"Yes. Who's calling?"

"Dan," he said and waited. If she acted unfriendly he would say, *Gosh, I'm sorry. I got mixed up on the numbers and dialed your home number instead of the store.*

"I heard you're sick." She sounded hoarse.

"You don't have a cold too, do you?"

"I'm fine. What's the matter with you?"

"Just the flu. I'm not going to work tonight."

"I had it last year. I thought I was going to die. My back hurt and my head hurt and I kept taking Empirins till they made me nauseous."

He listened for a while, the receiver against his ear.

"I couldn't do housework for a month after I had it."

"It's nice to have a night off," he said. "It's just lonely." He waited again. She could ignore what he had said, and again all he had to do then was say, *It was nice talking to you,* and hang up and that was that. He didn't want her to have to say yes or no openly so that they both heard it.

"What you need is someone to make you some hot chicken soup," she said. "Jewish penicillin."

"A beer would go better. Can you join me?"

"I was going to do my hair tonight, but I suppose I can do it tomorrow."

The despondency suddenly lightened and he said, "I can pick you up."

"I've got the car," she said. "Max walked to work."

He gave her the name of a bar he had often passed. It was on Vermont Avenue, several blocks away.

Sharon had been crying when Dan called, but she stopped when she heard his voice. After she hung up she washed her face and put a bandanna over her curlers. Then she called Max. "I'm going out," she said.

"Every time you get mad at me you run someplace. Now where?"

"Just out."

"Who with?"

"Never mind," she said and hung up. She had a momentary glow of satisfaction, but afterward she was annoyed at herself. She hesitated, on the point of calling him back, but she was aching to talk to somebody, and she couldn't talk to Max. He was what she wanted to talk about. She put on her coat and went out.

On the way to Vermont Avenue she wondered why Dan called and what he was going to offer. She became excited thinking about it.

She glanced up and down the street before she went into the bar. She wasn't likely to run into her friends at this end of Vermont, but she had never stepped out before and it would be just her luck if Max caught her the first time. The bar was dirty and some of the patrons were colored. She became angry at Dan for picking such a place. She considered walking out, but the bartender saw her and made a silent motion toward a table. Dan was sitting there, hair tousled, looking into a glass of beer, and she felt tender and frightened. She walked to the table, hearing the noise her heels made, expecting him to look up, but he kept staring at the beer. He finally looked up when she reached the table. His shirt was open, and even in the dim light she could see that his face was flushed with fever. She wanted to touch his cheek and kiss him but it was important that she hide what she felt, and she said, "Why did you have to pick this place for? It's creepy."

He stood up and awkwardly pulled her chair out. She sat down. He was handsome, too, she thought. Freckled and blond. A lot better looking than Max. He didn't have that silly stupid mustache, and he didn't chew on his words like they were spaghetti.

"There's a place like this over on Larchmont and the Board of Health made them close it up. Everybody got sick from eating there. The food was spoiled," she said.

"I've been sitting here a half hour and I haven't seen anybody eating," he said. "What can I get for you?"

"A Black Russian." It was a good drink to order and it didn't taste too bad either.

"I wouldn't gamble on it." He looked toward the bartender and the bartender came to the table. "I don't suppose you've got a drink called a Black Russian?"

"We don't get many calls for them. How about a gimlet with fresh lime juice?"

Dan looked at her, and she nodded. "Make it a gimlet," he said.

"I came over with my curlers on," she said. "I put a bandanna over them. It doesn't really look too bad, does it?"

"I've been thinking all day," he said. "I've been working on this cadaver for a year now and—"

"Your cadaver? What you practice anatomy on?"

"Yes. Today I found out—"

"Don't tell me about it. I don't like to hear about dead people. You don't mind my coming out this way? I just didn't want to get dressed. I sometimes go around the house all day barefooted on days like this. I have calluses on my feet from being barefooted, but I never had a corn in my life."

He was looking at his beer again, and she became provoked. He expected her to do all the talking. "You get corns from wearing shoes that rub too much. That comes from trying to make your feet look little. I have a size five." She saw by his face that he didn't know what a five was. "It's a real little size. I can wear the same size now that I wore when I was fourteen. I still got a few pairs around the house too." She tasted the gimlet. It was bitter. "You get all mixed up with a marriage," she started. "You don't know whose fault the trouble is. I don't know why I married Max. My father didn't want me to. He called him a *knebbish*."

He wasn't listening, and she stopped talking. She played with the gimlet and managed to swallow most of it.

He was telling her about someone falling down an elevator shaft.

"Don't they have safety things on the doors?" she said.

"Yes," he said, "but it didn't work. They were fixing the elevators and somebody must have just switched it off. Anyway—"

"What a case he would have against the elevator company! I told Max I was going out."

After a moment he said, "He doesn't mind?"

She shrugged. "Why should he mind? I let him go to his pharmacy meetings. When he wants to play poker I let him go. The rest of the time he goes to bed at eight o'clock. I'm only twenty-three. He won't see forty again. I don't want to stay in every night. If I don't have any fun now I won't have any in my life. It isn't my fault he's sick." She could see he wasn't listening and her voice became louder. "The way he acts you'd think it was my fault I don't want to go to bed with him. What can I do about that? Can you make yourself want to go to bed with somebody?"

She waited, but he didn't answer. Later he started speaking about somebody named Jesse Davis. When he paused she said, "If not for me he wouldn't even have the store. When we got married, he was plenty satisfied with just a job. I told him he's got to get a business of his own. A lot of our best customers are my friends. I called them up, and I told them that if they get their drugs anyplace else but from Max I would never speak to them again. They mail in the prescriptions and Max brings them out." He didn't say anything. Perhaps he was missing the point, and she went on a little more desperately: "At first I used to entertain a lot for Max. My friends. Some doctors I knew. But none of my friends like Max. When Francie comes to the house now all she does is say hello to him."

"How does your gimlet taste?" He reached for the glass and took a sip. "It's sour."

She waited. But there was nothing he seemed to want to say any more. He just kept sitting there.

She tried again: "Maybe I ought to go back to school. I wanted to study law when I finished high school. There aren't enough women lawyers. Women are afraid to go into professional fields."

She waited again, and he still said nothing, and her heart sank. She felt dry and empty and tired, and she knew for sure that there wasn't going to be any offer, and the things that she had told herself as she had driven over just weren't going to happen. When the evening was done she was going to go back to Max with his bad breath and his little mustache and his irritating habit of stumbling on words. She could have done something with this one. It would have been nice being married to him, and she would have helped him get ahead. She had a lot of friends. But there was no offer. He didn't make any. And she knew just why he had called her.

"I just live a few blocks from here," he said. "If you'd like we can go up and have some more beer there."

She started crying again and turned her face away so he couldn't see.

When they got to his room she looked around and said, "You should keep a window open. It smells bad in here."

"You get used to it."

"I had a girl friend who had an apartment around here. She was living with a colored fellow. She wouldn't live right in the colored neighborhood, and she couldn't live in the white neighborhood, so she got an apartment a couple of blocks away from here."

He nodded impatiently.

"I have to go soon," she said. "What time is it? Do you have a clock?"

"You have at least two hours."

"I don't want to leave too late. I want to finish with my hair tonight."

He put his arms around her and she smelled of perfume and the dry gritty smell that certain makeup carries.

"I want to talk to you," she said. "Wait a minute."

"All you do is complain about Max."

"Do you think I like hurting him all the time? I can't help it. What's the matter with me anyway? I keep trying—"

He put his hand over her mouth and said, "Be quiet," and then he kissed her. She broke away. "I'm aching to talk to somebody," she said. "What are you doing?"

"Taking your blouse off."

"Why?"

"Because I can't go to bed with you with your blouse on. The lousy buttons would scratch me," he said angrily.

"Don't stretch the material," she said. She got out of the blouse herself. He felt obliged to kiss her again as she was undressing. When she stopped short at her underpants, he slipped his hand under them and tugged them off.

"It's cold in here," she said, and got into bed.

In spite of her chattering his heart was beating hard and strong again. He dropped his own clothes to the floor, and rolled up next to her. She started talking and he said again, "Be quiet." She opened her mouth to answer and he kissed her. He reached down to separate her legs and in his nervousness brushed a small plastic ashtray from a bedside table. It fell a few inches against her face.

He pushed the ashtray aside. "Did it hurt you?"

"What was that?"

"Just an ashtray. It didn't hurt you, did it? It only fell a little bit." He started to move again but she abruptly rolled away and sat up on the edge of the bed. He lay in bed waiting. She got up and walked to the single mirror in the room. "Turn on the light," she said.

He reached over the bed and flicked the light switch.

She was standing, her hair still in the bandanna, curlers intact, her back and buttocks toward him.

"Your nose is all right. Come back to bed."

"Why?"

"You quit in the middle of things."

"Do you feel frustrated?"

"What do you think?"

"I couldn't care less," she said. She pulled on her underpants. "Go get yourself a call girl for ten dollars."

He didn't get angry. He thought instead, If ever a son of a bitch deserves what he's getting, I do.

"Did you have a good time? Am I a good lay?"

"You don't have to scream."

"All I wanted was to talk. All you needed to do was pat

me on the head and listen and you could have had everything."
She was shouting again. "Now I gave you a taste of your own
medicine. How does it feel?" Her face was bright red and tears
were streaming down her cheeks. She searched for her purse.
He got up and walked into the bathroom and came back with
some toilet paper. He gave it to her and she blew her nose
furiously. "Max is your best friend. You should hear how he
worries about you. Don't you have any shame?"

"Don't speak so loud."

"Let them all hear. You're a hypocrite too. You go to temple
on Yom Kippur in your hat all dressed up. I've seen you. But
at night when nobody's around you eat pork and beans." She
paused out of breath. "Next time do me a favor. Go get yourself
a call girl. I'll lend you the money." By then she was dressed.

Dan stepped into his pants. "I'll walk you to your car," he
said.

She raised her head high and marched to the door. At the
threshold she paused and said, "Now you can go play with
yourself," and she slammed the door hard.

When Dan went to work the next day he walked directly to
the back and put on his tan coat. He avoided talking with
Max, and he was greatly relieved when Max went home. That
night and for a long time afterward he worked unusually hard.
He dusted high shelves and cleaned seldom-used drawers. He
did not permit himself to rest or to sit down at work, thereby
doing a secret penance, and making amends to Max in the only
way he could.

Three

DAN DID UNUSUALLY WELL in his examinations at the year's end and received a note from the dean. Max arranged a summer job for him at a store on West Adams. He worked there days, and nights and weekends at Max's store. He bought an old convertible Dodge that brewed large clouds of blue smoke but which carried him promptly from one job to another. He put the Cunningham away on a top shelf in his closet. The book was blotched with formaldehyde and carbolic acid and had become old in the year he used it. He remembered most of its pages and illustrations, and its precise and ponderous wording, and this knowledge of anatomy colored his thoughts as no other knowledge ever had before. When eating he would occasionally stop and absently dissect the chicken leg on his plate, searching for the sciatic nerve and separating the various muscle groups. He began to think of people not as units but as assemblies of differently shaped and colored organs, protected by skin and supported by ingenious bony columns and plates. He listened to his own body all day long and would become fascinated by such things as the flow of saliva into his mouth, or the sensations arising from his stomach when he was hungry.

He thought frequently of Jesse Davis. He had found some of the answers he had sought. Davis died of Lysol poisoning. He had poisoned himself because, for some reason or another, he had emptied his own life of everything that might keep a man warm. But the underlying cause was still not explained, and he worried about it, fearful that what had destroyed Davis was also in him, and might destroy him, too, in time.

He worked sixteen hours a day, coming home tired and going to bed without turning the light on. The morning sadness stayed with him, and each night he wondered if he would get through it in the morning. Nevertheless he managed to work all summer without interruption, and he put aside enough money for his tuition.

In September he brought a cashier's check to the girl in the administration offices and registered for the fall term.

The subjects taught in the second year were livelier and more interesting than those he had finished. In one afternoon course the students were taught to do blood counts. At first they practiced on one another. Later they were sent to the County Hospital to do tests on the patients there.

Dan entered the huge building cautiously. Interns in white suits hurried down the halls. Orderlies pushed patients on tall carts, and hauled empty carts back. Only the nurses and the rest of the complex feminine matriarchy of the hospital in their various uniforms seemed unhurried and unharassed. He wondered uneasily, as he stood cramped against two dozen patients whether he would be likely to catch anything from them.

The students were assigned patients by the head nurse, a fat woman in a stiffly starched gown who wore so much face powder that her face also seemed starched. One afternoon in the second week of the course Dan and Noble found they had been given a patient named Effie Longham. As they were preparing their instruments Noble said, "All the patients we get are Negro, aren't they?"

Dan had noticed it too but all he said was, "They all have blood, haven't they?" He stuck the patient's finger with the lancet and filled his pipette. Noble walked out of the ward, and later Dan saw him talking to the head nurse. Dan went on into the ward laboratory and started doing the count. The other two Negro students were in the same room, working at a different microscope.

After a while Noble came in. "You get mostly Negroes to work on?" he asked.

One of the students, Kenneth Wiggins, was thin and light, and always well dressed. "I don't keep count," he said.

"She told me that some white patients object to Negro doctors."

Dan pushed Noble's pipettes toward him. "I filled them for you. Let's get finished."

"Why are you trying to shut me up? Where do you stand anyway?"

"What the hell are you going to do now?"

Noble ignored him. "Are you two colored or is that just a sun tan?"

Neither of them answered.

"I'm going to ask every white patient on this ward if they object to having a Negro working on them. Are you going to help?"

"All you'll do is stir up trouble," Wiggins said.

The other student, whose name was Greg, looked up from the microscope. "Colored patients are easier to work on than whites," he said.

"How long did it take to learn that fake English accent?"

"I'm not going to take any more of this," Greg said.

"You crawled on your butt to get into a white fraternity," Noble said. "Do they let you go out with their girls?"

"Don't get involved with him," Wiggins said. "He's sick."

Noble took off his glasses. Dan watched tensely but he merely wiped the lenses with a piece of paper toweling, and then set them back on his nose. He picked up a pad and a pencil and went out.

A half hour or so later, while Dan was finishing his last count, he heard the sound of shouting. He got up and hurried into the ward. Noble was holding an old man by the arm. The patient was in the short shirt provided by the hospital, and his naked gnarly legs seemed barely able to support him.

The fat nurse bustled in. "What's the matter here?"

"He's asking me a lot of questions," the old man shouted. "He's got no call to ask me questions."

"You better go back to bed, Mr. Starling."

"He asked me if I cared if a colored student worked on me. Sure I care. I don't want them working on me."

The nurse led him back to bed and fitted an oxygen mask about his face. "I'm going to give you a shot and then I'll report the whole thing to the nursing supervisor." Dan watched as she marched to the telephone. Later he saw her charting the incident, triumph showing in the rigid lines of her starched back.

The next day the dean came to the pathology laboratory and announced that Oney Noble was being suspended for two weeks. He showed bad judgment, the dean said, in arguing with a patient with an acute coronary thrombosis. Although the patient suffered an attack after the argument, he appeared to have recovered from it. If he had not, the disciplinary action would have been much more severe.

Several days later Dan went to the desk of one of the instructors, a young blond physician from Canada. "I want to take my partner his assignments," he said. "Will I be able to sign out the tissue slides?"

"Good idea," the Canadian said. "He has problems with his work anyway and if he falls behind two weeks more I think he'll have had it." After a moment he added, "I don't understand this kind of to-do. We have Nigerian students and Ghana students working in our wards back home and nobody says a word." He made some notes on a sheet of paper and handed it to Dan. "This is where we're going in the next two weeks. I'll leave instructions at the front desk so you can take the slides out."

Dan got Noble's address from the dean's office. It was on 103rd Street in Watts. Once through downtown, he found that every face on the street was black. The only exception were the occasional store owners he saw locking up for the day.

He passed stores that had been destroyed by fire and new apartment houses that were gutted, the windows torn out and the stucco chipped away until the chicken wire and studs beneath showed. He turned off Central and parked in front of a small frame house. A dozen colored children, the girls with their coarse hair in pigtails, the boys in levis, were playing in the street. They stopped and carefully watched him get out of his car. He walked up to the front porch and rang the doorbell. A man in his undershirt came to the door.

"Is Oney home?"

"They live in back," the man said and closed the door. Dan looked at the number he had written down, 1747-¾ 103rd Street. The door that was closing bore the number 1747-¼. The second door opening on the garage driveway in the middle of the house was 1747-½. Obviously the single stucco house, originally designed for one family, had been cut up into four units and fractional numbers were used to preserve the number sequence. He pressed the doorbell on the farthest door but it didn't ring. He then knocked, and after a while an elderly colored woman opened the door.

"Is Oney here?"

"What do you want him for?"

"I have some books and some slides for him." She closed the door and he waited, uncertain what to do next. Finally he knocked again and, when there was no answer, pushed the door open and came into a small kitchen. The old woman was sitting on a chair listening to the radio. "Isn't Oney here?"

She looked at him again, and he was amazed at the hatred in her eyes. "He's asleep," she said.

He started to put the slides down on a table when a young woman carrying a baby in one arm came out. She walked to the stove to stir something in a pot. Without looking at Dan she said, "Who you from?" The same hatred was there, but it showed only in the turned back, and in the tone of voice.

Dan began to get angry. "I'll take it to him," he said and walked by her into the hall and opened a door into a bedroom. A fully dressed man lay sleeping on an unmade bed. Noble was sitting on one of the cots. His eyes were puffy, and he reached for his glasses and put them on.

"I have your assignments," Dan said. "Here are the slides for the next two weeks. Do you want my notes too?"

"You write so lousy," Noble said. After a moment he said, "It's going to be hard to cover this stuff."

"You'd better, if you want to make it."

"They tell you that?"

Dan nodded. "Was it worth it?"

"I didn't know this fellow was a heart case."

"Why didn't you read the chart?"

"Because I was too damn mad." After a moment he said, "What happened to him?"

"I guess he's all right. He went home yesterday."

"I have another ten days of suspension."

"I'll run my notes out every couple of days. That fish place you work is the easiest to get to."

Noble nodded and followed Dan into the kitchen.

Dan paused at the door. "I wish the hell you'd cool it," he finally said. He saw the anger gathering in Noble's face and he added, "The first time you flipped I almost got a broken nose. Now I'm working without a partner."

"You want to change partners? Maybe Wiggins will work with you."

"What did you study in that divinity school?"

"Religion. New Testament history. Why?"

"No Jewish history?"

"Oh brother," Noble said.

"Do me a favor. It'll make my life easier. Go get Graetz's *History of the Jews*. Read it."

"Why?"

"Just read it."

Noble pondered the suggestion. Then he said, "How do you spell it?"

Dan wrote it down. He wanted to say something more but the spiteful eyes of the old woman remained fixed on him, following every movement, and he finally said, "I'll see you in a few days," and went out, glad to escape.

It had grown dark while he was in the house. The same children were in the street and once again they stopped when they saw him. He felt foreign with his naked white face. He wanted to hide it or paint it dark and get out of that artificial town that was more alien to him than a town in Spain, or Norway, or Siberia. He started his car quickly and was relieved when he finally turned into Vermont and saw white faces again.

At the end of the two weeks Noble walked into class, set his books down, and began working without having received or given a greeting to anyone in the class. Dan handed him two slides. "You haven't seen these yet," he said.

Noble put them under his scope. "What are they?"

"Two lung sections. 1011 is silicosis and 1012 is anthracosis."

The Canadian instructor stopped at Noble's bench. "I'm glad you're back, Mr. Noble," he said. "Any help I can give you just ask me."

Noble muttered, "Thanks," and the instructor moved on.

"Did you manage to keep up with the assignments?" Dan asked.

"I stayed out of work for the last three days."

"How did you do on the history?"

"Are you trying to convert me?"

"I think so," Dan said. "I'd like some peace."

"I'm up to the first dispersion. I'll give you a book report next year. If I'm still here."

Dan returned to his microscope. It was comfortable to have Noble back again, and the morning went more quickly, and he covered more ground than he did alone.

That Friday when he got his pay check he found himself with his tuition and rent paid, his books all bought, and free to spend the money on whatever he wanted. He carried the check about for several days, and then one early evening walking to work he saw the clown face in the art supply store and on a sudden impulse walked in. The owner was a small man who wore a double-breasted vest. "What can I do for you?"

"How much are you asking for that clown face?"

"The one in the window?"

Dan nodded. The storekeeper reached into the window and took it from its hook, and set it on the counter. The sadness and gentleness of the clown's eyes leaped out at Dan again, and he said, "I'm glad you haven't sold it."

"The artist isn't glad." The storekeeper had an English accent.

Dan looked at it for a while. "Is it good?" he finally asked.

"The girl has talent. She's going to have a show on La Cienega. Golden Galleries."

"She used to be a waitress at Hoagy's."

"So what? Gauguin was a bank teller. Toulouse-Lautrec was a pimp."

Dan smiled. "How much is she asking?"

"Seventy-five dollars."

"You better put it back."

"Can't manage it?"

"Nowhere close."

The storekeeper said, "Pity. It would do her good to sell a canvas. It's well worth it to you, particularly if her work takes on." He studied Dan for a moment. "I know you. Do you live around here?"

"I work at Wolfe's drugstore. You come in there once in a while."

"Of course," the storekeeper said. "Listen. I'd like to be able to call her and tell her that it's sold. I'll give it to you for half of what it's marked. I'll add my commission to the price when I tell her about it, and that way it won't be far from seventy-five. What do you say?"

Dan hesitated a long time, but he liked the painting and finally he handed the dealer the uncashed check. The small man was delighted. He dusted the canvas and cleaned the frame and took so long in wrapping it that Dan finally asked him to bring it to the store when he was done.

He hung it in his room that night. He hoped, if he saw it when he awoke in the morning, it might prevent the morning sadness that was still frightening him badly.

Two nights later while he was undressing, shirt off, sitting on the bed pulling off one shoe, the buzzer sounded. He took off the other shoe and opened the door and the red-headed girl was waiting. He stared at her in surprise.

"I decided to give you another chance," she said. Her face was pink from the cold and she smelled clean and fresh.

He was embarrassed. He was naked from the hips up, and besides he had forgotten her name again. "Oh, hello. Sure," he said. After a moment he said, "A second chance at what?"

"Me. Can I see where you hung it?"

He stepped aside and she came in. "Didn't you pay your electric bill?" she said.

"I don't get much company at two in the morning," he said and turned the light on.

She walked up to the clown face and looked at it. Then she looked at Dan. "I don't know how I managed to paint those eyes a year before I saw them."

Dan put his shirt on.

"Mr. Simon told me you paid sixty-five dollars. You must really appreciate art. You don't give me the impression of a big spender."

He sat down on the bed. "What's your name?"

She sighed in mock despair. "Joan Means."

"That's right. How are you?"

"Fine. I just sold a painting."

"You've quit waitressing?"

"I told you it was a penance."

"For what?"

"Do you mind if I sit down too?"

"Do you often do penance?"

"Sometimes I don't do anything else."

"I'm just finishing a spell of it myself."

"For what?"

"For the same thing, I suppose."

"Mine's mostly for drinking and the things I do when I drink. Why did you buy it?"

"Mr. Simon said it was good."

"Don't you like it?"

"I bought it, didn't I?"

"What do you like about it?"

"Do I have to know?"

"It's mine and I love it and I have to see if you love it too. Otherwise I'm going to give you your lousy sixty-five dollars back and take it home."

He thought a moment. "He's so miserably sad he makes me feel cheerful. Even when I shave."

"You talk in riddles. You're worse than I am. Do you have any tea?"

He got up and went into the kitchen. "I don't know why I'm looking," he called back. "I know there isn't any tea."

"Never mind," she said.

"I've only got one cup anyway."

She stood up, waiting, but for some reason he felt shy with her this time and he didn't take the invitation.

"Will you be nicer to me than you were the last time?" she said after a moment.

"I didn't do anything. You got angry for no reason."

"How did you know? You couldn't see me through that book."

He walked with her to the door.

"You take my number," she said and took out a little book and wrote a number on a page and gave him the page. "When are you going to call?"

"In a few days."

She didn't say anything. He realized she was waiting for him to kiss her, and he did. "That's better," she said. "Don't wait too long."

The next day in the pathology class the blond Canadian instructor interrupted the routine and talked briefly about enlargement of the heart. It was a sign of disease, he explained, and he listed a dozen or so causes of enlargement, among them arteriosclerosis of the coronary arteries that take blood to the heart.

Dan was puzzled. He remembered seeing in the pathology text the statement that arteriosclerosis in itself did not cause heart enlargement.

A half hour before the class was to end a short written quiz was given. The students were to mark right or wrong after certain sentences. One of them read, "Coronary arteriosclerosis can in itself cause cardiac enlargement." Dan hesitated and then underlined the word "Wrong." The instructor was in error, he decided.

When he left the store that night, he found the streets dim with fog. It dampened all noises. Cars with hazy headlights drove quietly and slowly. Orchid Street and the shabby old apartment houses on it became quiet and dignified, their blemishes covered by the fog.

He was startled to see light in the crack under his door. He opened it, and found Joan, hair tied behind her, standing in the middle of the room, ironing one of his shirts.

"What the hell?" he said surprised.

"Your landlord let me in," she said. "I could only find one shirt. Where are the rest?"

He looked about the room. Everything had been dusted and scrubbed. "I thought I was supposed to call you and ask you out to dinner," he finally said.

"I didn't want to wait," she said. "I did my best with the smell. It comes from that dumbwaiter. Have you ever been down to the bottom of that shaft?"

"What for?"

"There's garbage in there so old it's fossilized. An archaeologist could write a paper from the deposits on the bottom about the eating habits of four generations of Americans." She paused. "I spilled a bucket of pine oil deodorant down it. It was the best I could do." She sat down. "Where are your other shirts? I looked all over."

"I've only got the two."

The room was different. A vase of bright artificial flowers stood on the table, and an electric cord ran from a plug in the wall to an attachment on the frame above the clown's head painting.

"Do you get up when it's dark?" she said.

"In winter."

"And it's dark when you shave?"

He nodded.

"Just pull the cord and your buddy comes on." She pulled a small chain that hung from the attachment and the clown face lit up. "How's that?"

"It may just help," he said.

She stayed only a little while longer. She insisted on leaving most of the things she had brought. He walked her downstairs. She stopped at her car. "What's the matter with you?"

"What do you mean?"

"You haven't come within a foot of me."

After a moment he said, "I'm planning on it."

"Go up and get your toothbrush and the shirt I just ironed. I'll wait."

"Where do you live?"

"In the hills. You'll like it there."

He hurried upstairs and came back with what he needed. He hung his shirt in back and she started the car.

"You're different this time," she said. "You weren't shy before."

"I think it's . . ." He hesitated.

"You mean it's because I'm pushing so hard."

"Maybe," he said. "I'll get over it soon."

"It's dangerous to wait," she said. "Things can happen to spoil it if you wait."

"Other people?"

"That's one of the things."

"How can you afford a hill house on a waitress' salary?"

"My father is supporting me again. I showed him the contract I have with Golden—did I tell you about that?"

"Mr. Simon did."

"He's a nice old man. You must have liked him. He's Jewish too."

"What's that got to do with my liking him?"

"Take it easy," she said, and after a couple of minutes, "I was brought up in Idaho. In a little town. Then I went to a Catholic girl's college in Boise. You see?"

He was watching the streets. They drove down a broad boulevard that was lined with dozens of restaurants, some built like castles, others like Swiss chalets, or English inns, or ordinary delicatessens.

"Where are we?"

She laughed. "Haven't you been here before?"

"No." He kept watching, realizing that the town was even bigger than he had thought. They passed a hotel that occupied a whole block and she turned at the corner and said, "My father was staying there last week. He came down to see me."

"What does he do?"

"He owns a town."

"Where?"

"In Idaho. Means, Idaho. Mines, jail, hotel, and two stores."

They were climbing into the hills that ringed the city. The road had been laid along the bottom of a dry wash. The hillsides on either side were sharp and cut by water. The hills themselves were covered with scrub oak and thorny patches of flat-leafed cactuses. At one spot where there were no houses he saw something move in the dark brush ahead, and when they came closer he saw a deer hop daintily back into the shadows.

Joan's house stood back from the street and was shaded by trees with long leaves. Inside the house it was clean and quiet, and he heard crickets through the window. She brought out a bottle of whiskey and poured a drink for him.

"None for yourself?"

She shook her head.

"*Lekhayim,*" he said and drank it down. She filled it for him again. In a little while the whiskey took effect. His shyness disappeared and he kissed her.

She responded ferociously, and he became uneasy and started to pull away. "Now," she said. "Right now. Let's go to bed."

Once they were in bed and he felt the length of her body he became eager and excited. Afterward she said, "I'm safe now."

"From what?"

"From anybody." She fell asleep with her head on his shoulder. He waited until he was sure her sleep was sound. Then he got up silently, pulled his trousers on and brought the pathology book in from the car.

He closed the door to the bedroom and turned on a small lamp in the living room. The crickets were loud, and the street was quiet. It was a good house to study in.

He searched in the text and found again the clear statement that coronary arteriosclerosis does not produce enlargement of the heart. He then went back to bed and slept unusually well.

He awoke at four in the morning. Joan was sleeping softly beside him, her arm outstretched, her hair over the side of her face. He stole barefoot to the bathroom. His apartment had no tub. He filled her tub with hot water and soaked happily for a while. Then he dressed, and started the two-mile walk to Sunset, where he could catch a bus.

In the middle of the morning pathology session the quiz papers of the day before were returned, and Dan saw that his answer to the question on heart enlargement was marked incorrect. He picked up the text and went to the instructor and said, "You've made a mistake in grading my paper."

The Canadian physician looked at the paper. "This is an incorrect answer. We covered it yesterday in the lecture."

Dan brought out the text, the sentence underlined. "It's quite clear here."

"I know," the instructor said. "Kermer does say that. But in my experience uncomplicated coronary artery disease produces enlargement. I've seen it."

"How can my answer be wrong if it's what the text says?"

"Hold on a moment. Ben."

The other instructor left the student he was talking with and walked up. "Yes?"

"McDermott here just showed me where Kermer says that coronary arteriosclerosis doesn't produce cardiac enlargement."

"It can. I've seen it."

The instructor handed Dan's paper back. "There, you see, you lose. Listen to the lectures more carefully."

The deliberate contradiction of the text disturbed him. Perhaps Kermer was the one who made the mistake, he finally decided, and made his mind up to search the other texts on pathology in the library later when he could find the time.

When he got to the store that night Max was talking to Sharon and Dan had a few free minutes. He called Joan. "Would you like to have dinner with me tomorrow night?"

"I've been waiting all day for you to call."

"It's hard calling from school."

"Danny?"

"Yes."

"I love you."

At first he was surprised. Then he got angry. "Jesus Christ, what bullshit," he said. "You've only seen me three times."

"More than that. Don't get angry."

"But you don't even know me."

"It's a feeling," she said. "It hasn't anything to do with knowing." She started to cry. He was surprised again, and after a moment he said apologetically, "All right. We'll go to dinner. Stop crying."

"I can cry at a word from you. Doesn't that mean something?"

"Maybe your period's coming on."

"Go to hell," she said. "I'm not going to have dinner with you. You can kneel down and beg me. I've got some pride. What time do you want to pick me up?"

He laughed and set a time, and then they talked lightly awhile about how she was struggling to make frames for the pictures she was going to exhibit, and how unreliable her carpentry was. He hung up feeling cheerful, and went out to find Max.

Max was waiting on a customer. He completed the sale and Dan said, "I want to take a night off."

"You aren't sick again?"

"A hell of a life you lead, boss," Dan said. "Do you have to be sick to take a day off?"

"What then?"

"I haven't taken out a girl for a long time. I almost forgot what one feels like. Do you still remember?"

"I'm a married man."

"I don't mean wives. I mean girls."

"Hm," said Max. "You think they feel different?"

"Try it sometime."

"I just look at a girl and I feel guilty all week. How do you think I'd feel if I actually knocked off a piece?"

"You've got a Jewish conscience. It cripples a man."

"I never went to yeshiva. My family are freethinkers."

"The Torah says you can't even covet your neighbor's wife. Who can keep from coveting every so often?"

"What does covet mean?"

"Oh Christ," Dan said. "I'm alone in a desert. How about tomorrow night?"

Sharon walked up from the back of the store. "He's got a girl," Max said. "He wants to take a night off."

Sharon turned and walked out the front door.

"Don't misunderstand," Max said. "It's not the night off. She's just upset." He hesitated a moment. "She thinks she's pregnant."

"How did you manage that?"

"How did I manage? How does anyone manage?" Max said sharply. After a moment he shrugged. "Anyway she's not pregnant. You don't know what precautions she makes me take."

The next day after school Dan hurried to the library and took out six large pathology texts. Their combined weight made his arms ache as he carried them down to his car.

He drove down Sunset Boulevard to the canyon road and

found Joan's house. It was just getting dark. In one silent sweep all the streetlights of the long road went on.

He felt good about seeing Joan and he kissed her warmly. "Go ahead and finish dressing," he said. "Take your time. It's still early."

When he heard her splashing in the tub, he brought in the books and spread them out on the living-room floor. He was disappointed with several of them. One was in German and another was a history of medicine, the reference from the catalogue file referring to a chapter on the history of pathology.

"I'll be out soon," Joan called through the closed door.

"No hurry," he said. "You must be worn out from all that carpentering."

He quickly searched the other four texts. One of them made no statement on the point, but the other three said the same as the Kermer text. He felt victorious. He marked the passages in the books so he could find them readily the next day. He was about to close the books when his eyes fell on a paragraph about the remarkable deformities that birth defects produce in the heart. He read and lost track of the time.

Something was set down by his elbow. It was a plate of scrambled eggs and a cup of coffee. Joan stood above him in denim pants, her hair bright and her face shiny from her bath.

"I thought you were getting dressed."

"That was an hour ago," she said. "You'd better eat. It'll settle your stomach after all those pages you just swallowed."

"I'm sorry."

"It's too late for anything but bed," she said. She sat down on the floor next to him and started eating some of the scrambled eggs.

He found it easy to read with her close-by. When he got tired he helped her tack some of the frames together.

"The show's going to be in June," she said. "Mr. Simon arranged it for me. I used to buy my oils and brushes there, and he wanted to see something I had done. I showed him that clown and then he came out here all dressed up in his waistcoat and cardigan, and he looked at the others, and then he brought Mr. Golden out."

"It's hard to get a showing, isn't it?"

"It's not a very big gallery, and he's giving me a summer date. A lot of galleries are closed summers."

Later she questioned him about himself and Eddie. He barely answered her and finally she said, "You really should learn how to talk. It can be almost as much fun as going to bed."

The next morning he put the texts triumphantly on the instructor's desk and said, "I have some references I want to show you, Doctor."

The pathologist looked up from his microscope and saw the books. "You've been doing some reading, I see."

"All three of them say that coronary arteriosclerosis alone does not give cardiac enlargement."

The instructor opened the closest book. "This one is in German. You didn't wade through this last night, did you?"

"Parts of it."

"Don't waste your time on German texts." He looked at another one. "Here's Bowditch. He writes like a gentleman, simple and clear."

"He says the same thing."

The instructor read the passages Dan had underlined. Then he closed the books and piled them one on another. "I know what they say. They're all wrong. I've seen heart enlargement from coronary artery disease too many times to believe them."

Dan shook his head. "If you say one thing and the texts say something else, how do I know what to believe?"

The instructor tilted back in his chair and laughed. "That's an easy one. Now you believe whoever's grading your papers. Later, when you're practicing, you believe what you find out yourself." He went back to his microscope and after a moment Dan returned to his bench.

For the rest of the day, however, he puzzled over the instructor's words. Not only had he contradicted the texts, but he had then gone ahead and invited Dan's skepticism of what he himself was teaching.

It was a strange philosophy, since each physician would then be an authority to himself, and there would be no uniform opinions unless they were so clear that they couldn't be reasonably doubted. He wondered how such a philosophy could have developed in a field that was thought to be a science, and he took home the text on the history of medicine and started reading it in the store. The first paragraph snatched him up, and from then on he begrudged every minute he spent away from the book.

He found the explanation in the Middle Ages. The physicians' art—not the surgeons'—then consisted only of the rituals from the sterile writings of the Greeks and the Romans. In one week the plague swept all that mummery and chicanery away, and the physicians impotently watched their patients die and later ran away to the mountains to hide from the disease they were expected to treat. They were men though; their faith in the books hadn't robbed them of that, and afterward they were so ashamed they abandoned the books, each learning directly from the sick, slowly piecing together some degree of understanding of the diseases they saw. He realized that the victory over the books had been a great victory, and was still celebrated by each generation of physicians.

He was delighted with this discovery. He didn't know all the reasons that had led him to study medicine, but he was satisfied that he had chosen well and that he was learning a profession that would content him for the rest of his life.

Four

ON YOM KIPPUR EVE Dan went home before sundown. He took out the fedora and wiped it clean and put it on. He lay down to read. Joan came about seven with some sandwiches, and he said irritably, "I can't eat."

"Yom Kippur is tomorrow."

"It's sundown to sundown."

"Any rules about friends eating?"

"Be my guest."

She opened the wrapper and started eating. "What's the matter with you anyway?"

He lay silently in the bed, and after a moment she moved to the bed beside him. "You're not religious, are you?"

"No."

"Why then Yom Kippur?"

After a while he said, "It's like visiting my mother's grave and putting flowers on it. . . . I've been thinking about her all day."

"You think about her most of the time."

"Different ways," he said. "I was thinking today about the things that were important to her. When she was young it was men. When she was old my being Jewish was the biggest thing. She felt guilty about my father being Irish."

"Can you drink coffee?"

"Just water."

She brought him a glass.

"I've been thinking about something else. There were five million Jews at the time of the dispersion. And about then there were three million Englishmen. Why are there now only fourteen million Jews and maybe a hundred million people who live in England or whose families came from there?" He turned. "Are you going to light a cigarette?"

She stopped, the package half out of her purse. "Is that a sin or something?"

"I'm dying for one. You light one and puff it in my face and I'll boot you out on your butt."

"I'm Catholic and I can smoke on Yom Kippur." She got up and moved across the room and lit her cigarette. "Most of them have been killed, I suppose," she said.

"I don't think so. A lot of Englishmen were killed in their wars too, and they still got up there. I think there are a hundred million Jews that have become Gentiles one way or another. Only the stubborn ones are left."

"There's a new tribe in Israel named McDermott," she said. "What about sex on Yom Kippur?"

"I don't know," he said startled. "You'd have to ask a rabbi."

"Go call him up."

"I can't use a phone."

"What's his number?"

"You serious?"

"Sure I'm serious. Why should I be frustrated on Yom Kippur?"

He raised up to look at her and she rocked with laughter. "You should have seen your expression," she gasped, wiping tears away. "Holy and horny at the same time, and that's one hell of a combination!"

Later she started reading and he undressed and went to bed. She was gone in the morning when he awoke, and he washed and put on fresh clothes and his hat and started the walk to Fairfax Avenue.

He found the old men in the park and sat down among them. The one who had led the prayers put his glasses on and looked at Dan. "Weren't you here last year?"

"Yes."

"Good. Rosenzweig died and Josephson died and I was afraid there wouldn't be a *minyon*." He turned to the others and said in Yiddish, "It's Yom Kippur, Jews, and we have a *minyon* now." The synagogue doors closed and he struck his breast and started the prayer.

Eddie was one of Fidelity's senior claims executives, and most of the larger claims crossed his desk. He was careful and precise in his work, and the secretaries would go to special pains to present him with a neat file, all the papers punched and bound in proper order. Otherwise he was likely to become sarcastic, and sometimes he sent untidy secretaries back to their desks in tears.

He was examining the file of a claimant named Dostievsky when the outside secretary buzzed him. "There's a girl here to see you."

"It'll be a while," he said into the intercom, and flicked it off.

The strange name had caught his attention, and he was finding the file profitable reading. This Dostievsky, he saw, had submitted a bill for $480 for the treatment of a whiplash injury. The next sheet was the mechanic's estimate of the car damage in the accident. It was only $70. Those bastards always doubled or tripled their bill on an insured car. So figure $20 or $30 actual damages. A little tap on the bumper.

The outside secretary buzzed him again. "She's still waiting for you," she said.

"In a moment," he said. He turned a few more sheets and saw that Dostievsky had been struck by a man whose insurance was carried by Delaware. He lifted the phone. "See if you can get me Vernon Thomas over at Delaware," he said. "If you can't get him get me this other fellow—what's his name. You know who I mean?"

"Who?"

"Rutgers or Rogers or something."

"What do you want me to tell this girl?"

"Go ahead and put the call through. Then you can send her in."

He looked up when she came in and was surprised at how pretty she was. The office smelled good with her in it. "Be with you in a minute," he said. "Sit down."

She sat down. "You're Eddie McDermott?"

"Anything I can do for you?"

"I'd like you to come for dinner."

He stared at her. Nobody had pulled this on him for years. It used to work on him though. He had okayed a number of doubtful claims after a roll on the mattress. He looked at the girl considering, and then the buzzer sounded again.

"Here's Fred Rogers at Delaware," the secretary said.

"Hold my calls for a few minutes." He lit a cigarette and waited for the redhead to bring out her claim.

"I want to make dinner for you and Danny at his house," she said.

"Danny?"

"Yes," she said. "Your son."

"I haven't heard from him since last spring."

"It has to be on Monday. Do you know his address?" She started hunting in her purse.

"Forget it," Eddie said. "I'm not going."

"Why not?"

"He's been in town over a year. He called me when he got here, and once when he was sick or something and since then I haven't heard a goddamn word from him."

"I know," she said.

"I sent him a sweater. I knew he didn't have any clothes and people come out here thinking it's always warm. It was an expensive sweater too. I went down to Karp's for it. He didn't even call me up to thank me."

"He came down here because of you."

"He came down here to get something."

She turned away and looked out the window and Eddie said, "Are you going with him?"

"As much as anybody," she said. After a moment she added, "He is your son, isn't he?"

"I don't even know who you are. What's your name?"

She told him.

"How long have you been going with Dan?"

"Six months. Why?"

"Listen," he said, leaning forward. "I'm going to tell you something I can't tell him. His mother was a tramp. A real tramp. We were living together maybe a year. Maybe less. I don't remember. And she went to bed with everybody she felt sorry for, and God she felt sorry for half the city of San Francisco."

"I've done that," the girl said.

"What?"

"Gone to bed with somebody because I felt sorry for them. It's a pretty good reason."

"At least you're honest about it. She wasn't."

"Are you coming?"

Eddie sat back. "Why don't you feel sorry for me? I can give you a list of troubles a yard long."

The girl grinned, and he said, "I can't talk to that kid."

"You have any other children?"

"No."

"Then you better come to dinner."

He looked at her again. "I don't want to take any horseshit," he finally said.

"Maybe you'll have to take some. People don't usually die from it." She wrote an address down. "How's next Monday about seven or so? I can pick you up if you want me to."

"I'll grab a cab from here," Eddie said. "Do you know him well?"

"I keep trying."

"What kind of a kid is he?"

"Your kind, I think," she said. "Ever since I saw you I've been thinking what he'll be like thirty years from now."

He watched her walk out of the office, and he felt worried and uneasy about the dinner and about what she had said.

Then he got up and went into the bathroom and looked at the small gray face in the mirror and he felt even worse. He came back and pressed the buzzer. "I'm going out to dinner on Monday night. Mark it down. Then let me speak to Dr. Frazer. I want him to examine this Dostievsky joker."

When Dan came to his room on Monday evening he found Joan working. The room smelled warmly of cooking. A plastic covering had been thrown over the table and three chairs were set beside it. She kissed him and then stood back and looked at him. "What's the matter with you tonight?" she said.

"Why?"

"You're not your usual cheerful self."

"I didn't think it showed," he said. "I have to watch an autopsy and write a report on it."

"That's part of your work, isn't it?"

"I got so upset about a preserved cadaver I don't know how I'm going to take an autopsy."

"I'll bring you a drink."

"I don't have any liquor."

"I bought a fifth." She poured some whiskey into a tumbler. "Drink out of the side that isn't chipped."

He sipped at the whiskey. "What's this all about? What's happened? You pregnant?"

"I wish I were."

"Wish?"

"Sure," she said. "Wish. I'd take him back to Means with me and I'd clap my father on the back, that is if I could get him off of that whore he married, and I'd say to him, Pop, here's a new Means I picked up in Los Angeles."

"Why are you so nervous?"

"Your father's coming to dinner."

"Eddie?"

"You're not angry?"

"He's coming tonight?"

"I borrowed some pots from that cute little manager. He

lent me a skillet too. I'll make some lamb chops." She went back to the table and straightened the cover.

Eddie came promptly at seven-thirty. Dan was nervous. His hands trembled when he held a fork or lifted a cup. Joan returned to the kitchen, and Eddie talked about the insurance business and the wily thieves he dealt with. After dinner he pushed his plate aside and said, "You didn't tell me much about your mother. Does talking about her upset you?"

"Just with you."

"Why?"

"You did run off and leave her. For twenty-five years you never gave her a dime."

"Who knew where she was?"

"For twenty-five years you didn't know where she was?"

Eddie stared at him a moment. "I don't know why you're so touchy about her. She left you in an orphanage, didn't she?"

"How did you know about that?"

"Your uncle told me."

"I thought you didn't know where she was."

"He told me the last time I was in New York."

"She couldn't keep me and work too."

"Don't believe all that crap," Eddie said. "She was chasing around, shacking up here and there."

Joan came in from the kitchen. "Please," she said. "Don't fight for a minute. I have to make the coffee."

"Forget coffee," Eddie said. "Do you have something stronger?"

She brought in the open bottle and two glasses and left them. Eddie poured each one half full.

"Where did you find the redhead?" he said.

"She worked in the restaurant on the corner."

"I was fond of your mother. Don't you know that?" Eddie said. "But she was rough. Wait a minute. Don't get mad. I'm just going to tell you what happened." He finished his drink in two long drinks. "One day she comes to me and says, 'I'm pregnant.' Just like that. Nothing more."

Joan came back and sat down.

"I just started asking a few questions and she threw me out. Right then. Clothes and everything. And such yelling." He closed his eyes and shook his head. "It's all in the past. How's school?"

"Fine."

"Where do you stand in your class?"

"At the top," Joan said.

"Really?" Eddie licked his lips. He turned to Joan. "This kid hasn't asked me for a damn thing."

"You got anything?"

"Maybe a little," Eddie said. "Perhaps a bit more than most people think. Do you have a bathroom around here?"

Dan pointed and Eddie walked out of the room carefully.

"You two are alike," Joan said. She shook her head wonderingly. "Go figure that one out."

She looked pretty and he reached over and caressed her.

"What's that for?"

"I think it's the whiskey."

"Take a little more. Maybe you'll be able to be civil to your father, too."

"How do you know he's my father?"

"Leave me alone," she said. "I've been sweating over this ever since I dreamed it up."

"Every time I see him he bitches about my mother."

"He's here isn't he? He came when I asked him to, didn't he?"

"So what the hell does that mean?"

"Oh God, are the two of you alike," she said. "You want to live in a hotel room for the rest of your life?"

Eddie came back to the table, and poured out some more whiskey and drank it.

"You don't have much of a brogue," Joan said.

"I was just seventeen when I got here," Eddie said. "I remember the day I came. I was scared stiff they'd arrest me as I walked out of the ship. I was in that Easter Rebellion."

Dan knew of it only vaguely. "What?"

"We had this little fracas in Dublin. A big fellow by the name of O'Breen gets himself shot in the ass on Easter Day, and they dragged him up to my room, dripping blood all over the carpet, and the landlady yelling bloody murder." He looked at Dan and his voice dried up. Dan was swirling the whiskey in his glass, not listening, his mind obviously far away. Eddie snapped his fingers. "Come on back."

Dan looked up. "It's the whiskey," he said. "It makes me sleepy."

Eddie took an envelope out of his breast pocket. It held half a dozen yellowed snapshots. He gave Dan one. "That's my father's boat." The picture showed a sizable vessel hanging at anchor. Behind it were some hills. "My father fished in that inlet. I guess my brothers are fishing it now. Awful bunch of Christers." He brought out another picture. It was a young man in an odd, rather squarely cut suit, standing feet apart, planted firmly on the ground, in front of a tobacco shop. "That's me just after I came to Dublin."

Joan took the picture and studied it, tilting it so that the light of the single bulb hit it full. "Take a look at this," she said. "You want any more of a resemblance?"

Eddie took it back and looked at it and then looked at Dan.

"It could have been Dan," Joan said.

"Bullshit," Dan said. "You'd say that if it was a picture of Mahatma Gandhi."

"Look yourself," she said, taking the picture from Eddie and pushing it toward him.

"What the hell do I want to look like him for?"

"You have his name," she said.

"All right," Eddie said, tucking the pictures into his coat pocket. "Medical school must be pretty hard."

"Just a lot of work." He finished the whiskey in his glass.

"You know that nephew I told you about, the one I helped put through medical school? He flunked out at the end of his first year."

Dan didn't say anything.

Eddie turned to Joan. "Can you talk to this fellow?"

"Not much," Joan said. "But I just keep trying." She gathered up the empty plates and went into the kitchen.

"She sure breaks her ass for you," Eddie said. "You better buy her something. A coat. Maybe some clothes."

"She doesn't need anything."

"You got to pay for it. And believe me it's easier paying for it in cash." He paused. "I came to the hospital the day you were born. I didn't tell your mother anything about it. I hadn't seen her since she threw me out. I wanted to pay her hospital bill. I had to argue with them to take the money. They said she wasn't out yet and they didn't know what the bill would be, but I made them figure it for a week more." He shook his head. "You got to understand things were different then. Money was hard to get. I didn't have a trade. All I knew was selling liquor. You'll have it easier. You're going into the best racket of all."

"Medicine?"

"You better believe it. They come in with a backache from sleeping crooked and you tell them it's a fibrositis. You get ten dollars for a backache but you get fifty dollars for fibrositis. And then if they're really loaded you tell them they got myalgia. Do I know the lingo? Myalgia? Is that right?"

Joan came back with the coffee and Dan said, "I can't get drunk enough to stand this guy. I could throw up real easy now, but I still can't stand him."

Eddie got up and Joan said quickly, "Don't go. You'll both feel bad." To Dan she said, "After all he is your father."

Dan shook his head. "You're not saying it right. You're leaving out some words. He's my father maybe. Perhaps. According to the best of my knowledge and belief. According to the best of my mother's, *olav hashalom*, knowledge, and belief. I don't know what she got mixed up with Gentiles for anyway." He looked about uneasily. "I'm awfully sick to my stomach," he said.

"The kid looks green," Eddie said. "Why don't you bring him something to quiet his stomach?"

Joan brought him half a glass of milk. "Try this."

Dan carefully drank the milk.

"You know," Eddie said. "You're a Christer too. Just like my brothers. I never could stand Christers. Any kind."

"I haven't served the dessert yet," Joan said.

"It's past my bedtime hour." He picked up his coat and went out.

"I've been frightened ever since I saw him," Joan said. "I keep thinking that's you, thirty years from now. If I told you I was pregnant now, you'd say the same thing he did."

"I'm awfully drunk," he said. "When I close my eyes the room spins around."

"You didn't hear me, did you?"

"I heard you. What do you want me to do to change it?"

"I don't know," she said.

He tried to stand up and staggered and she caught him. "I let you drink too much," she said. "You'll have a hangover tomorrow."

"I'm not drinking any more coffee or milk."

"We'll go for a ride to my house."

"What good will that do?"

"The fresh air will oxidize the alcohol in your blood."

The drive did clear his head, and by the time they came to the canyon he was able to walk without help. They went directly to bed. He lay, open eyes, listening to the crickets. Joan's arms were around him. "Go to sleep," she said.

"I'm worrying about that autopsy," he said.

"Whatever the others can handle you can too," she said. "All the students must feel the same way."

"I don't know," he finally said. "If they do, they hide it better than I can."

Dan awoke the next morning with a headache. He dressed in the dark and drove Joan's car to school. He had coffee in the hospital cafeteria and then went upstairs to the pathology laboratory. O'Donnell came in about ten to eight and said, "Hi," and sat down beside him. One by one the group collected,

Noble being the last. Then they pushed together through the swinging doors and went into the long pathology hall. By this time Dan could identify the hierarchy of the hospital. The interns were the easiest to recognize. They wore white pants and white shirts, and they hurried about in a loping half run. Most of them were about twenty-three or twenty-four, and some still had adolescent pimples. They looked tired and soiled, and their half run implied unfinished work and emergencies. The residents were older and wore street clothes, or a mixture of street clothes and white. They walked at a more leisurely pace and were more likely to be seen chatting in the halls or waiting at the elevators. Above the residents were the attending physicians, but Dan had little interest in them. They were too far removed.

A little before eight the Canadian instructor came walking down the hall, hands in his pockets. He counted the six students and said, "There are three posts going on now. The most instructive is a case of chronic glomerular nephritis. Be sure and get all the organ weights and the measurements."

The students followed him into the autopsy laboratory. A resident, wearing a plastic apron, was standing at the head of one of the tables reading a chart.

"Mind if my little covey watches you?" the instructor said.

The resident looked up from the chart. "I'm delighted."

"I would appreciate it if you would call out the organ weights and measurements and let my boys record them."

"It'll save my making notes. Do you want his clinical history?"

"Go ahead."

"This is the third County Hospital admission for this nine-year-old boy," the resident said scanning the chart. "He came here first six years ago, when he was three." Dan's attention wandered to the quiet face of the boy. "In May he was put on the artificial kidney," the pathology resident was saying. Dan had seen these machines as they worked, drawing blood from the patient's veins, pumping it through plastic tubes and sheets, and returning the cleansed blood into the veins. He wondered why with such a wonderful and complex machine the boy lay dead on the autopsy table.

The pathology resident finished reading from the notes. He put the chart aside and picked up his scalpel and made the first two long incisions.

"This is the classical incision," the instructor said. "We've used it since Virchow's time. Before then the autopsy surgeon examined only individual organs. Like the autopsy on Napoleon, where only the stomach was examined, and doctors are still arguing whether it was cancer of the stomach or arsenic poisoning that killed him. You wouldn't make that same mistake again, would you, Doctor?"

"Not with an associate professor of pathology and six students watching me," the resident said, working. He cut carefully, his hands awkward from the gloves. He called out measurements and weights and the students marked them down. Later he started working with greater care and he said, "It feels like primary contracted kidneys."

The instructor looked over his shoulder. "Get closer," he said to the students. "It's a classical picture."

The resident was busy cutting away small pieces of tissue, which he dropped into a specimen bottle.

"Thanks for the demonstration," the pathologist said.

"Any time," the resident said.

The students filed out into the hall.

"Did you get those heart measurements?" O'Donnell said.

"Most of them," a boy named Moran said. They sat down and started comparing measurements.

Dan had seen the room marked DOCTOR'S LOUNGE at the head of the hall, and he hurried toward it. It was a small locker and bathroom. He went into one of the stalls and closed the door. Sweat poured over his forehead and dripped down behind his ears. He sat down, his head on his knees. Later he heard the sound of someone coming through the door. He wiped the sweat away with toilet paper and came out. The resident was standing at a sink, washing his hands, his white jacket hanging from a hook on the wall. He turned to look at Dan. "How are you doing?"

Dan shook his head.

"I've been watching you getting pale," the resident said. "I was wondering how long you'd last."

"If only it wasn't a kid."

"I know." The resident went back to washing his hands.

"He was on the artificial kidney. Why didn't that work?"

The resident dried his hands with a paper towel. "Why do you think we did an autopsy?" he asked. He took a package of Life Savers out of his pocket. "Here. These will help."

Dan took one. He washed his face. Outside the other five students were still comparing notes. "Do you have all the figures?" Dan asked Noble.

Noble looked up from his sheet. "All except the kidney size."

"I don't have that either," O'Donnell said. "I don't think he gave them."

"Let's do our writing upstairs," Dan said to Noble. "We can get what we're missing later."

They walked outside. The waiting room was crowded with patients. Dan stopped in front of a seven- or eight-year-old boy. "What are you waiting for, son?"

The boy looked up frightened. "I'm with my mother. She's getting a shot."

Dan searched through his pockets. Then he turned to Noble. "Do you have a quarter?"

Noble found a quarter, and Dan took it and gave it to the boy. The boy stared first at the coin and then at Dan.

"What's that for?" Noble asked.

"For having some color in his cheeks," Dan said. "Let's go."

They went up to the study room on the sixth floor and started to write the protocol, describing what they had seen, and interpreting as well as they could the meaning of the various findings. When the other students came Dan found that none of them had the measurements of the kidneys, and he wondered why the resident had failed to measure the organs which contained the actual cause of death. He thought about it during the morning, and he decided that perhaps what he had felt the resident had also felt, and that his horror and distress at the boy's death showed in this one error of omission.

Sharon came to the store about nine that night. Her hair was combed back and Dan thought again of the paintings on Cretan vases.

"Max's asleep. I thought I'd drop over," she said.

He wiped the counter in front of her and said, "Special on milk shakes tonight. No charge for the boss's wife."

"Where were you last night?"

"Why?"

"You slept out."

"Once in a while I do."

"I got in the car and I drove around and then I stopped at your place and there was nobody there. Where did you sleep? With that redhead?"

The pork and beans was warming and it gave off a spicy tomato aroma. He unplugged the cup silently.

"I thought you were going to call me again after that one time," she said.

"That was almost a year ago."

"Whose fault is that?"

"I'm going to eat this stuff in back."

"I wouldn't treat a dog this way. You get lonely for a night and you call me and I come running and then you're done."

"I'm sorry," he said.

"What good does that do?"

"I'm not trying to do any good."

"I'm going to get a divorce. What do you think about that?"

"Best thing in the world that could happen to that poor guy."

"You're a bastard," she snapped.

"If you can't get along with him you should get a divorce."

"I try all the time. I'm tired of trying."

"Why is it so hard?"

"Everything that man does makes me mad."

"Why?"

"Because he's a pig, that's why," she shouted. "Just like you. Look at you! You have pork and beans dripping from your chin!"

He wiped the tomato gravy from his chin with the back of his hand.

"I can't stand him near me. I can't let him touch me. What am I going to do?" she said.

"Suffer, I guess. Either way," he said.

"Did you ever try to go to bed with somebody that made you sick to your stomach?" Her face was strained, her lips were trembling, and the Cretan princess had turned into a nervous Jewish girl. "Sometimes when he's away I think I love him. I miss him. But when he gets home and starts messing around I want to kill him."

"Why don't you have a baby?"

"Are you off your rocker?"

Dan shrugged.

"I'm going home," she said. "I'll remember. I came to you and spoke about the most intimate things of my life, and I asked your help and all you said was, 'Suffer. Go have a baby!'" She gathered her coat around her. "I wonder what Max would say if I told him about us."

"Why would you ever want to tell him that?"

"Maybe he'll get a divorce then and that'll be that." Holding her coat tight around her she marched out the front door without looking back.

It rained about midnight and Dan drove through the rain to Joan's house. The house was dark and he was puzzled. She knew he was coming. He hurried up the steps and knocked. No one answered. The door was unlocked. He went in and turned the light on. She was sitting on the sofa. He noticed a long legal-looking envelope on the table beside her and picked it up. In the corner was printed the name of an attorney with an address in Wallace, Idaho. "What's this? Something happen to your father?"

She took the envelope away and put it in a drawer. "Daddy's all right the last I heard," she said. She made no further explanation that night, and when they went to bed she curled up sadly.

She nudged him awake. "How can you go to sleep so fast?"

"School was rough today, and then Sharon wore me out."

"What did she want?" she said, and he was surprised by the jealousy in her voice.

"She's cutting Max to pieces." He heard the rain beating on the roof.

"It's pretty when it rains here," she said. She got up and looked out the window into the street. "This is worth watching."

"I'm not getting up," he said, "and all I can see from here is your butt with freckles on it."

"I wish you'd learn there's more to life than sleeping, reading, and sex." She came back and tugged him out of bed. "Look."

The wet brush glistened in the yellow streetlight, and two splashing streams tumbled downhill in the gutters.

"Nobody knows how pretty it is," she said. "They all get up mad because it washes mud onto the driveway or spots up their cars." She started shivering in the cold and slipped back into bed.

He dozed again and she said, "No, listen. Do you love me?"

"Let me sleep."

"I'm miserable. Please answer me."

"It's a dirty word," he said after a moment. "I don't use it."

"Love?"

"The dirtiest."

"Why?"

"More fakes are excused by it than anything else except maybe believing in God. Every girl that wants to get laid has to tell herself she's in love first. If two people get married it's always because they're in love."

"A no or a yes would have done fine."

"Why the hell do you ask a question as big as a house at one in the morning?"

"What are you doing in my bed then?"

"Trying to sleep."

She didn't say anything for a while. Then he heard her strike a match. He fell asleep again, but awoke later and heard her talking. He tried to listen, but he drowsed in and out of sentences, and when he could he said "Yes" or "Uh-huh" so that she wouldn't get angry. He awoke once to hear her talking about some mountains. "He showed the ore and he got money from the bank and in six months he had a narrow gauge running out of there and thirty men working. They built a town and called it Means."

"Your father?"

"Have you been asleep?"

"No, no. I've been listening."

"He never came back to Pocatello. He just lived up there, digging the ore out. He got himself a girl from Boise and married her. She used to be a waitress. A real tramp. About twenty years younger than him. Her name is Carol. I walked in on them one day."

He was awake by then. "Well?"

"I walked in on them."

"What's so terrible about that?"

"I was only seventeen. I was just out of high school."

"So?"

"What do you mean, so? Haven't you any feelings?"

"I don't get it. You walked in on your father and found him screwing—"

"Shut up," she said.

He stared at her a moment. "All right," he said. "So then what?"

"I got a boy friend."

"Your first?"

"No. But this one was a man. A real hard-rock miner. Tanned and hairy and grimy. He was Dad's foreman."

"What then?"

"I got pregnant."

The words hung in the room for a moment. "I guess that was a reasonable outcome," he said.

"I have a little boy," she said carefully. "He's seven now."

"You're good at keeping secrets. . . . Where is he?"

"With my father. Carol's bringing him up."

"You gave him away?"

"I didn't have a choice."

"Is this what you've been upset about tonight?"

"Tonight and for the last seven years," she said. He couldn't see her face in the dark. "At first I didn't tell you because it was none of your business. Later I was afraid to. I didn't know what you'd do."

"What the hell difference should that make?"

"I'm always afraid you'll go off and leave me." After a moment she added, "I'm sorry, Danny. I know you don't get enough sleep, but I had to tell you about it. The lawyer up north has given up on another hearing. That's what the letter was about."

"You need any money?"

"I might. My father pays my rent and sends me fifty dollars a week."

"That's barely enough to live on."

"He's not about to put enough money in my hands to hire a lawyer to fight him."

"You've tried to talk to him?"

"He loves Turk a lot more than he ever loved me."

"Turk?"

"Everyone calls him that. His real name is Robert Turkel Means."

"What happened to this miner?"

"My dad tried to beat him up but instead he got his own jaw broken. Then he fired him and chased him out of Means. He doesn't matter anyway."

He stared at her in the dark. "Why the hell did you give the baby away?"

"There was a court hearing."

"Why would a court take a child away from its mother?"

"I was drinking," she shouted at him. "I was dead drunk every night. I didn't know when it was daytime and when it was dark."

"Oh," he said.

"Now you know why I drink."

"That's more bullshit."

"If I hear that word once more, I'll throw you out."

"Everyone who drinks has an excuse."

"It's the best excuse in the world. It's so good I could cut my throat over it right now."

"How long is it since you stopped drinking?"

"A while."

"Give me an answer."

"About a year. The only thing is I get into these lousy spells and I can't eat and I can't sleep. You don't know how hard the days can get."

"About Turk?"

"Mostly."

After a moment he said, "I know a little about this. All you've got to do is straighten out and the court will give him back. You do want him back, don't you?"

She started to cry and he held her and said, "All right."

"It's so hard to sit still," she said. "When I get this way, I do things. Do you know that one good drink would stop this whole lousy misery."

"For an hour."

"Then you take another one for the next hour."

He was stirred by the desolation in her voice. "That's enough for tonight," he said.

"I frighten myself. Once I got like this and I took pills."

"Sleeping pills? How many?"

"Not enough."

"Jesus," he said.

"What's the matter?"

"You're scaring the hell out of me."

"I don't think I'll do it again."

"Do you have any pills in the house?"

"A few in the bathroom. I was just a kid then."

She nestled against him like a child, and he waited until he thought she was asleep. Then he slipped out of bed. In the medicine cabinet he found a dozen red capsules that were probably Seconal. He emptied them into the toilet. As he lay down she said, "Did you find them?"

He didn't answer.

"I was going to get rid of them tomorrow anyway," she said. "I figured they'd upset you when you saw them. But what am I going to do when I get insomnia?"

"Read a good book," he said. He fell asleep soon afterward, but when he awoke in the night he found the bed empty. He walked into the living room and found her sitting in the dark.

"It's three o'clock," he said.

"I couldn't sleep."

"Are you going to sit in that chair all night?"

"Go to sleep, Danny," she said. "You have to be in school in a couple of hours."

He waited, and after a moment she got up and followed him to bed. But she remained restless, and moved frequently, keeping him awake for a time. When he awoke at six she was gone again. He found her in the same chair in the living room. He led her back to the still warm bed, and covered her.

That evening when he went into the store he found Max pacing between the prescription room and the cigarette counter. "Sharon wants to divorce me," he said. His chin trembled and his eyes were wet.

"I know."

"Who told you?"

"She did."

"What did you say?"

"That it was the best thing that could happen to you."

"You mind your own business," Max said, pointing a trembling finger at him. "Where do you get off saying something like that?"

Dan sighed and Max said again, "You mind your own business, you hear," and started toward the door.

"Max," Dan said.

He stopped. "Yes."

"You know the name of a good lawyer for custody cases?"

"I'm all mixed up and feel like crying inside and you ask me about lawyers. Who cares—" He stopped. "What's the matter? You in trouble?"

"It's for Joan."

"What's with her?"

"It's a long story."

"I'm all mixed up now," Max said. "I'll call you after a while."

He called about ten. "Seymour Gross," he said. "I asked my brother-in-law. Over on Wilshire in the Miracle Mile." He gave Dan the phone number and the address. "I'm sorry about getting mad. I got such a heartache with Sharon you don't know. Last night—"

"I have a customer," Dan said.

"Oh." After a moment he said, "Go take care of business. I'm sorry," and hung up.

Dan made the appointment the next day. He told Joan about it afterward, and later that week they visited the attorney. He was a sun-tanned man in his middle thirties. He kept watching Joan while they talked. He wrote the information she gave him on a yellow sheet of foolscap. Then he asked, "What kind of work do you do?"

"My father sends me some money each week," she said.

"Have you considered what this will cost?"

"I think we better find out," Dan said.

"Are you two planning to get married?"

"No."

"A shame," he said. "With a responsible husband, who'd make a good appearance in court, you would get the child back almost automatically." He looked at Joan. "There's a good deal of work in this matter. A reasonable fee is two thousand dollars."

"Jesus!" Dan said.

"Easily thirty or forty hours work just preparing motions and briefs alone. In about one month this folder will be two inches thick." He stood up. "I'll call Miss Means as soon as I get a reply to my letter to Boise."

She managed to eat some dinner in a restaurant on the corner, and then Dan left her and drove to the store. She phoned him a little after eight. She was excited. "The lawyer just called me."

"So soon?"

"Yes. He made a long-distance call to Boise and got some of the facts from Tom Bartlett, who represented me, and he thinks we have a chance. He talked to me for an hour."

"I've been worried about the money," Dan said. "I don't know how we're going to raise that much."

"He's interested in my case. He wants to see me get my baby back. We can work something out."

"Will you be able to sleep?"

"I'll take a hot bath. Don't worry, Danny. I told you I'd be all right."

He hesitated. "I'm short on sleep. I won't be over tonight."

"Oh damn. I have a clean shirt for you at my house."

"I can get by with this one for another day."

"Danny?"

"Yes."

"Let's get married."

"I'll see you tomorrow after work."

"All right," she said. "If I'm awake later I'll call you."

She didn't call, and he went back to his room, and this time turned on the light. He undressed, surprised that the room no longer bothered him.

Dan was awakened by the buzzing of the doorbell. He was confused and he reached for the alarm clock. The buzzer sounded again and he got out of bed and opened the door.

Max stood outside holding a small airline bag. "I'm sorry," he mumbled.

"What's the matter?"

"Sharon threw me out."

Dan stood aside and Max came in. "I hope you don't mind," he said. "I can go to a hotel if it's inconvenient."

"No, no," Dan said. He looked at the alarm clock. It was three o'clock.

"I didn't want to go stay with my family. Maybe it'll blow over and it's better they don't know."

"There's only the couch."

"That's fine," Max said. "I'd go crazy in a hotel room."

"What happened?"

"Do you know what she called me? Her own husband? A son of a bitch."

Dan got a sheet from the closet and a pillow from his bed and arranged the couch.

Max lay down fully clothed and Dan handed him a blanket. He covered himself and said, "I took four Libriums. I'm so dopey I could hardly drive over here. My heart's jumping. Maybe you ought to listen to it. You got your stethoscope?"

"It's in school."

"Feel it." Max opened his shirt and Dan put his hand on Max's chest and felt the prolonged rough heave of his heart.

"How does it feel?"

"I don't know."

"I think I've got palpitation."

"Why did you leave?"

"She threw me out. You should have heard her screaming. All the neighbors in the apartment house heard her calling me a son of a bitch and a bastard."

"What did you do?"

"She got mad because I wanted sex. Is that a reason? I haven't had it for two weeks. Is that natural?"

"I'm going back to sleep," Dan said.

"I'm sorry. I want you to know I appreciate very much." A little later he said, "You got a phone?"

"No. Why?"

"I want to call her. She got so wild maybe she might do something."

Dan rolled over and closed his eyes.

"She's high strung. Maybe I shouldn't have gotten mad. So what's one *shmeis* less? What's there to get mad at?"

Dan didn't say anything.

"You don't like her, do you? You never did like her."

"You're a jerk."

Max sat up. "I don't need you to call me names too."

"Why don't you go home and kick her ass out of bed?"

"I don't want to antagonize her."

"Sleep well."

Max stood up. "I have to find a phone. Maybe she calmed down."

"Leave the door open."

He was cold without the blanket and he got up and put on the sweater Eddie had sent him. In the morning when he awoke Max was snoring on the couch, still fully clothed, his mouth open, his sleeping face sad and empty. Dan put his own blanket over him and left.

Sharon called him at school. "Is Max staying at your place?"

"Yes."

"Why didn't he open the store yet?"

"He's probably still sleeping."

"His heart's all right isn't it?"

"How do I know?"

"I've had it with that man," she said. "I'm not taking him back."

"Good for you," Dan said and hung up.

Max stayed at the apartment for three days. He was lonely and unhappy, and he complained constantly to Dan that Sharon refused to talk to him. On the third evening, when Dan came into the store, Max said, "You just lost your boarder. I made up with Sharon."

"Congratulations."

"I have a backache from that couch anyway."

"Where are you going to sleep at home?"

Max shot him a sharp glance. "How do you know? Did you speak to Sharon?"

"It figures."

Max shrugged. "At least the couch at home is softer than yours. It's better built."

That week a new class started. When Dan went into the classroom on the sixth floor of the County Hospital, he found two instructors seated at the desk. One was a youngish bald-headed man and the other a plump middle-aged man in a beautifully tailored gray suit. The students waited, reading their notes or chatting among themselves.

The younger physician glanced at the clock and said, "We might as well start though we're a little early. You'll be assigned a ward and the intern will choose a patient for you. The purpose of this class is to start teaching you the reactions that go on between a patient and a doctor. Dr. Finch here is an internist and I'm a psychiatrist."

Dan listened with interest to the bald young man. He was a practitioner of the specialty that had failed so badly with Jesse Davis. The psychiatrist talked about the emotional reactions of patients. Apparently he liked to talk. When he was done at last he turned to the older man and said, "Anything you want to add, Dr. Finch?"

The internist nodded. "Whatever they're like you have to learn to treat them, and you might as well get started right now." He picked up a sheet of paper from the desk and read out a list of wards. Dan's was 6300. "You have the whole afternoon," he said. "Find out all you can about your patient. Read the chart. Look at the x-rays and then go in and sit down and talk to him. You can talk about his sickness. You can talk about how he's treated at the hospital. Anything. Then come back and we'll ask you some questions."

At ward 6300 Dan found a thin blond nurse writing at

the desk. Dan looked at his slip. "I'm supposed to get an assignment from Dr. Rosenthal," he said.

"Just a minute," she said. She went on writing. Then she picked up the phone and made a series of calls. Then she looked at Dan. "Oh yes. Dr. Rosenthal. I haven't seen him."

"Where should I look for him?"

"I don't know."

The ward consisted of a central charting room into which a dozen small and large rooms with beds opened. He walked from one room to another, looking for Rosenthal. Some of the patients were sitting at their bedsides reading, or listening to transistor radios. He stopped in front of a young colored woman. She was unconscious. Clear liquid dripped from a bottle into one arm. In the neighboring bed a young Mexican girl, her pajamas rolled to her knees, was sitting cross-legged filing her fingernails. He wondered why they left this unconscious girl unattended, and he went to the desk again. "There's a girl in the big ward who's unconscious," he said.

The nurse was busy on the phone and didn't hear him. He waited until she was off the phone and said it again.

"Which one?" the nurse said.

"The one by the door."

She nodded. Then the phone rang. She answered it and he waited longer, standing on one leg and then the other. Finally he resumed his search for Dr. Rosenthal. As an afterthought he looked in the room marked DOCTOR'S DRESSING ROOM, and he found a dark boy shaving in front of a mirror.

"Are you Dr. Rosenthal?"

The boy looked at him through the mirror. "Yes. What's up?"

"I've been looking for you since half-past one. You're supposed to assign me a patient."

Rosenthal grinned. "I've been here all the time. First chance I've had to take a shower since Monday."

"There's a girl in the middle ward who's unconscious."

"What's her name?"

"I don't know."

"The first bed to the right in seventy-three?"

"The middle room."

"Yes. I know. You're supposed to be assigned a patient?"

"That's what they said."

He finished one cheek and started on another. "Now let's see. What's this for?"

"Doctor-patient relationship."

"Oh. That's where they analyze your oedipus complex when you take a history. Let's see. Try that fellow in seventeen. I don't remember his name. Wait a minute." He left the sink and searched the pockets of a white jacket, finding a notebook. He ran down a list of names. "Yes. Hugh Avery. Try him." He went back to his shaving.

"Aren't you going to do anything about the girl?"

The intern shrugged. "She has disseminated lupus."

After a moment Dan said, "Thanks." He stopped at the door and said, "Aren't you going to do anything for her?"

"What would you do for a case of lupus in coma?"

"Why ask me? I don't know anything about that disease."

"You're in good company. Nobody else does either," the intern said.

Dan realized from his tone that whatever little could be done for her had already been done, and he closed the door and went back to the ward.

He tried to ask the nurse for the chart, but after waiting again while she marked figures on colored squares of cardboard he gave up and sorted through a basket of charts at the end of the desk, and finally found one with the name Hugh Avery. He sat at the desk-side stool and started reading. The first note was signed by Rosenthal, with a circled I after his name, no doubt standing for intern. It said that Avery had come into the hospital because of cough and paralysis of the left side of the face and left arm. Rosenthal had found something abnormal when he examined the chest. He had drawn a picture of the chest and in one part he had marked crosshatched lines to show an area of disease. Dan didn't understand the notes completely. They had many unfamiliar abbreviations.

He understood the diagnosis, however. It was cancer of the lung with spread to the brain. He remembered the vicious cancer cells he had seen on the pathology slides, and he wished he had not been given a patient with cancer. He asked the nurse, "Can I see the x-rays on Hugh Avery?"

"Medical students are not allowed to handle x-rays."

Rosenthal came around the corner, smelling of after-shave lotion, cheeks smooth, and looking less tired. "Got your chart?" he asked.

"Now I need his x-rays."

Rosenthal looked at the blackboard behind the desk. "I've got four new patients already so far. There goes the rest of the day." He turned back to Dan. "You want the x-rays on Avery?"

"I won't know what I'm looking at, but I'm supposed to see them."

Rosenthal searched through a pile of broad tan envelopes. "Not here," he said. The nurse was gone from her station, and he went into a small kitchen, Dan following close on his heels. She was leaning against the wall sipping on a cup of coffee. "Mrs. Roland, did you see the x-rays on Avery?"

"They were up for rounds this morning."

"Were they returned?"

"I don't know. Why don't you try looking?"

Rosenthal went back into the ward. "The nurses are overworked. They just don't have any time. Do you know where x-ray is?"

"I barely found my way here."

Another intern walked up to the desk and Rosenthal said, "Did we return Avery's x-rays?"

The second intern also seemed tired. "I brought them down myself," he said.

Rosenthal looked again at the four names on the blackboard and sighed. "All right. I better take you down," he said. "You can get lost there and nobody would hear from you till Christ-

mas. Come on." He started down the hall at a half run. Dan
found it hard to keep up. His new white coat interfered with
the long strides he had to take. He opened it and walked
better. They went downstairs, two steps at a time, and came
to a U-shaped room, one wall of which was occupied by
rows of white boxes fronted with translucent glass. Rosenthal
went to a window and waited. No one came out. After a while
he said, "I guess they're busy. I better get it myself." He
lifted the counter and went inside. In a few minutes he came
out with an envelope. He flipped a switch on one of the
viewboxes and put up the x-ray. "There."

"I don't know what I'm seeing," Dan said.

"It doesn't make any difference," Rosenthal said. "I don't
know what they want you to look at the x-rays for anyway."

"That's the heart, isn't it?"

Rosenthal nodded. Then he pointed toward a triangular
shadow three or four inches from the heart. "That's it."

"That's a lung cancer?"

"This guy was a smoker. Two packs of cigarettes a day."

"How do you know it's cancer?"

"The shape. And it spread to the brain." Rosenthal took a
cigarette out of his pocket, hesitated, and then put it back.
"I'll save it for after dinner," he said. He turned off the
light. "Take the middle elevator up to the ward. You won't
get lost that way."

"Thanks," Dan said, and Rosenthal nodded and carried the
x-rays back into the filing room.

Interns were hurrying past Dan, carrying books and instruments and pushing machines through the hall. Patients sat
about on benches, some in street clothes and others in the
gray shapeless gowns provided by the hospital. He took the
elevator back to the ward and walked into Avery's room.
There were three beds. In the first was a toothless old man
lying sideways, smiling foolishly and smelling as though he had
soiled himself.

Dan shook the old man's arm and said, "Are you Avery?"
The old man made no sign that he heard. Then he remem-

bered that Avery was only forty-eight. In the next bed an emaciated, baldheaded man lay against an upraised backrest smoking a cigarette. "Are you Avery?"

The man nodded and Dan found a chair and pulled it up to the bedside. He had no idea how to begin. "How are you?" he said.

Avery ground his cigarette out. "Are you going to take some more blood?"

"I've been assigned to your case."

"They stuck me forty times already." He pulled up his sleeve to show his arm. There were numerous puncture marks. "Every time somebody in a white coat comes around they stick you."

"I'm just supposed to talk to you."

"What good's that going to do?"

"How do you feel?"

Avery grimaced. Only the right side of his face moved. "The stink around here's enough to make you sick. Why don't they clean that guy up?"

"The nurses are busy," Dan said. "They're overworked."

Avery lay back without saying anything and Dan looked at the sick man, skin tight and yellow, complaining about smells, when inside his chest and in his brain his own miserable destruction was growing. He remembered something that happened when he was about seven. His mother had given him two dollars. He had hurried down Divisadero Street to a pet shop and bought two hamsters, soft, white little animals that twitched their noses like rabbits. The owner threw in a wire cage, and he took his pets home and fed them cabbage leaves and the tops of carrot bunches. A few days later when he went to play with them he saw translucent threads hanging down between the legs of one. It was the animal's intestine. He took the hamster out, turned it over, and saw the tear in its belly. He quickly put it back in the cage, and sat there sick, not knowing what to do.

The hamster moved about the cage dragging loops of intestine behind it, nibbling at cabbage leaves and lapping at the water. Dan spent three agonized days waiting for the hamster to die. It didn't die, and on the third day he took a needle and thread from his mother's sewing drawer and tried to sew up the wound, but again he became sick and wasn't able to finish. He took the cage to the alley and freed the two animals.

He felt the same way toward this dying man. He wished he had been given someone to whom he could talk more easily and who would not have reminded him of the torn-open hamster.

Avery started coughing. He wiped his lips with Kleenex and Dan saw blood. "Why don't they do something about my cough," Avery said. "All they do is blood tests on me and then they take some more x-rays, and then they do some more blood tests. I'm spitting up blood all the time. Why do they keep taking it out of my arms too? They don't tell me a damn thing here. I've been here three weeks and nobody's told me what's the matter with me. What's the matter with me?"

"I'm just here to get your history," Dan said.

Avery noted the long white coat for the first time. "You're not an intern?"

"I'm a medical student."

"What are you supposed to do? Experiment on me?"

"How do you feel?"

"If only I could get this lousy arm working and get this cough stopped. Why don't they give me some cough syrup?"

Dan got up. "Thanks," he said. "I'll stop around again."

"I need a physic," Avery said. "Tell them to give me a physic."

Dan found Rosenthal examining an old woman in another room.

"Can you assign me another patient?"

"What's the matter with Avery?"

"I can't get anything out of him."

"There's not much to get."

"I'm supposed to establish a doctor-patient relationship."

"At the County Hospital?" He looked at the clock. "It's too late anyway."

"He needs a physic."

"I gave him a standing order when he first came in. The nurses—"

"Yes, I know, they're too busy," Dan said.

Rosenthal grinned. "You're getting the picture, son. Anyway I'll write the order again." He went back to his examination.

Dan returned to the classroom, and sat and waited his turn. When it came, the internist, Dr. Finch, said, "All right, McDermott. Tell us about your patient."

Dan told him the patient's name, his age, and what the diagnosis was. He described the x-ray.

The psychiatrist was also listening. "Is that all you got out of it?"

"He needed a physic."

Finch smiled. The psychiatrist remained solemn. "Anything else?"

"No."

"Did you like him?" the psychiatrist said.

"I didn't have any reaction at all."

"None at all?"

"I didn't think he was an awfully good patient to work on."

"Why not?"

"He was so sick."

"That makes him a poor patient?" Finch asked.

"How did you feel about the sickness?" the psychiatrist cut in.

"It's miserable."

"Did you think you were going to catch it?"

Dan looked up in surprise. "You can't catch cancer."

"I know," the psychiatrist said. "But I'm trying to understand what you felt. Go ahead. What were your feelings?"

"I don't know how to answer you any better."

"It was painful for you?"

Dan thought about it again. "Yes."

"It was as though you had it?"

"No. It reminded me . . ." He stopped.

"Of what? Go on," the psychiatrist said.

"Two hamsters. One of them got its belly torn open."

"Did you do it?"

"Me? No." He was shocked. "Why would I do that?"

"How old were you?"

"Seven."

"You didn't do it?"

Dan shook his head. "You shouldn't keep hamsters in wire cages. They tear themselves open trying to get out."

"It seems to me you have a lot of guilt about this. You must have taken some pleasure in its suffering."

Dan didn't answer.

The internist said, "Let's get back to your patient. There was a barrier between you and this man."

"Why was that?" the psychiatrist asked.

"I couldn't talk to him. He was too sick," Dan said.

"You have to understand yourself. Patients react to you and you react to them. If you want to control the situation you have to first understand why you react. Why was it painful?"

"He had cancer."

"Did you feel as though you were in the patient's place?"

"I felt sorry for him but there was nothing I could do about it. I couldn't even get him a physic."

"You're not really trying to understand yourself here," the psychiatrist said. "You keep repeating the same thing. You must have had more feelings than that."

"No."

The psychiatrist stood up. "I've been asking you question after question, and I haven't gotten a warm or human response to any of them. You bring nothing but coldness and aloofness to this conference and I think this is what you brought to the patient."

"Wait a minute," Finch said. "This is a rough case. I still feel bad when I have to deal with a cancer of the lung."

"That's not the point," the psychiatrist said. "The point here is human relations with a patient. Did you demonstrate any kindness or any interest in this patient at all?"

"I told him I'd come back and see him."

"Are you going to?"

"No."

"Why not?"

"Because there's nothing I can do for him. I can't even give him a cigarette. It might make him worse."

"You could have given him some friendship, couldn't you?"

"How do you get friendly with a lung cancer?"

The psychiatrist turned away angrily and the older physician stood up and looked at his watch. "There's only one more student. Why don't you take him yourself, Fred. I think I'll spend some more time with this boy."

"Maybe it'll do some good," the psychiatrist said and settled back in his chair.

Dan followed Finch down the hall. "This is an experimental class," the physician said. "We really don't know how much we're going to manage to teach in it, and I guess it must be uncomfortable sometimes for the students."

They came to the ward and Dan showed him where Avery's bed was. The physician pulled out a chair and sat down. He seemed oblivious to the smell. "How's it coming?" he said.

Avery, who had been looking up at the ceiling, turned at the sound of his voice. "Pretty bad," he said. "I think my foot's getting numb too."

The doctor nodded and took Avery's pulse. Avery watched uneasily. "How is it?"

"Very good. Regular. Good quality."

"Really? You'd think with all this bleeding and this numbness and everything that there would be on the fritz too. I must have an awfully good heart."

"You certainly do," the doctor said. "How did all this start?"

Little by little Avery became talkative. He told the physician about the onset of the illness and his symptoms, stopping every so often to complain, but going ahead with the story, the doctor listening and nodding, and only once in a while asking a question.

It was well after six o'clock when they were done, and as they walked down the hall Dan said, "I couldn't get any of that from him. He just wasn't about to talk to me."

"There's only one trick," the doctor said. "I wasn't afraid of him." He looked down at Dan to see if Dan understood.

"Afraid?"

"That's what I mean," the physician said. "Look at the way people are fearful of hunchbacks or spastics or cripples. They confuse the disease with the sick person. This is the way patients think and you're still more of a patient than a doctor."

Dan understood and he was grateful. He said, "Thanks," and the physician waved and turned away into one of the elevators.

Five

THE STUDENTS took examinations during the next two weeks, and Dan saw Joan infrequently. Sometimes she was restless and silent. Other times she was suddenly and unpredictably loving, kissing him the moment he walked in the door and sitting by him all the time he studied.

He went to her house one Monday evening and found that the spot where he usually parked was taken by a large new car. He parked a block away and walked up the fragrant cool street and rang the bell. She opened the door almost immediately. She was in a white dress and seemed excited. "Oh Danny, I'm glad you came," she said. "I just called that landlord of yours."

"He's out."

"You ought to get yourself a phone. Come on in. Seymour's here." She led him into the living room. The attorney was holding a glass. He stood up when Dan came in, and shook hands. "I thought I'd drop around and get a few more facts," he said. "I'm filing Joan's action tomorrow."

"She doesn't seem to remember much," Dan said.

"Background material is what I'm after. You'd be surprised how much judges these days are swayed by psychiatric concepts."

"Sit down, honey," Joan said. "I'll fix you a drink."

Dan looked about quickly and saw her glass on a chair-side table.

"Just a little flavored water," Gross said. "I don't think she put a teaspoonful of vodka in it."

"Seymour came over to cheer me up," she said.

"I'm glad you're cheerful again," Dan said. "Why feel bad about filing your action?"

"Some people might feel bad about starting a court battle against their father," Gross said.

"Lime juice or on the rocks?" Joan said.

"Give me some coffee."

"We were talking about skiing," Gross said. "Have you ever done much?"

Dan was watching Joan. She went into the kitchen and he heard the tinkle of glass. "What?" he asked.

"Have you ever skiied?"

"Once, and I fell flat on my ass every time I stood up."

"She's quite a skiier, that girl of yours. Apparently up in Idaho they start skiing just about the time they start walking."

Dan got up and went into the kitchen. She was pouring from a bottle of vodka that bore the double Romanoff eagle. "Did you buy that?"

"Not me. It's too expensive," she said. "Here. Have one drink. It'll make you less of a grouch."

"I thought you were all done."

"Listen," she said, speaking in a whisper, "he's nice enough to come out here to talk to me. Why shouldn't he have a drink if he wants one? You heard what he said. All I had was a little flavored water." She thrust the drink at him, and they went back into the living room.

"There's a place up near Wallace called Whiteslip. It has a run two miles long," she said. "It's the closest thing I know to flying."

"Have you tried Mammoth?" Gross said.

"I haven't taken my skis out of the closet this year."

"We'll have to go. It's only a morning's drive. I think Dan here might enjoy it."

"You break a leg every seven seasons of skiing," Dan said.

"Did you hear that?" Joan said. "We're speaking about fun and he worries about broken legs."

Gross was lying back in his chair, legs stretched out, watching Joan.

"They're all my own," Joan said.

"Nice too," Gross said.

"Isn't she supposed to be building up a good character?" Dan said.

"That's right."

"Might as well start now then." He got up and took the drink out of Joan's hand and walked into the kitchen and poured it into the sink. Joan followed him. "Just who do you think you are?" she whispered fiercely.

Gross walked into the kitchen. "Did I hear quarreling?"

"You sure did," Dan said. "Why do you bring her something to drink when you know what her problem is?"

"Wait a minute," Gross said.

"Wait a minute hell." Dan emptied the whole bottle into the sink.

"It seems to me you can go a little too far in this policing," Gross said. "A little support and encouragement would probably do more good."

Dan turned his back on the attorney. "I came over to take you to dinner. You want to go?"

"I can fix something for all of us," she said hesitantly.

"I have to leave anyway," Gross said. He reached out and again shook hands warmly with Dan. To Joan he said, "I'll call you if I need any more information."

After he left, Joan said, "What was that all about? This man is trying to be nice and you almost get into a fist fight."

"I think you better get a different lawyer."

She was putting her coat on. "He's done more in a couple of weeks than Tom Bartlett did in five years."

"I don't like him and that fee is too much."

"I know what's bothering you," she said. "Forget it, Danny. All I want is my baby back."

He held the door open and she went out. They ate in a restaurant on Sunset. It was crowded and service was slow and it took them almost two hours to get through their meal. By this time her excitement and sparkle had disappeared, and she was silent and dispirited. He took her home, and he tried to kiss her but she turned her face away. He stayed only a few minutes, and then drove back to his room, where he studied pathology, preparing for the final examination.

The pathology course ended with the examination, and the afternoons were then devoted to a new course, physical diagnosis, in which the students practiced the technique of examination on one another. Dan and Noble again were partners and, after the lecture, one of them would strip to the waist and the other would gravely and tediously examine him by percussing, inspecting, or listening.

Dan was slimly built, and his heart tones and the sound of his breathing were clear and loud. On the other hand, Noble was squat and thick-chested, and Dan had to thump hard to determine the position of his heart, or the upper margins of his liver, or the outlines of his spleen.

They spent a whole week learning how to use a stethoscope. Finally Dan had grown accustomed to the strange instrument pressing against his ears, and he was able to make some sense of the noises he heard when he put it against Noble's chest.

"Come on, count," Dan said.

"One, two, three," Noble said.

"Now whisper."

"One, two, three."

"Take a deep breath. Now hold it. Now cough. Go on cough, for Christ sake." After the cough Dan heard something odd. It sounded like the crackling of tissue paper. He lifted off his stethoscope, blew into the mouthpiece, and set it back on the same spot. "Take a deep breath. Come on. Deep."

Noble breathed again and there was a shower of cracklings in the right lung just under the collar bone.

"Let's do it again. Breathe deep."

"I'm getting dizzy from all this breathing," Noble said, but he breathed again, and again crackling noises came out.

Dan put the stethoscope down. "I think you've got rales in the right upper lobe."

"They're not supposed to be there."

"I can't help it. They are there."

Noble took the stethoscope away from Dan, fitted it into his own ears, and listened. "I don't hear anything."

"You're not taking a deep enough breath. Come on. Breathe deeply."

Noble took a deep breath, and then frowned. He listened for four or five breaths, and then he said, "Come here. Let me listen to you."

Dan took off his shirt, and Noble put the stethoscope on the corresponding spot on Dan's chest and listened.

"Hear anything?"

Noble shook his head. "Just normal breathing." He went back to listening to the spot on his own chest. "What do you think it means?"

"Maybe a cold."

Noble looked around. Then he said quietly. "My mother and father both died of tuberculosis."

"You're probably just full of snot," Dan said.

"I've lost eleven pounds."

"Have you been swimming lately? Maybe you got some water in your lungs."

Noble put on his shirt. "I had a chest plate two years ago when I started in school. They found a scar. Nothing active though."

"So what are you worried about?" Dan said and rolled up the instruments and tied them together.

That evening, however, he reread carefully the portion on tuberculosis of the lung in the text of physical diagnosis. The next morning it was his turn to act as a patient, but instead he said, "I better work on you again today."

Noble had apparently also read the text during the night. Without a word he pulled his shirt and undershirt off and sat on the small stool. Dan listened meticulously over his chest, and once again he heard the crackles. "I don't know," he finally said. "Maybe you ought to go get an x-ray."

"Be quiet," Noble whispered fiercely. "If they find out about this I'll be put in a sanitorium. I won't get out for a couple of years, and I won't make it then. I'll be out of money."

"Are you sweating at night?"

"Sometimes."

"A lot?"

"I don't know. Sometimes I sweat. Don't you?"

"Not much. You ever run a fever?"

Noble felt his own forehead. "I don't know," he said.

"Get a thermometer. Take your temperature whenever you get a chance, particularly in the late afternoon. That's when you get the rise."

Noble looked at him. "Don't tell anybody about this," he said.

"You ought to see a doctor. The school doesn't have to know anything about it."

"It's a reportable disease."

Dan had forgotten. All cases of tuberculosis discovered by a physician had to be reported to the Board of Health. In turn the Board of Health would undoubtedly notify the school.

They sat idly, the stethoscope hanging between them. After a while Noble said, "I don't feel that sick."

"You don't have to feel very sick when it first begins. Besides you lost eleven pounds."

"I was on a diet. I was too fat." After a moment he said, "I don't know what to do."

"You ought to see a doctor."

"A lot of cases of tuberculosis get better. I have a scar in my lung. That means I had it once and I got over it, and if I did it once I can do it again."

"What happened to your father?"

"He was sick a long time," Noble said. "Then he had a hemorrhage. One day he spit blood up all over the place. They took him to Cook County Hospital. They couldn't stop his bleeding. I don't even know whether they tried." He sat thinking. "Most of the time it goes away. It calcifies."

"It didn't for your father," Dan said.

At noon he went to ward 6300 at the County Hospital. The same blond nurse sat at the desk. "Is Dr. Rosenthal around?"

The nurse pushed the phone toward him. "Check with the operator."

He pushed the phone back to her. "Where is Dr. Rosenthal?"

"I haven't time—"

"You're the only one around here with any time. Where's Dr. Rosenthal?"

She hesitated, measuring him, and then she said waspishly, "He's been transferred to the jail ward."

He took the elevator up to the eighteenth floor, his white coat getting him past the guard. He wondered about the dullness of prisoners, and how easily they could escape if they would provide themselves with white students' or interns' uniforms. Inside the barred door the wards looked just the same as those downstairs. He found Rosenthal dressing a long knife wound on a young Mexican boy.

"Got a minute?" Dan asked.

"As soon as I'm done." Rosenthal wiped the wound with a roll of moistened cotton. The youth winced and Rosenthal said, "There. That's not bad. It'll be a distinguished-looking scar."

The youth looked at the shoulder and then at Rosenthal. "You want a distinguished-looking scar too? All I've got to do is put in a word for you with a friend."

Rosenthal grinned. "I get all my scars on my duodenum. Hold still."

The youth held still and Rosenthal wrapped the bandage around his shoulder and passed it under the arm and fastened it in place with safety pins. "All done," he said. "I'll work on you tomorrow if you're still here."

"I'll be here longer than you will," the youth said and sauntered away.

"How did he get that?" Dan asked.

Rosenthal went to the wall sink to wash his hands. "You're not supposed to ask them about their crimes. If you do you can get cross-examined about it in court. I guess somebody cut him."

"So why is he in jail?"

"Probably he cut the other guy too," Rosenthal said. "What are you back for this time? Doctor-jailbird relationship? I could teach a hell of a course in that. I'm a professor of dope addicts, whores, holdup men, and weenie wavers."

"Do rales in the right lung under the clavicle mean tuberculosis?"

"It sure could. Why?"

"It's a friend."

Rosenthal dried his hands. "Have you been hearing things in your own chest?"

"I'm not that crazy. I'd go to a doctor. I want to run a sputum on him to see if he's contagious."

"You can't run around making diagnoses of tuberculosis. It's a reportable disease. You can get into trouble."

"He's a student."

"Oh." After a moment Rosenthal said, "I see." He shook his head. "Every year a few of the interns come down with it. Kids from the country. They come out here and we get a patient we think's got pneumonia or a lung abscess and he turns out to have sputum just crawling with TB and these country kids catch it. That may have been what's happened to your buddy." He took him into the laboratory. "You know how to do an acid-fast stain?"

Dan nodded.

"Well, here's all the fixings." He set out some slides and a bottle of red liquid. "I want you to know something else. If I find out who this student is I'm going to report him for his own sake. Besides, he might be giving it to patients."

"You won't find out."

"The scope's in the corner. It's kind of dirty."

Rosenthal went out and Dan cleaned the microscope lens and then put the slides and the stain carefully away where he could find them again.

He called Max and told him he would be late to work. After school he and Noble went up to the jail ward. It was six by then, and the interns and residents were gone. A male nurse and several male attendants watched them go by without interest. Once in the laboratory Dan found a wax-paper cup and gave it to Noble. "Go ahead. Cough up some sputum."

Noble took the cup and struggled, managing to bring up a

fleck of mucus. "It's not much," Dan said, "but I suppose we can try it." He smeared it on a slide, and he stained it with the hot dye. He washed it and restained it and looked at it under the microscope.

After a while Noble said, "Say something. Don't just sit there. What do you see?"

Dan was looking at thin red rods that could have been the acid-fast bacillus of tuberculosis. They also could be the harmless bacteria that are occasionally found in saliva, particularly after the patient has eaten butter. Later on he said, "Here, take a look."

Noble sat down at the scope. "Oh Christ," he said. "They're there. Goddamned slide's loaded with them."

"I didn't see that many," Dan said. He pushed Noble's head aside and looked. "Those are mucus streaks. They're not even red."

"You're color blind," Noble said. "They look like TB germs to me."

Dan looked again. "It could be just plain junk."

"I've been sweating an awful lot at night," Noble said. "Last night I had to get up and change my pajamas. I lost three more pounds. I can't eat at all now."

Dan looked at him. His shirt fit loosely about his neck. "You haven't spit up any blood?"

"I tasted something funny yesterday. I took a deep breath and it felt like something broke in my chest." He looked at Dan, his eyes blinking behind the round glasses.

"You ought to go to a doctor," Dan said. "Maybe you have a cavity."

"How do you know when you have a cavity?"

"Just on x-rays."

"I'm not going to a doctor," Noble said. "Don't you give me away. You don't know how hard I've sweated to get into school. Even cavities heal up."

"Sometimes they don't. You have to get an x-ray."

"I ran a fever last night. It got up to ninety-nine eight."

Dan passed his hand over his face. After a while he said, "Let's walk down to x-ray."

"They'll report me."

"Let me take care of it," Dan said. They wandered into x-ray unnoticed, their white coats serving as camouflage. "Settle someplace," Dan said, and Noble sat down on one of the benches.

Dan chose one of the x-ray rooms and went in. A short, female technician was pushing heavily against a fat woman on the x-ray table.

"Mind if I hang around and watch you take some pictures?"

The technician looked at his white coat. "Fine," she said. "Give me a hand."

Dan helped her push, and they moved the patient into position. The technician took the picture, explaining the technique, and how the pictures were to be labeled.

"How do you take a chest x-ray?"

"That's the easiest of all," she said. She showed him how the dials on the machine should be set, and he looked about and discovered himself where the blank film was kept. Later on he followed her into the darkroom and watched her mark the x-rays and feed them into another machine that developed them.

When he came out Noble was sitting in the same spot, hands folded in his lap, looking down at his feet, and Dan said, "Listen, if we can get in and out of there fast we can get an x-ray later."

"What'll I do if it shows a cavity?"

"I don't know," Dan said. "Let's get something to eat."

They went across the street to the hamburger stand and ordered hamburgers and fried potatoes. Noble took one mouthful and then pushed his plate back. He coughed from time to time, turning his head away from Dan and holding a napkin in front of his mouth.

Dan called Max again and told him he wouldn't be in at all that night. Then he called Joan. "Hi. What are you doing?"

"Getting ready for the showing. Making frames mostly. Why?"

"I can't come over tonight."

"Anything wrong?"

"Not with me."

"We ought to go out once in a while," she said. "Everytime I close my eyes I see frames."

"Are you feeling any better?"

"When I get Turk back I'll feel better."

"Yes," he said. "Get busy on those frames. Don't waste time."

Noble was waiting outside the booth. "I'm kind of nauseated," he said. "Is that one of the symptoms?"

"Not early," Dan said. They went back into the hospital. Only one technician was still working. The other rooms were empty. Dan chose the room he knew. "Come on. Hurry up," he said nervously to Noble.

Noble went in and stood in front of the cassette.

"Take off your shirt," Dan whispered sharply, and Noble unbuttoned the top button and pulled his shirt and undershirt off with one tug.

"Take a deep breath." Noble breathed and Dan pressed the button. Then he said, "Go sit out in the hall. Look like you're waiting for somebody." He took the cassette and went into the darkroom and took the film out. He did not mark it but fed it directly into the developing machine. He went outside afterward. "It'll be out in a minute," he said to Noble.

The wheels of the machine rolled, and finally the film came sliding out. Noble snatched it up and walked to the battery of viewboxes and put it into one. He pressed the switch.

"That's the wrong side up," Dan said.

"How do you know?"

"This is the diaphragm, isn't it?"

Noble studied it a few moments, and then reversed the film. They both stared at it.

"Look at this," Noble finally said.

"I think that's the pulmonary artery."

"The pulmonary artery comes out lower down. That's tuberculosis."

"I don't know," Dan said. "Let's go back up to the jail ward."

Noble took the x-ray, wrapped it around his waist, and buttoned his white coat firmly over it.

Rosenthal wasn't in the jail ward. Dan called the operator and discovered that he was in the plaster room. They went down to the fourth floor. Dan looked through the door and saw him applying a cast to a patient's leg. "Wait outside," he said to Noble. "This is a bright guy. He'll know what it's all about the moment we walk in together." He took the x-ray and went in. "Hi," he said.

"What kind of hours are you keeping?" Rosenthal said. "I thought students fold up at six."

"I want to show you an x-ray picture."

"You're like my kid brother. Always bugging me." Rosenthal gently lowered the patient's casted leg to the table. He took the film with one hand, being careful not to soil it with the moist white powder of the plaster that coated his hands. "It's a lousy picture. It's overexposed." He handed it back.

"Is there any tuberculosis in it?"

Rosenthal took the x-ray again. "Your buddy?" He carried the picture to a desk lamp and held it against the lighted bulb. "I can't tell a thing. Everything's all burned out. Who shot this?" Then he said, "There's no name on this. Whose is it?"

"I wouldn't want you to have to report anybody," Dan said. He took the x-ray and went outside. "The picture's no good. I overshot it," he told Noble.

They sat down on the bench and watched the stretchers going into the plaster room and coming out bearing patients with new white casts on their legs and arms.

"I'm beat," Dan finally said. He stood up.

Noble stood up too. "Mind if I stay at your place? You know, my sister's got a little kid."

Noble slept on the couch, but whenever Dan awoke during the night he heard him either moving restlessly or coughing. Once during the night he found Noble standing in his shorts holding his undershirt up against the gas heater. "What are you doing?"

"I'm sweating. Night sweats," Noble said. "I'm just drying my shirt out."

In the morning Dan did not pull into the school lot but drove directly into the hospital lot. "You're going to get examined. Right now," he said.

"You think I'm crazy? I'll be out of school."

"There are worse things. Like bleeding to death. Or spreading this goddamned disease around. Now come on."

Noble remained in the car. "You think I've given it to anybody yet? You know they do have trouble with that baby. They think he's got asthma. You don't think it's really tuberculosis?"

"Come on," Dan said.

Noble got out of the car. "What am I going to do? You don't know what these sanitoriums are like."

"Let's go."

They marched across the street back into the County Hospital and started another search for Rosenthal. This time they found him finishing breakfast in the intern's cafeteria. Rosenthal kicked out a chair. "Go ahead," Dan said to Noble and Noble sat down.

"This is your patient?" Rosenthal said.

"His name is Noble."

"Hi." Rosenthal reached out his hand and Noble shook it.

Rosenthal finished his coffee. Then he got up. "We'll go to Admitting," he said.

On the admitting ward he chose a small cubicle and said to Noble, "Go ahead. Let's take off some clothes." Noble took off his shirt and his undershirt, and stood blinking, his black skin moist with sweat.

Rosenthal pulled the stethoscope out of his pocket and listened and didn't say anything. "Over there," Dan said, and pointed to the spot. Rosenthal moved his stethoscope and listened. After a while he took the stethoscope off and said, "Where did you hear these rales?"

Dan pointed again.

Rosenthal handed him the scope. "Find them for me."

Dan put the scope on and listened. "Breath deeper," he said. Noble took a deep breath, and Dan heard nothing but the soft movement of air.

"What's going on?" Noble said. "What do you hear?"

"Be quiet," Dan said. "Everytime you speak it hurts my eardrums."

He continued to listen and then he gave the stethoscope back to Rosenthal, who listened again.

"Have you had a cold?"

Noble nodded. "I'm just getting over one."

Rosenthal shrugged. "All you heard was some mucus in the bronchi. You got mixed up between coarse rales and fine rales."

"What?" Noble said. After a while he said, "I can't eat and I've been sweating and I've been feeling lousy."

"I'd feel the same way if I thought I had tuberculosis." He filled out a slip. "If you want a chest x-ray, just take this upstairs. But it'll be negative. All you have is a cold. I have to get back to work." He walked out.

Noble stared at Dan. "You dumb prick," he said.

"I'm sure there were rales. Give me that stethoscope."

"You don't listen to me again," Noble said menacingly. "Stay away from me."

Dan put the stethoscope down. "Better get that x-ray anyway."

"I'm going to," Noble said. "But I mean it. You're not putting a hand on me for the rest of the year. Go find yourself another pigeon."

Noble got to the physical diagnosis class about an hour late. Dan, having no partner to work on, was reading the text.

"How was the picture? he said.

"Nothing there."

"Then what took you so long?"

"I went out and had a couple of hamburgers. I'm hungry. I haven't eaten for three days."

Joan's show was scheduled for June. When Dan visited her he found canvases strewn all over the living-room floor. She did strange imaginative things to the frames. Some she coated with colored grains of sand. She wiped other pieces with bleaching solution and scraped and sanded them until the wood seemed sun-whitened and bony. She no longer talked much about Turk, and Dan felt, since she had to wait, it was good fortune that the show was at this time. By the end of the month she was delivering the paintings to the gallery. She slept well and was no longer restless, and Dan stopped worrying.

The show was to open on Monday. He came up on Sunday night after work and found her dressed in a skirt and brassiere, sitting with a mouthful of tacks nailing a frame together.

"Haven't you finished?" he said annoyed. "You should have had them all down there already."

She spit the tacks out and laughed. "They're all there. All that Golden has room for. It's not a very big gallery. These extras are to rotate in."

"What commission does Golden get?"

"Forty per cent."

"That sounds reasonable."

"Danny, what would you do if the President of the United States had to have an operation suddenly and there was nobody but you there to do it?"

"Piss in my pants," he said. "Why?"

"Not a bad idea. I might just do that tomorrow."

He laughed again and joked with her, but she kept working and he had to go to bed by himself that night.

He awoke and found her bare figure by his bed.

"What's the matter?"

"There's someone outside the window."

He got up sleepily and listened. "It's probably a dog."

"That coughs?"

He put on his shoes and went outside. The street was empty except for a light sedan on the corner. He walked about the house, up to the hillside, and then back again.

"Panthers cough," he said. "Maybe it's that black panther that's supposed to live in these hills."

"I could have sworn I heard somebody."

"Come to bed."

"Later," she said and kissed him.

The light sedan was still there when he left in the morning. A man sat in the right front seat reading a paper.

At seven-thirty that evening he drove to LaCienega Avenue. He had to search for a place to park, and he saw the Monday-night walk going by, dozens of strangely mismatched people walking up one side of the street and then down the other, going from gallery to gallery. Some were ordinary middle-aged homeowners shopping for a picture to hang over the mantel. Many of the young girls were untidy and wore long stockings. Most of the young men had oddly trimmed beards, and some of them wore red ribbons about their hair and resembled Apache Indians.

The Golden Gallery was an ornate two-story building with tropical plants growing in the foyer. Dan climbed terrazzo steps to the second floor. A woman sat before an open door, a stack of pamphlets in front of her. "So glad you came," she said and gave him one of the folders. He signed his name in a book and went in.

Joan's paintings and pastels lined the walls of a long room. In the corners of the frames were small stickers with prices. He saw they ranged from a hundred to five hundred dollars.

The whole gallery held only a half-dozen people. Joan came rushing up, wearing a long gown. Her face was tight with strain. "Nobody's come yet," she said. "Those people are friends of Mr. Golden."

"I didn't see anything in the *Herald* this morning."

"He put it in the *Times*."

"You'd think he'd put it in all the papers," he said angrily.

She took him by the arm and led him to a sturdy white-haired man. "This is Rudolph Golden. Daniel McDermott." They shook hands.

A man came in the door. "Just a moment," she said and hurried toward him.

"How's it going?" Dan asked.

The art dealer shrugged. "She's an exotic painter. Are you a friend?"

Dan nodded.

"Come here." He led Dan to a large canvas. "What do you think?"

"I don't know anything about art."

"It's exciting." He paused. "Rather disturbing too."

"It shows?"

"It certainly does."

Dan looked about the room. "Not much of a crowd."

The art dealer smiled. "It's summer. It's not an art-buying season. It's a time to show unknown artists. Once in a while one takes hold and it pays for the others. Excuse me." He went to greet another newcomer.

Two of the strangely dressed young people were standing beside Dan. The girl said, "What do you think of this one?"

The boy was barefooted. He glanced at the canvas. "Flamboyant crap. Art Student League variety."

"I never could get that red to work for me either," the girl said. They walked out, the girl's behind wobbling in her tight pants.

Dan found Joan after a few minutes. "Take it easy."

"That fellow who just came in is from *Art Forum*," she said.

"What?"

"It's an art journal. He likes my nudes. Do you think he's queer?"

"Who cares? Business is picking up. I got to go. Call me later." He kissed her.

Joan dreaded calling Dan. She put it off until she got home. Then she sat down and dialed the drugstore. He answered on the second ring. "Hi Danny. How's the pill business?" she asked brightly.

"How's it going?"

She could picture him in the drugstore phone booth, his hair untidy, his thin face scowling with concern, and a sudden wave of tenderness for him wiped some of the disappointment away. "I was lonely for you all evening," she said.

"You're not answering me. How did it go tonight?"

"It didn't go."

"Any other critics?"

"No."

"Will there be any reviews in the paper?"

"No."

"It takes a while for a new artist to get—"

"Shut up," she said.

"It seems to me painters always—"

"Damn it, shut up."

They were silent a while. Then she said, "Come over tonight, Danny."

"Fine."

"And bring me a few pills. I haven't slept for a couple of nights. Please."

He hesitated, and then he said, "You're better off without them. I'll see you about twelve-thirty."

She paced until it was almost time for him to come. Then she undressed and took a shower. As soon as he came she took him to bed, but it didn't help much.

He started to fall asleep and she shook him. "Listen," she said. "Are you awake?"

He rolled over on his back. "Not really."

"I want to get married."

"What?"

"Right now."

"Who do you want to marry?"

"I'm not joking. I want to get married. We can get to Vegas by eight. No blood tests. Nothing. I even have a ring we can use."

"You really mean it, don't you?"

"I never meant anything more in my life."

"No," he said. "I don't want—"

"Right now. Let's get married right now. You don't know how much pain it would save us. Both of us."

"Now I wish I had brought a pill. You could use one."

"Do you love me?"

He didn't answer.

"I have a right to some answers."

"Go ahead."

"Do you want to get married?"

"Not now."

"Now," she said. "Right now. We'll get in the car and drive over the hill to Ventura, and we'll take Ventura to Sepulveda, and then we'll follow Sepulveda past the mountains to the other side of the valley, and then we'll start across the desert and by the time we're in Bishop the sun will be up and by the time it's broad warm daylight we'll be in Vegas, and we don't have to change clothes or anything, just get married."

The room was quiet except for the crickets. Then he said, "Go to sleep. You're all worn out."

"You don't know what a good wife is. I don't even think you ever had a girl all your own before."

"No," he said.

"I'll be good to you. I'll keep myself so pretty that whenever you go anyplace with me everyone will look and the men will all want to be you. I'll work and I'll get some money from my father and you won't have to work any more. You can study in the evenings and go to bed at eleven and drive to school in an open convertible." She saw his face. "I mean it," she said.

"So do I."

"But why won't you marry me? You love me."

The phone rang. Joan answered it. "It's for you."

Dan took the receiver. It was Goldie. "Thank God I got you. It was my last dime," Goldie said.

"What's the matter?"

"I'm in a little bit of trouble."

"What happened?"

"You have to do me a favor. A very big favor."

"What?"

"I need some money. How much can you spare?"

"About forty dollars."

"I need two hundred and seventy-five. There's a hundred and forty in the apartment." He told Dan how to get in, and where the money was hidden. "You haven't any more than forty?"

"That's all," Dan said. There was silence on the other end of the phone. Then Goldie said, "I'll need another seventy-five."

"What for?"

"I'm in jail."

Dan started to ask why, and then stopped himself. He knew why. "It's two in the morning," he said finally. "It's not going to be easy." He put his hand over the receiver. "You have any money here?"

"Just a few dollars," Joan said. "Why?"

"Goldie's in jail." He went back to the phone.

"Can you borrow it from anybody?" Goldie said. "I'll give it to you back on your rent."

"When do you have to have it?"

"Right now. I want to get out tonight."

"I think I can get it for you."

"Pay it to Fred Benjamin. His office is right across the street from the precinct house. Fred Benjamin, the bail bondsman. Remember."

"Fred Benjamin. Sure."

"It's for me and for a friend whose name is Ronnie."

"All right," Dan said.

"Be sure you get my name right. It's Osborne. Harold Osborne." He spelled it.

"All right."

"God bless you," Goldie said and hung up.

Dan put the phone down. "I have to get seventy-five dollars in cash."

"Why did he call you? Hasn't he any friends?"

"That's what I'm wondering." He dialed Max's number. The phone rang a half-dozen times and then Sharon's sleepy voice came on.

"Can I speak to Max?"

"What's the matter? Anything wrong at the store?"

"I need some money."

"You call in the middle of the night to ask for money?"

"Someone's in jail."

"I'm not waking him up. He's got heart trouble." She hung up the phone.

"That'll teach you," Joan said.

He dialed again and rang Eddie's room at the St. Regis Hotel. "Do you have any cash with you?"

"What for?"

"I need seventy-five dollars."

"Where are you?"

"At Joan's house."

"What do you need seventy-five dollars for?"

"This fellow Goldie. The manager. He's in jail."

"You wouldn't be lying to me now?" For the first time Dan noticed a brogue. Maybe it came out only when he was sleepy.

"What do you mean?"

"Give me the number. I'll call you back."

He called back in just a moment. "At least I know where you are. I thought maybe you were the one who's in jail instead. Why give that queer anything? They never pay you back."

"He wouldn't call me if he had anybody else to ask."

"I'll want it back in a week," Eddie said. "If you want to throw your own money away, that's up to you. But you're not throwing mine away." He hung up.

Dan started dressing.

Joan sat up nervously and said, "Don't go."

He paused, one foot in his trouser leg. "Why not?"

"Stay with me tonight."

He hesitated. Then he finally said, "He's in jail. I think they just get a few dimes to make calls, and he's already used up all his dimes."

She got up and started pacing again and he watched her a moment and said, "You better get some rest. You're kind of wild."

"Thanks," she said. "It's a remarkably fine suggestion."

Dan was surprised by the great number of books in Eddie's room. A whole wall floor to ceiling was covered with shelves. Eddie was in a robe. He handed Dan the seventy-five dollars. "Just kiss it good-bye if you're lending it to a queer."

Dan found the rest of the money in Goldie's apartment, and drove to the Lincoln Heights jail. It was just off the freeway, close to North Figueroa. The street across from the jail was brightly lit by neon signs advertising the bondsmen's offices. An elderly man was behind the counter at Benjamin's, and Dan gave him the money and said, "It's for Harold Osborne and another fellow named Ronnie. I don't know his last name."

The bondsman examined a list. "There's a Ronald Herlihy. That's probably the one." He took the money, and then gave Dan several yellow sheets of paper filled with fine print to sign. Dan signed them quickly. He took the number from Dan's driver's license. Then he made a phone call. "They'll be out soon. You can wait across the street," he said.

Dan went into the precinct waiting room and sat down. He had never been in a police station before and he was nervous and uneasy. After a while he went up to the desk. "I just posted bail on a man you're holding. His name is Osborne."

The sergeant glanced at his book. "Yes, Osborne. He didn't show any identification." He studied Dan for a moment. "Friend of yours?"

"He runs the apartment house I live in."

The sergeant picked up a pencil. "Where's that?"

Dan hesitated. "I think you better ask him," he said after a moment.

The sergeant shrugged. "He'll be coming out the side door," he said. "You can watch for him."

Dan went back and sat down. He waited a very long time and finally Goldie came out, still fresh in his sharply pressed suit. A young man was with him.

Dan stood up. "Don't say anything in here," Goldie said quickly. "We can talk outside."

He stopped on the steps. "This is Ronnie Herlihy. We met in the hoosegow. He's going to stay with me till we get this business straight." He turned to Ronnie. "Did you say what I told you?"

"Sure did," Ronnie said. "I think they believed me."

"Remember," Goldie said, "mouths are a felony. Hands are just a misdemeanor." He turned to Dan. "Did they make you sign any papers over at Benjamin's?"

"A whole stack of them."

"Don't worry about it. All they can get me on is a misdemeanor, and I can plead entrapment. They'll have to reduce the bail at the arraignment." He seemed quite gay. "Let's all go for some ham and eggs. It's still early."

"Not for me," Dan said.

"That's the trouble with you," Goldie said. "No fun in your life. Anyway I left my car at Coffee Joe's."

Dan drove them there. Goldie chatted gaily with the young man, and the last Dan saw of him he was holding Ronnie's arm fondly as they walked together across the dark parking lot.

The next day Dan took the last of the final examinations. It went well, and by four he was finished with that year's work. Max had once again arranged a summer job for him at the West Jefferson store, and he drove there to complete his negotiations with the owner. He had no chance to call Joan until that evening. He found the line busy then, and finally closed the store at midnight and walked home. A light was on in Goldie's apartment. He knocked.

"Hello," he said. "Mind if I use your phone?"

"Come on in," Goldie said. "We were just talking about you. You remember Ronnie."

"Hi," Dan said. He sat down to dial.

"You in any rush on that money?" Goldie said.

"I've got to pay some of it back."

"You'll get it," Goldie said. "It'll take a little while though. Something else has come up. Don't worry."

"I'm beginning to worry plenty," Dan said. He dialed Joan's number and it was still busy.

"Ron is interested in studying medicine."

"How many years does it take?" Ronnie asked.

"Eight after high school," Dan said. He dialed the operator and asked her to check the line.

"How much do doctors make?"

"What?"

"He's thinking of studying medicine," Goldie said.

"Oh, I don't know. Twenty-five, thirty-five thousand or so a year."

"My uncle makes that and he's only an engineer," Ronnie said.

"One of the best families in Little Rock," Goldie said.

"Accounting's a pretty good field," Ronnie said. "You start as an accountant for a firm that's just being set up, and you can work yourself into a piece of it."

"That line is out of order," the operator said. "I will report it."

Dan hung up. He looked at Goldie and was struck by how happy he seemed. "Aren't you worried about your trial?"

"I'll be in hock for the next six months, but I'm not even going to be arraigned."

"They dropped the charges?"

"Well it's this way. Two businessmen from vice came out to see my lawyer the first thing this morning, and my lawyer thinks fifteen hundred will do it. I'm going to have to borrow it but it's better than digging up carrots on the farm for three months."

Dan looked puzzled and both Goldie and the boy grinned. "Jesus, he's square," the boy said.

"I've been booked six times," Goldie said. "The only thing that happens is they keep raising the ante."

"Oh," Dan said.

"Don't worry about the money," Goldie said. "When you get some time though it would be nice if you sat down and had a little talk with Ronnie here about medical school. I really don't think the boy has found himself yet."

The phone rang, and Dan waited, but it wasn't Joan. He debated with himself whether he should drive to her house. Most likely her phone had fallen from the receiver, and when she discovered it she would call him. He stood up. "If Joan calls, wake me up," he said.

"I owe you money," Goldie said. "How can I refuse?"

The next morning he found the art critic's comments on Joan's show in the paper. The comments were favorable. The critic used words like "imaginative" and "warm" and "extravagantly original." Dan tried to call her then, but the line was still out of order. He decided to drive out after work. Just before he closed the drugstore the phone rang. "I have a long-distance call from Wallace, Idaho, for Daniel McDermott," the operator said.

"I'm McDermott."

A man's voice came in on the line. "I'm Joe Means. Joan's father."

Dan was startled. "Yes?"

"Have you heard from Joan in the last two days?"

"I can't reach her."

"You better go up there and see what's happened."

"Why?"

"She hasn't been out of the house for two days. Her car's still in the garage. No one's been there except a delivery boy."

Dan remembered the sedan in front of Joan's house and he said, "Did you get any good pictures?"

"I'm not detectiving now," Means said. "I'm just worried about my daughter." After a moment he added, "She's probably drinking again."

The line hummed gently. Dan said, "I think she's worn out. She's been up every night making frames. She hasn't had one night's sleep in the last two weeks."

"You better take a look anyway. Did anything go wrong that might start her off?"

"She thinks the show went badly."

"Didn't it?"

Dan told him about the critic.

"Anything else?"

"She wanted to get married."

"Do you?"

"No."

"I see." After a moment Means said, "Call me after you see her." He left a number.

Dan found the sedan still on the corner beyond Joan's house. A different man was sitting next to the empty driver's seat, listening or pretending to listen to the radio.

Dan walked around the house, opened a window into the bedroom, and climbed in and turned the light on. Joan was sleeping deeply. Blood was spattered over the sheets and the carpet. He pulled the bedclothes back and searched for its source. Shreds of toilet paper clung to a deep scratch on her leg. He shook her savagely. Her eyelids were swollen, and when she opened them her eyes were crossed.

"Danny is here," she said. "Hi Danny."

He led her into the toilet and sat her down on the closed seat. He handed her the toothpaste and her toothbrush. "You better wash."

He left and he heard the sound of retching from the bathroom. He put coffee on to boil. When he came back to the bathroom the brush was still in her hand, some paste on it, and some on the floor. He put the paste on the brush, and then she scrubbed at her teeth. Then he led her to the bed. "How do you feel?"

"Awful."

"How much did you drink?"

"I don't know." She looked up at him, eyes still not focused. "Hardly anybody came to the show tonight."

He gave her the cup of coffee and she held it unsteadily with both hands. "Should I drink it?"

"It won't hurt you to throw up."

She drank some. After a while she said, "I guess it'll stay down."

"What happened to you Monday?"

"Monday?"

"That was the night you started drinking."

She saw the cut on her leg. "Will it have to be sewed?"

"It'll heal."

"I always cut myself or burn myself when I drink." She kept her face averted. "Did you find the vodka?"

"I didn't look for it."

"I have the shakes. Do you have any paraldehyde?"

He shook his head and she said, "It's too bad you haven't studied this in school yet. Paraldehyde would have done it. Listen, Danny, I'm going to have another drink."

He said nothing.

"All I'm going to do is take a drink so I can stop shaking. I'd like to feel better. Do you mind?"

She tried to light a cigarette and he saw she was truly shaking. He lit it for her. "Will one do it?"

"Just one. I'll pour the rest out."

"Go ahead."

"It's not so easy. I'm a secretive drunk. I hide the bottles." She looked around the bedroom. "You're sure you didn't see it?"

He shook his head again. She got out of bed and, supporting herself against the wall, managed to get to the kitchen. She opened the oven, and then she looked under the sink, and then on the shelf where the canned goods were kept.

"Try the dresser. One of the drawers was open when I came in," he said.

She went into the bedroom and came back with the vodka. She filled a tumbler about a quarter full, and gave him the bottle. "Pour it out. This is all I need."

He emptied it into the sink. She took the glass in both hands, and carefully brought it up to her mouth. She drank two long swallows, and started retching again.

"Please get out," she gasped, holding onto the long chrome spigot.

He walked into the living room and waited. When he heard water splashing he went back. She was washing her face. "I can't stand the taste of vomit and booze mixed," she said between clenched teeth. "Get me some Lavoris from the bathroom." He brought her the red bottle and she washed her mouth.

She held out her hand. It was still shaking badly. "In a minute," she said. "You'll see."

It wasn't much more than a minute. She straightened up and said, "The hair of the dog that bit you. The poison of the snake that got you going through the tall grass. Don't doctors use poison to kill poison?"

He was watching her. "I think they pump stomachs now. How do you feel?"

"Fine," she said. "In the pink. Rolling. Are you disappointed? Do you want me to be sick in proper Jewish atonement?"

He didn't answer.

"Why did you leave me alone last night?"

"How did I know you were going to start drinking?"

"I was in misery last night. The—"

"Monday night."

"Sorry. I stand corrected. Monday night. Okay? The show went badly. I wanted the man I love here in my bed. Anything wrong with that?"

He didn't answer.

"And where were you? Bailing a queer out of jail!" She shook her head angrily. "Just what do you think you're doing for me that I should put up with the crap you hand out? The sex? Listen, you need a few years seasoning. I feel like a den mother with you sometimes." She lit a cigarette with a steady hand. "Come on. You've been learning to talk. Let's talk."

He was very angry. He dragged her to the bedroom and found a pair of underpants in the drawer. He tugged her pajama bottoms off and got her into the underpants. He threw a dress at her. "Put it on."

"Drinking is a sickness," she said. "You can't get mad at somebody for having a fever or the measles. Right?"

"Do you have a key?"

"What do I need a key for?"

"Never mind." He pushed the button below the latch so the door would be unlocked.

"Just who do you think you are?" she snapped and pulled away and fell against the door frame. "Who put that there?"

she said and covered her face with her hands. Blood was running down her chin and he pulled her hands away and saw her nose was bleeding. He got a kitchen towel and wiped the blood, and pinched her nostrils together. She stood obediently waiting, peering at him over the towel. "What's the matter with you?" she said. "You look beat."

"I haven't had much sleep lately."

"What are you putting up with this for? Nobody else ever put up with it this long."

He didn't answer.

"I think you got some kind of Jesus Christ complex."

He managed to get her into his car and drove her to the apartment house. By then the sky was already showing a vague pallor. He led her upstairs to his room and put her into his bed. He washed and shaved, and when he came out she was fast asleep.

He went to the corner, bought some milk and doughnuts, and put them into the refrigerator. As he was closing the door a second time he heard the sound of footsteps running up the stairs and he turned quickly and saw Goldie coming up two steps at a time, his eyes red and his thin gray hair disheveled. "Did you see Ronnie?" Goldie panted.

"Who?"

"The kid that's been staying with me."

"I wasn't here last night. What's wrong?"

Goldie spun around without answering and ran downstairs. Dan came down after him and found his door ajar. Goldie was sitting on the couch dialing furiously. He listened to the receiver for a moment and then slammed it down in exasperation.

"What happened?"

"That son of a bitching poggie! That lying faggot bastard! He stole my gray suit and my Italian silk and two sets of gold cuff links and a brand new pair of shoes. Here. Look!" He sprang up and threw open the closet door. "I'm going to report him. I know some people in the vice squad."

"He can't wear your clothes. They're too big."

"He's going to sell them. That son of a bitch. I caught him yesterday messing around with Bender."

"Who?"

"Oh the fellow that lives across the hall from you, and I—"

"The fellow that plays the drums? He's married."

"What the hell difference does that make?" Goldie said. "I dragged the little bitch down here and I kicked his ass good and when I got up this morning my best suits were gone." He started dialing again. "Let me have the University precinct house," he said into the receiver. He waited a moment breathlessly. Then he gave Ronnie's age, his description, and then a description of the stolen merchandise. "Listen. This boy is a male prostitute. He was picked up a couple of days ago by the vice squad and he's got a record. And I can identify him. I'll identify him for you any time. Day or night. And I want to tell you something about that time he was arrested. He said he was just groping with this other kid. Well, they were performing fellatio. You know what that is?" He listened a moment, and then he said, "All right. I'll report it to them. And I'll give them a signed statement. That psychopath should be behind bars. He's just a common ordinary thief." He hung up the phone and looked at Dan.

Dan glanced at his watch and saw that he had only a half hour to get to work. He was walking toward the door when he heard the sound of sobbing. He looked back at Goldie. Goldie's hands lay in his lap, and he was looking straight ahead, his face twisting rhythmically into sobs. Tears ran down his cheeks, and shiny mucus dripped from one nostril. "Oh God, oh God, oh God," he sobbed. Dan was puzzled and didn't know what to say and he closed the door and left Goldie still sobbing.

When Dan came home from work in the evening he knocked at Goldie's door. After a while a thickened voice answered, "Who is it?"

"Me. Dan."

"My doctor came out and gave me a shot."

"How do you feel?"

"I don't know," Goldie said. "I'm going back to bed."

Dan listened to Goldie's feet padding away from the door. Then he climbed the stairs and went into his own apartment. The bed was empty and the bathroom door locked. He became frightened and pushed on the door and the flimsy latch sprung open. Joan sat on the floor, one arm over the curved pipe below the sink. She looked up at him. "I thought I could take a shower. I didn't know how weak I was," she said.

He helped her up.

"I did manage to take it," she said. "I'm clean. But then I threw up some blood and I got weaker."

He led her back to the bed. "How much blood?"

"I always do that when I drink. A doctor once told me it's alcoholic gastritis. I don't think it's dangerous."

"Did you drink the milk?"

"I threw it up. Then I found a can of sardines and I threw it up too. I won't be able to eat for a couple of days."

He took off his shoes. "School ended today and I've taken two days off work. Two solid days." He undressed and hunted out a pair of pajamas. He washed and set about preparing the couch.

"It's not contagious," she said, watching him. "It's a hereditary and environmental disorder."

He pulled the wool blanket over him. "This couch is wet."

"I cleaned it," she said. "Matter of fact I've cleaned your whole room. I was doing my penance."

"You've just started."

"What do you mean."

"There's somebody parked in a light sedan outside who I'll just bet has infrared pictures of me dragging you out of your house last night, and you staggering all over the place, bloody nose and all."

"He's having me watched again?"

"Yes."

"Oh God, dear God," she said, and then was quiet.

He tried to fall asleep but he was restless. Finally he got up and lay down in the bed next to her. She was sleeping heavily as though she were very tired. He felt sad and sorry for her, and he put his arm around her.

She awakened him by sitting up. It was still dark. He sat up too. "Get back in bed," he said.

"I'm not going to drink," she said. "That isn't the way it goes with me. I hit the end of the string and I'm good for a while."

She started pulling her clothes on. "I'm going back to my place to get a canvas. I'll bring it over here and I'll paint in the kitchen with the door closed. I won't keep you awake."

He hesitated a long time.

"It'll make me feel better. It always does."

"If you're not here when I wake up in the morning I won't even wonder what happened," he said.

"I'll be here," she said. "Don't get up. I'll take a cab." She stooped down and kissed him.

She wasn't there in the morning, and he got up sadly and washed and drove to work. He didn't expect to hear from her, and she didn't call. After several days he called her. Her voice was thick and indistinct, and he hung up unhappily. He missed her badly, and for relief he forced himself to work hard at both drugstores, getting up early and going to bed late.

The work failed to lessen his yearning, and finally he phoned again. She was out and he kept phoning every chance he found that evening. He reached her at midnight. "Where were you?"

"Went to a show."

He couldn't tell from her voice whether she was drinking. "What did you see?"

"Something with Paul Newman," she said. "Bandits and Indians and that sort of stuff."

He spoke to her for a few minutes and then hung up. Afterward he wasn't sure. Her voice was thick but what she said had made sense.

The next morning was a Sunday, and Max planned to keep the store closed for inventory. Dan awoke early and suddenly decided he would see her again. He became excited at the idea. It had been three whole weeks. He stopped at a delicatessen and bought white fish and bagels and corned beef. He drove up to her house, the heavy bag on the seat beside him. He walked gaily up to her door, and pressed the doorbell. No one answered. Then he heard the sound of a door closing inside, and he became angry. She was probably drunk again. He pushed a window screen aside and stepped over the sill into the living room. In full view on a coffee table was an almost empty bottle of vodka, the Romanoff eagles viciously marking the label. He strode into the bedroom, his mouth open, ready to demand an explanation, and was amazed to see a tall man lying propped up against the pillows puffing on a cigarette. It took him a few seconds to realize that it was Gross.

"She's in the bathroom," Gross said. "I don't think I'd try to see her."

Two empty glasses were standing on the bedside table. Gross's clothes, Dan saw, had been hung away carefully in the closet.

Dan turned and walked to the toilet door.

"I'd leave her alone," Gross said. "This spying of yours is going to upset her."

"Don't talk to me about spying, you miserable bastard," Dan said. "If I had done a little I would have known about this a month ago."

"You know now."

Dan rapped on the toilet door. "Be sure you get a receipt for the bill," he shouted. He went out shutting the door firmly behind him.

The anger lasted only a few minutes, and then he felt relieved. It was done and he was clean out of it. He stopped on Sunset Boulevard to take the top of the convertible down, and drove on toward Orchid Street, the wind flipping his tie and ballooning his shirt.

He knocked on Goldie's door. Goldie looked at the groceries. "What's with you this morning?"

"I've come to invite you to a nice kosher Jewish breakfast. Lox and white fish and bagels with cream cheese. It should be a Saturday morning breakfast, on *Shabbas,* but owing to the pressure of Anglo-Saxon civilization it is now eaten on Sunday morning. Can I come in?"

"What are you celebrating?"

"Freedom," Dan said. He emptied the bag on the table, and the packages rolled out.

"I can't eat very much so early in the morning."

"You'll eat it," Dan said. "And you'll enjoy it too." Goldie brought out the dishes, and they ate with enjoyment the white fish and the bagels and the cream cheese and the rich sweet butter.

At noon Dan went to work. He helped finish the inventory, and then worked the rest of the day alone. From time to time he worried about himself—that he could live with a girl for many months and then take her loss with only a transient annoyance.

But by the following morning he realized he had no cause for worry. He was lonely and ferociously angry at Joan and Gross that day. The following days were chaotic and miserable. His anger would sometimes stifle him, and to relieve it he would pace restlessly until it eased. He thought of savage things to say to her, relishing the contempt and fury of the words. At other times the anger disappeared and he thought of appeals to make to her that would move her to love him again. The morning sadness came back harshly. It stayed all day, and was waiting each morning when he awoke.

At the end of the month he stopped at Goldie's apartment. "Let me have a receipt for my rent," he said.

Goldie sat down with the receipt book. "Where's your check?"

"You're paying it. Out of the money you owe me."

"Not this month. I had to raise—"

"Give me a receipt."

"I'm just the manager. I got to turn the money over to the owner." His voice was shrill. "You can't get blood out of a turnip. Everybody's squeezing me. My lawyer. The vicers. You."

"Quit yelling, and give me a receipt."

Goldie changed tactics. "I can give you a little bit of it now. Later—"

"The whole month's rent. I have to pay my father back."

"Listen—"

"I don't want to. The rest comes out of next month's rent too."

Goldie stared at him. "A fine friend you are." He sat down and wrote out the receipt.

Dan picked up the phone and started to dial Eddie. Goldie snatched the receiver. "Don't you ever use my phone again," he screamed and slammed the receiver back into its cradle.

Dan stopped in a gas station and called Eddie and told him he was coming with the money.

Eddie had been reading when he got Dan's phone call. The call upset him, and he put down the book. He called room service and had them send up two glasses with ice. He filled one glass half full of bourbon, and sipped on it and waited. Dan knocked a little after midnight and Eddie opened the door and found the boy outside, shirt open, collar a little soiled, the check in his hand. "Come on in," he said. He ignored the check. Dan sat down in one of the chairs, cautious, ready to get up, and Eddie said irritably, "For God's sakes, relax. Have a drink." He poured some bourbon into the second glass and handed it to Dan.

Dan put it down. "Here's the check," he said. "Thanks."

Eddie didn't take it. "Why don't you get yourself some clothes? Look at the way you're dressed. Your suit's unpressed. Your shoes need shining."

"I'm getting along."

Eddie got angry. "What do you want now? I only see you when you want something."

"Oh Christ," Dan said and looked up at the ceiling and Eddie felt like hitting him. Instead he took a drink and was silent until the anger passed. "I'm a hell of a lot better off than you think," he said. "I own a hunk of this hotel. If I sold everything I own right now I would have at least on today's market a couple of hundred grand." He watched Dan's face, and the boy looked as though he was thinking of something else instead of listening and Eddie got angry again. "Do you know how hard it is to accumulate that much money?"

"I don't suppose too much of it comes from your salary."

"I'm one of the best-paid men they got," Eddie said. "I've saved that company millions of dollars since I've been with them. But most of it comes from investments. In '46 when I first moved into this place it was going on the rocks. I bought a nice piece for ten thousand dollars."

Dan nodded.

Eddie watched him a moment. "How's the redhead?"

The boy's face twisted and he said, "I haven't seen her for a while."

"What happened?"

Dan told him about her drinking. Then he told him about Gross.

Eddie got up and walked around the room. "That bitch!" he said. Then he stopped at the phone and ordered two more glasses with ice. "It's your fault," he said. "It'll always be your fault, just as it was always mine. You didn't give her enough. You've got to pay them."

"She's not a prostitute."

Eddie shook his head. "Maybe I'm using the wrong word. You don't feel this way very often in your life. How many times in my life do you think I felt about anybody the way you feel about this redhead? Twice, three times maybe. You have to give them what they want. You have to work like hell to make them happy. Otherwise they go away on you, and if they think they've been cheated they go away mean and nasty." Eddie shook his head. "The worst was with your mother. You remember her as old, don't you?"

Dan was listening. "She always acted like it," he said.

Eddie shut his eyes. "I wasn't a kid when I met her. I was thirty-eight and I didn't think anybody would ever get to me again. But in ten minutes I was a kid. She was maybe twenty-two. She had been married once and it had blown up on her." There was a knock at the door and Eddie let in the bellboy and took the two glasses. "Do you have any idea what your mother looked like when she was twenty-two?"

Dan shook his head.

"She was so pretty you wouldn't believe it," Eddie said, "and after a while, after we were in it, every time I'd look at her she'd get prettier. It got where there was nothing important but her. And yet I didn't trust her." He shook his head wonderingly. "I figured that she was too damned pretty for me, and that any minute she'd break away. I thought I was too old for her."

"Sixteen years older?"

"A hundred years older," Eddie said. "I'd been shot at in this goddamned Sinn Fein Rebellion, I'd slept with a thousand women, I'd been on my own battling and scratching since I could button my pants."

"Why didn't you marry her?"

"It happened too fast. It started like it started with all the others, and I figured it was good only for a month or two. Anyhow, I got hooked the way you get hooked on morphine, and I began to get worried, and the more I worried the less I trusted her. Then she stepped out with some son of a bitch of a schoolteacher, and when I found out about that I came down on her with both feet. I was mad, and I waited for her to come and say, 'I'm sorry,' but she didn't and it got worse. She quit seeing the schoolteacher, but then she took up with some bastard that was supposed to be composing a symphony. I was so suspicious by then I was watching everything she did, and I still didn't give her a thing. I wasn't about to get married. I wasn't about to make her happy." He stopped. "You can't do it that way. You have to give it to them first."

"What happened?"

"I threw her out on this musician bit, but after that nothing was any good. I didn't feel like living. So I went back and found her, and begged her to quit him, and after a while she did." He looked out of the window and Dan thought of Jesse Davis. "I'd come home and I'd threaten to leave, or she'd be excited because of somebody she met, or the phone would ring, and they'd hang up." He put his hand up to his face and said, "Jesus, the men she went to bed with. Every time we had a fight she chased out and found somebody."

"You couldn't have lived with her."

"You've got to give them everything you have. You can't hold anything back. What if they do drink once in a while? What the hell is a little screwing?" He stopped and looked at Dan. "It makes you mad. You feel like somebody kicked you in the balls. What is it really? If you've got something going, you can cut hell out of it and it heals up after a while."

He got up and walked around the room again. "The last time with your mother was sudden death. I was mad as hell about this screwing around. Then I came home one night and she says she's pregnant. All I said was, 'Whose is it?' That was the last thing I ever said to her."

"Whose was it?"

"What the hell difference does it make?" Eddie said. "But like a prick all I could say was, 'Whose is it?'"

"Yes," Dan said.

Eddie remembered him. He sat down. "Better go on back there, kid," he said.

"I can't."

"You mean this fellow Gross? He's married. It's not going to last. The worst that can happen to you is that you get another kick in the balls. But maybe you'll get her back." He looked at the clock. "What time do you get up in the morning?"

"Six."

"You sleeping?"

"Sometimes."

"Yes," Eddie said. He put his arm around the boy's shoulders and walked him to the door. "Watch the way you drive," he said.

Dan called Joan the next morning. "I can take part of this morning off. How about my coming up?" He waited, his mouth dry.

"I just woke up."

"I've been sweating," he said.

"Give me ten minutes to get my face washed."

"Do you need anything?"

"Just some coffee."

He bought a can of coffee at a corner market and drove to the house on Beverly Glen. When she opened the door he reached out and hugged her. She let him hold her a moment. "Where's the coffee?"

He handed her the can.

"I have to get my housework done. I have to be at the bank at noon." She busied herself with the pots.

"I was afraid to call this morning."

"Why?" She looked at him over her shoulder.

"I was afraid Gross would be here."

"I went to bed early last night."

The ache went out of his stomach, and when she brought him the cup of coffee he was able to drink some of it. He reached for her again but she pulled away. "What's the matter?" he said.

"There are so many things."

The knot tightened in his stomach again. "Nothing that we can't straighten out."

She didn't say anything.

"Is there?"

She brought him a small pitcher of milk.

He stood up and started walking around the room.

"Calm down," she said. "You'll get yourself an ulcer."

He passed the open door to the bedroom, and saw the unmade bed with the two rumpled pillows and the two troughs made by two bodies, and like a small boy he suddenly fought back tears.

He went back into the living room and sat down. "Let me have the cream," he said.

She had been watching him all the time. "I should have made the bed," she said.

"Go to hell," he said. "Go straight to hell." He stared at the cup of coffee in front of him for a few minutes and then he got up and left the house.

Dan waited several weeks until his agitation quieted enough so that he could conceal it. Then he called Eddie. "Are you still up?"

"Reading," Eddie said. "Why?"

"Don't go to bed for about fifteen minutes."

He went up to his room and opened the large bag he had brought from San Francisco, and took out a twine-tied shoe box. He sorted through the snapshots and put several in an envelope. He drove to Eddie's hotel and knocked at his door. "What's up now?" Eddie asked.

Dan gave him the envelope. "Here are some pictures. I thought you might want them."

Eddie sat down under the lamp and looked at the snapshots.

"They're all I've got," Dan said. "I think that's all that she ever had taken."

Eddie was studying the first one. He turned it over and looked at the back. "Sure," he finally said. "I remember this one. I paid for it." He looked up at Dan. "I didn't think I was going to keep her very long, and I got the idea I wanted a picture made." He went back to the photo. "You could watch her for hours. It was fun just looking at her."

Dan watched, finding it odd and unfamiliar that he no longer hated his father. Something was gone from his life and he thought it would never be quite the same again.

When he left Eddie was still sitting in the chair under the lamp going over each photo.

Six

DURING THE SUMMER Max worried a good deal about Dan. He cornered Dan one evening. "All you eat is pork and beans seven nights a week. You can get beriberi. You look like hell. Why don't you take some vitamins?"

"They're a waste of money."

"So eat a steak once in a while."

"I can't broil steak in that chocolate hot-cup."

Max took a jar down from the shelf. "Don't argue." He shook out two capsules. "Go ahead. Fifteen milligrams of ribo-flavin."

Dan shrugged and swallowed the capsules.

"Two every morning." Max put his suit jacket on. "I don't see that redhead around. Broke up?"

Dan didn't answer.

"It's not such a tragedy," Max said. "There are lots of girls. You can always get a new one. So you feel bad for a month. So what? You don't die. You don't even get sick. You just feel bad, that's all." He patted Dan on the arm. "You won't die, I promise you." He chewed on his mustache awhile. "Can nervousness make you late in your period?"

"How late are you?"

Max grimaced humorlessly. "Sharon's two weeks late this time." He sighed. "She's all upset about it again. I told her it's just nerves. Do you think it could be?"

"How do I know?"

"After two years of medical school you don't know? Don't they teach you anything?"

"I get obstetrics next year."

"I told her it's nerves anyway. Maybe she'll let me have some peace for a while," he said.

For the next several days Max was quiet and preoccupied. Then on a Sunday morning about ten he burst into the store, his eyes red and his hair awry. Dan had been trying to study. He closed the book and said, "What's the matter? Anything wrong? Did you have another fight with Sharon?"

"She's pregnant."

"She always thinks she's pregnant."

"She's pregnant this time. She's good and pregnant. I know." He was waving his arms in agitation. "I spoke to the doctor myself. Two frog tests. I feel so sick you wouldn't believe it."

"Your heart?"

"Heartburn. I can't stop it."

Dan emptied a small carton of milk into a glass. "Amphoteric. Good for heartburn."

Max drank the milk. "I can't talk to her. Honest to God, she's crazy. She says it's my fault she got pregnant. She raised such a fuss yesterday she was screaming for an hour. All night she was walking up and down until it was light. Today she says she going to get an abortion. She wants to go to Tijuana."

"Why doesn't she want the baby?"

"You ask her. You see what kind of answer you get." After a minute, he said, "There was this daughter of a friend of mine. A sixteen-year-old girl and she went to get an abortion and she died and they threw her in the alley. Then when the police did an autopsy on her they found she wasn't even pregnant." He shook his head. "What did she get married for if she doesn't want to have children?" He paused. "I want you to talk to her."

Dan was startled. "I can't talk to Sharon."

Max pressed his hand over his heart as though he were pushing it back in place. "You have to. I get too excited. She gets pregnant and she acts like it's a cancer."

"Why don't you let her have her own way?"

"What kind of a question is that?" After a moment he said, "I'll tell you. We'll get old and we'll hate each other. I'll hate her for not having any children and she'll hate me because there won't be anything else for her. Am I right? Is that what will happen?"

"I think so," Dan said after a moment.

"So be a man," Max said. "Let's go. We'll close up the store. What difference does it make if she gets mad at you?"

"It's the middle of the morning."

"The hell with business. You think I care about business now?"

They found Sharon talking on the phone. She turned an angry back toward them. Dan could see only the side of her face. It was taut, and the hollows about the eyes were dark. "Honey," Max said.

She spun around in a fury. "Get the hell out of here," she shouted.

"Please," Max said. "Don't get upset. I brought Dan over. He wants to talk to you. I'll go out." He walked into the kitchen.

"You can get the hell out too," she said.

He remained standing in the center of the room.

"Do you mind? I want a little privacy. Okay?"

He sat down. "I told Max I'd talk to you."

She glared at him, and then dropped her voice so that he couldn't hear what she was saying. Dan waited and it was twenty minutes before she was done. Then she stood up. "I'm going out. You can stay and play pinochle with your buddy." She went off to the bedroom.

Max ran out of the kitchen. "I'll stop that right now." He ran into the bedroom and came back with a set of car keys. "She was in the bathroom," he explained, and sat down. "It's so distasteful."

Sharon came out in a few minutes, her hair up, makeup covering the marks of weariness on her face. "Have fun you two," she said and strode toward the door.

"You haven't got your car keys," Dan said.

She stopped and searched through her purse. "What did you do with them?"

"Sit down," Max said. "He just wants to talk to you."

"Give me back my car keys, you bastard son of a bitch," she shouted.

"What's it going to hurt you if he talks to you?"

"Why do you get your employee into our personal business?"

"He's no employee. He's a friend," Max shouted back, and she hesitated and then she said to Dan, "I'm very nervous. It's hard for me to sit still."

"Sit down a minute," Max said.

She sat down and looked at Dan. "You're going to talk to me? You with your life all screwed up with this crazy girl you're running around with? You're going to give me a lecture?"

"He's studying to be a doctor."

"Even if he was a doctor what good could he do? I don't want a baby. Period. Okay?"

"Abortions are dangerous," Dan said. "Particularly criminal abortions."

"You telling me about abortions? This morning I've spoken to fifteen of my girl friends that had abortions. I know everything that they went through, and I'd rather have an abortion right now than to stay another day the way I am." She hunted in her purse for a Kleenex. Max hurried into the kitchen and brought her an absorbent paper towel. She wiped her eyes and nose with it.

"I'll tell you the truth," she said. "I don't want a baby with him. He knows it and I've told it to him and now I'm telling it to you. So what he brings you here for I don't know." The girl dabbed at her face with the paper towel.

"You came to talk to her. So talk," Max said.

"What the hell can I say when she says something like that?"

"I'll go out for a walk. It might make it easier." Max walked toward the front door.

"Put your sweater on," Sharon said. Max stopped at the closet and took out a wool sweater, and pulled it over his head and went out.

"I can't even let him touch me," Sharon said. "I tried for a while. I had to hold my breath. And then this is what happened." Her face flushed. "He talked me into it and then he got me pregnant. He drives me crazy. You should see how he acts. He cried all last night."

"Cried?"

"All night long. He doesn't want me killing his baby. His baby! He should be the woman and I should be the man."

Max strode in. "Ask her what she got married for if she doesn't want children. Ask her!" He slammed out again.

"You want me to have a nervous breakdown?" she shouted. "You want me to get sick and go to a sanitarium?" She blew her nose. "How can I carry his baby around in me for nine months? I've only known I've been pregnant one day and I already have almost a breakdown. I'm so nervous I shake. Look." She held out two bluish small hands that trembled. "I'm having an abortion just as soon as I can arrange it. There's no point talking."

"I better get back to the store," Dan said.

Max came running in and shouted, "I'm sick of your craziness. You're supposed to be happy when you're pregnant. You're supposed to make plans for your baby. But all you want is some quack to scrape it out and throw it in the garbage."

"It's not a baby yet," she shouted back.

Max sighed and turned to Dan. "Ai, it's so distasteful. I'm sorry I got you into my troubles. You got enough of your own. I'll drive you back."

"I can walk."

"I'm sorry. I know you have good intentions," Sharon said.

He closed the door. He heard them shouting again before he was halfway down the steps.

In the late afternoon Max phoned. "Sharon been in?" His voice trembled.

"No. Why?"

"She's gone already then. I was so tired I lay down for ten minutes, and when I got up she was gone."

"She have any money?"

"There's always some money around the house." After a moment, he said, "Even if it kills me I'm going to stop her this time. You'll see."

"Sure," Dan said.

"I mean it. I need a car. She took the Chevy."

"You can have mine for all the good it'll do you."

Max hesitated as though he wanted to say something more. "What is it?" Dan said.

"Never mind. I'll take a cab over."

When he came in his eyes were gleaming and his cheeks were flushed. "She's going to kill me, that woman. All day long my heart's been beating like crazy. I get short of breath. Does that mean anything?"

"It's just excitement."

"I took an extra digitalis anyway."

Dan went in back to get his car keys. He came out with his jacket over his arm. Max saw the jacket. "I didn't want to ask you, the way you've been feeling. But who else can I ask? Who?" Dan started once again to set the burglar alarm but Max said, "Come on. We have to hurry," and they went out, merely locking the door.

Dan swung into the driver's seat and started the Dodge. "I called my brother-in-law," Max said. "He's supposed to be a big lawyer but he doesn't know a thing. I asked him if I can stop her at the border gate. He says he thinks so. He's not sure." Max stopped and wiped his lips. Froth had formed in the corners. "He says he thinks we would have to have a restraining order, and to have a restraining order we would have to show a civil tort. You know what that is, a civil tort?"

"What?"

"I don't either. I thought maybe you would. Anyway he says the only civil tort he can think of is that she's destroying my property. The baby. My property. You see?"

"Getting an abortion is a crime. Can't they stop her for that?"

Max sighed. "He said it's a state crime, and the border guards are federal. Besides he said you can't do anything before a crime is committed. Anyway I argued and he said that he thinks if he can get a federal judge to sign a restraining order maybe he can get the border guards to cooperate and stop her. He's getting it drawn up now and I'm supposed to call him."

Dan was dodging between slow-moving cars and driving as fast as he dared in city traffic.

"She's not a fast driver, but she's been gone an hour." Max looked at the car clock. "We have to get to Tijuana in three hours. Hurry up!"

Dan increased his speed even more, and finally came onto the freeway. Then he swung out to the left lane, and brought the gas pedal down to the floorboard. The Dodge smoked and trembled but the speedometer crept up to seventy miles an hour. The old car steadied, and they rolled smoothly over the broad concrete roadway that sliced through the town. In a few minutes they had passed the downtown section, and a little while later they were whistling between the factories of East Los Angeles. Dan was watching the speedometer and the roadside mileage signs. "We'll make it in two and a half hours if we don't hit any heavy traffic," he said.

When they reached Santa Ana it was twilight. Max began watching the slower cars to the right, searching for the bright red Chevrolet.

"How much gas did the Chevy have?" Dan asked.

"What difference does that make?"

"Maybe when she stops off to get gas she'll stop to eat."

"About half a tank," Max said. "But if she's going to eat, it'll be at Victor Hugo's. She likes fancy places."

They stopped for gas on the outskirts of Santa Ana, and Max went to phone. When he came back he said, "Are you hungry? We can run in and get a hot dog."

"Let's go," Dan said. "We lost about ten minutes with you being on the phone so long." He started the car and turned back into the freeway.

"I had to," Max said. "That was Irv. My brother-in-law. He got the restraining order signed by Judge Rander."

"Did he call the border guards?"

"I told him to wait. I don't want everybody to know my

wife don't love me. It's bad enough I know it and you know it." He rocked back and forth.

"I'm sorry," Dan said.

"I know how you feel," Max said. "I know you can't say things easily." He patted Dan's hand. A little later he complained, "Why does every car have to be red?"

They raced along the freeway through Costa Mesa, and then along the dark road toward San Diego. Max was leaning forward in his seat like a hunter. At the Laguna cutoff, he said, "Turn here! We must be almost up with her now. Shoot over to Laguna and we'll catch her at Victor Hugo's."

They drove along a side road that ran through a canyon with stone walls. Finally they rounded a curve and came into Laguna. It was, Dan knew, a summer beach resort, popular with artists and young people. Max said, "Turn right. That's Victor Hugo's."

Dan turned into the parking lot behind the restaurant. An attendant came hurrying toward them. "Just looking for somebody," Max shouted out the window.

Dan drove along the lines of parked cars. "Not here," he finally said.

"I don't understand it. Here's where she would stop for supper."

Dan swung the car around and turned back into the highway. "I don't think we can make it now. We lost a lot of time when we got off the freeway."

"So I'll go to every abortionist in Tijuana," Max shouted, "and when I find her I'll call the police."

The road followed the edge of the ocean, sometimes curving around small, perfect bays. The air was cool with the inland breeze.

"There's a restaurant," Max cried and they slowed down and examined the cars parked before it. There was no red Chevrolet and they went on through South Laguna and Dana Point and San Clemente. They were passing through Del Mar when Dan saw a red car parked slantingly against a building. He slowed down.

"Is that it?"

Max was staring at it. "Back up," he cried. "All right. All right. Stop here." He got out and opened the door of the Chevrolet. "It's mine, all right," he yelled.

A red-uniformed attendant came up. "Dinner parking?" he asked.

"Never mind," Max cried and ran into the building. Dan left the car with the attendant and went in a side door and walked through a corridor lined with paintings of the sea into a large dark room with candles flickering on the tables. He hesitated and then he heard Sharon's angry voice. He couldn't make her out in the half darkness. He stumbled over chairs and outstretched feet, and found Max holding Sharon by her arm. "You want to make a scene in a restaurant?" she was shouting. "Go ahead! Let everybody know!"

Max started dragging her silently toward the door.

"Let go or I'll call the police," she shouted.

A waiter hurried up to them. "Just a minute," he said.

"It's all right," Dan said. "It's his wife."

"We can't have a disturbance in here."

"Don't interfere then," Dan said. The waiter hesitated and then tore a check off his pad. Dan paid it. He came out of the restaurant just in time to see Sharon hit Max in the face with her fist. An elderly couple passed by, pretending not to see them. Sharon twisted suddenly and pulled herself free. Holding her shoes in one hand, she raced full speed toward the beach, and close behind her, head down, mouth open, ran Max. Several people had gathered to watch. A tall man, smelling of whiskey, said, "They're probably stoned," and the watchers grinned.

By the time Dan got down the hill Sharon was already on the beach, and he had to run as hard as he could to catch up with her. The sand filled his shoes and the cuffs of his trousers, and he slipped and fell, and got up quickly. Max was closer to the water and still running. Sharon tried to cut back to the road but Dan turned quickly and caught her and threw her down. "Max," he called, not seeing him in the darkness. Then he saw him standing fifty yards or so away, head down and gasping. "Max," he called again. When Max didn't answer, he let go of the girl and walked to where he was standing. Max was coughing repeatedly.

"What's the matter?"

Max shook his head and kept coughing.

"You better sit down," Dan said and pushed him down. Max sat on the sand, his head resting on his knees. He kept coughing, and after a while he began to spit up a thin froth, very like the froth that the waves were leaving on the sand a few feet away. "You ran too much," Dan said.

"Where did she go?"

"Who the hell cares? You have edema of the lungs."

Max raised his head from his knees, looked at him a moment, and then said, "Get me up. Then you better go after her."

They walked very slowly up the slope of the sand, and climbed the stairs, a step at a time. When Dan saw Max in the light he became frightened. His face was gray and his lips were purple. Sweat stood out on his nose, and had collected in small droplets on his mustache.

"I think I ought to get a doctor for you. Maybe there's a hospital close-by."

"Take me to the car," Max gasped, and Dan led him across the parking lot to the Dodge. The red Chevrolet was gone. Dan started the motor and turned into the main street. The town was small, and in a few minutes they were past the lights and out on the highway. For almost ten minutes he listened to the sound of Max's gasping and then he pulled off at a motel. "You're going in here, and I'm calling a doctor."

"Can you handle her if you catch her?"

"Why are you so worried about her? You can't even breathe."

"I don't care what you do to her," Max said between coughs. "You stop her. Anything. You've got my permission."

Dan hesitated, and Max shouted, "I haven't got breath to argue with." He got out of the car and Dan backed out onto the highway. A rapidly approaching car screeched its brakes and turned angrily aside. Dan pressed the gas pedal and sped along the road as it turned a hundred feet or so above the beach. He slowed at each gas station or town, looking for the red Chevrolet. He caught his first sight of Sharon on the elegantly curved highway on the outskirts of San Diego. Traffic was heavy then and he stayed just behind her. He followed her through San Diego, and over the twelve-mile stretch of road to San Ysidro, waiting for the border gate where he knew she would have to stop.

She stopped about a hundred yards before the gate and he realized she had seen him. He parked in front of her and slipped out of his seat, leaving the motor running. She suddenly shifted gears, and he sprang back into his car, and before she could re-enter the highway he cut her off. She screeched her brakes to a halt. "Get out of the way, you bastard," she screamed. "You want to get killed?"

Several of the tourists standing at the border gate heard her and turned. Dan backed up the Dodge and struck her front end resoundingly. Then he got out again.

"You could have caused an accident," she shouted.

He unlatched her door and pushed her away from the wheel. He sat down and turned the key off. She tried to turn it on again but he slapped her hand away.

"You can't force me to have a baby. You can't stop me." Her face was red, and her tears had carried mascara onto her cheeks.

"I think Max can. He's got a restraining order."

"A what?"

"A judge signed it."

She jammed her elbow into his chest and when he turned in surprise she threw her small body on him. The attack was unexpected and carried him to the floor. While he was struggling to get up she kicked him hard in the groin. The pain was tremendous. He let go of her and she sprang out of the door and started running toward the gate. He managed to crawl back to the driver's seat, and, hunched over from pain, he started the car again and drove ahead of her. She turned to run around the car but he was out in time and hit her open-handed across the face and knocked her down. She jumped up screaming with rage and scratched his arm and he closed his fists and struck her hard on the shoulder and high on the face, throwing her against the fender. She raised her hand to her face and he slapped her and said, "Shut up. Don't say anything. Get in the car." He opened the door and pushed her in and slipped in beside her. For a few moments they both sat panting, the girl holding a hand against her face and Dan bent forward, waiting for the throbbing in his groin to lessen.

She reached inside her mouth and felt about. "You're insane. You're crazy," she said. "I think you loosened a tooth."

Dan wiped the cold sweat from his face with his sleeve. "You couldn't get through the gate anyway. All I have to do is tell them what you're here for."

"You'd do that?"

"After that kick in the balls? Just try it."

"Why didn't he come down? Why did he send you to fight his battles for him?"

He didn't answer and she grabbed his sleeve. "Did something happen to Max?"

After a moment he said, "He's having heart trouble."

"You left him? Without a doctor?"

Dan's groin was aching and he was still angry and he would have enjoyed hitting her again. "Shut up," he said. "Just shut up."

She reached over to turn the key and he tore her hand away. "Let me alone," she said. "Where is he?"

"Some motel on the highway outside of San Juan."

"Go call him."

"I can't walk. Besides I don't know the name of the motel."

"After all he's done for you, you run off and leave him when he's sick? He thinks more of you than of his own flesh and blood."

"You're weird," Dan said. "I don't understand you."

She suddenly broke into tears. "Oh God, what I've done to him! Forgive me, God. Please forgive me. Don't let him die."

"He's not going to die," Dan said disgustedly. "He's got edema of the lungs. It'll get better if he rests." He hesitated a moment. "I'm not taking any chances. I'll get into my car.

You wait. Then you turn around in the highway slowly and so help me God if you try to break away I'm going to crash right into you."

"Are you crazy?" she said. She waited and Dan limped to his car. They drove the sixty miles back to San Juan and found the motel about one in the morning. Dan aroused the sleepy manager, who gave him Max's cottage number.

"What kind of a hole is this? Couldn't you find a better place?" she said.

Dan was watching the numbers. "Here," he said. He knocked, and after a moment Max said, "Yes?"

He opened the door and they went in. Max was propped up against the back of the bed, his knees drawn up.

"What happened to you?" Sharon asked.

Max acted as though she wasn't there. "What took you so long?" he asked Dan.

Dan wearily sat in a chair. "What difference does it make? She's back. She's still pregnant. How do you feel?"

"I feel like hamburger. Like I've been through the grinder. My heart beats so bad I can't breathe." He glowered at Sharon.

"Why didn't you call a doctor?" she said.

"I asked him to," Dan said.

"You asked me to," Max repeated angrily. "How could I call a doctor and get a shot when I didn't know whether my wife was going to get an abortion or not?"

"Go call a doctor," Sharon said to Dan. "A heart specialist. A good one."

"Tell her I don't want a doctor," Max shouted. "She's the cause of my heart trouble."

Dan went out and roused the manager again. He phoned the doctor the manager recommended. After about an hour the physician came. He was small and wore glasses, and he examined Max's heart carefully. "Acute congestive failure," he said. "Probably brought on by his running."

"Shouldn't he go to a hospital?"

He considered the suggestion. "We have a modern hospital here. If you'd like I can put him in."

"I'm not going to a hospital," Max said. "All I need to do is get home." He leaned toward the doctor. "It's not only the running that brought this on. It's something else. Family trouble. You know what I mean. You can't treat that in a hospital."

The doctor nodded noncommittally and said, "I can give you a shot. I think that will help some. But I don't think you ought to drive. You should have your wife drive you back tomorrow if you feel better."

He gave Max the injection, and just as he was ready to leave Dan said, "I wonder if you can look at me for a moment, doctor?"

"What happened to you?"

There was no place but the bathroom and Dan walked into it followed by the physician.

"I bumped myself," he said, and showed him where.

The doctor whistled when he saw it. "That must have hurt. Stay off your feet a couple of days. Soaks might help."

"Hot or cold?"

"It's a good question," the doctor said. "Try cold first."

The doctor left. When Dan came out Sharon was sitting on the edge of the bed. "You ought to have called the doctor before," she said. "You just left him here. He could have died."

Dan suddenly exploded. "Goddamnit," he shouted at the top of his voice. "I've just driven nearly three hundred miles at seventy miles an hour to keep you from having an abortion. I've been kicked in the balls. I can barely walk. I've fought with both of you and you're both bitching."

He started for the door and Max said, "You don't have to get excited. I know what you did."

"I'm sorry," Sharon said. "Does it hurt?"

"Goddamned right it hurts. I've got to go home and put cold compresses on it."

"You'll have to open the store tomorrow," Max said. "If I can I'll come in tomorrow evening so you can get some sleep."

"Go to sleep," Sharon said to Max. "You shouldn't get excited."

Seven

DAN WORKED Monday morning, but Max came in before noon. He looked gray and tired. "We just got in from Laguna. I still don't feel so good. You think you can change your hours around at the other store and work for me tonight?"

"I guess so. How's Sharon?"

"How should she be? She didn't get her own way for the first time in her life." He grinned sadly. "Did you really beat her up like she says?"

"You wanted her stopped, didn't you?"

"You were like a crazy man, she says. You scared her. She says you're so mad at that redhead that you were taking it out by hitting her. She's all black and blue." He was watching Dan.

"If you don't like the way I stopped her, the next time do it yourself."

Max patted him on the arm. "Don't be so touchy. I'm worried about you, not her."

"What if she tries it again?"

"We stopped her once, we can do it again. She knows it. She won't run so fast. Have a good day," and he waved to Dan.

Dan noticed afterward that Max coughed a great deal and was short of breath. After about a week Max said, "I tore something loose, I think. It rattles when I breathe. Do you know a good heart doctor from the hospital? I don't want to go to my regular doctor. He's Sharon's doctor too and he'll tell her."

Dan remembered Dr. Finch, the physician who had helped him so greatly with the patient with the lung cancer. He got the address and phone number from the book and gave it to Max.

After his visit Max came directly to the store. He looked somber.

"Is he a good doctor?"

"The best I've found so far."

"He said it was all right for you to call him. I was so nervous I don't remember anything he said."

Dan called the physician. Max waited impatiently outside the phone booth. The moment Dan hung up the receiver he said, "What did he say?"

"You have a double lesion—"

"Don't talk to me in medical terms," Max said sharply. "That's what he did and I didn't know what he was talking about. Tell me so I can understand."

"Two of the valves of your heart are stiff and leaky. They keep blood from flowing in and blood leaks out when it shouldn't. See?"

"No," Max said. "But that part doesn't matter. What kind of an operation do I have to do?"

"Didn't he tell you?"

"Sure he told me, but who understood? Don't keep anything from me. I have plans to make."

"It's open heart surgery." He watched Max's face.

"They cut the heart open?"

"They put a pump in its place so that you get oxygen while it's being worked on."

"Is the heart beating all the time?"

"They stop it."

Max closed his eyes a moment. "Can they always start it up again?"

After a minute Dan said, "No."

"What's my chances?"

"Pretty good."

"How good?"

"It's a dangerous operation," Dan said. "But you don't have any choice."

"I know I don't have any choice," Max said irritably. "All right. Now you forget everything. You hear? I don't want you telling this to Sharon."

"You should," Dan said.

"I'm not getting any operation until she has the baby." He walked into the back of the store. He opened a jar of pills and took one. "You know, she's a little bit happy now once in a while. I don't know what happened to her."

"I do," Dan said.

Max looked at him, mouth open. "Well?"

"You were a man for once in your life."

"It almost killed me," Max said. "It's hard to be a man with a bad heart." He took some papers out of his jacket. "Put these away where you can find them if you need them."

After Max left Dan examined the papers. There was a pass book to a saving's account holding three hundred dollars, and two insurance policies. One was a druggists' group policy for five thousand dollars for which Sharon was the beneficiary. To it was clipped a photostat of Max's application, and Dan saw Max had lied. He denied having any heart disease. If he should die in the contestable two-year period not a dime could be collected. The other policy was for a burial plot at Gromeyer's Mortuary. Dan put the papers in a drawer and put an old pharmacopoeia on top of them. A thief breaking in might think the drawer held nothing but books.

School started again in September, and once more Dan gave his tuition check to the girl with the glasses. She was pregnant this time and was sweating in the heat. She wrote out the receipt. Dan said, "I guess you won't be here next year."

"One of the family will be. My husband's a first-year student."

"Does he get a reduction on his tuition?"

She smiled for the first time in two years. "He says he's the only man in history that ever had a wife and baby in medical school along with him." She gave him the mimeographed list. Cecil's *Textbook of Medicine*. Christopher's *Text of Surgery*. Holt's *Pediatrics*. Wintrobe's *Diseases of the Blood*. "Here starts another nine months," he said.

She arranged her glasses. "I got a head start on you. I have only three months to go."

He bought his books. They were too heavy for him to carry in one load, and he made two trips to the car.

The next day he started the school year. The mornings were taken up by lectures on disease and the afternoons by the examination of patients in the clinics or on the wards.

The morning sadness got better as soon as school started and in a week he had no more than a few minutes of despondency while he shaved. It disappeared completely once he was at work at the County Hospital. The wards fascinated him, and he would have liked to work late every evening, reading charts and talking to patients. However Max had trouble getting through his day's work, and Dan left promptly at five and drove directly to the store without stopping. Max was silently grateful.

Business at the store fell off, no doubt because Max could no longer take care of trade properly. Dan soon found he could read almost without interruption from nine to midnight.

His distress over Joan had disappeared. He studied well, and slept well. Only one thing bothered him—hunger for a girl. Both Max and Eddie were amazed that he had nobody. Max usually affected not to believe him. He would wave his hand in a skeptical gesture and say, "Probably getting *shtupt* every night on those cases of Kotex in the back room. Just don't screw the customers, please. Just stick with your girl friends."

Eddie called Dan from time to time, and occasionally they had dinner together. One evening he came in a taxi. He walked in, and looked the store over, and said, "Let's go out and get a bite. I just got out of the office."

It was about midnight. Dan put the day's receipts away in the hiding place in the "B" drawer and set up the alarms. They walked to Hoagy's. Eddie ordered steaks. "Seen anything of the redhead?"

"Not since I was up there last."

"You're better off without her." After a while he said, "Have you started going with anyone yet?"

"No."

"Get yourself a girl for Christ sake. This is no way to live. All you've got to do is be nice to them, and then you're in bed with them. As easy as all that."

"You know what hours I work."

"Then get a call girl," Eddie said. He took a small notebook out of his breast pocket and spun the pages, and Dan suddenly had the sickening fear that he was about to recommend a girl that he himself also used. Eddie stopped at one page and copied a name and a number onto the paper napkin. "Here. I've never seen her, but one of the fellows at the office was raving about her the other day. She'll ask for fifty but she'll take twenty-five and she'll go anyplace."

Dan looked at the name and the number but left the napkin lying on the table.

"A little screwing would improve your disposition," Eddie said and stirred his coffee.

Later when Dan got home and emptied his pockets he found the napkin tucked into his jacket pocket, and between its folds was a twenty-dollar bill and a five-dollar bill. He carried the napkin around in his pocket for several days, the twenty-five dollars still in its folds, hungrily thinking of a girl, but worrying at the same time about the diseases such girls might carry. Finally the hunger got the better of the fear and he dialed the number. A girl's voice answered. He looked hastily at the slip. "Is this Gwen Kelley?"

"Yes. Who's this?"

He stuttered when he told her his name. Then he said, "Somebody told me you sometimes go out on calls." It seemed like a reasonable way to say it.

"Who gave you my name?"

He looked down at the napkin again. "Brougham, a William Brougham."

"Oh Billy," she said. The sharpness was gone. "Sure. He sends me the nicest clients. Are you a friend of his?"

"Someone got your name from him for me."

"What's your number?"

He gave her the phone-booth number.

"Call you back in five minutes. Don't go way, hear?"

"Sure," he said and hung up the phone. It rang back in a few minutes.

"Billy says you're a relative of the boss's," she said. "Why didn't you tell me? They're a nice bunch of boys up there. Just name your time."

"How's tonight?"

She hesitated. "I have another call to make first. I guess I can make it at midnight."

"Twelve-thirty," he said and told her where. He hung up the phone excited, but the thought of the call just before his distressed him. He wondered what they did in between calls. Did they go home and douche or did they carry the douche about with them? Or perhaps they didn't douche at all. He felt queasy and he went back to the phone to call her and tell her not to come. The number rang without an answer. He wrote out a note that said, *Gwen Kelley—I couldn't make it tonight. Call you some other night. McDermott.* When he closed the store he went up to his room and stuck the note to the door with Scotch tape. Then he went to Hoagy's restaurant and read and ate. At one-thirty he decided she would have come already and gone, and he came back. The note was still attached to the door. He was brushing his teeth when the buzzer rang. He spat out a mouthful of toothpaste, and opened the door. The girl in the hall was lovely. She was slim and dark, with a delicate clean face. "I'm Gwen Kelley," she said. "I'm sorry I'm late."

"You must have really worked hard on that last call."

"Now don't be that way," she said. "It wasn't that kind of a call. I was just having dinner with a girl friend."

He knew it was a lie, but even so it was comforting.

She walked to the window, pulled the blind aside, and looked down on the street as if she was searching for somebody. "Did Billy tell you how to take care of me?"

Dan found the money and gave it to her.

"Where's the rest?"

"That's all."

She shook her head. "Fifty dollars, sonny."

He started laughing. "Just give me twenty-five dollars worth," he said. After a moment she shrugged and put the money into her purse. "I generally charge fifty to screen the schmucks out. But Billy sends me a lot of work." She undressed and piled her clothes neatly on the chair, and then, naked, got into bed with him. She smelled warm and nubile and he seized her hungrily. At first she moved mechanically, but then suddenly she cried out in excitement, buried her face into his shoulder, and dug her nails into his back. At the moment of climax she twisted and jerked convulsively. Dan, emerging slowly from his own convulsion, marveled at her skill in simulation, until suddenly she turned and buried her face in the pillow. She was sobbing, her bare shoulders shaking. Dan couldn't understand the reason for this bit of acting. He lifted her head up gently and touched her face with his fingers and found that she was truly crying tears. "What's the matter? Did I hurt you?"

She wiped her face on the pillow case and then took a deep breath and sat up. "You caught me," she said. "Once in a while that happens. And whenever it's good I cry. I can't help it."

It was a puzzle and Dan didn't understand it. He sat up, waiting, and the girl got out of bed and looked out of the window again.

"Who are you looking for?"

"My husband. He drove me down here."

"You're married?"

"Where's the light?" she said. He reached over and turned

it on. "I think I'll wash at home," she said. She stepped into her underpants when she caught sight of the large text on medicine. "Are you a doctor or something?"

"Medical student."

She sat down on the chair. "Got a cigarette?"

He wanted her to go. He was worrying about infection, and he was anxious to bathe. He hesitated and then he found the pack on the bedside table and tossed it to her. She lit one. "Do you know why I cry like that?"

He shook his head.

"Guilt," she said. "Hustling makes me feel guilty. I feel unworthy. You know what I mean?"

Dan got out of bed. "I'm going to take a shower," he said.

She followed him into the bathroom, and pulled down the lid of the toilet and sat on it watching him while he adjusted the water taps.

"Aren't you worried about your husband waiting in the street?"

"Let him wait," she said.

He turned down the water, and started scrubbing.

"I go to a doctor regularly," she said. "I see him twice a week."

Dan's heart sank. He put his head out of the shower curtain. "You have an infection?"

"Just in the head," she said. "He's a psychiatrist. You see I get this guilt from hustling. I have guilt from all kinds of sex, but it's worse from hustling. And after I hustle for a while I get real depressed. Can't sleep. Can't eat. Then I get these stomach cramps. I talked it over with my husband and we decided I'd go see this doctor. So I've been going for two years. He's real good. I call him Harry. He wants me to quit hustling. And after I've been seeing him for a while, I get over the guilt and I start feeling better, and I usually do stop." She shrugged. "The only problem is that I run up such a bill that I have to hustle again to pay it off. He charges me thirty dollars an hour. That's ninety dollars a week. I owe six hundred dollars now, because I didn't work all last fall. I'll hustle till Christmas, and then maybe I can get him paid off."

Dan came out of the shower dripping. She handed him the towel. "Do you have a shower cap around here?"

"No."

She shrugged. "I'll do my hair tomorrow." She took off her underpants and stepped in the shower. "He started me on deep analysis," she said over the noise of the water. "Harry says when I understand why I hustle I'll be able to stop."

She got out of the shower. Her face, washed of its makeup, was pale and tired. She wiped the water away with a towel, and brushed the loose strands of hair. She sat on the edge of the tub wearily and said, "Jesus, I'm tired. I could die right now. It wouldn't have been so bad if you hadn't caught me, but when I get caught I start crying and that's what really hurts."

He was afraid she was going to start crying again. He went into the other room and gathered her clothes up and brought them to her.

"What year are you in?"

He told her, and she thought a moment. "Have you studied anything about skin trouble yet?"

"A little."

"Take a look at my husband," she said. "He's got some kind of a rash that's been bothering him for the last few months. He's been to a couple of doctors, but all they give him is ointment to rub on and it doesn't help." She went to the window, opened it, and put her head out. "Lionel," she called.

"Wait a minute," Dan said angrily. "I'm not even dressed."

"He doesn't care," she said over her shoulder. "Lionel, come on up. Second floor. I'll leave the door open."

Dan was in a fury. "I don't want to examine your husband."

"You don't have to be so hostile," she said. "He's a nice fellow. The only thing the matter with him is that he's a pimp."

Dan pulled his trousers on in a silent rage.

"He's pretty decent most of the time. He lets me pay my

psychiatric bill out of what I make. It doesn't leave much over for him. He's an actor. You know how they work. A day here. A day there. He's the one that ought to see a psychiatrist, believe you me. There's something the matter with a man who has his wife whoring for him, don't you think?"

"I don't want to have anything to do with your husband. Here's the rest of your clothes."

The buzzer rang. "All right," she said. "I'll explain it to him." She opened the door, and the man said, "Hi honey."

"He's a medical student or something," she said to the unseen man in the hall. "And I told him about your rash but he's embarrassed."

"Nothing for him to be embarrassed about," the man's voice said.

"Come on in," she said.

A tall young man, hair long about his ears and the back of his neck, came in and held his hand out to Dan. "Hi Doc," he said.

"Yeah," Dan said not moving.

"It's my rash," the man said. "Here on the back of my hands. You want some light?" He walked over and held it under the lamp. "You see. I've got it on both hands and my neck."

"What do you think it is?" the girl said.

In spite of himself Dan looked at the rash. It was an angry red eczema. "It's a contact dermatitis," he said.

"What do I do for it?"

Dan hesitated and then told him a simple remedy he could buy in a drugstore.

The girl picked up her purse. "All I got was fifteen," she said winking at Dan. "He doesn't have much money."

The man was writing down the name of the lotion in a small notebook. "Well, if the stuff helps it's worth it," he said cheerfully. He dismissed the girl with a nod of his head. After she left he said, "I have others besides this one. She's a little bit kooky. You know. With the psychiatrist and that bit. You want a fresh piece of tail you just call me." He took a card out of his pocket and left it on Dan's dresser. "Anytime. Particularly if that stuff you told me about works." He waved and went out the door, shutting it carefully and silently.

After she left Dan wondered about the girl and her husband, and most of all he wondered about the psychiatrist named Harry. He thought about Jesse Davis again and Goldie. The next day he told Noble about Gwen Kelley.

"Her only problem is having two pimps," Noble said. "It's a good business if they don't get involved with pimps. They can make three or four hundred dollars a day and no income tax."

Dan sat back. "What do you say we take a psychiatry clinic?"

Noble took the schedule out of his notebook. "We've got a choice of that or general medicine or arthritis."

"We get medical cases on the ward all the time."

Noble thought a moment. "All right. Just don't get involved."

"What do you mean?"

Noble sighed. "Like with the cadaver and what killed him. And scaring me sick about tuberculosis. Let's have a nice quiet clinic and learn something for a change."

They entered their names in the register in the dean's office and two days later, with the change of services at the month's end, they were assigned to a psychiatry clinic that met in the afternoon. One of their first patients was a small man with a grayish stubble of beard who oddly enough wore the same round, gold-rimmed spectacles that Oney Noble wore. Noble started taking the history. He said stiffly, "Why are you here?"

"My attendance is a condition of my probation."

Dan was leafing through the chart. The man's name was Walter Grenell. A formal-looking document in his chart gave a list of orders of probation, one of which was that he was to report to the psychiatric clinic at the Los Angeles County Hospital weekly or more often on the recommendation of the physicians.

Noble made a note. He said, "Why are you on probation?"

"The judges in this state are naïve to the point of incompetence." He had false teeth, and whistled a little on the s's.

Noble nodded. "Do you have a drinking problem?"

"Is the young doctor asking me whether I'm an alcoholic?"

"Well . . . yes," Noble said.

"I might be," Grenell said. "It depends on how the word is defined. But my probation is on another matter. What actually happened is that I went into an alley to relieve myself. Many fine people do. You can't always find a public bathroom in time. This youngster was there and she told the police some things that weren't true."

A weenie waver, Dan thought. He searched the chart again but there was no mention of the nature of the man's offense. The judge had been lenient, imposing only a period of probation with psychiatric care.

Noble went on with his questions, and Grenell answered them. He spoke in a courtly and even artificial manner, using long words when shorter ones would do.

Noble finished the usual questions about his childhood and his parents and then came to his occupation.

"I've been called a mathematical genius," Grenell said.

Noble showed no surprise. Dan looked over his shoulder. In his tiny concise script Noble had written, *Patient states he is considered to be a mathematical genius.*

"What field of mathematics?" Dan asked.

"I'm a general mathematician. I've taught the subject for years." He looked from Dan to Noble, his eyes bland under the round lenses. "Try me out. There are some tricks I can show you. It's not true mathematics but it might impress the young doctors." He waited. "Let me have an arithmetical problem."

"Eighteen times forty-two," said Noble.

The patient shrugged in annoyance. "A real problem," he said. "Five figures in the multiplier and five in the multiplicand."

"All right," Dan said. "Try this. 14,392 times 81,643." He said the numbers just as they popped into his mind. Grenell looked up at the ceiling and pursed his lips. After a minute he said, "You have me in the billions on this one." A little later he said, "I'll give it to you from right to left. You better mark the numbers down." Dan picked up a pencil. "6506005711," said Grenell. "One billion one hundred seventy-five million six thousand and fifty-six."

"What was he supposed to be multiplying?" Noble finally asked.

Grenell shook his head. "You always should mark the problem down. Otherwise there's no way of checking the answer. It was 14,392 times 81,643."

Noble pulled out a fresh sheet of paper. He wrote the numbers down and painfully started multiplying.

"How did you do it?" Dan said.

Grenell waved his small hand. "Principles of factorization," he said. "What day were you born on?"

"November fourteenth, 1938."

"A Friday," Grenell said. He said it definitely, not asking for a confirmation, and Dan was surprised.

"It was a Friday," he said.

"That's only a trick for amusement's sake," Grenell said. "How's the other young doctor coming?"

Noble looked up from his sheet, half covered with figures. "Done in a minute," he said.

"There's a beauty in mathematics," Grenell said. "You can play games with it. It's like water skiing. I've never water skiied but I've seen it on television and when I imagine myself water skiing it feels like mathematics."

"You're wrong," Noble said.

"The young doctor says I'm wrong," Grenell said. He got up and looked over Noble's shoulder. "You've made three mistakes." He picked up Noble's pen and made three corrections. Then he sat down and said, "Do you want to try quadratic equations? Or powers?"

"It's right," Noble said.

"Of course it's right," Grenell said. "Do the young doctors want to prescribe any paraldehyde?"

"I don't know how he does this," Noble said.

"Talent and training. I can use some paraldehyde."

"We can't write prescriptions," Dan said. He took the sheet of figures from Noble and studied it.

The psychiatry instructor walked into the room and sat down. He read Noble's notes. Then he looked up at the old man. "How are you, Grenell?"

"Very well, sir, all things considered," Grenell said. "I'm losing my jail pallor. I could use some paraldehyde."

The psychiatrist wrote out a prescription and handed it to him. Grenell arose. "Thank you, sir, and thank you, too, both of you young doctors. If you'd like I'll be glad to return for the next clinic."

"Tomorrow," Noble said and started writing a slip.

"Tomorrow's Yom Kippur," Dan said.

Noble changed the date and gave the new slip to Grenell. He took his tattered topcoat and walked out with an air of distinction.

"Intriguing problem," the psychiatrist said, grinning.

"How do you think he does it?" Noble said. "It took me ten minutes to work it out on paper and I made three mistakes."

"Don't look at me. I barely got through algebra one," the psychiatrist said. "Some of these simple schizophrenics are amazing characters." He spoke for a while on the nature and symptoms of simple schizophrenia, and then went on to the next pair of students.

They were free for a moment and Dan said, "How did the summer go?"

"Fine."

"You don't look sleepy any more. Aren't you still working in that fish place?"

"Managing an apartment house." Noble went back to his notes.

"How can you make enough that way. They usually only give you a little off your rent."

"Free rent and three hundred dollars a month."

Dan whistled. "Must be a hundred units."

Noble shook his head. "Twelve. It belongs to a friend of

mine." He continued writing in the chart for a while. Then he examined what he had written. "That fellow worries me."

"Why?"

"He used to teach mathematics."

"That's probably bullshit," Dan said. "His lying is part of his exhibitionism."

Noble handed Dan the chart opened to a typewritten page. It was a social worker's report and Grenell had taught mathematics for years at Fordham University.

"So it's true. What difference does it make?"

"I don't know. It just worries me," Noble said.

That evening Dan left school about an hour early and got home before sundown. He cleaned the old hat, and polished his shoes. He set out a fresh shirt and tie for the morning and lay down and read the pediatrics text. Early in the morning, while the brown summer-burned grass in front of the apartment houses was still moist, he started walking the half-dozen miles to Fairfax Avenue.

It was his third trip and he was no longer walking through a strange town. The street names, once so oddly Spanish and unpronounceable, were familiar, and he passed restaurants where he had eaten with Joan, or theaters they had gone to.

The handful of old men were sitting in the park waiting. Dan sat down on the bench beside two of them. The leader of the prayer sat across from him, looking down at the ground. After a while he looked up and said in Yiddish, "How many?" Only the right side of his face moved. Dan realized he had suffered a stroke in the past year.

"Eight," Dan said.

The old man looked at Dan. "You were here last year?"

"And the year before."

The old man nodded and held his hand out. "Barenholtz," he said.

Dan shook hands. "McDermott," he said.

"What?"

"McDermott."

"An Irish Jew," one of the other old men said. "They have plenty of Jews in Ireland. You don't expect an Irish Jew to have a Russian name?"

Barenholtz shrugged. Then he looked down at the ground again and waited. No one else came, and after a while the doors to the synagogue closed. There was no *minyan*. They could not pray.

One of the old men started to get up uncertainly, and Dan said, "Wait a minute."

"I'm just going to the bathroom," the old man said. "I'll be right back."

Dan got up and walked across the street to the synagogue and waited on the steps for a few minutes. No one came by. He tried the doors and found one open. The ticket taker, in his small black hat, came up, ready to collect his ticket, and Dan shook his head and walked by him. The rabbi was already talking, and the people were sitting quietly in the pews listening.

Dan reached over and tapped the shoulder of a man who was sitting by the aisle. "I need two Jews for a *minyan*," he said. The man shrugged his shoulder away. "Shh," he said.

Dan walked farther down the aisle. "I need two Jews for a *minyan*," he said loudly, looking around. The ticket taker behind him said in an angry whisper, "You're making a disturbance."

"I need two Jews for a *minyan*," Dan said again. "Isn't this synagogue a good place to find Jews?"

The rabbi had noticed Dan and was watching him as he talked.

The ticket taker took Dan by the arm. "They have all paid for their seats," he said, still whispering. "They're not going out in the park."

Dan pulled himself away. He walked a few feet farther down the aisle. A bald man who had been watching stood up as Dan came close. "Where are you praying?" he said.

"In the park."

The man nodded. "The old men." He stood up and squeezed his way into the aisle.

"I need two," Dan said.

"You have them." He beckoned and a boy about thirteen, plump, in a fresh dark suit, rose from his seat and joined them. "My son."

The three of them walked up the aisle, down the steps, and across the street. They sat down on the bench.

"Mr. Barenholtz," one of the old Jews said, "there's a *minyan* now."

The prayer leader looked up from the ground, and then from one face to another, counting slowly. He stopped at the boy. "Has he been bar mitzvahed?"

"He's a Jew," his father said.

"So it's Yom Kippur and we have a *minyan*." He started praying, striking his breast with his right hand.

The boy was sitting very straight, his face clean and shiny, his hands in his lap.

"And for the sin of perjury," said the prayer leader and struck himself.

Some of them whispered the prayers and the rest listened until the morning was done and the synagogue doors opened.

Grenell did not keep his clinic appointment. After a half hour Dan and Noble walked out to the desk. "Our patient isn't showing," Noble told the clerk.

"Do you want me to assign you another patient?"

"He's on probation and has to attend every clinic."

"Oh, that's easy then." She picked up the chart. "I'll call his probation officer."

They waited while she talked. She hung up and said, "He's in the hospital now. A new complaint has been filed against him."

They got permission from the psychiatrist to leave the clinic, and then they walked down the long ramp to the locked psychiatric unit. An orderly unlocked the door for them and they found Grenell reading a newspaper in a small room with a half dozen other patients. He stood up when he saw them. "The young doctors," he said. He waited expectantly, and after a moment Dan held out his hand. "A great privilege," Grenell said and shook hands with Dan and then with Noble. He tapped a nearby patient on the shoulder. "I wonder if you would mind getting up and moving. My doctors have come to visit me." The other patient, a lean, scarred man who was chewing on his lip, got up angrily and stalked out of the room.

"A very sick man," Grenell said. "Highly irritable. Do sit down. There's room for you now."

Dan sat down. Noble remained standing, holding the chart.

"One gets so few visitors here," Grenell said. "It's such a delight to have one's own doctors come through those terrible barred doors for a visit."

"What brought you back here?" Noble asked.

"It's all quite unreasonable," Grenell said. "I rent a small room from a couple. Nice people. Elderly. Quiet. But they drink more than they should. They have a small dog, and I don't mind people drinking but I do get distressed about maltreatment of animals." He went on, the story becoming involved, and Dan finally said, "We've been wondering how you work those problems."

Grenell smiled. "Would the young doctors really like to know?"

Dan nodded and Grenell disappeared into the hall. Noble looked up from the chart. "Child molesting again," he said.

"What did you expect?"

"They picked him up in an alley. Drunk. A bottle of rubbing alcohol in his pocket. The people he rooms with are the ones who called the police."

"This time he's ending up in jail, I guess," Dan said. "He's broken probation, hasn't he?"

"Not if he's sick."

Grenell came back with a paper bag. He opened it and dumped out a variety of rolls of paper. Some of them were adding-machine tapes, and others were letter-sized sheets that had been carefully Scotch-taped together into scrolls.

"You showed so much interest the last time I saw you that I asked a friend to bring these down. We'll start with the easy ones." Grenell rolled out one of the smallest scrolls. It was covered from one end to another with equations. Dan saw equation within equation, with superscripts and many puzzling mathematical symbols. "This is the simplest?"

"Oh yes," Grenell said. "I'll be able to explain it very easily." He started talking, pointing to one equation and then to another. Dan was completely unable to follow him. He looked at Noble, and saw Noble shaking his head.

"We don't understand this at all," Dan said.

"Very simple," Grenell said and started the explanation over again.

"Where did you learn this?" Noble said.

Grenell paused. "I see you young doctors are not as interested in mathematics as I had thought."

"Just a minute," Noble said. He shone his pen light into Grenell's eyes.

"I have a little trick of square root," Grenell said. "Why don't you try a square root on me?" He sat, hands on his knees, leaning forward, his blue eyes patiently looking into the light.

"49,140," Noble said.

"That root is an irrational number. How many decimal places do you want?"

"Take off your slippers," Noble said.

Grenell reached down and pulled off his slippers and his socks. "Four seven nine point naught six one five roughly. If you want to take it a little further, the last figure goes on to four eight seven three." He hesitated. "I'm getting mixed up now. I'm not perfectly sure I'm right. A rational square root would be easier."

"What did you do with this kid in the alley?" Noble said.

"You're not supposed to ask about the crimes. You might get cross-examined if it comes to trial," Dan said.

"I won't write it in the chart," Noble said. "What happened?"

"I'd rather not discuss it," Grenell said.

"Repeat specific electricity," Noble said.

"Why?"

"Just repeat it," Dan said.

"Pacific electricity."

Dan was listening carefully and it sounded as though the syllables were incomplete. "Say it again."

"Say what?"

"Specific electricity."

"Pacific electricity," Grenell said.

"When you were teaching, did you ever have any trouble with the students?" Noble asked.

"Students are the same breed all over the world," Grenell said. "Sometimes they don't do their lessons. Sometimes they try to bluff. Sometimes they cheat." He shrugged. "They generally respected me. I was firm but fair."

"Say, round and round the rugged rock the ragged rascal ran," Noble said.

Grenell shook his small head. "What's the purpose of that?"

"Just say it," Dan said.

"What for?"

"To test your control of speech."

"That's foolish. I can speak fine."

"You're married?" Noble asked.

Grenell nodded.

"How many children?"

"Three."

"Do you see them?"

"Not recently," Grenell said. "My wife has turned them against me. She's portrayed me as a drunkard to them."

"What happened first?" Noble asked.

"When?"

"When things began to go wrong."

Grenell leaned back in his chair and thought. "I really don't know," he finally said. "I suppose I had a nervous breakdown. You see I was working on the Manhattan Project all during—"

Dan looked up. "The Manhattan Project?"

Grenell nodded. "It's all right to talk about it now. There was, however, a time when I didn't mention it. With Dr. Oppenheimer and the others. And then after the war I was very busy trying to get ahead in my field, teaching and writing papers. You'd be surprised the amount of research that is being done in mathematics. The more esoteric aspects of mathematics have just exploded." He paused, then scowled, obviously trying to remember his point.

"Were you very religious?" Noble said.

"Oh come on," Dan said. "We're taking a psychiatric history."

"If you have something else to do, go ahead and do it," Noble said. "I'm going to spend some time here."

"I went to church regularly up until I got sick," Grenell said.

"You mean when you started getting into trouble with children," Noble said.

"I don't know why you're questioning me like this," Grenell said. "You sound like a detective instead of a doctor."

"I don't mean to," Noble said. "I'm just trying to understand you. It's not easy."

"I'm going back to the clinic," Dan said. "See you tomorrow."

He went back and examined the next patient by himself. When he got to the store that evening he found that Max had left the day's delivery of drugs in disarray on the prescription counter. Dan set about restoring order. About nine the phone rang. It was Noble. "I've been thinking about this fellow Grenell," he said.

"Aren't you working?"

"I fixed a leaky toilet an hour ago. He was a decent sort of a guy before he got into trouble. He treated his wife well. He was good to his kids. He was pretty well respected in his field."

"I keep forgetting what business you used to be in," Dan said.

"This case has got me upset."

"He's an old-man child molester. They're a dime a dozen."

"His speech was thick, wasn't it?"

"He's being given sedatives. Besides he has false teeth."

"Syphilis could do it too."

"His Wassermann's negative. It's on the chart."

"You can't tell brain syphilis without a spinal."

Dan sighed. "He has no signs," he said.

"Listen, when you were upset about our cadaver and spent more time trying to figure out what killed him than what his anatomy was like, I didn't bitch, did I?"

"A little."

"I just called because I know the way you read the books. I was wondering if you knew anything about this that I didn't."

"No," Dan said.

"That's all I wanted to know," Noble said and hung up.

The next afternoon Noble did not show up at the psychiatric clinic. Dan again saw the new patient alone. She was a thin, nervous young girl who had ulcerative colitis. He wrote his notes carefully so Noble would be able to read them. The girl took only an hour or so, and with the afternoon still unfinished he went to the locked unit. He found Noble sitting beside Grenell, talking to him. "He had a sore on his penis when he was seventeen," Noble said excitedly.

Dan picked up the chart. "A dozen men have examined him already," he said.

"He still could have it."

"If my aunt had balls, she'd be my uncle."

Noble took his glasses off and Dan backed away and said, "You don't have to start swinging again just because I disagree with you."

"There's some dirt on them," Noble said and wiped the lenses. "He needs a spinal tap. He could have brain syphilis. That would explain the whole thing. I'm going to find the resident."

They found the psychiatric resident, a dark young man with horn-rimmed glasses, in one of the side rooms talking to an elderly woman. Noble walked up to him and said, "I think we ought to have a spinal tap on this patient Grenell."

"Just a minute," the resident said to his patient. He looked at Noble. "Who?"

"Grenell."

"Who are you?"

"Third-year medical student," Noble said. "He's a very interesting case."

"He doesn't need a tap," the resident said. "He's a typical case of simple schizophrenia with infantile sexual behavior."

"But why now?"

"He's always had strong latent homosexual tendencies his whole life, and has had rather poor heterosexual adjustments. Gradually the adjustment has broken down and his latent infantile structure has become exposed. I interviewed him myself half a dozen times."

"But his speech is slurred."

"He's taking Thorazine."

"A spinal tap wouldn't hurt," Dan said.

"We can't do a spinal tap every time one of you medical students gets an idea in his head," the resident said. "We'd be doing taps on everybody in the ward. It's expensive to do a tap. If you were out in private practice and the patient was paying the bills, you wouldn't go doing a spinal tap on him for no good reason at all, would you?"

"We can do it ourselves," Dan said. "We've done about twenty of them already in the outpatient department."

"This patient's case has been studied thoroughly already. Besides, I have to present him at conference tomorrow and I don't want him with a spinal-tap headache." He turned back to his patient.

"Your last patient of the day?" Dan asked.

The resident looked at the clock and nodded. He started writing on the chart on his knee.

Dan and Noble walked away. Noble was furious. "Why were you so friendly? That bastard sounds like a John Bircher. Looks like one too."

"More Democrats among psychiatrists than any other specialty," Dan said. "Sit down." He picked up a tired old magazine and started leafing through it. After a while Noble sat down beside him. "I have to be home by six."

"So do I," Dan said. "What's that resident's name?"

Noble looked at the chart again. "Berger. Frederick Berger."

They waited, and the resident finished his interview. A few minutes after five Dan went over to the nurse's station and picked up the telephone. "I'd like to speak to the resident for psychiatry two," he told the operator. There was a pause. Then she said, "That's Dr. Berger. He just signed out."

"Who's on call for him?"

"Dr. Furnish," she said. "I'll try to reach him for you." He waited and after a while the line clicked and a voice said, "Furnish."

"This is McDermott," Dan said. "I'm a third-year medical student. There's a fellow over here by the name of Grenell who should have a spinal tap."

"That's Berger's ward."

"He's signed out to you."

"Can't it wait until tomorrow?"

"He's being presented at rounds tomorrow."

"Oh. I suppose they'll want the results by then. What's the problem?"

Dan told him about the slurred speech. He didn't say anything about the Thorazine, and the resident finally said, "I'm at dinner now but I'll walk over as soon as I'm done."

They waited, and in about a half hour a sandy-haired boy walked in with a blood pressure machine under his arm. He spoke briefly to Grenell, had him repeat the phrases, and then said, "Well, if they need a tap for rounds I guess we better do it."

"My partner here's done about twenty of them," Dan said.

"I'll have to supervise," Furnish said. "You're only students."

Furnish stood around watching and smoking while Grenell's back was draped. Noble, his hands trembling slightly, picked up the needle and put it in position.

Furnish sighted along the needle. "A little lower and to the right," he said.

Noble adjusted the needle. "Go ahead," said Furnish, and Noble pushed the needle in and Dan was delighted to see the clear fluid come through the bore.

"Good shot," Furnish said. "Be sure and keep him down for

the rest of the night." He went back upstairs, the blood pressure machine still under his arm.

Noble removed the needle and applied a bandage. "Stay on your back, Mr. Grenell," he told the patient. "Don't get up until tomorrow morning."

"That's the way you get these things done around here," Dan said gaily.

Noble marked the laboratory request urgent. "I'll just bet it's positive," he said. "He must have syphilis."

Twice during the morning lecture on gastrointestinal diseases Noble got up and left the classroom. After the first trip he whispered to Dan, "I had to argue with the laboratory technicians. But they're running it right now. I'll be able to get the results in an hour." He was silent when he came back from the second trip. After class Dan said, "It was negative."

"How'd you know?"

"One look at your face."

"We shouldn't have done that tap," Noble said. "What if we introduced an infection or something?"

"You thought it was worthwhile taking that risk yesterday."

"I wouldn't have done anything after Berger said no, but you went ahead and played that cute trick with the night resident."

"You ungrateful bastard," Dan said. "I was just helping you out."

"I'm going to walk over there now. I'd feel awful if he got some kind of infection. They can get meningitis from a spinal tap."

"Look at those that we've done without infections."

"Maybe we were lucky," Noble said glumly. He started toward the psychiatric ward, and after a moment's hesitation Dan followed him. Berger was at the nurse's desk. "I want to talk to you," he said to Noble. Noble didn't answer. After a moment Dan said, "We're listening. Go ahead."

"Were you in on this too?"

Dan nodded.

"I'm glad to know that," Berger said. "I just reported Mr.

Noble to the superintendent's office for doing this tap without permission. Now I'll add your name. What is it?"

Dan told him his name and spelled it out.

Berger picked up the phone and dialed and then said, "Miss Collie, I want to add another name. There were two students in on that spinal tap without permission. The other one's name was McDermott." He spelled it again. He hung up the phone. "I don't know what they're going to do to you for this but whatever it is you certainly have it coming. You can't take on responsibility like that. Not without authorization. What if something happens to this fellow as a result of your tap?"

"He hasn't got a fever, has he?" Noble said.

"He's got a headache," Berger said. "We couldn't present him at rounds."

"We had permission," Dan said. "Dr. Furnish gave it."

Berger spun around in his chair. "This isn't his ward."

"He was on call last night. He supervised."

"That's not going to work," Berger said. "Not after I get done speaking to the superintendent." He turned his back coldly.

For the next week Dan expected at any moment to be called to the dean's office. No such summons came, however, and he grew puzzled. At the end of the week, while going to see another patient, he met Berger in the hall. Berger stopped when he saw Dan. "I spoke to the superintendent's office about that tap," he said. "I told them it was a misunderstanding and that I had authorized it."

"You didn't have to do that. It really was authorized."

"I didn't want you fellows getting into trouble," Berger said. "It could be pretty serious. They suspended a fellow last year for pulling the same thing. I just figured you two had learned your lesson enough from what I told you."

He went ahead, turning into a conference room. Dan was about to go on when he saw Grenell in a wheelchair being pushed along by an orderly. Grenell reached over and caught Dan's sleeve. "I'm being presented again today, Doctor," he said. "I thought you might like to attend, you being so interested in my case and all. Where's the other young doctor?"

"He's having lunch I think," Dan said.

"Please come," Grenell said. "I'm a very instructive case."

Dan followed the wheelchair into the conference room. He sat down and waited. After a while a physician, who was probably the chief of service, said, "We're going to represent a case that we've seen twice before. He was originally considered an example of infantile sexual disturbance along with alcoholism. Due to some excellent diagnostic work by our resident, we've made some changes in our diagnosis. Go ahead, Dr. Berger. The show is all yours." He sat down and Berger stood up, cleared his throat, and began reading Grenell's history. Dan was listening attentively. Berger reviewed Grenell's various criminal citations and his behavior in the ward. Then he read, "A spinal tap showed a protein of a hundred and ten milligrams, with a negative Wassermann."

Dan leaned toward the intern sitting next to him. "What's the normal spinal fluid protein?"

"Less than forty," the intern said. "With a hundred and ten this fellow probably has a brain tumor."

When Berger was done another physician in street clothes stood up. He was a neurosurgeon and he had also examined Mr. Grenell in view of the recent information that Dr. Berger had turned up. He was satisfied that all of the aberrations in Mr. Grenell's personality were the result of a tumor, and surgery was scheduled for six in the evening.

Grenell was brought in from the anteroom, and the doctors questioned him. He demonstrated once more his remarkable power with figures. Several of the doctors came over and tapped his reflexes and shone lights in his eyes. As he was wheeled out he turned his head and winked at Dan. The chief psychiatrist stood up. "It's amazing how we all fall in the same old trap every so often," he said. "I want to thank our resident and compliment him on his diagnostic acumen. Good work, Dr. Berger."

"Thank you sir," Berger said.

Dan got up and left. Mr. Grenell was being slowly wheeled down the hall. "Very instructive wasn't it?" he said.

"Indeed it was," Dan said. "I'll be seeing you later."

That evening when class was over he took Noble by the arm. "Your tenants are going to have to fix their own toilets tonight."

"Why?"

"Come on," Dan said. He lead Noble to an elevator, and they rode up to the twelfth floor.

"What are you up to now?" Noble said suspiciously.

Dan had found a schedule posted to the wall. Grenell's name was on it, along with the number of the operating room. "There's a friend of yours being operated on," Dan said. They went into a small locker room, and pulled on the gray surgical gowns over their street clothes, and went down the hall and turned into the room with the proper number on it. Through the glass window they saw the surgeon drawing a line on a shaven scalp.

"Who's that?" Noble said.

"Grenell."

"What?"

Berger walked in. "Hi fellows," he said. He sat down at the very farthest end of the narrow glassed-in room.

"Fine diagnosis," Dan said.

Berger nodded.

"We're both very grateful to you for covering up for us on the spinal tap."

"What the hell is this about?" Noble said.

"Wait awhile," Dan said.

They waited, and the surgeon opened the scalp, and then carefully working with thin saws he opened the front of the skull. They saw the large, dull white tumor compressing the frontal lobes of the brain.

"My God!" Noble said. "Where did that come from? Who suspected that?"

"You did," Dan said. "The spinal fluid protein in that tap you did was a hundred and ten milligrams."

"What's it supposed to be?"

"Not more than forty."

Noble suddenly understood. "Yes," he said, turning back and watching while the surgeon worked cautiously, slipping smooth instruments about the edge of the tumor, working it loose. Finally he lifted it out and set it in a pan. Then he replaced the bone and sutured the scalp.

Berger squeezed by them on his way out and Dan said, "Thanks again, Doctor, for sparing us."

"Screw you," Berger said and went out the door.

Dan grinned. Then he clapped Noble on the shoulder. "Well, friend, you brought a man back to God."

"I bet I did at that," Noble said. "I'll just bet I did. You think he'll go back to teaching?"

"Why not? That big tumor is out and in the pan."

"You don't think he'll die or anything?"

"Nobody seemed very worried."

They discarded their gowns and walked to the elevator. Noble was chewing on his lip thoughtfully. Suddenly he reached down, hooked one arm around Dan's waist, and gave him a tremendous hug. "You ever drink?"

Dan pulled out of his grasp. "Sure. Why?"

"Because I've got something to celebrate," Noble said. "I did do that, didn't I?"

"Yes."

"Well then let's celebrate. There's a bar on the corner."

They sat in the bar and they each had two drinks and their speech became slurred.

"I'm not getting much out of this psychiatry clinic," Dan said. "I still don't know why that girl was hustling when it made her so miserable."

"Who?"

"The call girl I told you about."

"Oh. That's easy. For the money."

"She's in debt. Her pimp and her psychiatrist take it all."

"We still got three more weeks in this clinic."

"You think I'll find out then?"

"What's eating you now?" Noble said.

"Jesse Davis."

Noble scowled. "I must be drunk. I can't follow you. Who's Jesse Davis?"

"Our cadaver."

"Very clear."

"You think I can follow your reasoning? What the hell difference does it make if Grenell's weenie waving comes from a brain tumor or from a psychiatric character defect?"

"Because we all have character defects and most of us don't scare kids with our peckers," Noble said. "You see?"

"No." Dan belched. The whiskey was giving him heartburn.

"It has something to do with the origin of sin," Noble said. "The only thing is I don't know quite what."

"He had a tumor. That's the only meaning."

"You lonely bastard. You should have another drink. You can't even celebrate well."

"I'm stoned already." Dan stood up. "I have to work. I've got a boss with a bum heart."

"Even if I flunked out of school right now," Noble said, "it would still be worthwhile just for what happened today." His black face shone.

Dan started unsteadily for the door, and Noble got up and took him by the arm and said, "Let's go into practice together. We'll finish up and we'll open up an office together. What do you say?"

"Who the hell wants to practice with you? The only thing you're interested in is sin. They took a tumor out and all you're thinking about is God."

They were in the street and Noble said, "Don't stagger so much. Some of the instructors are walking by on the other side of the street."

"They didn't diagnose a brain tumor today and bring a man back to God like we did. We have a right to stagger," Dan said. He pulled away and started searching for his car in the dimly lit parking lot. His last sight was Noble's dark face staring at him worriedly through the open car window and asking,

"Are you sure you're able to drive? Do you want me to drive you home?"

Later that week the phone rang in the store about eleven. The voice on the other end was hoarse and distant. "Dan?" He heard a clatter as the receiver dropped. Then the voice said hoarsely again, "Danny?"

"Yes?"

"Oh Danny." There was a long silence and he finally said, "Joan? Is that you?"

"Danny," she said again and he realized she was drunk.

"What do you want?"

"I've been calling you every night," she said. "Danny, I need you. I can't make it without you. I made a terrible mistake. Can you forgive me?"

The alcoholic drama sickened him and he said, "Jesus, what crap!" and hung up.

Two days later when he came home he found a note Goldie had tacked to his door. It said, "Come downstairs. I want to talk to you. G. R. Lechinski."

Goldie was angry. "She keeps calling every night late," he said. "I had to have my number changed. It cost me three dollars to get an unlisted number." He glared at Dan.

Dan took three dollars out of his wallet and put them on the table. Goldie counted the bills and stuffed them into his pocket. "All right. Don't you give her my new number. You better get yourself a phone too. I can't be harassed like this."

"She's drunk."

"I got enough drunk friends of my own without yours keeping me up all night," Goldie said and slammed the door.

After that Dan started dreaming of Joan again. She was sober and loving in his dreams. He talked to her and fondled her, and when he awoke he was sad and longed for her again.

From time to time she called him at the store. Sometimes her voice would be hoarse and drunk, and he would quickly escape. Other times the drunkenness would not be so obvious, and he would hesitate and listen for a while, hoping that she had changed, but he would catch an awkward intonation or the slurring of a word and he would cut the conversation short.

Later when he answered the store phone, he would hear only the sound of someone breathing on the other end. He would wait and say "Hello" a few times and then hang up. One Thursday, in late November, he answered the phone and said "Hello," and there was the usual silence and he was going to hang up when suddenly she said, "I can't stand it any more. I can't stand it another day. Not even another ten minutes." He was puzzled and worried and he said, "Stand what?" She hung up without answering.

The next morning he was drowsing through a dull lecture on diseases of the ear, a subject in which he had little interest, when a student nurse came hesitantly into the lecture room and handed a note to the instructor. He stopped and read it. "An emergency call for Mr. McDermott," he said.

Dan got up and went into the hall. A tall man was waiting for him. "I'm sorry to get you out of class, but it really is an emergency."

It took Dan a few moments to realize that it was Gross. The lawyer's face had lost its tan, and his eyes were red and watery. Dan recognized the yellow slip in his hands. It was the patient location slip given out at the information desk on the first floor.

"Joan's in here," Gross said.

"Sleeping pills?"

He nodded. "I spoke to her on the phone last night and she seemed fine. Better than she'd been in weeks. She hadn't had a drink all day. She was reading a book of plays by Paddy Chayefsky, and she was going to start painting again. This morning I called her. I just had a feeling something was wrong and I couldn't get an answer. I went to her house and she was out ice cold." He was suffering, and Dan felt a small malicious gleam of satisfaction. "How sick is she?"

"She's not breathing."

The satisfaction disappeared. "They have her on a respirator?"

Gross nodded.

"What floor?"

"Six."

Dan went up the stairs two at a time, Gross behind him. They hurried down the hall of the sixth floor to the admitting ward. "Couldn't you afford a private hospital for her?"

"I didn't know what to do. I just called the police."

Dan went into the intensive care room. Most of its occupants were the strange and alien people that made up the bulk of the County Hospital patients—old people, drunkards, and addicts. Many were getting infusions, bottles hung high above their beds, and thin plastic tubes strapped to their arms. He walked to her bed. A respirator mask was strapped tightly across her mouth. The machine clicked mechanically. He watched the small rise and fall of the wool blanket over her chest. He touched her. Her head felt cold.

"How is she?" Gross said.

"She must have taken an awful lot."

She wore a thin hospital gown. It was split open in the front, exposing her breasts.

An intern who was going from patient to patient stopped at Joan's bed and silently counted the drip of the fluid from the bottle. He adjusted the small key and slowed the rate. "How's she doing?" Dan said.

The intern continued watching the drip. Then he shrugged. "Not very good," he said. "We haven't got her barb level back, but I bet it'll be five."

The three of them watched the drip of fluid in the glass container.

"I called the police and they went out and searched her place," the intern said. "One thing in her favor. She sure has been taking the sleeping pills. They brought me about six empty bottles, and from the dates on them I figure she's been taking four or five a night. She must have had a chance to build up a tolerance." He looked at Dan. "Do you know her?"

"Yes."

"A drinker, isn't she?"

"Periodic," Gross said.

"That's against her," the intern said. "We lose most of the alcoholics." He went on to the next bed.

Dan followed him.

"Are you going to dialyze her?"

"I've been arguing with the resident about it," the intern said. "She's pretty shocky. He wants to see if we can't get her blood pressure up first."

"What was that all about?" Gross asked when Dan came back.

"Nothing," Dan said. He stood there silently, watching the drip and watching her breathing, and after a little his legs began to hurt him. He glanced at Gross. The lawyer was standing at the same kind of vigil, his hand clasped around the enameled iron of the foot of the bed, the knuckles white. "How long have you been here?"

"Since this morning."

"In the room all the time?"

"Watching this bottle. I figured so long as it keeps dripping she's still alive. Sometimes I can't see her breathe." He went back to watching the drip.

"I think they ought to dialyze her," Dan said again.

"What's that?"

"They put a needle into her abdomen and they drip liquid into it and then suck it back out again. It washes out the barbiturates. The drug in the sleeping pills."

"Why don't they?"

"I have to find the resident." He went out in the hall, Gross behind him. He found the resident in the doctor's reading room, studying a thick journal.

"I'm a friend of this patient, Joan Means," Dan said.

The resident was thin and dark. He looked up and said, "Who?"

"That barbiturate suicide."

"Oh. Do you know her?"

Dan nodded.

"Her blood pressure's been slipping. It's touch and go," the resident said.

"What about dialyzing her?"

The resident looked at Gross, who was standing behind Dan. "Are you the husband?"

"A friend."

"Do you mind waiting outside?"

Gross nodded and went outside. The resident opened the journal he had been reading. "Here's a series on dialyzation in barb poisoning. Dialyzing helps. But I don't know what it will do when they're in shock. It might just finish her off." He was very distressed.

"How long are you going to let her go then?"

"I don't know," the resident said. "I've been sitting here worrying about her for the last hour." He took a bottle of white medicine from a drawer, drank some and then grimaced. "I guess it all depends on her condition. If she comes out of shock we'll dialyze her." Dan nodded and went back into the hall. He pushed the elevator button. Gross came up. "Where are you going?"

"To the library."

The elevator came up and the door opened, and he and Dan stepped in. "I don't suppose there's any point in my staying around any more, is there?" Gross said.

"No," Dan said.

Gross looked at him. "It's been rough. A lot rougher than you know. For the last month every time the phone rang I thought it was the police calling to tell me she had taken an overdose. I haven't had my hair cut or gone to dinner without being afraid of what she might do." He opened his wallet and took out a card and gave it to Dan. "Here. Call me as soon as there's a change."

For an hour Dan read everything he could find on sleeping-pill suicide, and most particularly on dialyzation for the desperately ill patient. He checked out several journals and carried them up to the sixth floor.

Joan's condition was unchanged when he got back. He sat

down by her bedside and later the resident and his two interns came in. One of the interns listened to Joan's heart.

"What's her pressure?" the resident said.

Dan took it. "Eighty over sixty," he said.

The resident nodded. "Keep checking it," he said, and closed the key that controlled the drip of fluid.

"I can't get it at all now."

The resident turned the key up and Dan said, "It's coming up a little now. About forty." Later on he said, "She's back up to eighty again."

The resident put his hands in his pockets and studied the drip of fluid from the bottle. Then he sighed. "What do you think?" he asked one of the interns.

"Nothing to lose," the intern said.

"I think we're waiting too long," the second intern said.

"She's getting worse," the first intern said. "In a little while it won't make any difference what we do."

The resident sighed again. Then he said, "Let's put in a call for Claude. See if he's around."

One of the interns went out. Dan and the resident and the second intern stood at the bedside, watching the dripping fluid and listened to the clicking of the machine. In about five minutes the intern returned with a heavy blond young man. Dan recognized him. He was in some way connected with the school. He held the title of super-resident. He listened to the history and nodded and then took the blood pressure. After a moment he said, "Dialysis would help her, but it would be better to get her out of shock first. It's risky when she's in shock."

"What if she doesn't come out of shock?" the intern said. "Do we just sit on our hands until she's dead?"

"If a patient dies of what ails them, then that's outside a doctor's control," Claude said. "But if they die of a procedure, that's something else." He watched the dripping bottle. "That's the way it looks to me," he said and nodded and left.

"No-guts Claude we call him," the intern said.

The resident took her blood pressure again. "I don't know," he said.

"She's not going to last long this way," the intern said.

"Most of the articles I read show it'll probably help," Dan said. "I brought a couple to the ward."

The resident turned on him fiercely. "The last thing I need is a third-year medical student telling me what to do. My interns do a good enough job. If you want to do anything, son, you stand there and take the blood pressure when I ask you to." He sighed again. "All right. Let's get set up."

After he left, Dan said, "Thanks."

The intern looked up from the chart. "What for?"

"For talking him into it."

"Supposing she dies. What do you say to me then?"

Dan went out to the desk phone and dialed the operator. He put in a call to Joan's father.

"Yes?"

"Dan McDermott," he said, and told him what had happened.

Means was quiet. Dan could hear the sound of his breathing. "In the County Hospital?"

"In the intensive care ward."

"Does she have good doctors?"

"She's sure got enough of them." Dan told him about the dialysis. Means listened and said, "Do you think it'll do any good?"

"I don't know."

"Can't you get somebody who does?"

"There's no time now any more."

"I'll be down in about ten hours," Means said. "Get her everything she needs. I'll cover it when I get down." He hung up the phone.

Dan went back into the ward. He didn't see the interns or the resident again for what seemed a long time. Finally one of the interns wheeled in a large cart carrying plastic tubes and containers. The resident followed him.

"Let's get started, boss," the intern said. He laid out a pair of gloves. Then he pulled the bed covers back, painted Joan's abdomen with an orange antiseptic, and handed the resident the needle. "It's all yours."

The resident pushed the needle through the skin and muscle of the abdominal wall. The girl did not move. He clamped the needle in place, removed the stylet, and connected the tubes. He told the intern what to do, and then he stood and watched while the fluid entered the abdomen.

"How's her pressure?" the resident asked.

Dan checked it. "Seventy over forty."

"Maybe we should have done a tracheotomy first," the resident said. "Maybe we'll run into problems with breathing."

All four of them watched her breathing. "We still can do it," the intern said. "I and this medical student will scrunch down on one side, and you two can work on the other side."

"Better speed up that drip."

Dan turned the key and fluid went a little more quickly.

"These suicides worry you to death," the resident said. "You always figure if you can get them through the next couple of hours, they'll make it."

"There's something I learned in school that might help you, boss," the intern said. "You don't have to cure everybody. All you have to do is give them the right treatment."

The resident gave orders, and the interns worked, doing as they were bid, until it was almost two o'clock. Then the intern removed the needle and the dialysis was complete. The resident sat down then. He asked Dan to take her blood pressure, and it was the same as it had been for the past several hours. He pursed his lips and watched her breathing. He looked very tired. The intern said, "Why don't you knock off? If anything goes wrong I can call you."

The resident turned to Dan. "Did you bring up some articles?"

"They're on the nurse's desk."

"I'll read them now," the resident said. He got up stiffly and walked out.

The intern pushed away the paraphernalia and pulled the blanket over Joan.

"What are you going to do now?" Dan said.

"We've done it," the intern said. "It's all done. Either she makes it now or she doesn't." He washed his hands in the nearby sink and then went out. Dan sat down by the bedside. The room was brightly lit, and the nurses kept coming in to check one or another patient. From time to time one of them took Joan's pulse or her pressure, and made notes in a small book.

A thought kept going in and out of his mind. Gross had discovered Joan while there was still something to fight about. No one had gone to see his mother. Perhaps if he had gone the night before there would have been the same sort of a battle in a hospital in San Francisco and she would be alive now. The thought ached like a rotten tooth, and it kept him sitting rigidly, waiting and watching.

He fell asleep without intending to, and he was awakened by somebody's hand on his shoulder. It was the resident. "I thought you were going to fall out of that chair," he said.

Dan shook his head and reached over to take her blood pressure.

"I already took it," the resident said. "It's up around a hundred. The drip's been off for five minutes and the pressure is still staying up." He went back into the hall, and after a moment Dan followed him. The resident sat down at the nurse's desk. The clock over his head said five o'clock.

"I guess I better make some notes on this girl," he said. "What's her name?"

The intern at the other side of the desk shook his head. "I don't know."

"Joan Means," Dan said.

The resident wrote it down. "She's doing a little better," he said to the intern. "Her pressure is staying up."

"I know," the intern said. "I heard her coughing a few minutes ago."

"You did?"

The intern nodded. "Not very effective, but a real cough."

The resident blinked his eyes and yawned. He looked at the

clock. "An hour before we can have any breakfast. I sure would like some coffee."

"What do you think?" Dan said.

"She might make it now if she doesn't get pneumonia, or peritonitis from the dialysis, or go into vascular collapse all of a sudden," the resident said. He yawned again. "I'm going to get some sleep. If anything goes sour call me." He walked down the hall wearily.

Dan went to class that morning unwashed. At noon he borrowed a razor from Noble and shaved. Then he returned to the intensive care unit. Joan's color was pink again, and her skin was warm. She still was unconscious, but the complex respirator had been replaced by a simple oxygen mask. He went out to the desk and called Gross's office. His secretary didn't know where he was. He dialed the home number. A woman answered. "Hello," he said. "I was calling Seymour Gross."

"This is Mrs. Gross. Who is this?"

"McDermott. Do you know where I can reach him?"

"Are you calling from the County Hospital?"

He hesitated, and then said, "Yes."

"It's about Joan Means, isn't it? How is she?"

He didn't know what to say.

"Is she all right?"

"I think so."

He asked her to tell Gross to call him, and hung up wondering what pivate agony Goss and his wife were suffering. The lawyer did not call him back, and he didn't hear from Gross again.

When he returned to the ward after his last clinic, Joan was gone. She had been transferred to St. John's Hospital. About seven Joe Means called him at the store. "I've got a fellow by the name of Wharton taking care of her. Do you know him?"

"No."

"She's coming out of it. I tried to give that resident something. I wrote him out a check that would probably take him six

months to earn and he acted like I had insulted him. Don't
they teach you anything about money in school?"

"They never mention it."

Means snorted. "How about running up and having dinner
with me?"

Dan arranged to meet him a little after midnight. He drove
out Sunset and then turned into the curved driveway of the
huge, brightly lit hotel.

Means was waiting in one of the booths in the restaurant.
He was about sixty. His cheeks had a high color and he was
small and deeply tanned. They shook hands. "Good food here,"
Means said. "All I ever get to eat up north is steak and stew.
I'm having some lobster salad. Do you want the same?"

Dan ordered a sandwich.

"How is she?"

"She's still asleep," Means said. "But this fellow Wharton
checked her blood and it was down to two, whatever that means."

"It was six yesterday."

"Why did she do it?"

The question was sharp and direct, and after a moment Dan
said, "I haven't seen her for months."

"Was that the reason?"

"She was involved with a married lawyer."

Means was playing with matches, and Dan noticed that his
fingernails were bluish and clubbed. He was breathing rapidly.
"Did you ever do any hard-rock mining?"

Means looked at him for a few moments. Then he smiled.
"How did you figure that out?"

"You have silicosis?"

Means nodded. "Is there anything new for it?"

Dan shook his head.

"They tell me if you don't get tuberculosis you're good for
a while," Means said. He wiped his mouth. "I can't stay in
this town. The smog in the air chokes me up. It's so big and
full of people I can't sleep either. I'll go back tomorrow."

"Aren't you going to take her?"

"She wouldn't come," Means said.

They chatted about small things for a while. Dan, who was very tired, left as soon as he could, and once in bed fell asleep promptly without turning the light on.

Dan called St. John's Hospital daily and spoke to the ward nurse. Joan continued to do well and he was relieved. After a week he stopped worrying and was able to turn his full attention to school.

The psychiatry clinic had ended and he and Noble attended a new clinic in pediatrics. Dan had been weighing the idea of becoming a pediatrician, and he spent a good deal of time talking to the children or to their mothers. He enjoyed playing with the children brought in for examinations and when a child showed affection for him or trust in him he was greatly pleased.

In the third week of the clinic a middle-aged Mexican woman brought in a baby wrapped in a blanket. A boy of about six followed her. Dan wasn't sure which child was to be examined. "Which one's sick?" he said.

"Yes?" she said.

"She doesn't understand English," Noble said. *"Que muchacho es infermo?"*

"It must be this one," Dan said. "He's all bruised up. What's your name, son?"

"He doesn't understand English either," Noble said.

"Who's sick?" Dan said again speaking slowly, hoping the woman would understand the simple words.

She started talking quickly. Her hands pointed to the infant and then swept upward in a strong gesture.

"I think she means the baby's been throwing up," Dan said. "Better get somebody to interpret."

Noble put his pen down and went out of the room. He came back with a woman in the gray uniform of a ward maid.

"Ask her what's wrong with the baby," Dan said.

The maid said something in Spanish. The woman answered and the maid grinned. "She says that's what she brought her here to find out."

"What symptoms does she have?"

There was actually very little wrong with the infant. From time to time she took her bottle too fast, and then spit up part of the milk and sugar mixture. Dan completed his examination, calling out the findings to Noble, who marked them in the chart. When he was done he turned to the interpreter and said, "Do we examine the boy too?"

"She says there's nothing the matter with him."

"Why doesn't he talk?"

The interpreter listened. "He never talks. He's not her son. It's her husband's sister's son. She doesn't know where the mother is."

Dan sat down on a little stool and looked at the boy again. He was small for his age. The toe of one shoe was worn through and patched with newspaper on which Dan could see the printing.

"Make a noise," Dan said to Noble.

"What for?"

"Just make it."

Noble shrugged and clapped his hand down hard on the desk. The boy jumped in surprise. The baby started crying and the mother soothed it.

"Anyway he's not deaf," Dan said. He took the boy by his hand, led him to the far end of the hall, and left him there. He returned to the cubicle and beckoned to the boy. He walked toward Dan, easily, balance perfect.

"It's not a birth injury either," Dan said. "What's his name?"

The interpreter said, "Ramon Jorge Benson."

"Tell her we want to examine him."

The Mexican woman became annoyed. "She says there's nothing the matter with him," the interpreter said. "She didn't bring him to see the doctor. He just came along."

"He doesn't talk. That's enough."

"We can't see him anyway today," Noble said. "We still have to write a report on the baby."

"Tell her to make another appointment for the boy tomorrow."

"She doesn't want to," the interpreter said, listening. "It costs her seventy cents on the bus to come out here."

Dan opened his wallet and took out a dollar bill. "Here," he said. "Bus fare."

The woman took the dollar and slapped it into her purse.

Dan followed her out to the desk. "See that she makes an appointment for Ramon Jorge Benson," he told the clerk.

"It'll have to be a new chart," the clerk said. "He's never been here before."

"Tomorrow, the first patient," Dan said.

He went back into the cubicle. "It wasn't brain damage," he said to Noble.

"Why can't he talk then?"

"I knew a kid like this once," Dan said, remembering. He took a cigarette out of the pack and lit it. "They used to think I talked to him." He looked at the clock. There was some free time and Noble seemed interested, and he told him the story.

It was after he had come out of the orphanage. His mother had tried that year to keep him with her. He didn't tell Noble why she had failed, but he remembered. A tall man had moved in with her, and the two were usually at each other's throats. He often awakened at night to hear them fighting, and his mother cried a good deal, and was distraught. Then she had him put into a boarding house. It was run by a German couple. The man was gross and dull. The woman had an odd rancid smell, and usually dressed in black. His mother rarely came to see him. He didn't know what had happened to her. After a time he developed the habit of waiting on a certain piece of half-buried concrete in the yard. He would watch the people that walked past the gate.

From time to time other children stayed at the boarding house. He was too busy watching to play with any of them. One night he was awakened by the bedroom light being turned on. Two men and a boy were in the room. The men wore leather jackets. They called the boy Buddy. He was about Dan's age, five or six, and wore a wool cap with a tuft on the end of it. Dan sat up and watched. The new boy silently undressed

down to his underwear, and crawled into the other bed still
wearing the wool cap. The light was turned off and Dan fell
asleep again. When he awoke in the morning, the new boy was
still sleeping, his wool cap protruding above the covers. Dan
dressed, and went downstairs. Mrs. Shafer was in the kitchen,
and the plates were on the little table where the boarding
children ate. He hesitated and then he went back upstairs and
shook the boy. "You've got to eat now," he said. "She doesn't
give you anything to eat if you don't come down right away."

Buddy got up out of bed and slowly started dressing. Dan
didn't want to miss breakfast and he went downstairs alone.
Without a word Mrs. Shafer gave him the dish of mashed
potatoes, and poured the gravy over it.

When he was done Dan walked outside and took his position
on the piece of concrete. The rule was that he had to be
watching, because if he wasn't watching she would go right
on by. After a while the boy came out and stood next to him.
"You've got to get up right away," Dan said. Then, "There's
some rabbits over there. They're fun. You go over behind the
barn between the cages, and you lay down and then you can
look at the rabbits. You can touch them too. Mr. Shafer gets
real mad if he sees you, but if you lay down he can't see you."
The boy walked behind the barn. He must have liked the
rabbits because he stayed there a long time, and when he came
back there was straw and dirt on his clothes.

"You want to see the ducks?" Dan asked. The boy neither
nodded nor made any sign that he understood.

"They walk awful funny," Dan said. "There's a mamma duck
and four baby ducks and they walk right after one another.
There's a barrel, too, and he keeps a turtle in there. But you
mustn't put your finger in. It'll bite your finger."

Buddy went off to look at the ducks. Dan wanted to look at
the ducks too, but he had to watch the gate.

When it was lunchtime Dan left his stone and went around
the far side of the house, and found Buddy, sitting in the mud
at the edge of the pond, watching the ducks, and he said,
"We've got to eat now." Buddy got up and followed him and

they went in the house and they sat down at the little table, Dan sitting at the far end so he could still see the gate through the window. She gave them mashed potatoes and gravy again. When Dan went out to the stone Buddy followed him, waiting beside him. Dan told him about the chickens. Then he told him about the rats that made holes in the ground. He told him the bad things too, about how Mr. Shafer chopped the heads off chickens, and he showed him where the chopping block was, with the ax still in the wood and the blood and feathers on its blade.

In the middle of the next morning, while he was watching with Buddy, Dan got thirsty and went back into the kitchen. The sink was too high for him to reach and he asked Mrs. Shafer and she gave him a glass of water. Then he said, "Buddy's thirsty too." She gave him a second glass, and he handed it to Buddy and Buddy drank it. Later when Mr. Shafer went to feed the chickens Dan said, "Buddy likes to watch the chickens being fed. Can he watch?" Shafer looked at him oddly and then shrugged and let the boy follow him to the yard where the chickens were kept.

From then on he spoke for Buddy. If he was thirsty he asked for water for Buddy too. If he wanted to go to the bathroom he thought Buddy would want to also. Buddy never disappointed him. When he asked for water, Buddy always drank it. When he came in and said, "Buddy's got to go to the bathroom," Buddy always went.

One night after Buddy had been there several months the two men came to visit again. Mr. Shafer went into the parlor to talk to them. One of the men walked to Dan and took him by the arm. "Buddy talks to you, doesn't he?"

Dan was too startled to answer. The man shook Dan and said again, "Come on. Buddy does talk to you, doesn't he?"

Dan still didn't answer and the man shook him once more, this time very hard. "What does he say?"

"He can't talk," Dan finally said, frightened.

"The hell with it," the man said. "He keeps telling you things and you run in and tell the Shafers."

It was as far as the story went. "I don't know what happened afterward," Dan told Noble. "They moved him out of there right after that."

Noble scratched his nose with the end of his pen. "Probably a schizophrenic little kid. He understood everything you said?"

"He just wouldn't talk."

"A pair you two made," Noble said. "We'll see this kid. Probably the same thing."

All that morning Dan looked forward to seeing the mute boy again. But in the afternoon Dan did not see the Mexican woman in the waiting room.

"Who are we going to see?" he asked Noble.

Noble handed him two charts. Neither of them bore the name of Benson.

Dan went out to the desk. "What happened to that woman that made the appointment yesterday."

The clerk looked at her appointment book. "She just didn't show," she said. "We worked another patient in."

"Call her," Dan said.

"She doesn't have a phone."

"What's her address?"

The clerk wrote it on a slip of paper. The next day Dan drove out to the address. He turned off the freeway into a neighborhood of small wooden houses. Again he was passing through an alien island in the town, but it was different from what he had seen of Watts when he visited Noble. He didn't feel the anger. The people in the streets paid no attention to him. He found Rivera Drive, and he parked and walked up creaking unpainted wooden steps onto a porch that groaned unpleasantly under his weight. The doorbell had been pulled out, and two bare wire roots remained. He touched the wires together and heard a buzzer inside the house. A bald Mexican man came to the door. His abdomen bulged over his belt. His shirt was open, and he held a newspaper in one hand. "Allo?" he said.

"I wanted to speak to your wife about bringing your boy, Ramon, to the clinic."

"You from the State Aid?"

"No," Dan said and explained who he was. The man shrugged and opened the door. Dan walked by him and caught the odor of stale beer.

"Just a minute. You sit here. I go get the missus."

Dan sat down on the old sofa. In a few moments the man was back with the woman he had seen in the clinic. She started speaking rapidly the moment she saw him.

"She says she hasn't got no time to go running to the clinic," the man said. "She takes the baby because she's sick, but Ramon isn't sick. Nothing the matter with him." He shook his head. "He's a mean boy. He makes lots of trouble."

"Can I see the boy?"

"You from the State Aid? You here to look around?"

"I've already told you. I'm a student."

"*Es estudiante,*" the man said and the woman started talking again. The man grinned. "She don't like students very much. But she brings Ramon. I tell her to."

She came back with the boy. He wore the same shoes, the same trousers, and the same small, patched red shirt. If he had had a wool cap with a tassel on it he would have looked just like Buddy. Dan unwrapped the package of instruments he had brought and laid them out on a table. The boy looked at them without curiosity and Dan wondered if he had ever been to a doctor before. "Do you take him to get his shots?"

"All the time," the man said. "She takes very good care of them."

"Where?"

"The big hospital. Where she takes the baby." It was a lie. The boy had no County Hospital chart. Dan nodded and said, "Take off your shirt."

The boy did nothing.

"*Quítate la camisa,*" the man said and the boy reached down and pulled his shirt up.

"You see?" the man said. "There's nothing the matter with him. He understands everything. Just very stubborn."

"Take off your pants too."

"Los pantalones," the man said and the boy unhooked the top button on his worn trousers and let them slide down to his ankles. Dan was startled. There were bruises all over the boy's body, standing out dully under the dirt. Dan pulled his underpants down and across his small buttocks was a jagged line of cruel half-healed scratches. Dan puzzled over them. "What happened to him?"

"Maybe he fall down," the man said.

"Awfully thin."

"The state only gives us forty dollars to take care of him. You can't eat so good on forty dollars with clothes and with bus fare to the hospital and medicines. You can tell them downtown they give us more money we feed him more."

"I'm not from the State Aid," Dan said. He touched the scratches and the boy winced and stepped away.

"All right," Dan said. "I won't do that again. Come back here." He led the boy closer and listened to his lungs and his heart. He shone a light in his eyes, and examined his reflexes. When he was done he knew no more than when he started.

"You find anything wrong?" the man asked.

"How did he get these bruises?"

"He fell down. You want some beer. I got some good beer."

"No," Dan said.

"You want to see the rest of the house? Everything's clean. The baby is clean. Everything's fine."

Dan shook his head, and rolled up his instruments.

He thought about the boy Ramon frequently as he worked that evening. He wondered why the child wouldn't talk, and he thought again about Buddy, wondering why he didn't talk, and in his thinking the two became confused. He worried about the bruises and he wondered uneasily how a small child could fall so often.

The next day he went to the hospital cafeteria for lunch. With his tray balanced on his hands, he looked over the room and saw Rosenthal eating with another resident. He hurried over.

Rosenthal looked up. "Haven't seen you around. Figured maybe they flunked you out."

"I'm working in pediatrics." Dan sat down and unloaded his tray. "Where are you now?"

"Cardiology resident. Have you ever been in that new room they set up?"

Dan shook his head.

"Every patient is monitored. Two hundred thousand dollars of monitors, and every time anybody's heart skips a beat, or their blood pressure goes up, the alarm lights start flickering, and when you've got three or four alarms going off all at once you get indigestion." He looked at Dan. "What kind of trouble are you in now?"

"No trouble."

Rosenthal ground his cigarette out. "Okay," he said and started to get up.

"Just a minute," Dan said. "I did want to ask you something. What's a battered child syndrome?"

Rosenthal sat down again. "Have you found a case?"

"I don't know. Do you see many of them?"

"Ask Ben here. He's a pediatric resident," Rosenthal said.

"All the time," the other resident said. "Beaten up. Legs broken. Skull fractures. You wouldn't believe it."

"How can you tell whether the bruises came from falling down?"

"What difference does it make?" the pediatric resident said. "If a kid's all beat up, and it keeps happening, it doesn't make any difference whether it's by beating or by neglect."

"What do you do when you suspect a case?"

"Call the police," Rosenthal said. "Put the sons of bitches in jail."

"Wait a minute," the pediatrician said. "Don't go off half cocked. If you call the police and they make an investigation and don't find anything, the first thing you know the kid's brought in dead a week or so afterward. Last month we saw this little girl with two broken legs. She had a chart three inches thick. All kinds of fractures. Every couple of months. So we called the police. They went out but didn't do anything. Then a week or so later the coroner's office called us. She was dead and we still couldn't prove anything."

"I saw the autopsy," Rosenthal said. "Forty-seven bones broken. Ruptured lung. As well as we could figure they must have put this kid down on the floor and just walked back and forth on her."

Dan was agitated. He stood up. "See you later," he said and left his meal half finished. He went to the hospital superintendent's office. He was out to lunch and Dan told the secretary the story.

"These things come up once in a while," she said. "We got homicidal poisonings, beatings, rapes. The admitting resident will have to check the patient and he'll have to make the report to the police."

"The boy isn't a patient," Dan said. "He's never been here. The mother won't bring him."

"Oh. That's different. Then the hospital doesn't have any part in it. You report it as an ordinary citizen. Juvenile Hall is just across the street."

He started to leave and she said, "You better see that they make a good investigation the first time. Last month we had this little girl and—"

"I know about her. I'll go out with them," Dan said.

He told his story at Juvenile Hall to a detective named Jorgenson. Jorgenson typed out a report. Then he and Dan drove to the house in City Terrace. Ramon Benson wasn't there. The fat man told them he didn't know where the boy was. He had run away in the morning.

The detective drove Dan back to Juvenile Hall. "I'll turn in a missing persons report, and if he turns up we ought to recognize him right away. Not much problem in identifying a boy of six who doesn't talk. If you want to go further you can go down to the district attorney's office as a private citizen and sign a complaint and they'll call her in for a hearing."

"What do you think happened to the boy?"

"I don't know," the detective said. "That's why you better go down and sign that complaint."

Dan managed to get to the district attorney's office before five. He told his story and signed the complaint.

Dan spent a restless night thinking about the Mexican boy and his bruises and about Buddy and his silence. He was angry with himself for not having shown more courage when he first visited the house. He should simply have picked the child up and taken him directly to Juvenile Hall. The act was probably illegal, but it would be unlikely that he would have been prosecuted for it in view of the obvious signs of maltreatment on the boy's body. The dull woman and the sly, oily man infuriated him, and he wondered, looking at the clock, if they were beating the boy now—drunk, getting pleasure from striking him. He thought of the thin bones of children, and how easily they break. Rosenthal had said the girl's body had looked as though it had been walked on. He imagined the crunching of a child's bones under somebody's shoes and he broke into a sweat, and got out of bed and walked about the room in a fury.

Next morning at seven he was at the house in City Terrace. The buzzer brought no answer and he rapped loudly. The woman finally opened it. "I want to see that boy," he said and pushed into the apartment.

The man came out in his underwear. "What do you want now? Why do you wake us up and scare the baby?"

"Is Ramon back?"

"Sure he's back. He always comes back."

"Where is he?"

"There's nothing the matter with him," the man shouted. "You leave us alone."

"Show him to me."

"I call the police," the man shouted.

Dan walked through the house again, and in the kitchen, lying on a mattress on the floor, he found the boy. He was naked except for remarkably dirty underpants. Dan lifted the window shade and let some light into the room. There were dozens of bruises on his shoulders, thighs, and back. He touched the ribs and the boy winced and pulled away. He rolled the underwear back and saw the cuts on his buttocks. He was satisfied, and he started searching the kitchen for the boy's trousers.

The woman started shouting in Spanish.

Dan found the trousers under the stove, and he gave them to the boy and said, "Put them on. *Los pantalones.*"

The boy stepped into the pants and Dan said, "That's enough. Let's go." He took the boy's hand and turned. The fat man stepped quickly out of his way. The woman threw herself down on her knees, tears running down her cheeks.

"She says don't take the boy. He's sick," the man said.

"Sure. With broken ribs and bruises. What did you beat him with?"

The man shook his head. "She tell the truth. She don't hit him. I don't hit him. He does it to himself. He's sick." The man waited, looking at Dan. "He's sick in the head. She's very ashamed. That's why she don't tell you."

Dan took two more steps. The man took him by the arm. "You wait. Please wait. No harm. She want to tell you something." The woman stood up and started talking. "She say it's her son. She don't know where the father is. He's a North American like you. He run away and leave her. The boy acts funny. He hurts himself. You wait and see. Please wait. Sit down please." He led Dan to the couch, and after a moment Dan sat down. The boy remained standing in the middle of the room.

"She love the boy," the man said. "Me, I don't care very much. I don't love him. I don't hate him. He's sick. But she love him. She's very ashamed. It's a great shame among our people to be sick in the head. She try to keep it hidden. You wait."

Dan sat on the couch and waited, not sure what he was waiting for. The man sat in one chair and the woman remained standing. Ten minutes or so passed. The boy remained motionless in the center of the floor, looking down, blinking occasionally. Then suddenly he made a gesture toward his mouth. It was so quick that Dan almost missed it. It was the gesture of a Roman emperor too haughty to talk. The woman turned and hurried toward the kitchen. She came out with a glass of milk. The boy didn't look at it.

She returned to the kitchen, and came back with a slice of bread with butter on it. The boy suddenly threw himself against the molding of the doorway, striking his left shoulder, and falling back on his buttocks. Dan sprang up, but the woman was there before, catching the boy and holding him. He kicked violently, battling to get out of her hands. She said something to the man, and he went into the kitchen and came back with a bottle of Coca-Cola. She held it to the boy's lips, and he stopped struggling and started sipping contentedly on the bottle.

"That's all he wants to eat for breakfast is Coca-Cola," the man said. "She try to give him milk. She try to give him bread like you see. You don't give him what he want, he jumps against the door. Sometimes he jumps against the door even when he gets what he wants. For no good reason at all. And he doesn't talk." He looked at Dan. "She's very ashamed. She do everything she can. She don't want nobody to know."

Dan stood up. "I'm awfully sorry," he said.

"Stubborn boy," the man said. "What can you do?"

Later that morning Dan told the chief pediatrician at the clinic about the child. The physician was a thin elderly man who spoke with an east European accent. "You had it all backward," he finally said. "It's a little Hitler syndrome."

After he left Dan said to Noble, "You don't suppose Buddy was a little Hitler too?"

"Sure had you running all over the place for him. Talking for him. Arranging his meals."

Dan thought about it a long time. "I never saw him beat himself. He was a nice kid."

Noble sighed. "There's one thing that's worrying me though."

"What's that?"

"You better call the district attorney's office and get them off that kid's mother. She's got troubles enough already."

"Sure," Dan said rising. "I think I'll go across the street to Juvenile again. Maybe they'd send out a psychiatric social worker who speaks Spanish."

Noble looked at him a moment, opened his mouth to say something, and then closed it. "Go ahead," he finally said. "I'm beginning to enjoy working by myself."

About a week later Dan found a note tacked to his door. It read, *There is a package for you in my place. Goldie.* He rang Goldie's bell. Goldie looked much slimmer. "Lost some weight?"

Goldie smiled. He took Dan's hand and pressed it against his abdomen. Dan could feel steel stays.

"Can you breathe with it on?"

Goldie did a pirouette and came down on one knee, hands outstretched. "See?" He disappeared into the bedroom and came back wearing a gay yellow wig, the hair curling down to his ears. "Well?"

Dan grinned. "You look like a nellie queen."

"Don't I though?" Goldie said, looking at himself in the mirror. "I paid off the vicers. I paid off my lawyer, and I went shopping today."

"Where's my package?"

Goldie pointed to a box in the corner of the room. "Books," he said. The carton was already open. It was Wilson's *Practice of Pediatrics,* a fourteen-volume set that Dan often had admired in the library. The card with it said, *Many thanks. Means.*

"Interesting," Goldie said. "I got started on the first volume on infectious diseases. Reading all day."

Dan was delighted with the gift. He carried the heavy box upstairs, and took the books out one by one and set them on the table. He lay down in bed and read for several hours about mutism and autistic children and he was amazed at how little he had known. The next day he called Joan. He no longer remembered her number, and he had to look it up in the book.

She sounded sad and very sober. "I'm glad you like the books," she said. "Daddy wanted to get you something. He's funny that way. He's always has to pay his debts. I told him what you wanted."

"He couldn't have given me anything nicer. How are you feeling?"

"I don't think those pills are all out of my system yet. I'm still bumping into things."

"Yes," he said. "I imagine. Thanks for suggesting the Wilson."

She wanted to talk more but he remembered too vividly his vigil in the hospital and was fearful she would say something that would in some way entrap him again. He quickly said good-bye and hung up.

The days were getting colder and clearer. He had felt well and cheerful all autumn, the morning despondency troubling him only a little when he first awakened.

By state decree daylight-saving time ended and all clocks were set back an hour. Afterward when Dan left school it was already twilight and by the time he got to the store it was night. After a few weeks of this he drove home down Wilshire and saw colored lights and cardboard reindeer hanging over the street and he realized uncomfortably that Christmas was close. Thereafter each subsequent day deepened his uneasiness, and finally he called Eddie. "How's it coming?"

"The same as always. Why?"

"What are you doing on Christmas?"

"Vegas," Eddie said. "I go every year." He offered no invitation, and Dan realized he was not going by himself.

"Take care of yourself," Dan said. "Win some money."

"I'll do that," Eddie said. "Call you when I get back."

Later Dan tried to persuade Max to keep the store open on Christmas. "There's no business on Christmas day," Max said. "Everybody's sleeping their hangovers off. I'm going to take Sharon to Palm Springs."

"How is she?"

Max shook his head. "How should she be? She throws up in the morning and her stomach hurts her and she's constipated and she's mad at me. Every time she throws up you'd think it was me that stuck my finger down her throat." He hesitated. "Why don't you come with us? Sharon will have you to fight with. It'll give me a rest for a while."

Dan shrugged. "I'll study," he said.

That same night after work he was reading in Hoagy's and someone sat down beside him. Without looking up he knew it was Joan.

"I've been waiting an hour trying to get up enough courage to come in," she said.

He looked at her. She was thinner. She wore a sweater and a wool skirt. "Hungry?"

She shook her head. "I'm too nervous to eat. I'm going to give you an explanation."

"Why don't you wait a few months? It's too close to Christmas."

"Just listen."

"I already know it."

"If you know what a heartache I've had why are you so angry at me?"

"Because everybody's got a heartache," he said. "You're no different from the rest of us. Ask her. Come here, miss."

The waitress looked around. "Yes sir?"

"Ask her about her heartache," Dan said. "I don't know anything about her but I know it'll be as big as yours."

"Did you want something?" the waitress said.

"We're just talking about heartaches," Dan said. "Do you have any?"

She stared at him, uncertain how to understand his words, and Joan said to her, "He always talks that way. Don't pay any attention." To Dan she said, "You're upsetting the girl."

"She probably has six heartaches, and the last thing in the world she wants to do is talk about them. Because otherwise she'll start crying. The one difference between her and you is that she doesn't run and yell and scream and get herself stinking and sleep with the first son of a bitch that she can find."

"That's what I was going to say," Joan said. "I'll have some coffee."

Dan ate quietly. Joan's hands shook badly when she raised the cup of coffee to her lips.

"Those pills wreck your constitution," she said.

"You need a couple more weeks."

"There are a lot of things I could tell you that might make it better. The only trouble is they'd be lies. I knew if I talked to you again I'd have to tell the truth."

"Forget it," he said.

"I can't," she said. She stood up next to him, her body against his shoulder. "I've decided what my penance is going to be. A real rough one this time. I'm going to crawl on my behind wherever I have to, and do whatever I have to until you take me back."

"Why?"

"The only way I'll get this one wiped away is when you forgive me."

"I forgave you last week. Or maybe six months ago. I forget. Anyway you're forgiven. Go find another penance. Work in the Salvation Army scrubbing bums. Put pebbles in your shoes. You can even shove a pineapple up your ass. That's a good one too. Just leave me out of your penances."

She bent over and kissed him. "I'll see you later," she said.

After she left the waitress looked at him peculiarly. "What was that about heartaches?" she said.

"I'm sorry," he said. "I just got carried away."

"If that redhead wants to hear something about heartaches, I can tell her."

"She used to work here," Dan said irrelevantly.

"I have a boy that's four and he can't talk."

Dan looked up, suddenly interested. "A deaf-mute?"

"The doctors don't know. They're giving him psychological testing. If she wants a heartache she can have that one."

After a moment Dan said, "Any dessert go with this?"

"Oh. Orange or pineapple sherbet, cherry, apple, or pumpkin pie."

"Never mind," he said, suddenly weary. "I guess that's enough." He left a tip, and outside he looked for Joan's red car but it was gone. He walked up to his room. It was scrubbed from one end to another. Every item was in place. Someone had gone over the sink with bleach so that the ancient ceramic seemed pure and white. His bed was made, and the corner of it turned down. A small Mason jar with flowers sat on the table. The pediatric books were lying right next to it. He opened the dresser drawer and found his pajamas folded neatly, smelling of laundry soap. He put them on and went to bed uneasily in the strangely tidy room.

On Christmas Eve school finished at noon. He went to his room, lay down, determined to study, but he heard the radios and their carols, and the sound of people moving about and shouting at one another. He turned the light off and tried to sleep. Almost immediately he heard a scratching noise on his door and he thought at first it was one of the Christmas Eve revelers brushing by, but when it was repeated, he knew who it was. He turned on the light. Joan was standing outside, rosy-cheeked from the cold, a package under her arm. "Your cleaning woman is here," she said. She stepped by him, and set the package on the table and unwrapped it. It was a small tape recorder. She fed a tape into it, pressed a lever, and it sang, *There were two ships came sailing in, came sailing in, came sailing in. There were two ships came sailing in on Christmas day in the morning.*

"That's all I need," he said.

"How's my penance coming?"

"I wish you'd stop it. This room is too clean. I don't feel at home."

She shook her head. "You don't have to scowl so much. I'm here. I'm going to stay." She went out into the hall and came back with a paper bag. "I know you. You were lying in here looking up at the ceiling and feeling as empty as an old beer bottle until I came in. Now I'm going to make your night a little better." She went into the kitchen and he heard cupboards opening. "It's all a Jewish plot anyway," she called back. "One Jew starts this whole business off by getting born. The rest of the Jews make a prophet out of him, and the garment industry and the toy shops and the moving picture moguls all cash in. It's amazing how we Gentiles always catch Jewish insanities. First Christianity, then Socialism, then atom bombs. Speaking of Jewish insanities, I'm going to go to a psychiatrist."

He was startled. "You are?"

"Yes." She came out in the living room, her sweater sleeves rolled to her elbow, and her hands wet. "I've got to do something. Anytime anybody loves me I do my best to rip them apart."

"It might help," he said.

"I lined up a job last week. Art director for Security First National."

"Why does a bank need an artist?"

"Advertising. They gave me a tentative assignment and I drew them up a few layouts and they liked it. It'll help pay my head-shrinking bills. Who should I go see?"

"You really mean it?"

"I never meant anything more in my life."

After a while he said, "What happened?"

"I don't know which came first," she said. "The drinking or the getting mad. Maybe they both came together. Anyhow I got good and mad. I started out to hurt you and then before I knew it you were gone and I had to keep drinking to feel better."

"You're leaving out a few parts."

"Yes," she said. "I am. I'll tell you about those later if you want me to."

"That son of a bitch hasn't even called to ask how you are."

"Chasing around for a man is almost as bad as drinking. And that poor fellow will chase and never find what he's hunting for and get a divorce and get married again and the same thing will happen." She shook her head. "Toward the end I felt sorry for both of us."

"I don't know anybody better for a psychiatrist to work on. You're young. You're bright. And maybe you've had your ass kicked enough."

"This last time hurt."

"Soon as I get back to school I'll find a doctor for you."

Later she set the food out and they ate and talked. She told him about her new job and he was surprised at how much she was being paid. "I'll need it," she said. "How much do they charge?"

"Thirty dollars an hour."

"You haven't said anything nasty for a half hour. I think my penance is working."

He helped her carry the dishes to the sink. "There's something I've been wondering for years," he said. "When I first met you you were also doing a penance. What was that for?"

"When I came out here I went to work for this advertising firm, Cramoline and Blake. I was drinking some then, not enough so I couldn't work, but enough so that I was good and damp every night when I went to sleep. About twenty-five men worked there and then one day after I'd been there six months or so I walked through the office and I realized that I had been to bed with every one of them. Do you know how that felt? To see twenty-five men, some old, some young, some married, some single, all in the same office?"

"Have a merry Christmas," he said. "God rest you merry gentlemen. Let nothing you dismay. I'm going to read."

"I told you I was going to be honest," she said.

"Don't overdo it. It's your penance. Not mine." Nevertheless when he lay down to read with Joan in the apartment he felt happier than he had felt in months and Christmas no longer distressed him. Even after she left he read comfortably and happily, and fell asleep easily.

Dan was awakened during the night by a thump on his floor. It sounded like an angry downstairs neighbor striking a broom handle against the ceiling. It came from Goldie's apartment and Dan wondered what sort of strange thumping orgy Goldie was celebrating Christmas with. The irregular thumping kept on and finally he pulled his trousers on and padded down barefooted to Goldie's apartment. The door was locked. He listened and again he heard the thump and then something hitting the floor. Someone inside was throwing something up against the ceiling. He ran outside and around the apartment house, his bare feet bruising against the wet pebbles and cement shards. He overturned a garbage can and stood on it and looked into the window. The living room had been torn apart. Drapes lay on the floor. Tables were overturned. Books were scattered about with torn pages lying where they had settled. He rattled the window and shouted Goldie's name. Then he broke the window open with a garbage-can lid and climbed in. A wet mumbling sound came from the hall. He ran through the small kitchen and found Goldie crawling painfully along the floor on his elbows. His face was bloody. His jaw was pushed to the right and several of his teeth jutted out between his lips. His blond wig was spotted with red jellied clots. He crawled to a shoe and rolled over on his back and threw it up at the ceiling.

"I'm here," Dan said. He knelt down but Goldie seemed only dimly aware that he had come. Dan noticed his pockets were turned inside out.

"What happened?"

Goldie mumbled and Dan said, "Never mind. Lie still." He got a blanket from the bedroom. Someone had taken the time to cut open the pillows and scatter the down over the bathroom and bedroom floors. He covered Goldie. "I'm going to call the ambulance," he said. "Take it easy."

He called the receiving hospital and the police. Afterward he sat down on the floor and wiped the blood away from Goldie's face with a wet towel.

The police came first, two young officers, their blue jackets buttoned to the neck. One of them stood at the door and looked in. The other walked through the small apartment and then knelt down alongside Goldie. "Is he conscious?" he said.

"His jaw is broken. He can't talk."

Goldie mumbled, bloody bubbles forming on his lips.

"Take it easy," the officer said. "The ambulance will be here any minute." He stood up, took out his notebook, and asked questions. Dan told him all he could.

A siren screamed outside, and in a few moments two men came in with a stretcher and lifted Goldie onto it.

One of the policemen stooped over and picked up two loose teeth. "Here," he said and handed them to one of the attendants. "You better give them to him. Sometimes the dentist can graft them back in." He wiped his hands on the blanket. They watched Goldie being carried out.

"Did you see anybody here?" one of the police officers said.

"I wasn't out of my room."

"He's a faggot, isn't he?" He was prodding the yellow wig with his toe.

"Yes."

The officer shook his head. "They pick up these queer kids and bring them home with them and then the kids turn out to be sadists and beat the hell out of them. Remember that old fag up on Silverlake?"

The other officer came inside. "Last month?"

"They damn near killed him. They get their kicks that way." He put the notebook in his pocket. "Better leave things alone. If he dies we'll want to fingerprint the place. Anyway we'll show up later on at the County and see if he'll be able to give us a statement."

Dan picked Goldie's key chain up from the floor. He looked about for a moment. Every small thing that Goldie had brought into it to give the apartment some air of elegance was torn down and the rooms were squalid and ferociously ugly again.

"These queers depress me," one of the policemen said.

Dan closed the door and locked it.

"Good night," the policeman said.

Dan watched them go. "Good night," he said.

The next morning was Christmas. He got up at six and drove to the County Hospital. He looked for Rosenthal in the intern's cafeteria and couldn't find him. However, he saw Berger eating by himself and in spite of his dislike for the psychiatric resident he walked over and sat down beside him. "I want to ask you about a referral," he said.

Berger was eating thin oatmeal on which floated blue skim milk. He swallowed a spoonful and said, "For yourself?"

"An alcoholic girl."

"I thought it might be for you. You do have a problem with hostility."

Dan grinned. "You mean Grenell?"

"I was very upset about your attitude. As a matter of fact I discussed it with my analyst."

"Who's your analyst?"

Berger hesitated. Then he said, "Akenside. Harold Akenside."

"Is he good?"

"He's a teaching analyst."

"Will he be good for this girl?"

"She'll need analysis. It's not worthwhile just trying to patch up an alcoholic's personality. They have too many severe dependencies."

"Should I send her to him?"

"I just hope he has time to take her." Berger hunted around in his pocket. He couldn't find any paper and he wrote the doctor's name and number down on the cover of a matchbook. Dan put the matchbook in his pocket and went upstairs to visit Goldie. He found him in one of the wards on the fourth floor. His jaws had been wired shut and his mouth was greatly swollen. Dan sat down beside him. "Can you talk?"

"A little."

"What happened?"

Dan couldn't make much out of Goldie's answer. "Anything you need?"

Goldie tugged at Dan's sleeve. "Get me out of here," he managed to say.

"There's nobody to take care of you at home."

Goldie made the sign of a pencil, and Dan took one out of his pocket and handed it to him. On a pad at his bedside Goldie wrote, *Call Marie ex-wife. EX 4-1454.*

Dan remembered Goldie once mentioning that he had been married. He wondered what kind of a woman this Marie would be. He called her from the hall phone. She sounded brisk and energetic. "I knew something was wrong," she said. "We always spend Christmas together."

"Do you see him often now?"

"Maybe every week." She asked about Goldie's injuries and readily agreed to take care of him. Dan was surprised. He hung up and went back into the ward and said, "I guess I can run you back here when you need to go to clinic. All you've got to do now is get yourself discharged."

Goldie nodded and wrote down on the slip, *I'll be sprung this afternoon. You'll see.*

After Dan left the hospital he had nothing to do and Christmas day lay ahead of him like a desert. He drove about for a while, and then turned his car westward into Beverly Glen. He hadn't seen Joan's house for a year. It looked the same. He rang the doorbell and she promptly opened the door.

"Do you want to do something?" he said. "Go to a show?"

"Christmas is a day for staying home. Come on in."

At first he was uneasy with her. Later, tentatively, he put his arms around her and the old desire came back just as strong as ever. They went to bed and afterward he fell asleep. He was awakened by the clatter of pans and dishes. He drowsed for a while. Then she came in with a list. "There's an open market on Pico and Doheny," she said. "Here's what we need for dinner." He took the list and then took the match packet out of his trouser pocket and gave it to her. "There's a doctor's name on this. He's the one."

She unfolded the packet. "How do I know he'll take me?"

"You have everything going for you."

"You think so? Danny, I'll work like hell on it. I'll—"

"No speeches," he said. "Just do it."

After dinner Joan insisted on going out. "You live a somber

life," she said. "The only playing you ever do is in bed. Come on. Get dressed."

He dressed reluctantly and they went to a nightclub, which was gaily decorated for Christmas. Joan sipped coffee and Dan drank and watched three girls, naked from the waist up, twist and stamp in a Spanish dance. The girls looked young under their makeup, but the skin about the nipples on two was darkened, and he knew they had borne children. He watched carefully as they came stamping by his table, sweating and taut, the music crashing. He saw the faint white scar of an old midline incision on the abdomen of the third.

"What are you thinking about?" Joan said.

"Just enjoying the dance."

"I'll bet," she said.

He smiled. "The third one's never been pregnant. She had a hysterectomy real young."

The next evening he stopped at Goldie's apartment. Marie was a thin, bright-eyed woman who was busily repairing the damage. The drapes were back up. The intricate bedspread was on the bed. The blood spots were out of the carpet. Goldie lay on the couch, propped up on pillows, drinking some juice through a straw.

"Hello, hello," Marie said. "Is this patient a complainer! It's a good thing his jaws are wired shut. He doesn't like the way I cook. The couch is too hard. He doesn't like the way I make his bed." She smiled. "I don't know how I stayed married to him for so long."

"How long?"

"Six weeks. Sit down. I'll bring you some tea."

He sat down alongside Goldie. "How is it coming?"

"Can't talk good," Goldie said through clenched teeth. "My head hurts."

"What happened?"

Goldie grimaced. "These two guys were freaks," he mumbled. "You get them that way once in a while."

"Has this ever happened to you before?"

"Once I got a fractured skull."

"What the hell for?"

"You can't tell what they're like. You only find out when it's too late."

"Why go out and pick these guys up anyway?"

"Sex," Goldie mumbled. "You've heard of it haven't you?"

Dan watched Marie through the kitchen door. "Why don't you get married again?"

"I can't go to bed with her."

"So jack off."

"You're very coarse sometimes," Goldie mumbled. "Anyway you've got a thing about people changing. It's a kick you're on."

In the week between Christmas and New Year's Dan fell back into his old relationship with Joan. Again when he was not working he was at her house, reading, sleeping, or eating and again they talked a great deal. She fed him and cared for him. She supervised his dressing in the morning, and complained if his shirt wasn't clean or if his tie was stained. She often stayed up at night, washing his shirts and laying out his clothes for the morning.

He was happy with her again and became cheerful. He joked with customers in the store and with patients at the hospital. He enjoyed school even more than before, and studied well again.

Her first appointment with the psychiatrist was for the seventh of January. "When I phoned him he didn't know if he could fit me into his schedule," she said uneasily the night before.

"This town's full of psychiatrists."

"But this one's a teaching analyst."

"There are other teaching analysts."

"What's a teaching analyst?"

Dan sighed and put his book down. "They treat other psychiatrists."

"Is that good?"

"Only the best do that."

"He'll want only the best patients, and I'm terrible. I lie and I drink." After a while she added, "Am I supposed to tell him about masturbation, or about wanting to sleep with my father?"

"Don't screw around. Tell him about your drinking."

"I guess the treatment's beginning to work already. My conscience is bothering me about things that happened years ago. You're not listening."

"I've just started a new clinic in obstetrics and if I don't study I'll mess it up."

She kissed him. "I'll worry silently," she said.

Dan was truly concerned about the obstetrics clinic. He had found himself shy and ill at ease with the women, and was reluctant to ask them certain questions. The instructor had criticized Dan's meager histories.

He had wondered, when he first started the clinic, whether, with so intimate a state as pregnancy, the white women would be distressed to have a Negro medical student attend them. So far as he could tell in the first couple of days it made no difference. They came in with their small symptoms, gladly told them either to Noble or to him, and seemed genuinely pleased with Noble's stolid courtesy. Neither did the Negro patients prefer Noble to him. Dan knew there were many white doctors throughout the town who did not want colored patients in their reception rooms, and perhaps some colored doctors who did not want white patients. Yet he saw none of this in the clinic and he wondered about the long unwritten but firmly enforced prohibition that had kept colored physicians out of white hospitals for so many generations.

One of their early patients in the clinic was a girl whose name was Dorothy Harris. She was seventeen, blond, and overweight. Noble had been complaining about doing all the writing and Dan had taken over her history. He scanned the chart.

"The pills that the other doctor gave me helped," she said.

"No problems?"

"I'd just like to have this baby and get it over with. Can you arrange that?"

"We just take your history," Noble said. "The resident comes in later on and he does the arranging."

"I know," she said. "I always see medical students. It's easier to talk to them than to real doctors."

Dan was back to the beginning of her chart, and the first note startled him. It read, *This seventeen-year-old girl was assaulted and raped by a colored assailant last night. Physical examinations this morning reveals bruising of the thighs and arms. Six hundred thousand units of penicillin given as prophylaxis against syphilis and gonorrhea.*

"You were raped?"

"Yes."

"Is that how you got pregnant?"

"Yes."

"You're not married?"

"No," the girl said. "When do you think I'll have my baby?"

Dan studied the obstetrical table thumbtacked to the wall and told her the day.

"Let me see her chart," Noble said. He started reading it.

"I'm supposed to give the baby away," she said.

Dan led her to the long examining table and took her blood pressure. Later he adjusted the head stethoscope and listened over her abdomen.

"Are you listening to my baby's heart?" she said, looking down from above.

"I think so." Dan counted the beats. "A hundred and forty," he said. "Here, Oney, you want to check this?"

Noble put on the stethoscope and timed the beat by his wristwatch. "I get one forty-five," he said.

"Don't fight over five beats, boys," she said. "How does the baby's heart sound?"

"Good," Dan said. He remembered Dr. Finch and the man with the cancerous lung and he said, "A very fine-sounding heart. Quite splendid."

The girl smiled. "There is a hand over here," she said. She

took Dan's hand and pressed it to her stomach. "It's a hand, isn't it?"

"It might be a foot."

"He doesn't kick with it. He just sort of moves it back and forth."

Noble felt it too. "It could be a hand," he said.

"Where's his head then?"

Dan felt her abdomen. "Way down low where it's supposed to be."

The girl was delighted. "He is a lefty then. If his head is down there and his hand is over to my left side and if he is looking backward like they're supposed to and he keeps using that arm then he must be left-handed. My whole family is left-handed." She looked at Dan expectantly and Dan nodded and said, "That figures."

The obstetrics resident sauntered in. He picked up the chart. "How is she doing?"

"She's doing fine," the girl said. "She is just wondering what's taking so long on this baby."

The resident put on the head stethoscope and listened. "Very good fetal heart sounds. Good strong baby. When the pains start coming regularly you're supposed to come right on in."

"I read the booklet you gave me."

"What do you know? We have a patient who can read." The resident grinned and said to Dan, "Better have her come back in a week. She's just about ready to pop." He went out.

Dan started writing notes on the chart.

The girl sat up. "Will you deliver my baby?"

"I can't do a delivery. I'm a student."

"I want you to be there anyway."

"I have classes during the day."

"I'll try to have my baby at night then. If I start having pains during the day I'll lie down and I'll put cold packs on my stomach. My mother told me how." She waited.

"All right," Dan said. "If I can."

"It's a promise you made now. You can't break it. Remember my name. Dorothy Harris."

"I'll remember," Dan said. He gave her a note for a second appointment in a week.

After she left Noble said, "What a mess she's in!"

"You believe that rape story?"

"It's in the chart."

Dan shrugged. "All the intern wrote down is what she told him. She could have told him anything. How would he know?"

"I don't know," Noble said.

"Of course you don't. What you have is faith."

When Dan returned the chart to the desk, he found the resident smoking and chatting with the nurse.

"Are you going to deliver this baby?" he asked.

The resident nodded. "If I'm on call when it comes."

"Will you call me?"

"Why?"

Dan was embarrassed. "She wants me to be there," he said, and then, "Do you believe the story about her being raped?"

The resident looked annoyed. "Why shouldn't I believe it? There was a police investigation and they caught that fellow. It was in all the papers. He is in prison at Chino right now."

"Oh," Dan said.

"Yes, oh," the resident said and went back to chatting with the nurse.

That night Joan started talking as soon as he walked through the door. She was very excited. "He's a wonderful man, so kind and so gentle. He thinks I can take analysis. They don't do that except with the most promising sort of patient. He wants to start me off right away three days a week. He is going to undertake a character change. I thought it was going to be so hard to talk, but it wasn't. He listened, and he helped me already in just one visit."

"Three times a week? That's about four hundred dollars a month."

"I've got to do it. It's my whole life. My life is worth four hundred dollars a month for a while."

"Your father will have to help."

"I'd rather die than take anything from him."

"Why?"

"Just let him get a hold on me through my analysis and my life won't be my own. Besides, when I start pushing to get Turk back—"

"You still planning that?"

"Why do you think I'm going to a psychiatrist?"

"I don't know now," he said uneasily.

"I've been thinking. I can live on almost nothing once I stop buying booze. I can give him three hundred a month out of my own salary. Can you give me a hundred a month?"

"I'm a tyrant too."

"I can handle you. You can eat all your meals here. But you have to buy the food. Okay?"

"Food and a hundred dollars a month?"

"I'll be able to make it with that."

Dan calculated his expenses. "I guess so," he said after a moment. "It'll be tight though."

"I'll try to sell some pictures and pay you back."

"Scramble me up some eggs," he said. "I didn't have time for dinner." Later he phoned the obstetrics ward and left Joan's number so they could call him if Dorothy Harris was admitted that night.

He got the call three days later while he was attending his afternoon clinic. He was shy about visiting her. "I don't know what she wants to see me for anyway," he told Noble.

"So stay away."

"Come on upstairs with me."

"You're going to get yourself involved again in something. You just got through with that mute kid that you thought was your old friend Buddy. You ended up there by calling the cops. You don't know how to stay uninvolved. You can afford it, but I'm not that good a student."

"Come on," Dan said.

"Shove it, friend," Noble said firmly.

Dorothy Harris shared an obstetrics ward with eighteen other women. She was lying on her back, her abdomen a large mound under the blankets. Dan pulled up a chair and she promptly took his hand.

"I had pains today," she said. "They were coming every fifteen minutes. My mother got all nervous and she rushed me down here. Then the pains stopped. I feel like a dope."

"That's the least of your worries."

"Do you think I'll have my baby anyway?"

"The pains will start again. They always do."

"Move over a little closer. I feel better with you here. I told them I was unmarried downstairs. My mother thinks I should have said my husband left me. Can you stay awhile?"

"A few minutes."

"If one of the parents is a criminal or maybe psychologically sick, does the child inherit it?"

"That depends on the way he's brought up, not on the parents."

"The baby can't inherit it?"

"No."

"I've changed my mind. I'm going to keep my baby," she said.

A nurse came in and said, "How are your pains?"

"They're gone."

The nurse wrote in her book and went away.

"You can't give a colored baby away for adoption very easy," she said. "Nobody really wants them. The city would have to take him and put him in an orphanage or a foster home. They weren't even going to let me see him. The social worker said that if I saw him it might be harder for me to give him up." She licked her lips.

"How will you bring up a baby by yourself?"

She shrugged. "I had to stop high school. I felt peculiar walking around school with this stomach. But I was a pretty good typist. Maybe I can do typing at home and make enough."

"Won't your mother help you?"

"She'll be mad."

The visitors' bell sounded and Dan stood up. "I have to get to work now."

"Wait, please. I'd like you to meet my mother. She'll be here in a minute. I've been telling her about you."

He waited, and with the rush of visitors a fat woman, heavily made up, swept into the room. She dropped a paper bag on the girl's bed. "Here's your bed jacket, my fair lady," she said.

"This is the doctor I told you about."

The fat woman smiled. "So you're the charming young man my little jewel has a secret crush on."

The girl shook open the bag. She started to slip her shoulders out of her gray, hospital half gown, when her mother said sharply, "Pull the curtain, young lady." Dan stood up and closed them around her. He waited and in a moment she said, "You can open them now. Does this look better?"

The bed jacket was too large for her. It was obviously her mother's. "Looks good," he said.

"Come back tomorrow," the girl said. "Please."

He nodded and as he turned to go he saw a black-button eye glistening at him from the bed. He stared at it. "It's Bogi Bear," the girl said. She pushed the teddy bear a little further under the covers. "I can't sleep without him. Don't tell the nurses."

Joan's phone rang at four o'clock on Saturday morning, and Dan got up and pulled on his clothes and still warm with sleep started the long drive to the County Hospital. The building was somber in the darkness, and inside he met only an occasional intern or nurse walking quietly from one ward to another.

When he reached the obstetrics ward, he found that Dorothy Harris had already had her baby. She was in the recovery room, still drowsy. He walked to the glass-walled crib room and knocked. The nurse opened the door and handed him a gown and a surgical mask. He put them on. "Who are you here to see?" she asked.

"The Harris baby."

She nodded and said, "Third crib second row." She watched

him apprehensively. "If you're going to examine the baby, you have to use sterile technique, Doctor."

"I'm a medical student. I'm just going to look at the baby. What's its name?"

"None yet."

"A girl?"

"A boy."

He walked to the bassinette and looked down at the infant. The nurse stood alongside him.

"That mother sure had me fooled," she said. "She doesn't look colored."

"She isn't," Dan said. "The father is."

After a moment the nurse said, "That's what they get with this antisegregation bit."

"It was a rape."

The nurse snorted.

"It really was."

"Why didn't she have an abortion then?"

"She's Catholic."

"I'm a Catholic and I'd have an abortion."

"He looks fine."

"That's the way it goes," she said.

Dan went out into the hall. Dorothy was being wheeled out of the labor room. Fluid from a bottle was dripping into one of her arms. She recognized him. "It's a boy."

"I know."

"What's he doing?"

"Sleeping."

"Sleeping? He just got born. What do they do, get born and go right back to sleep again?"

"Lot of times."

"He's going to be a sleepyhead," she said. "I've got a sleepyhead for a baby." She grinned and then she said, "Mother and Father Packard are waiting to talk to you." She fell asleep while Dan was still watching her.

The fat woman and a middle-aged man in clerical dress were

waiting for him by the desk. "Took your time about getting here, didn't you?" the woman said.

He didn't want to talk to her, but the priest stopped him. "I'm Father Packard," he said.

"I've been in a sickbed because of that girl and I'm not going to let a fresh young kid come along and talk her out of what we planned," the mother said.

"Is the baby all right?" the priest asked.

"Fine."

"What color?" the woman asked.

"Pretty definitely Negro."

"Babies dying every day and that one had to be strong," she said.

"Maybe we can sit down someplace," the priest said. They walked to the visitors' room. In the corner a man sat, his head against the wall, legs outstretched, snoring quietly. They found a place on the far side of the room.

"I haven't given her any advice," Dan said.

"That child's been through a real tragedy," the priest said. "She's only seventeen. She can't possibly know all that's going to happen to her if she makes the decision to keep the child."

"I'm not involved in this," Dan said. "I just came to make her feel better." He got up and walked away. He took the elevator down to the basement, started up his car, and turned into the street. He was dissatisfied, however, and felt cowardly. All the way along Sunset Boulevard he kept thinking of the half-grown girl making decisions boldly when she should make them with fear, and finally he turned around and drove back to the County Hospital. When he got to the ward the breakfast trays were being passed out, and Dorothy was awake. "Were you here when I had the baby?"

"Right afterward." He sat down.

"They're going to bring him to me after breakfast."

"You shouldn't see him."

"Why not?"

"Because you should go ahead with what your mother decided. You should give him away."

She let loose of his hand and pulled the covers up about her as though she was cold.

One by one he went down the important points. She listened without answering. When he was done he said, "Is what I'm saying true?"

"I guess so," she said.

"Then that's what you should do."

"All right," she said. "Thanks."

He went to the desk and phoned Joan and told her he would be home in twenty minutes. When he passed the door again he saw that Dorothy was arranging the teddy bear in bed next to her. She looked very young, maybe fourteen or so, and he hurried on by.

He had breakfast with Joan and he told her the story carefully and truthfully and waited to see what she would say. She didn't say anything for a long while. Then, when she had gathered up the dishes in the kitchen, she said, "She should have had an abortion."

"But she didn't."

"I know," Joan said, and went on scrubbing at the dishes with vehemence. Finally she said, "I guess you're right. There's no way out of it. I was standing here thinking what I would do after all I know now about giving children up, and I think I would still give that baby up. So I guess she ought to. Look at us. How much harder would it be if Turk were colored?"

"It might be easier. Your father might not want to keep him."

"Would you marry me with a colored baby?"

"That's a hard question."

"You're not answering me."

After a while he said painfully, "It would be a big obstacle."

"Don't bring me any more stories like this. They upset me."

Later on in the morning he told the same story to Max. Max stood and listened, becoming impatient when Dan was interrupted by customers, and at last he said, "What else could she do? She has to give the baby away."

"What would have happened if Sharon had a colored baby?"

"I'd break her goddamn neck."

"I mean before you were married."

Max chewed on his mustache. "It's not fair asking about Sharon," he finally said. "She's my wife. If I knew what I know now, even if she had seventeen colored children, I'd still marry her. But what if I didn't know her and I just started going with her and she told me she had a colored baby? Then it'd be different. I'd say, 'Oh, that's nice. You're a very fine woman. You practice what the rest of us preach.' And I wouldn't see her again." He chewed on his mustache some more. "You gave her good advice. Don't worry."

Dan stayed away from the obstetrics ward until the fifth day. That would be the day Dorothy would be going home. He went to the ward then, and was amazed to find her nursing the baby. She looked up when she saw him. "He's going to be a good eater," she said. "He just gobbles and gobbles."

The baby's eyes were screwed shut, his cheeks working furiously, and he had the appearance of a tiny man concentrating on some exquisite pleasure.

"Don't start anything," she said. "Arguing can sour a mother's milk."

"I won't argue," Dan said. He sat down and watched the child gulping the milk. "He is a good eater."

"He's gained six ounces. Most of the babies lose weight while they're still in the hospital."

"I'll still be in pediatrics clinic for two more weeks. When you bring him in next week, ask for me."

"If you won't argue with me."

"I've studied about formulas and baby feeding."

"I'm not angry at you," she said. "What you told me—"

"Was true and for your own good. That's the worst kind of thing to tell a person. It can really choke them. I know," he said.

She adjusted the nipple in the baby's mouth. "You talk funny sometimes," she said. "Sometimes I don't understand what you mean."

"Never mind," he said and leaned over and kissed her. "Ask for me next week."

He arose and saw a nurse watching him and he blushed with embarrassment as he went by.

He got to the classroom early and looked for Noble. "That Dorothy Harris is in 4600. I want you to go see her," he said.

"You've got yourself involved again," Noble said.

"I've just got out of it. Now you go on up there."

"Why?"

"Go on."

"Why are you so insistent?"

"Go on up and find out."

At one o'clock Noble came down and said, "Why didn't you tell me about this? Did you see what kind of a bitch she's got for a mother? She practically threw me out of the room."

"She should," Dan said. "Think how much more effective that speech would have been coming from a real black doctor instead of me."

"She told me about that speech," Noble said. He rubbed his nose. "I guess you get it with your mother's milk, and it ties up with the calcium and phosphorus and sets up in your bones."

"I couldn't find anyone to tell me I was wrong."

"You have friends with poisoned bones. Like your own."

"Why didn't you go see her? Why did I go up alone?"

"I didn't know what the problem was."

"The hell you didn't," Dan said angrily. "You knew the facts of the rape and the pregnancy. The rest of it follows. Including the mother and the priest and the speeches." He waited. "Well? Doesn't it?"

"Yes," Noble said after a while.

"And while I and my lousy poisoned bones were sweating, you stayed away because you were afraid you might have to give her the same speech I did."

"I wouldn't have," Noble said.

"You sure would have had a hell of a time deciding," Dan said. "It's in your bones too, friend."

"Calm down."

"Hell," Dan said. "I finally figured out what you've been mad about for so long."

"I've known it for years," Noble said placidly. He took off his glasses and thoughtfully wiped them. "I hope for that girl's sake that the father isn't a moron or an epileptic. How would you check on someone in Chino? Do you think Social Service could find something out?"

"Forget it. You're too late," Dan said. He went out and brought in the next patient. Noble was gone when he came back.

Eight

AS JOAN'S TREATMENT CONTINUED it absorbed all of her ener-
gies and her interests. She spoke of little else. Sometimes when
Dan came home she would tell him of the wonderful things
her doctor had discovered about her. At first he was interested
and he would question her, but each time when she finally
revealed the discovery it was always some strange and inhuman
motive that he failed to understand. He would puzzle about
what she told him, and then would ask, "Do you really feel
that?"

"Oh, I know he's right," she would say. "I've gone thirty
hours already, and he knows me now better than anybody else
in my whole life. That man can see right through me."

She became preoccupied with her dreams. Once he awoke
and found her standing by the bedside, the light on, scribbling
something on a pad.

"What's that?" he asked.

"My dream. I wanted to write it down before I forget about
it."

"Can't you remember it?"

"If it's a bad dream your unconscious represses the memory."

"Was it bad?"

"I don't know yet. I'll have to tell him about it."

Her moods became unpredictable. One Monday night, when
he had taken off work early so they could eat out together,
he came home and found the house empty. He waited in grow-

ing annoyance, and then finally opened up a can of sardines and ate them with bread, studying the meanwhile. She came in about ten o'clock.

"Where were you?"

"I felt like doing some window-shopping."

"What about dinner?"

"I wasn't hungry."

"Why didn't you call me up?"

She flew into a rage. "I'm an individual in my own right and if I want to go window-shopping I'm going to go. I'm declaring my independence here and now. I'm not going to stand for this type of tyranny. I'm done with it. Do you understand. Done. D-o-n-e. Right now."

He stared at her. "What's the matter with you?"

She stopped, and turned inward a moment. "Isn't it wonderful," she said. "I got mad. I finally was able to express anger. That's what Dr. Akenside says was the matter with me. I can't express anger. Now I expressed it."

"Being able to yell at me for no reason at all means you're better?"

"Oh Danny, don't you understand? All my life I've lived with repressed anger and I've had to act it out and do things. Now I can really shout. I really got mad."

"Why window-shopping tonight?"

"Because I wanted to," she said. "Because I don't have to do things to please other people any more. Now I can do things to please myself."

He thought about what she said. After a while he decided that maybe it did make sense. If she were truly sickened by sealed-in anger, then if she did feel it openly she might understand it better and even later get rid of it completely. He didn't know what to make of her sudden desire to go window-shopping, but then it might be unhealthy to try too much to please others. He let it go at that.

Later on that evening she said, "I have to talk to you about something else."

"What?"

"The hearing about Turk."

"You haven't got a lawyer."

"I do."

"Gross?"

"My old lawyer. Tom Bartlett. He's agreed to handle it again."

"Have you paid Gross's bill?"

"We're nasty tonight, aren't we?"

"How much are you paying Bartlett?"

"All he wants is four hundred dollars. I borrowed it on my car and sent it to him last week."

"I'm not sure you ought to have the boy just now."

"I guess it's time I asked you. Danny, are you going to help?"

He didn't answer.

"I promised you I would get treatment and I would change. I'm borderline. With a little help I can make it. But if you pull me down I'll fail."

After a while he said, "I know."

"Do you still love me?"

"Why do you ask me that? You know how I'll answer."

"I'll be going up north in a month."

"Where? To Wallace?"

"That's where the hearing is. Are you coming?"

He sighed uneasily.

"Are you?"

"You have a lawyer. You don't really need me."

"Are you coming?"

"All right," he said at last.

"You may not be sure you love me, but I know I love you," she said. "I've never been this close to anybody in my life. You mean more to me than anybody else in the world, except maybe Turk, and I don't know what I would do if I had a choice between the two of you."

"I already said I was coming."

"You feel all weighed down by commitments?"

"Up to my neck."

"It's good for you. You have to join the human race."

"Aren't you going to eat anything tonight?"

"I'm too nervous." She went to the kitchen and brought a glass of milk into the living room. By then he was lying on the couch reading. "Thanks," he said.

"You might think about seeing a psychiatrist too," she said.

"Why? I'm fine."

"Dr. Akenside said something about you today."

He looked up from his book. "What?"

"He said you're a sick boy."

"He doesn't know me."

"I talk as much about you as I do about myself."

"I'll see how it works on you first." He went on with his reading.

She took the book away. "He wants me to come four times a week now."

"That'll be a hundred and twenty dollars a week!"

"I've got no one to turn to but you."

"I'm already giving you a hundred a month."

"Why don't you give up your room?"

"And move in here?" For some reason obscure even to himself his sense of morals was offended. He shook his head. "No. I'll keep it."

"There's one place you can get more money. Get a raise from Max."

"He can't afford it."

"That's one of your problems," she said. "You're so hostile you let people take advantage of you."

He considered her words. "You think—"

"You're making four dollars an hour now, aren't you? Union scale is five fifty."

"Nobody would pay me five fifty an hour and let me study three or four hours a night. Besides Max isn't taking in that kind of money."

"It's the only way I can do it, Danny. There's no other way."

"I can't ask Max for a raise."

"It's either me or him," she said. "Who's more important to you?"

"That's not the point."

"It is the point. He's underpaying you. He should be paying you full union wages. He couldn't hire anybody for less than five fifty an hour and you know it. If you got a raise of only a dollar an hour it would make the difference."

Dan thought about it for several days, the meanwhile watching her. He thought again about Jesse Davis, wondering if he would be alive if, when he was twenty-five, he had had the money for treatment and the wisdom to take it.

He finally cornered Max at the end of the week. "Wait," he said when he came in. "Don't run off. I have to talk to you."

"Sharon had some false labor pains today and she's afraid to be alone. She's called me up three times already today."

"It can't wait," Dan said. "I need a raise."

"Are you crazy? You know what I'm making here," Max said angrily.

"Union scale is five fifty an hour now. I'll take five dollars. That'll make up for my studying some in the evenings."

"That increases wages about a hundred and eighty dollars a month. I can't do that." Max took the small blue notebook out of the drawer. "Look for yourself. Last month our profit was nine hundred and fifty. You got more than half of that. If I raise you one eighty a month I won't be able to make ends meet."

"I have to have the raise."

"Why?"

"I need it."

"You never needed it before."

"I have to have it or I'm going to leave."

Max stared at him a long time. "You know I can't get along without you. I'm too sick to put the merchandise away. If I try to work a full day I get so short of breath I can't walk across the store." He looked gray and miserable. "Why don't you let it go for a few months until after I have the operation.

If it's a success I'll be able to run the store myself and I can cut your hours down and pay you more by the hour."

"It'll have to be this week."

"It can't come out of the store," Max shouted. "There isn't enough. Do you want me to borrow it?"

"I'm sorry," Dan said.

"So you're sorry. What good does that do? You're squeezing me like a sponge and you're sorry. Don't you tell Sharon, do you hear?" He stalked out of the store.

Dan called Joan then. "All right," he said fiercely. "You can go four times a week. I just got a hundred and eighty bucks a month more out of Max."

She was silent a long time. Then she said, "Thanks Danny. When I'm better I can cut down. Then you can go back and work at the old salary. I know how you feel about Max."

He hung up the phone, angry with her and with himself. Then since he was now making almost union wages, he plunged into work, working faster than he usually did arranging and putting stock away, and whenever a customer came in he tried stubbornly to increase the sale.

As Joan's hearing came closer he worried more and more about it. However, he didn't talk of his doubts, and one evening he came home and found her sorting through her clothes.

"I've already packed your stuff," she said. "I won't take very much. We can get it all in one bag."

He sat down. "How long will it take?"

"It was a week last time."

"I don't like to stay out of school more than three days. Besides it's hard for Max to run the store alone. Sharon can't help much now."

"The airplane tickets for both of us will be about three hundred. Put another hundred on that for hotel bills and food."

"Will they give you an advance at the bank?"

"I already took one. I needed some clothes."

"I guess I'll have to borrow it," he said after a while. "I'll speak to my father."

"Not Max?"

"I've already squeezed him dry," he said. "There's nobody left but my father."

He called Eddie in the morning and met him after work at the bar near the insurance company. Eddie's hair was carefully combed. He smelled as usual of cologne and looked as though he wouldn't put up with any kind of fraud for a moment.

"How have you been doing?" Dan said.

"Same old stuff," Eddie said. "I'm fed up with this claims-adjusting bit. I'm thinking about retiring. I could go off and live like a millionaire in Argentina or Brazil right now. There's a very favorable currency exchange rate. Half a dozen servants. A different girl every week. Own my own *finca*. I've been speaking to one of the vice presidents. We might go partners." He looked at Dan. "Come to the point. What do you need, kid?"

"Four hundred dollars."

"What for?"

He had to tell the whole story. Eddie listened, and when Dan was finished he said, "This psychiatry is a pile of crap."

"What do you know about it?"

"Half the people I know have gone to a psychiatrist at one time or another, and they're just the same. Maybe even worse. There's this fellow down at the office who was having trouble with his wife, and—"

"Joan's getting analysis."

"What's that?"

"It's intended to change character."

Eddie puffed on his cigarette. After a while he said, "I guess you should know. It's your profession. But you need other things a hell of a lot more than you need a trip to Wallace."

"I have to go."

"The worst thing in the world for that kid would be living with his mother."

"She's getting psychiatric care. What more can she do?"

"How do you know it will help her?"

"There's a promise in treatment," Dan said. "The doctor knows how much we're sweating to pay for it, and if he's treating her, he's making a promise."

Eddie was quiet for a few moments. Then he took out his checkbook and wrote out a check.

Dan put it into his breast pocket. "You'll start getting this back this summer."

"Be careful," Eddie said. He gulped his drink down.

"Yes," Dan said, "I know."

Eddie paid for the drinks. "Have a nice trip," he said.

The trip was wearisome. The last part of the journey, from Boise to Wallace, was made in a small two-motor plane that bounced badly. Joan was silent during most of the trip, and she remained tight and silent in the cab ride to the attorney's office.

Bartlett was about sixty. He shook hands with Dan and said, "I ought to have my head examined for getting back into this case. Joe Means used to be one of my best clients." He looked Joan over. "You look prettier than ever. That ought to help a little. On the other hand we got the same judge we had for the hearing before. Old Judge Kroger. When you first called me and asked me to represent you again I was hoping he would be retired by the time the hearing came up. He has prostate trouble and he's getting pretty forgetful. But he still hangs on."

"What do you think the chances are?" Dan said.

The attorney shrugged. "The judge can change the order if he wants to. But I don't know if I can talk him into wanting to. I'll try."

About noon they walked across the street to the county courthouse. Joe Means was standing outside the door to the courtroom, talking to a younger man. Means shook hands with Dan.

"Hello daddy," Joan said.

"Hello baby," Means said. "How are you getting along?"

"All right."

"You're sure you want to go through with this? It might get rough."

"I want to go through with it," Joan said. "Where's Carol?"

"Not feeling well. She wanted to stay home."

He went into the courtroom with his lawyer and after a few moments Dan and Joan followed with Bartlett.

An elderly dewlapped judge sat at the bench, listening impatiently to a traffic violation hearing. Dan looked at Joan. She was sitting rigidly, hands in her lap, her face strained. He felt sorry for her and he folded one hand over her knuckles. "Take it easy, honey," he said. "I like this lawyer of yours. I think he probably knows how to handle a country judge."

"Carol would never let him come down to Wallace by himself. She always goes on a buying spree when he comes here, and she'd come if she were dying. I think there's trouble between them," she said. Then she leaned over and whispered to Bartlett.

The court clerk called the names, Means *vs.* Means, and Joan and her father and their two attorneys moved up to the table before the bench. Bartlett stood up first. "May it please Your Honor," he said. "I'm going to show that there are changed circumstances in the character of this girl which warrant her having her child back again."

The judge sorted through the papers on his desk. "Didn't I hear this case originally?"

"That's right, Your Honor," Bartlett said. "It was back about seven years ago."

The judge put on his glasses and read the papers. Then he looked up. "I don't want to go through a hearing on this unless there are changed circumstances. I'm warning you right now I'll give the same verdict unless you can show me some changes."

"I'll have a change or two to show Your Honor, both in the girl and perhaps in the home circumstances of the grandfather." He put Joan on the stand. She told of her job, and she demonstrated pay stubs to show what she was earning. The two attorneys argued whether pay stubs were admissible, but the old judge grunted angrily and said, "Get on with your

case. I'll accept the witness' statement that she is gainfully
employed." Bartlett then led Joan into describing her psychiatric care.

"This is an effort to correct a prior emotional problem, isn't
it?"

"Yes," Joan said.

"What progress are you making?"

"A great deal."

Bartlett took a letter out of his file. "Your doctor is Dr.
Akenside at 9730 Wilshire Boulevard in Beverly Hills?"

"Yes."

"I have a report from Dr. Akenside here which I received
in the mail last week," Bartlett said. "If it please Your Honor,
I'd like to submit this to the court."

The other attorney stood up. "This type of evidence is not
admissible," he said. "If Mr. Bartlett wants to introduce a
doctor's opinion, let him bring the doctor here so I can test his
qualifications and cross-examine him."

"His qualifications are in his letter," Bartlett said.

The judge waved Bartlett down. "You know it's not admissible. You can't put in a doctor's report without proper foundation. Here, let me read it." He took the letter, read it, and
handed it back to Bartlett.

"This is prejudicial to the court," the younger lawyer said.

"Just a minute," the judge said. He got up and left the bench
and walked around to his chambers.

"We get a recess every ten minutes in this court," Bartlett
said.

"Can I see that letter?" Means said.

"Sure." Bartlett handed him the letter.

"The old man's reading of this letter is grounds enough for
a new trial," the younger lawyer said.

Means walked back to Dan with the letter. "Let me know
what this doctor says. I can't understand his medical terms."

Dan read the letter over. In it Joan was described as suffering from a character disorder characterized by recurrent bouts
of alcoholism and self-destructive behavior. She was responding

well to psychoanalysis, was proving an intelligent and cooper-
ative patient, and Dr. Akenside had every reason to expect an
excellent result. Dan explained the technical words.

"You believe it?" Means asked.

"One of the best psychiatrists in Los Angeles."

Means returned the letter to Bartlett, and turned to Joan.
"You know, baby, when this is all done, it would be nice if we
could take a few days off hunting. It's still cold yet, with some
snow in the mountains up around Pebble Flats. We might have
some fun."

Joan shook her head without answering.

The judge came back into the room and sat down.

"Your witness," Bartlett said.

The other lawyer stood up. He was very gentle, apparently
under orders from Means, and asked only a few questions. "It
is true that you were drinking too much a good portion of last
year, isn't it?" he asked.

Joan hesitated, and the lawyer took out a folder. "Let me
see. I have reports here that will enable me to refresh your
memory."

"What are those?" the judge asked.

"Reports from a detective agency in Los Angeles, Your
Honor."

"If you're going to use that sort of material, bring the wit-
nesses up."

"I wasn't going to introduce a report," the attorney said.
"I was just using it to refresh this young lady's memory.
Do you want to answer the question, Miss Means?"

"Yes."

"You were drinking a good portion of last year?"

"Yes."

"You're not married, are you?"

"No."

"Do you plan to get married?"

She hesitated. Then she said, "I don't know."

He nodded courteously and said, "That's all," and Joan

stepped down trembling. She looked as though she might break into tears.

"I'll ask Mr. Means to step up to the witness' chair," Bartlett said.

Joe Means walked up to the chair, raised his hand for the oath, and then sat down.

"The boy, Turkell Means, is in your custody?"

"Yes."

"And that of your wife?"

"Yes."

"Where is your wife now?"

"She couldn't come down."

"Couldn't or wouldn't?"

"She's in Salt Lake City."

"Are you and your wife having any trouble, Mr. Means?"

"None that's any concern of yours."

The old judge leaned across the bench. "Listen, Means, anything that I decide is proper is the concern of this court. You go ahead and answer that question."

"Go ahead and answer, Mr. Means," Bartlett said.

After a moment Means said, "We've separated."

"Any particular reason?"

The other lawyer was on his feet. "That's irrelevant and immaterial. I object to the question."

"Answer it," the judge said.

"Just a minute Your honor—"

"Sit down," the judge said.

"There's been a disagreement," Means said.

"How long has she been in Salt Lake City?" Bartlett asked.

"Three months."

After a moment Bartlett asked, "Has she filed for divorce yet?"

"No."

"Did you persuade her to wait until this hearing is over?"

The young lawyer objected and Bartlett said, "All right. I'll withdraw the question."

That was that. The whole hearing had taken less than fifteen minutes. Dan followed Bartlett into the hall. "That went fine," he said excitedly. "I think you did a wonderful job."

"We lost."

"He didn't give a verdict."

"I don't need one. I know this judge. He wouldn't let all of my stuff get in unless he was pretty sure from the beginning what he was going to find against me. That's the way he works."

"Are you sure?"

"Dead sure," Bartlett said. "I've tried most of my cases before him." He sighed. "You know I told Joan it was pretty much of a dead issue. The only hope we had was that the old crow would retire. Maybe when he does it's worth another crack at it." He shrugged.

"When will that be?"

The attorney smiled. "Depends on whether he gets operated on or not."

"What sort of justice is this? What was the purpose of this hearing?"

The lawyer raised his eyebrows. "Tell me, son," he said, "if you were sitting in his bench and all you wanted to do was the right thing, who would you give the boy to?"

"What if she gets married?"

"Somebody of good character?"

"Yes."

"He'd probably grant change of custody then. I can almost guarantee it." He shook hands with Dan. "It'll be official in a couple of days. There's no point in your waiting around. You can get the bad news back home."

"If there's a change in the next day or so can you still do something about it?"

The lawyer looked at him a moment. "Yes. I think so. Any time up until he delivers the verdict. He'll let us bring in additional evidence."

"Thanks," Dan said. He sat on the bench in the hall waiting for Joan.

They went to a dingy doctor's office across the street from the courthouse to have their blood tests taken. At four o'clock they were married by a justice of the peace. Joan had her own ring. She gave it to Dan and he put it on her finger. The justice looked up from the form he was signing. "You can kiss each other," he said.

Joan called Bartlett and told him. Then they went to a hotel called the Commercial Hotel and took a room. They were both very tired and they bathed and went to bed while it still was light.

"Nothing much new about going to bed with me any more, is there?" Joan said.

Dan had been looking up at the ceiling. "Just worn out," he said. "It's been a rough twenty-four hours. That plane ride and then the hearing and then getting married."

She was lying on his arm, her face close to his cheek. "Why did you marry me?"

"For the same reason anybody else gets married."

"I'm not a fool, Danny."

He sighed. "All right," he said. "I'm committed. You're under analysis and if there's any value to it, and God knows I have to believe there is, then you'll be all right and things will go fine."

"A hell of a way to get married." Later she said, "I know what you're saying. I promise you I won't quit being analyzed. I'll keep working on it until I'm well. I'll make you a good wife. You will be good to the boy, won't you?"

"Why shouldn't I?"

"You're awfully young to be a stepfather."

"Is it hard?"

"Not with Turk."

He kissed her. "Go to sleep. You must be as tired as I am."

The next day, as soon as court had adjourned, they spent another ten minutes in Judge Kroger's courtroom. The judge listened to Bartlett's statement, and then examined the marriage certificate. Dan then went up on the stand and told his age, his occupation, his present employment, and his expected income. When he was done the judge looked from one lawyer to the other. "Well, can't you two get together now? Do you still want me to render a decision?"

The attorney who represented Joe Means stood up. "My client would like to withdraw his objections to a change of custody, and ask the court to grant the custody of the child, Turkell Means, to his natural mother."

"Saves time that way," the judge said. "Granted."

Joe Means turned Turk over to them at the airport. The boy was about seven. He had dark hair and brown eyes and, oddly enough, an olive skin. He let his mother kiss him. He cried when Joe Means kissed him good-bye, and Joan started talking quickly, telling him about the sights he would see in Los Angeles. He listened to her, still crying, but once on the plane he became excited and interested. He waved good-bye to his grandfather through the window. On the flight out of Salt Lake City across the desert he fell asleep and was still sleeping when they landed in Los Angeles. Dan got him home without awaking him and put him to bed and covered him. Joan was unpacking.

"You're going to make him something to eat, aren't you?" he asked.

"He'll wake up if he's hungry."

"He hasn't eaten since we left Wallace."

She smiled at him. "He's not a baby. He's seven. If he's hungry he can say so."

"How do you feel?"

"Grand," she said. "I have my baby and I have a husband."

"I'm going to the store."

"Look," she said. "You went up north a lonely bachelor and you've come back with a family. Now relax and enjoy your family. Take a bath. I'll make some bacon and eggs and later on when Turk wakes up we'll feed him. We can take him for a ride and show him the city. He's never seen a big city before."

"I'm worried about Max."

"He has a wife to worry about him. You just work there."

"I'll call you later." He went out the door and drove to the store. Max was sitting in back. "Well, how did it go?" he said.

"Fine." After a moment Dan added, "I'm married."

Max stared at him. "Married?" Then he shrugged. "What can I say? Be happy. Another time I'd get you a wedding present. I'd give you a week off with pay. But what can I do now?" Later on he said, "You have any troubles you come and talk to me about it. I've gone through such trouble with Sharon you wouldn't believe."

The store had been neglected during Dan's absence, and he persuaded Max to go home. He set about putting stock on shelves and listing items that needed reordering.

He got home after midnight. Joan was very quiet. She set some eggs before him, and she sat down with him while he ate.

"Turk's been up all afternoon asking for you," she said.

"Did he eat all right?"

"Is that all you worry about?"

"There are some other things. We're going to have to move over to my place. That's the only way we'll make ends meet."

"I don't want Turk living in that miserable place of yours."

"There's no way out. We're paying your doctor about five hundred dollars a month. Between the both of us we take home barely nine hundred. Tuition's got to come out of that too."

"I've been thinking too," she said. "Danny, I don't want to ask you to stop school. I know how important it is to you. But if you could just interrupt for a year. If you worked full time as a pharmacist you could bring home a thousand dollars a month and then with what I made it would be easy. We wouldn't have to scratch. We'd be able to take better care of Turk. I wouldn't have to see you running around in those old clothes and driving that beat up car."

He didn't say anything.

"It's not like I'm asking you to give anything up. Just interrupt for a year. At the end of a year maybe I'll be done with my treatment. We'll have some money saved up. Then you can go back."

"No," he said.

"It'll only be for a year," she said. "Look, you're twenty-seven now. You could take out a year and you'd still be only twenty-nine when you graduate. That's young enough."

He stood up. "Better get yourself packed tomorrow. We can start moving after work." He undressed and lay down and read from one of the volumes on pediatrics. After a while she came in and lay down next to him. "Will you think about it?"

"What?"

"Stopping school for a while."

"I'm not going to," he said. "Let me read. I have to cover the lectures I missed."

The next night they moved to Dan's apartment. He bought Turk a cot that could be folded away into a closet during the day. Goldie agreed to conceal the new tenants from the building owners. "They'd want to raise the rent," he said. "But listen, if anybody comes around, she's just visiting, see?"

The crowding in the small apartment did not seem to bother the boy. When Dan awoke in the morning he usually found Turk up and sitting on the edge of his cot. Dan would get up in his pajamas and the two would go into the kitchen, carefully closing the door so that Joan wouldn't waken. Turk would perch on a high stool that Joan had brought from her house, and Dan would cook bacon and eggs. Later in the morning they would get dressed and steal out of the apartment to a school playground a few blocks away where Dan would read and Turk would swing on the swings or hand himself along the monkey bars until it was time for both of them to go to school.

Dan found it easy to like the boy, and he soon looked forward to the mornings and the weekends when they could play together. Joan turned out to be a cautious and fretful mother. She had rest schedules and diet schedules arranged for Turk, and Dan marveled at the patience the child showed.

For several days after they returned Joan was cheerful and

loving. Gradually, however, she again became immersed in her psychotherapy, and her interests turned inward again. She complained a great deal about how small and shabby the apartment was and how little money they had. Oddly enough she began to resent the affection between Dan and Turk. She brought Turk into the store one evening, but after a half hour she suddenly stood up and said, "I'm fed up with this. I'm going home."

"What's the matter?"

"You haven't said a word to me."

"The kid's always asleep when I get home. I barely have any time with him."

"What time do you have with me?"

"I can talk to you at night."

"You'll just have to learn to change," she said. "I'm not the girl I used to be. I don't drink any more and I don't need rejection." She took the boy from his half-eaten sundae and led him out of the store. She didn't bring him back the rest of that week, and at night, for a while, when Dan made advances to her she turned her back coldly and would have nothing to do with him.

Dan thought her mood would pass as her other moods had, but instead it deepened and she became morose and sullen, given to sudden bursts of anger at him and at the boy. If Turk woke her she would spring out of bed in a fury, shouting at him. Small infractions of discipline readily provoked her anger. One night when Dan was tussling on the bed with Turk he found large bruises on the boy's back. "How did you get these?"

"Mommy hit me with the hairbrush."

Dan strode into the bathroom, where Joan was lolling in the tub. "Why the hell did you hit the kid with a hairbrush?"

"I lost my temper," she said. "I shouldn't have."

"You lost your temper with a hairbrush?"

"I'm sorry about it. What more do you want?"

"You can hurt him with a hairbrush."

"Goddamn it be quiet," she shouted at him at the top of her

voice. "I'm fed up with this. I'm not going to stand it any more." She suddenly began to cry and Dan lost his anger. He sat down. "What's been so bad lately? You have Turk. We're married."

The tears were streaming down her face. "I know," she said. "That's it. It's all here and I feel worse than ever. I feel like I'm going to blow up. I can't go from one minute to another without gritting my teeth and telling myself I've got to do it. I can't paint. I can't stand that job at the bank. Christ almighty, I can't stand you."

"Why?"

She closed her eyes. "It has something to do with my relations with my mother. I felt trapped there too. I've been having terrible dreams lately. I think I'm beginning to understand it though. You're my mother."

"What bullshit!"

"You're ignorant," she shouted. "You don't know anything about psychoanalysis. I'm telling you that you're my mother to me."

He found the hairbrush in a drawer and broke it in half and threw the pieces away. "Don't take it out on the kid again," he said. She nodded dumbly and he went back to his studies.

She did not strike Turk again, but she remained morose and depressed. Dan tried from time to time to lighten her mood. He would beg evenings off from Max, and would take her and Turk out to dinner. The boy would be delighted, and sit wide-eyed, watching the waiters and the patrons. Sometimes Joan would try to be cheerful, and would talk constantly and brightly. On other occasions she wouldn't even pretend, but would sit glumly through dinner, and Dan would be relieved when the evening was over and he could go back to the store.

About a month after they got back from Wallace she began changing again, however, and he found that occasionally they would enjoy talking and lovemaking. At first he thought that her psychotherapy was finally working. Then he discovered a simpler cause. He shaved on Sunday morning and, finding his own bottle of shaving lotion empty, he took a bottle of her cologne, which had a pleasing scent, and splashed it on his face. He was surprised. It was colorless and had only the sharp odor of alcohol. He came out of the bathroom. "What do you keep in that cologne bottle of yours? Rubbing alcohol?"

"What are you doing with that?"

"Using it for shaving lotion."

"Leave it alone," she snapped irritably, and ran into the bathroom and snatched up the cologne and carried it out to the kitchen, where she set it in a cupboard. Later Dan took the bottle down and tasted it. It was vodka.

He said nothing, but watched her carefully for several days. He discovered that each evening during the several hours between his coming home and their going to bed, she made a number of trips to the bathroom, her mood lightening and her speech thickening with each trip.

She didn't want Turk to see her drunk, he realized, and she was compressing her drinking to the hours he was asleep.

Finally he followed her into the bathroom and took the cologne bottle away and emptied it into the sink. She watched him and then shrugged. "So I'll have another sleepless night." She went back to the living room.

He followed her. "What the hell's the matter with you?" he asked.

"There's something you ought to learn," she said. "Drinking isn't the worse thing in the world."

"Why are you going to a psychiatrist then?"

"To resolve my problems. When they're done I won't have to drink any more. But until then I need something to help me get through the day, to help me live in this hole of an apartment, and to work in that bank."

"We have to pay for your treatment."

"You could make a lot more money. You could interrupt school for one year. But not you. Nothing before school. Not me. Not Turk. Nobody. Not even yourself."

"I'm not going to have enough money for next year's tuition the way things are going."

"Good!" she said.

He was amazed at how much he hated her and how quickly it had come. He passed his hand over his face. "I think I better go see this psychiatrist of yours," he said.

She looked up frightened. "Why do you want to see him?"

"I want to know what we can expect."

"Don't you think he's helping me?"

"Do you?"

"Of course," she said. "Before psychiatry I could never have stood up and fought for my rights with you this way. I would just have gone along with whatever you wanted, just the way I always went along with my mother and my father. Pressed down. Pushed around. Rejected. Now I stand up and fight."

"With a cologne bottle full of vodka?"

"That's one way," she said. "Maybe it's not the best, but it's better than not having any identity at all."

The next morning he set up an appointment. He went about four o'clock and waited in a small reception room. About ten after four the psychiatrist called him in. He was a big man with a mustache and glasses.

"I want to talk to you about my wife," Dan started.

"Go ahead."

"What progress are you making?"

"What do you think?"

"I can't see any." Dan told him about the moods and the sullenness and the drinking.

"It's a painful treatment," the psychiatrist said. "Unfortunately there's no anesthetic for it. The patient just has to look at himself and in the process he suffers a good deal. When he suffers his disposition gets a little soured. It's just human."

"But she's here to stop drinking."

"It's only a symptom."

"It's the whole sickness."

"It is? How about the promiscuity? The homosexuality?"

"The homosexuality?"

"Latent. I'm not saying that she ever practiced it, but it certainly shows itself in her dreams."

"Her dreams aren't doing any harm," Dan said. "It's her drinking."

"You're a medical student, aren't you?"

"Just finishing my third year."

"These problems go very far back. You know, we are able to trace some early infantile disturbances to intrauterine masturbation."

Dan stared at the physician.

"I'm serious," he said. "There's been extensive psychoanalytical studies on this subject. But what I would like to discuss with you is your part in all this."

"I've been thinking about it."

"Why did you marry her in the first place?"

"There was a year we got along fine," Dan said. "I thought if she had the boy and was coming here we'd get along the way we used to."

"It was a sick kind of happiness. It wasn't founded on true emotional health. You're much better off now. You're working from a realistic foundation. I want to know more about you."

"I'm worried about her. Not myself."

"We're talking about her. How do we know you're not encouraging this drinking?"

"I can't stand her when she drinks."

"On the conscious level. But how about the unconscious level?"

After a while Dan said, "I don't know."

"Of course you don't. From what I've heard about you you're a rigid personality. Withdrawn. Friendless. Tell me about your background."

Dan told him a little, feeling foolish as he talked.

"You should be in analysis too."

"I don't drink."

"You're a sick boy. You need help."

"What kind of a sickness do I have?"

"Look how angry you are. Is that a healthy response to a doctor's suggestion for treatment?"

"You've been telling my wife it's a great sign of health."

The psychiatrist wrote a name and a phone number on a slip of paper. "Here. A very fine analyst. A woman. I think it will do you a world of good. Why don't you go see her?"

He left confused. During the next several days he puzzled uneasily about himself, fearing that in some way he was encouraging Joan's drinking. Perhaps her humiliation gave him a secret satisfaction. It was hard to judge.

When he finally made up his mind he told Joan about it. "I'm not going. I'd have to give up school to go, and I won't do it. I guess you have to keep on though. There's nothing else for us to do."

She was softened by vodka and she said, "It's helped me so much. I don't know why you're even thinking about my stopping."

"Because I keep wondering if the fact that there's nothing else to do makes doing something worthwhile."

"It's new," she said. "The old rules that you doctors measure treatment by don't apply here."

The phone awakened Dan. He reached over Joan, fumbled with it, and heard Max's quivering voice. "She just called the doctor. She's got to go to the hospital."

"Can she wait ten minutes?"

"Hurry up," Max whispered. "I'm having a heart attack. I don't want Sharon to know."

Dan pulled his trousers and his shirt on over his pajamas and thrust his bare feet into his shoes. He drove very fast and found Max, half-dressed, gasping in the middle of the living room. In the bedroom Sharon, in her nightgown, was tossing clothes from her dresser into a bag.

"Get dressed," Dan said.

"What for? I just have to get undressed when I get there."

"You can't walk bare-assed into the hospital."

She shrugged and took a robe down from a closet hook and wrapped herself in it. "How's that?"

"Are you having pains regularly."

"Every five minutes." She looked at a clock on the table. "It's due in a minute and a half."

Dan clamped the lid of the bag shut. "Come on."

"Don't get hysterical," she said and went into the bathroom.

Max walked into the bedroom. "I can't make it," he said. "I can't breathe."

"You're going down to the hospital and see this baby born," Dan said angrily. "I've sweated my balls off nine months worrying and you're not going to conk out on me at the last minute."

"You better get me a shot then," Max said. "I'm choking."

"Where's the stuff?"

Max pointed to a drawer. It held two plastic syringes and several ampules of Dilaudid. Dan filled one syringe. "Calm down. You're just nervous. Give me your arm."

Sharon started screaming from the bathroom and Dan dropped the syringe. "Wait a minute," he shouted back. He got the other syringe and quickly gave Max his injection.

Sharon was screaming even louder. Dan tried the bathroom door and found it locked.

"Screwdriver," Max shouted. "In the hole in the knob."

Dan snatched a nail file from the dresser and thrust it into the knob and twisted it and the door opened. Sharon was sitting on the toilet, holding her stomach and screaming. Tears were running down her face.

"Fine time to go to the toilet," Max shouted. "The baby's ready to get born and she decides to go to the toilet."

"It makes you feel that way when the head comes down," Dan said. He took Sharon by the arm. "Come on."

She stopped her screaming long enough to say, "Wait a minute," and then started screaming again.

Dan hauled her off the toilet. "Let's go."

"I'm not done yet."

"Who the hell cares." He wrapped her in her coat and

dragged her out of the house, Max following behind, staggering from the injection.

When they got in the car Sharon said suddenly, "I forgot to lock the door. Max, go back and lock the door."

"Forget the door," Dan said, starting up the car.

"I've got my fur in there," she cried. "Wait a minute. Don't get hysterical. Max, go lock the door."

Dan took the keys and ran up the stairs and locked the door. Before he was back Sharon was screaming again. "That couldn't have been more than three minutes," he said. He drove through the dark residential street and turned on Santa Monica Boulevard.

"What does it mean when it's only three minutes?" Max said.

"We better hurry."

She started screaming again when Dan stopped for a light at Fairfax. A motorist in a neighboring car looked them over curiously. "What are you looking at?" Max shouted. "Why don't you mind your own business?"

"I feel wet," Sharon said.

"I'm going through the lights," Dan said. "You just watch the corners, Max."

Max put his head out of the window and watched. Dan sped up, passing through red lights. He was sweating and when the girl started to scream again he trembled. He pulled up at the ambulance entrance of the hospital. He took one of her arms and Max took the other and they marched her into the admitting room. She was taken immediately to the fourth floor.

A ward attendant showed them a small room. "Here's where the fathers wait," she said brightly. "The doctor will come out and give father the good news later."

"Is the doctor here?" Dan said.

"He's in the labor room," she said. "You can watch television if you like."

Dan tried to turn the set on but it had no knobs. He looked at Max for a moment. "Sit down," he said. "It's easier on your heart." Dan sat down, closed his eyes, and stretched his legs out. After a while he fell asleep.

Max shook him awake. "It's taking so long. Go down and see what's happening."

"I don't think they want me wandering around."

"It's my baby. You go look."

Dan walked down the hall. He met an obstetrician coming out of the labor room. "How's she doing?" he said.

"Mrs. Wolfe told me you're a medical student."

Dan nodded.

"It's a chin presentation."

"That's not deliverable, is it?"

The obstetrician shook his head. "If it stays this way we'll have to do a section. You want some coffee?"

Dan nodded and followed the physician back to the doctors' lounge. The obstetrician poured some black coffee from an electric pot into two cardboard cups. "I hate to do a section. It increases the chances of losing the baby."

Dan was trying to remember what he had learned in obstetrics. "Can't you manipulate the head so that it presents normally?"

"I've been trying. I'll go in and try again after a while. But if it doesn't straighten out in an hour I'm going to do a caesarean. We'll already be in trouble and that'll be the best way out." He picked up a newspaper and Dan returned down the hall.

"Did you find out anything?" Max said.

"They're all in the delivery room."

"Didn't you talk to anyone?"

"No."

"What are you lying to me for? I saw you speaking to this doctor."

Dan didn't answer.

"Don't you hold anything back from me. It's my baby."

Dan told him about the chin presentation.

"Maybe he ought to get another specialist."

"One's enough."

Max started pacing again. Dan stood up. "I'll be back in a little while," he said. He walked down the stairs and found an open liquor store two blocks away. He bought a pint of scotch and took it back to the waiting room. "This will help," he said.

"I don't drink."

"It'll help your heart."

Max unscrewed the bottle cap, and took a remarkably long swallow. His face turned red and sweat appeared on his forehead. He handed the bottle back to Dan. Dan took a swallow and set it out on the table. "You might need some more," he said.

The time went painfully slow. Sometimes Dan listened to the clock and sometimes he watched Max pacing. Finally he got up. "I'll see what I can find out now," he said.

The obstetrician was sitting at the table in the lounge playing solitaire. "I haven't been able to move the head," he said. "I've just ordered them to set up the room for a section."

"How much greater is the infant mortality with a section?"

"Triple." He reshuffled the deck. "Nothing else we can do."

An old man walked into the room and hung his coat on the rack.

"I thought you quit night deliveries," the younger obstetrician said.

The old man shrugged. "One of my assistants is on vacation and the other one has the flu."

The younger obstetrician put his cards down. "I have a girl with a chin presentation and I can't turn it. I'm getting ready to do a section."

The old man smiled. "Maybe I've got a trick or two."

Dan followed them into Sharon's room. She was wide awake, her eyes large with fear.

"Good," the old man said, "not too much sedation." He began feeling her abdomen.

"Who's he?" Sharon said.

"Be quiet a moment," the younger obstetrician said.

The old man felt about thoughtfully. "It's the chin all right," he said to himself. "Impacted too. And engaged."

"What do you think?"

"I've done a few of these. Maybe it'll go. Just push up when I tell you." He felt a moment longer and then nodded. The younger obstetrician leaned forward, pushing vigorously. Sharon screamed and slapped at his hairy forearms.

The old man said, "Be quiet, miss," impatiently and Sharon cut her scream off in the middle and stared at him openmouthed.

"A little more effort," he said to the younger man. His hands quickly kneaded the lower part of the bulge in Sharon's middle. He suddenly pressed down again and Dan thought he saw something give.

Sharon tore away and flung herself about the bed. "You broke something loose," she screamed. "It's killing me."

The old man started washing his hands. "The head's where it ought to be now. There goes your section out of the window."

The younger physician smiled. "Put her in the delivery room," he said to the nurse. "It'll go fast now."

Dan went back to the waiting room. "Everything's all right. An old doctor came along and flexed the baby's—"

"Speak English!"

"What difference does it make? She won't have to have a caesarean."

"What's his name?"

"Whose?"

"The old doctor."

"How do I know?"

"He saved my baby and I don't even know his name." Max started pacing again.

For a long time nothing new happened. By four they had finished the pint of scotch and Max, gray and short of breath, was still pacing the small room.

He stopped for a moment. "You know we haven't decided on a name yet. Sharon keeps saying it's going to be a girl and inventing girl's names and she gets mad at me if I think

of a boy's name. I like Bartholomew. It's an old Jewish name."
He looked questioningly at Dan.

"When he gets to school they'll call him Bart the fart."

"I've got to name him with a B for my father." He sat down.
"Listen. I want you to tell me about my operation."

"I keep explaining it over and over again."

"Tell me again."

"They have to open up the heart," Dan said uneasily.

"Start from the beginning."

"They give you an anesthetic."

"The whole thing. Don't leave anything out."

"They start with a by-pass. They expose—"

"Tell it to me so I can understand."

Dan sighed. "They cut in the leg and they expose the big
artery and the vein and then they connect a machine to the
vein that draws the blood out. The blood is mixed with oxygen
and pumped back into the artery."

"Remarkable. Go ahead."

"Then they expose the heart and correct the defect."

"You're skipping," Max said. "Tell me exactly."

"They cut into the chest and they expose the heart and
then they operate on it."

"How?"

"They stop it first."

Max cracked his knuckles. "That's enough," he said. He got
up and started pacing again.

They heard the footsteps coming down the hall and Max
looked out the door. "He's coming now," he said breathlessly.
Dan stood up and the obstetrician walked in. "You're Wolfe,
aren't you?"

Max nodded.

"It's a boy," he said. "Everything went fine. He weighs
seven pounds six ounces. Your wife's in good shape."

Max took the doctor's hand in both of his own.

"Everything went all right?" Dan said.

The doctor was trying to get his hand away from Max.
"The usual primipara delivery," he said.

"The baby's breathing all right?"

The doctor tried to free his hand again. "No problem," he said. "We didn't give the mother much sedation and we got a wide-awake baby."

"Thanks," Dan said.

"You can see her if you want to."

"Let go of him," Dan said.

Max let go and the doctor walked out.

Tears were running down Max's cheeks and hanging in droplets from his mustache. He suddenly kissed Dan wetly on his cheek. "It's a boy," he said. "It's a boy and I'm still alive. I'll make the *briss* too."

Sharon lay asleep, still under the anesthetic. They did catch a glimpse of the nurse bathing a small, bright red baby and Max was delighted. He talked constantly all the way home. "You'll stop in and have a drink. I've got some real good French brandy."

When they got in the apartment he started looking for the brandy in the cupboards, but before he found it he sat down. He closed his eyes, his head fell back, and in a few seconds he was snoring, his face suddenly empty.

Dan pulled the slippers off his feet, which were badly swollen. He got a pillow from the bed, and put it on the couch, and pulled Max down so that he lay on it. He went out, carefully locking the door, remembering Sharon's fur.

Max called him at school about noon. "I'm in the hospital too," he said.

"What do you mean?"

"I woke up sick after you left. I couldn't breathe. I called Dr. Finch and he sent an ambulance for me. You better hire a pharmacist for the store."

"How long is he going to keep you?"

"He says I can't wait any more."

After a while Dan said, "You'll be out in two weeks."

"From your mouth to God's ears," Max said. "Put an ad in the paper. Hire a pharmacist."

After school Dan went directly to Cedars of Lebanon Hospital. Max was pale and his lips were purple. "It was a terrible attack. I thought I was going to die."

"You look fine," Dan said, sitting down.

"Really?" Max got out of bed and looked at himself in the mirror. "Maybe a little tired," he said. "Did you put the ad in?"

"I called it in from school."

"Don't be choosy. Hire anybody so long as he's honest." He went back to bed. "Did you see the baby?"

"Not yet."

"I made them wheel me up. He's red-headed."

"They turn brunette after a while."

"I've got two hundred dollars in cash in a bag in the B pull drawer. Better deposit it." After a moment he said, "It's a shame you and Sharon don't get along better. She thinks a lot of you. Why do you always fight with her?"

Dan didn't say anything.

"You be nice to her. I don't care what she says. Do you hear?"

"Sure."

"Everybody's got some kind of craziness. You have plenty of your own." He lay back. "Go bring her something even if it's only a fifteen-cent get-well card. Then you better go to the store and hire a pharmacist." He waved good-bye to Dan.

Dan brought Sharon some flowers, and visited with her briefly. He then went to open the store. He worried what would happen if no one answered his ad, but the next evening a small elderly man named Tompkins came to the store.

"I came out here to retire," he said with a Midwestern accent, "but I can't make ends meet and I have to fill in with part-time work." Dan agreed to pay him union scale. He would have to let the store eat up its inventory until Max was able to work again.

After this Dan had extra work, checking stock and keeping a running inventory. He started getting home later at night. Joan usually waited for him, and would quietly start drinking after he got home. He said nothing. He was relieved she didn't drink when she was alone with Turk.

Dan went to the hospital early on the morning of Max's operation. No one else was there. Sharon lay in bed at home six days after the delivery. Max's mother was an old woman who had had several strokes and lived in a rest home on Pico Boulevard.

Dan went up to the surgical floor and put on the hospital cap and gown. A baldheaded anesthetist was adjusting a drip that ran into Max's arm. Dan explained who he was, and the anesthetist said, "Don't look so worried. This is the third open heart this week."

"The other two all right?"

"Sure." He looked at the chart. "Kielguld's doing this one. They don't come any better."

By then Max was well under the anesthetic and was breathing deeply and slowly. Dr. Finch came in, also in surgical pants, and took Max's pulse and listened to his heart.

An orderly wheeled Max into the operating room. The anesthetist connected the electrocardiographic leads and on a large oscilloscopic screen Dan saw a little glowing ball of light that wrote waves and left a slowly fading fluorescent line behind it.

"A few irregularities," Finch said, looking at the screen. "They'll disappear when the anesthetic gets deeper."

The surgeon and his assistant came in, gloved hands covered with towels, and stepped cautiously around the table. The nurses arranged the sheets over Max's chest.

Two men and a woman, smocked and capped, pushed a sizable, square apparatus into the room. One of the men was older and was probably, Dan thought, a physician.

"Morning," Finch said.

"Hello Fred," the surgeon said. "He looked pretty good last night when I saw him. How is he this morning?"

"A few extra systoles."

"I have a few myself this morning," the surgeon said. "I

was working until about one last night and decided to eat
a pizza on the way home and I haven't felt the same since."

"I think he's ready," the anesthetist said.

The surgeon looked over his shoulder at Finch. "Are you
going to be able to stay?"

"I've canceled everything out."

"I always feel more secure with you watching those waves
up there," the surgeon said. "Let's get the pump in." He
picked up the scalpel and made an incision into Max's thigh.
Dan walked out of the room through the double door and
phoned Sharon. "I didn't want you to worry," he said. "They're
just getting started."

"I thought maybe they'd be done already. It's nine o'clock,"
she said.

"Take it easy. Nobody dies of an operation these days. They
have an artificial heart in there as big as a Volkswagen and a
doctor and two technicians to run it."

He went back into the operating room and watched. The
surgeon had found the vessels in the leg and had put tubes
into them. He stood aside while the nurses exposed Max's
antiseptic, stained, and shaven chest. Then the surgeon chose
a fresh scalpel. He kept changing instruments, cutting deeper,
his assistant wiping the blood away and clamping hemostats.
The anesthetist sat at the head of the table, isolated by a fold
of sheet hung on a curved steel guard. He watched the flow
of liquid in the drip and from time to time wrote notes in
a chart. Finch stood behind the surgeon, sometimes watching
what they were doing and sometimes watching the dancing
point of light on the fluorescent screen. He seemed nervous
and under his mask Dan could see him lick his lips every
so often.

The surgeon opened the chest and Dan saw the heart clasp
and unclasp. "Not bad," the surgeon said, looking at the clock.
He started working more slowly and with greater care, and
put two more tubes into the great vessels. He fitted the tubes
into the connections on the machine, and then unloosened the
ties and said, "Let it go." One of the technicians at the machine

turned a switch and the blood passed through a translucent section of tubing. "We're going right down to twenty degrees," the surgeon said. "Call the temperature every couple of minutes."

"Thirty-seven degrees," the technician at the machine said.

Dan suddenly felt sweaty. He thought it came from standing too long in one place and he walked out of the operating room and leaned against the wall outside. Later he called Sharon again. "It's going fine. Everything's connected beautifully. They're beginning to take his temperature down."

"How low do they take it?"

"Twenty degrees."

"Twenty? That's below freezing."

"No, no," he said quickly. "It's centigrade." He didn't want to tell her about stopping the heart so he said, "It's a lot easier on the system that way."

He went back into the operating room. The technician at the machine said, "Thirty-two degrees."

"Dropping a little fast isn't it?" Finch said nervously.

"Oh, I don't think so," the surgeon said.

Finch sighed. "Ever see one of these before?" he said to Dan.

"No."

"When it hits twenty-six degrees the heart generally starts fibrillating. It doesn't stop completely until about twenty-two or twenty degrees or so." He looked at the fluorescent screen. Dan did too. The waves were changed. They were broader and slower.

"He's got some sort of a heart block," Dan said suddenly.

"They all get it. Everything is going fine."

"Twenty-seven degrees," the technician said.

The surgeon looked at the anesthetist. "How is he doing?"

"Pretty good," the anesthetist said. "Pressure is a little low."

"Want some more blood?"

"Probably a good idea."

One of the technicians went out and came back with the bottle of blood and attached it to the pump.

"There it goes," Finch said tightly. They all looked at the screen. The point of light was moving irregularly in a jagged uneasy line.

"Fibrillating," the surgeon said. "What's the temperature?"

"Twenty-four degrees," the technician said.

"The by-pass is working fine," the surgeon said. "Set up your pumping volume."

The technician turned a dial and the pitch of the machine changed.

"Just twitching a little," the surgeon said. "We ought to be able to start working any minute." He picked up a scalpel and waited.

"Twenty-two degrees," the technician said.

The light on the screen was perfectly straight. Finch was leaning against the wall studying his shoes. The surgeon was working intently, his hands inside the chest. The assistant, holding several retractors, was looking off into space.

From time to time the technician called the temperature. It was generally about twenty degrees.

"All done here," the surgeon finally said. He dropped his instruments into a tray and turned around and washed his gloves in a basin. "Better start warming him."

Dan went out and called Sharon. "It's all over. He did a fine job. He repaired the valves."

He heard her crying.

"They're starting to warm him up."

"How cold is he?"

"Pretty cold. I'll call you back. Don't worry."

He sat down on a bench in the hall and took his cap off and wiped his face with it. For a while he watched the orderlies wheeling patients through the hall. Then he got up and went back into the operating room.

The line on the screen was straight. Finch was still studying his shoes.

"How's it going?" he said.

"I'd like to see some activity on that oscilloscope," Finch said.

"Twenty-eight degrees," the technician said.

Finch walked to the operating table. "Maybe there's a bad connection."

The surgeon watched the heart carefully. "Motionless," he said.

The anesthetist suddenly stood up, arched his back, and then sat down again.

"I guess we better try a few shocks," Finch said.

"Give it a few more degrees," the surgeon said. He waited until the temperature was thirty degrees and then he said, "Let me have a pacemaker set."

The technician was ready with it. The new machine was wheeled in and the surgeon connected the electrodes. He stepped back and said, "All right." The technician flipped a switch and the fluorescent line jumped a little.

"Step up the voltage," the surgeon said.

She made the adjustment and the point of light jumped again.

"What's it doing?" the anesthetist said from behind his barrier.

"Just an ineffectual twitch," Finch said.

The men stood around quietly, watching, and rhythmically the small point of light jumped. Dan could not see the heart. He started to sweat again. He walked to the head of the table. The anesthetist was busy writing notes on his chart.

"Thirty-four degrees," the technician said.

"You don't have to call it any more," the surgeon said.

They waited. Then the surgeon picked up a fine scissors from the tray. "Stop that pacemaker. I'm going to open again." The assistant nodded and they started working again.

Finch went back to the wall. The doctor at the machine and his two technicians watched the dials and made notes of the readings. The anesthetist sat hunched up and silent.

"I was afraid I had caught one of the coronary arteries in my sutures," the surgeon said. "But they look fine to me."

"Valves are all patent," the assistant said.

The surgeon started sewing back what he had just opened.

The pacemaker was connected again, but Dan thought it produced even a lesser movement of the luminescent point.

"How long now?" the surgeon said.

The anesthetist looked at the wall clock. "Three hours."

"Turn off this gadget. It's not doing anything." He lifted the electrode away and reached in and closed his hand firmly on the heart. The luminescent point moved in a wide curve.

"We'll see what we can do this way," the surgeon said. He too watched the screen and regularly closed his fist firmly and held and let go and waited, and then closed it again. After about ten minutes, his assistant said, "Better let me spell you awhile."

"Warm water," the surgeon said. The nurse brought a basin of water and he let his hand rest in it a few moments. Then he took over from the assistant.

The anesthetist got up and walked to the door and back and then sat down again. "It's four hours," he said. "I guess that's it."

"Not yet it isn't," the surgeon said. "Let me have some Adrenalin." He made the injection and he resumed the compression of the heart. After a while Finch sat down on a stool. Dan stood beside him. "It's four hours," Finch said. He looked at the clock. "More than four hours."

"What does that mean?"

"They don't start up again after four hours."

"He's still alive isn't he?"

"Technically. Where's his wife?"

"Just had a baby six days ago. Still in bed."

"How is it coming?" Finch asked the surgeon.

"Fingers ache," the surgeon said. "This lousy rheumatism of mine."

No one said anything for a long time.

"You want me to keep this respirator going?" the anesthetist asked suddenly.

"I'll tell you when to stop," the surgeon said. "If my fingers can take this so can your back."

The surgeon kept working, the machines making a gentle

noise. Dan stood dully, flat-footed, thinking, this is a punishment in some way. He wondered if the rest of them felt that way too.

At three o'clock the surgeon looked over his shoulder at Finch. "How long is it now?"

"Six hours."

He let go of the heart and washed his hands. "Go ahead and disconnect," he said to the assistant. He went out of the swinging doors.

"What's that?" Dan said.

"He was gone four hours ago," the anesthetist said. "We've been working on a dead man for four hours." He turned off his machine. The assistant was taking the tubes out of the vessels.

Dan walked into the operating-room door, striking his head. The blow made him dizzy. He rested a few moments in the hall and then went to the dressing room. The surgeon, his mask and cap off, was leaning against the sink. He was gray. When he saw Dan he dipped his hands into water and washed his face. Then he sat down on a bench and slowly started removing his white surgical shoes.

Max's funeral was the next day. Dan went by himself, since Joan had a psychiatrist's appointment at the same time. Eddie was among the mourners. He sat alone, his hat squarely on his head. Dan remembered telling him of Max's death over the phone. He sat down next to his father. The handful of people listened and the rabbi prayed. "Oh Lord, our God, who called down our father Abraham from the city of Ur of the Chaldees and made a covenant with him in the desert, hear while we pray over a son of Abraham, Max Wolfe."

Later in the same day the baby was circumcised. Dan came a few minutes early to speak to Sharon. "I want you to be the *zendick*," she said.

"It should be your father," Dan said.

Sharon started crying. "Max wanted you to be the *zendick*. He told me."

Dan waited. When the *mohel* said, "Who will be the pious man?" he stepped forward. The *mohel* took the baby from Sharon and handed him to Dan. Dan held him while the *mohel* prayed and made the cut.

When he got home he found Joan sober. "Oh Jesus, I don't want to have to go through that again," he said.

"What did they name the baby?"

"Max. It's a tribal mutilation. I got scared that the circumcision wouldn't stop bleeding. It's a hell of a way to do a surgical procedure."

"Did it?"

"What?"

"Stop bleeding."

"Sure, but I sweated for five minutes until it did."

"Danny you look terrible. You're going to get sick." After a moment she said, "What went wrong with Max's operation?"

"The heart didn't start up."

"Why not?"

"I don't know," he said. "It happens."

"I didn't drink last night."

"Feel better?"

"No. I started to shake. How bad was it with Max?"

"Pretty bad. I don't know how Sharon will make out. She's going to have to borrow to pay the hospital bills."

"How about her father?"

"He's living on old-age security."

"Danny?"

"Look at me. I'm trying to talk to you."

"I know you are." He looked at her. She was sad and chastened and her hands trembled. She got up and took the bottle of cologne down from the cupboard and emptied it into the sink. "All right?"

"Yes," he said. Then, "Make some dinner. I'll get Turk."

He picked the boy up at school. Later they had dinner, and afterward he studied from the obstetrics text. A test was scheduled for the next day.

Nine

THE WEATHER was warm again. The hillside cactuses were growing soft leaves and the lawn grass had turned green. On most days breezes swept the smog from the valley and one could see not only the Santa Monica hills, which are in the city, but beyond them the sharp, tall San Gabriel Mountains that kept the desert out.

Although Dan didn't speak of it often, Max's death had hurt him badly. Partly to distract himself from his dejection and partly from need he worked unusually hard in the store. He spent a good deal of time going over the scanty store records. Finally he called Eddie. Eddie came one evening and sat down on one of the fountain stools and watched the customers and what they bought. Then he took the bills and the cash register tapes that Dan had prepared and studied them, adding figures on the back of an envelope. Then he said, "The way I figure it if you tore out the fountain and left a hole there you'd be fifty dollars ahead each month. The cosmetic counter is a good idea. Can you sell thirty dollars worth of cosmetics a day?"

Dan thought. "Easy," he said. "More if we push them."

"An inexpensive line from the look of your customers. You need a fifty per cent markup." He looked over the fountain. "You ought to be able to get away with two thousand for the counters and displays. Spend three thousand. Fancy it up. Hidden lighting. All glass shelves. It'll give the store a little class. It needs it."

Dan thought about it for several days. Then he went to the bank where Max had the drugstore account and spoke to the loan officer. Then he went to see Sharon. It was the middle of the day but she opened the door wearing a nightgown. He was startled at how thin she was. Her gown hung loosely and her face was dark and drawn.

He walked by her into the bedroom. The baby, two weeks old, kicked in his crib. Dan lifted the corner of the diaper. "It's healing all right," he said. He turned. "How are you doing?"

"How do you think?"

"I brought some coffee cake." He went into the kitchen and turned on the coffee pot. Then he emptied the bag of sweet rolls onto a plate and set them on the table.

"I miss Max," she said. "I'm so lonely I can't stop crying."

He waited by the stove, and she said, "Why don't you say something?"

"What the hell can I say about dying?" he said savagely.

"What should I do? I hurt all the time."

"Wash your face."

She washed her face in the kitchen sink.

"You're a human being. Your husband died. It has to hurt," he said.

She started crying again.

"I came to talk to you about the store," he said.

"My father says I ought to sell it."

"The store is run-down. The stock is low. You won't get much now."

She wiped her nose. "I don't know," she finally said.

"I can borrow four thousand dollars from the bank, but I'll have to pay four points—"

"What's points?"

"Never mind," he said. "Anyway I want to close the fountain and let the fountain girl go." He told her his plans. "The rest of the money I'll put into the prescription stock. Then I'll go up and visit all the doctors around here."

She felt inside her mouth. "Two fillings came out. Yesterday somebody told me that breast-feeding the baby draws the calcium out of your teeth. Should I take calcium pills?"

"Drink plenty of milk. The school year ends pretty soon. Then I'll let the pharmacist go for the summer and run the store by myself. I figure if we can make some money on the cosmetics you'll be able to draw a few hundred a month. Then if I can build up the prescription business we'll start paying on the loan."

"All right," she said.

He stood up.

"Where are you going?"

"I want to get to the bank before it closes."

He brought her the papers a few days later and she signed them. He got the name of a contractor from Eddie. The contractor came in one afternoon with a crew of men and tore the entire fountain out. A few days later he came back with the same crew and set in a series of bright, new glass cases. Dan put in his orders and filled the cases with the colorful bottles and jars that women are so fond of. He still had a thousand dollars left over, and he spent it replenishing the depleted stock and filling the prescription room with new drugs.

The third year of school ended, leaving only one last year. Dan gave the summer wholeheartedly to the store. During the afternoons he visited the physicians practicing in the neighborhood, trying to persuade them to refer their prescription patients to the store. He cleaned and swept and sold stock and filled prescriptions and at night he often made deliveries.

Business increased promptly. Just before Max died, the store was taking in two hundred dollars a day. By July it was doing at least three hundred a day and sometimes more. And best of all the increase was largely in prescriptions, where the profit percentage was often several hundred per cent, and in cosmetics where it was about fifty per cent. He was able to give Sharon three hundred a month and he paid another five hundred each month on the bank loan. Sharon trusted him just as

Max had, although once, for no reason he knew, she decided to have her brother-in-law check the books. He was a bald-headed man in the shoe business who came in and examined the register tapes, the checkbook, and the bills, and ended up by taking a dozen cartons of cigarettes without paying for them. Actually Dan paid himself his full wages only one of the three months of the summer, the month of August. In June he paid himself $3.50 an hour and in July $3.75 an hour. Even so, he was able to pay Eddie back all the money he had borrowed for the trip to Wallace.

In the middle of August Joan's psychiatrist went on vacation and her drinking became worse. Dan worried about Turk, who was out of school and spent all day with her. One afternoon when he failed to get an answer to his calls he closed the store and drove home. The air in the apartment was almost unbreathable with gas. An empty pot lay on the kitchen floor and an unlit burner was on. He turned it off and opened the window. Turk was playing with an electric automobile. "It smells bad here," he said. "My head hurts."

Joan was too drunk to be awakened, and he took Turk back to the store. They both ate pork and beans heated in the hot chocolate cup that Dan had rescued from the destruction of the fountain. Later when it got dark Dan put the boy to bed in the prescription room.

Sharon came in about ten o'clock and when she saw the sleeping boy she said, "What's the matter with you?"

"There's no place else."

"You're crazy," she shouted. "A little kid like this and you put him to sleep on Kotex cases. I'll take him home tonight and you can pick him up at my house."

"That's a good idea."

"What time does she start?"

"Pretty early today."

"Bring him to the store and I'll take him home with me every night."

Joan was still asleep when Dan got home. Early the next day he enrolled Turk at a private summer school.

Joan called him in the morning. "Is Turk at the store with you?"

"He's at school. I'll bring him home with me."

"You put him in school without asking me?" She sounded angry. "I am his mother."

"You were drunk yesterday. Who the hell could ask you anything?"

"Drunk? With Turk here?"

"Don't you remember?" He told her about the gas.

"Oh God," she said. Then, "I didn't think I could do anything like that."

Thereafter she started drinking in the morning. She no longer went to work. The apartment, which she had always kept tidy, grew disorderly. At night, after Dan put Turk to bed, he would pile the dirty laundry into his car and drive it to a coin-operated laundromat and put the clothes in the machine while he sat nodding sleepily. In the mornings he fed the boy and took him off to school. He was always careful that Turk was never alone in the care of his mother.

Ten

THE FIRST OF SEPTEMBER Dan borrowed back from Eddie most of the money he had repaid during the summer. The girl with the glasses was no longer in the school office and he gave his check to another secretary. In return she gave him the list and he bought a dozen heavy and expensive books at the bookstore.

The night before Yom Kippur eve he stopped at Sharon's apartment. She was in a rage. "You have to put that boy in boarding school or send him back to his grandfather. I can't stay locked up in the house—"

"What started all this?"

"I'm tired of being taken advantage of."

"It was your idea."

"Have you said thanks once? Have you bought me anything to show your appreciation?"

Dan yawned. "Day after tomorrow is Yom Kippur."

"You don't listen to anything I say, do you?"

"How's the baby?"

"He's starting to teethe. Just like me. I started to teethe early. When I was six months old I had a full mouth of teeth and the doctor said he had never seen anything like it before. Perfect teeth too. Everybody in my family—"

"I think you could start working at the store now."

"Working?" she screamed at him. "How am I going to work and take care of Turk and the baby? I'm only one person. I've only got two arms and two legs. What do you want me to do? Be in six places at once?"

"This Sol Tompkins is all right. He's an honest pharmacist. But the cosmetics don't move when he's there. I don't think he knows anything about them and he doesn't like to sell them. The baby's asleep in the afternoon, isn't he?"

"I take a nap every day. I'm run down. I'm just going on nervous energy. After all I've been through—"

"Get your mother to come down and stay with the baby. Come in every day about noon and stay until it's just about time for Turk to come home from school. Start taking care of the cosmetics and see that they move."

She glared at him. "Anything else?"

"You want to make Yom Kippur dinner?"

"Who for?"

"Me and Turk."

"I was supposed to go to my father's."

"Stay home. Make a good dinner. Do you know how?"

"You're something else," she said.

"The bills for the cosmetics are in a folder in the prescription-room drawer. Read them over tomorrow. You should know the items we make the most money on."

He went into the bedroom and picked Turk up and carried him out.

"Do you like beef and noodles?" she said.

"Any old thing."

"What time do you want to eat?"

"After sundown."

"My mother used to make the food the day before, and then she'd put it away in the refrigerator, and then—"

"That's the right way to do it," he said and nodded and went out.

The next day, while it was still light, he closed the store. He took Turk to Hoagy's for dinner. Afterward he gave the boy two dollars in change. "Tomorrow you'll get hungry. You may want to buy something," he said.

Joan was asleep when they got home. They went to bed promptly, and in the morning they both bathed and Dan shaved. Then he put on his hat and they started the long walk to Fairfax Avenue. They walked slowly, stopped to look in store windows, or to rest on bus-station benches. When they got to the park it was already fairly late in the morning and most of the old men were there.

"Go and play," Dan said. "Don't go out of the park. If you get hungry buy a sandwich." He showed him where.

The boy ran off and Dan sat down on the bench and waited. Later the baldheaded man from the last year came with two boys. "My nephew from Newark," he said and sat down.

The prayer leader was missing. When the synagogue doors closed Dan turned to one of the old men and said, "Where's Mr. Barenholtz?"

"I hear he's got a bad heart," the old man said.

"Did he have an attack?"

"Maybe. Who knows?"

Dan looked around. "Who else can say the prayers?"

"Not me," the baldheaded man said. "I can't even talk Yiddish."

"Can any of you?"

Several of the old men shook their heads. One of them said, "I have cataracts. Even with glasses I can't tell the difference between an alef and a yod."

The baldheaded man started to get up and Dan said quickly, "Wait a minute. All I need is a book."

He walked across the street to the synagogue. It was the same usher as the year before. He saw Dan coming and hurried out to meet him on the stairs. "Please no commotion," he said. "The services have started."

"I need a prayer book."

"Wait here. Don't go in. I'll bring it out."

Dan waited for the book. He carried it across the street and sat down and said in Yiddish the formula, "It's Yom Kippur and there are ten Jews."

At first he stumbled over the square letters he hadn't read since he was a child. After a while he remembered better and read more fluently, pausing every so often to watch Turk, making sure the boy didn't leave the park or run into the street.

Eleven

BY THEN, Joan knew the days only dimly. When she awakened in the morning she tried not to look at her body. The bruises frightened her. Later, after the diarrhea and cramps subsided, she would drink some coffee and then, still shaking, she would drive to the psychiatrist's office in Beverly Hills. She was comfortable there in the dark and she felt as though she had come home. He would sit behind her and she would talk and tell him how much things hurt. It was bad though when the hour was finished. When she came out of the dim office into the street the light struck her across the face and her vision danced so badly that it was hard for her to keep from stumbling. She would hurry back to the apartment, driving as quickly as she dared, and find the vodka she had put away.

By late morning she was comfortable again, and by mid-afternoon she dozed peacefully, and if she fell and bumped herself she didn't feel it.

She knew vaguely that the school year had started again and that Dan was back at school. Sometimes she pretended Turk was at home and she talked to him. Other times she pretended he was as a small baby and she held him and fed him. She talked to her mother and her father, and sometimes to Dan. She was confused about Dan. He had two different natures. When she spoke to him during the day he was understanding and gentle and loving, but at night when he came home he was angry with her and often didn't speak to her at all. She couldn't decide which one was in her mind and which one was real.

She first talked to her psychiatrist of killing herself sometime in September. It popped out while she was lying on the couch. "I wish I were dead," she said. "I think it would be a good idea." It didn't seem to startle him, and she repeated it. "I wish I were dead."

He said, "What does death mean to you?"

She thought about it. "Being buried. Like my sister. Like my mother."

He didn't say anything and she sighed. "I think I could do something to myself again if I wanted to. It's not much different than drinking. I'm not really afraid."

"Are you planning to do anything?"

"I don't know. It just occurred to me."

"Death is the great castration. It's the final destruction. The final act of contempt and anger."

He often spoke that way. Sometimes she didn't know exactly what he meant.

She scratched her nose. "I could go to sleep and sleep forever right here."

"That's what you really want to do, isn't it? Do something to yourself so you can sleep comfortably forever and not be troubled?"

"Yes," she said after a while. "That's just the way I feel."

They went on to other things, but at the end of the session, when she sat up to leave, he said, "I have to take a threat of suicide seriously. I want you to answer me honestly. Is it really in your mind?"

She realized then that she had frightened him. And she knew why. It would be his failure if she killed herself. All psychiatrists must be afraid of that. It would be like a surgeon having a patient die on the operating table. Like Max did. "I don't know," she said. "I'm just supposed to say what pops into my head."

"If your thoughts are at all serious it may be necessary to in-

stitutionalize you for a while. I am going to have to rely on you
to tell me the truth."

She didn't want to go into an institution. She said, "It was
just a thought that went through my head. I don't suppose
it means any more than the other crazy thoughts that go
through my head. I think about it once in a while." She went
out of his office feeling triumphant.

She went directly home. She pulled the shades down and
took a drink, enjoying the biting burn of the alcohol. Then she
set about looking for the pills she had taken from the store.
She found them in an aspirin bottle on the top shelf in the
kitchen. She poured them out. She found seventy the first time
she counted and sixty-eight the second time. She got her oil
paints and painted the aspirin bottle black. Then she put it
back on the shelf, handling it carefully so as not to smear the
paint.

A few days later she spoke to him again about dying. He
didn't seem to worry this time. She became angry, but she refused to tell him what she was angry about. If he really understood her, as he pretended, he would know.

She came home out of the bright sunshine and drank some
vodka and vomited. She smoked a cigarette and afterward drank
some more. The doorbell rang. She lay down in bed and ignored
it but it kept ringing. Then she heard Turk's voice outside. She
got up and opened the door and he came in carrying his school-
books. She was surprised. Turk usually went someplace to
school and didn't come home until Dan did.

"Hello, son. How are you doing?" she boomed.

"The nurse sent me home from school. I've got a fever," he
said.

"It must be lunchtime," she said. "I'll make you some eggs."
She got up and managed to get into the kitchen, but then she
fell asleep. She awoke and found the kitchen full of smoke and
the eggs black. She turned off the gas and opened the window.
She started scratching the burnt egg out of the pan. After a
while she remembered Turk. She thought he was playing a
game with her and she looked under the beds and into the

closets. She called Dan at the school. "I can't find Turk. He's hiding on me," she said.

"I don't understand what you're saying," he said.

"Where is Turk?"

"Turk?"

"That's right," she said speaking very slowly. "He's gone. I looked under the beds and in the closets and no Turk."

"Goldie's taking care of him," Dan said. "I called him up and asked him to get him."

"Who?"

"They called me from school and told me he was sent home sick. I called up Goldie and asked him to get him and put him to bed until I get home."

"I can't find Turk," she said again.

"Never mind," he said angrily. "You can finish your bottle." He hung up.

She called him back. "Where is Turk?"

"He's staying with Goldie," he said. "He's sick."

This time she understood. "I've got to make him lunch," she said. "I'll go get him."

"He's sick. Just leave him alone. I'll get home as soon as I can."

"If he's sick I'll take care of him," she said. She started to go out and then realized she was in her underpants. She put on a pair of capris, went downstairs, and knocked on Goldie's door. He opened it.

"I want to make Turk some lunch," she said.

Goldie didn't understand her either. "He's sick," he said. "Dan asked me to take care of him. I'm giving him some hot soup."

"I don't want you taking care of him," she said. She tried to push past him but he stood in the center of the doorway.

"Dan said for me to take care of him."

"Get out of my way, you faggot," she said, pushing hard.

"You should be ashamed of yourself," he screamed. "So drunk you can't even take care of your child. Other people have to take care of him for you." He slammed the door in her face. She stood open-mouthed, trying to decide what to do next. She tried kicking at the door, but she was barefooted and the wood hurt. She banged on it with her fist. Goldie opened it again. "Get away," he screamed. "I've got good friends in the police force. I can send you to the drunk tank where you belong." He slammed the door again.

She went back upstairs and phoned Dan again at the hospital. It was hard to make the operator understand who she wanted. She finally got a nurse who said, "Wait a minute," and then came back and said, "He said to take a message. He's with a patient." She dialed another familiar number. "Dr. Akenside's office," a strange voice said. It was the telephone exchange.

"I want to talk to the doctor," she said slowly.

"Excuse me? What was that?"

"The doctor. Dr. Akenside."

"What is your name, please?"

"It's an emergency."

"An emergency?"

"Yes. Emergency. I need to speak to him right now."

"What number are you calling from?"

"Listen," she said to the operator. "My little boy is sick. I can't get to him. They have him downstairs. I don't know what to do."

"I can't understand you," the operator said. "Would you speak more distinctly?"

"I have to talk to Dr. Akenside," she said, separating the syllables.

"He's between locations," the operator said. "If you leave your number I'll have him call you."

She gave her number and then waited for him to call, restlessly walking from room to room, bumping against doors and tables. She snatched the receiver up on the first ring. "Hello?"

"Doctor Akenside," he said.

"This is Joan," she said. "I'm so relieved I reached you."

"What?"

"I want to talk to you." She spoke very slowly again.

"You sound like you've had a little too much to drink."

"I'm frightened."

"What?"

"Frightened," she shouted.

"About what?"

"They took my little boy away. I don't know what happened to him."

She heard a woman's voice laughing in the background and the psychiatrist said, "Just a moment." He must have put his hand over the mouthpiece, because then she didn't hear anything for a while. When he came back he said, "You're in a panic state again. We've talked about this many times. If you'll only remember the mechanisms it'll go away."

"Who's laughing?" she said.

"What?"

"I'm frightened," she said again.

"I'm with a patient. I can't talk very well now."

"I'm sorry," she said.

"We'll talk at your visit tomorrow," he said and hung up.

She sat still, thinking of mechanisms a while, but it didn't help. Then she decided to go to church. She hadn't been there for a long time. She drank some coffee and put on a dress. She drove very carefully. She didn't want the police to stop her again. The church lot was almost full, and when she got inside she saw that mass was going on. She puzzled over that. She didn't think it was Sunday. It probably was a holy day. She fell in the church aisle and a man helped her up. "I caught my heel," she said.

"Are you all right, miss?"

"Fine," she said. "Thank you very much."

She followed an usher to one of the pews. She sat down and pulled her dress over her abraded knees. The kneeling bench was folded away and she tried to open it. The boy next to her had his feet propped up against it.

"Do you mind?" she asked.

"Sorry," the boy said and took his feet away.

She knelt, her abraded knees hurting her exquisitely. When she raised her head she saw the people coming up the aisle to take communion. She rose and managed to get up to the rail. She knelt again, but when the priest came by he didn't offer her the wafer. "He's right," she said to the woman next to her. "I'm not in a state of grace. I don't know how he knew."

She got up. The usher came up and took her arm again. "Would you like to sit down?"

"I want to go to confession. Where's the rectory?"

He helped her to a door, and then opened it. "The priest is at Mass now but I'll tell him you're waiting," he said. She sat down in the chair and fell asleep. When she awakened she felt sick and wasn't sure where she was. She opened the door into the church but it was empty.

She drove back home and got into bed and felt better. Later she got up for some more vodka and she saw the black bottle. She took it down from the shelf and poured the pills into a red mound. She could swallow them anytime she wanted and down would come the big buildings and the streets and all the ships at sea.

She walked around the apartment and then stopped in front of the pills and swallowed three of them without water, gulping them down on saliva.

She sat down at the table to write a note. She saw the letters double. She closed one eye and printed, *You will be better off without me. Dear Dan, I want you to marry someone else, a fine girl, who will take care of you and Turk.* She wanted to write something for her psychiatrist. Last week she was lying on the couch and she had thought of something good to say. She had said, "I know veterinarians who have more feeling for their patients than you do." She had relished it all day. She would like to think of something else like that, but nothing occurred to her. She printed, *I know you did the best you could for me. I don't blame you for anything.*

The last time she took pills she swallowed water after every two or three, and she threw up before she was done. That's probably why she didn't die. She went back to the sink and threw a handful of pills into her mouth. Holding them tight with her tongue she filled up half a glass of vodka and tried to wash them down. Some of the pills went down, but the rest stuck to the roof of her mouth. She worked them free with her tongue. Then she filled her mouth with the rest of the pills, and drank one glass of water and they washed down. She went back to the table and tried to think of something else to write on the note, but then, all of a sudden, she remembered the undertakers' parlor and and the terrible wounds they make in the neck and stomach when they pump in formaldehyde. That's what they had done to her sister. She crawled to the phone and, holding one eye shut so she wouldn't see double, she dialed the hospital number. The number kept ringing and the operator didn't answer. She couldn't wait any longer. She hung up the phone quickly and then she dialed O. "Give me the police," she said.

In a few minutes a man's voice came on.

"My little boy died," she said. "And I took a lot of sleeping pills. Seventy of them."

"I can't understand you," the man said.

"Sleeping pills," she shouted. "Seventy."

"Speak more distinctly. I can't understand you. Did you say pills?"

"Sleeping pills. Sleeping pills," she shouted. "Red ones."

"Did you take them?"

"All of them. My little boy is dying and—"

"What's your name?"

"Joanie," she said.

"Joan E. what?" He kept asking questions and she kept trying to answer them, but he couldn't understand anything she said. She was getting very sleepy and she thought she ought to throw up the pills. Maybe if she drank some warm water and tickled the back of her throat she would vomit. She hung the phone up and tried to stand up. She had no idea where her feet were and instead of standing she rolled against the dust-smelling thin carpet. She was cold and she felt terrible. The room was turning and twisting and she retched without bringing anything up.

When Dan got home he went directly to Goldie's apartment. Turk had a little fever and a runny nose. He watched with delight as Dan listened to his lungs and thumped him on the chest. He put the stethoscope on his own ears and gravely and wonderingly listened to his heart.

"I don't even think you need any medicine," Dan said.

Turk opened his mouth and put his tongue out. "Look."

"It looks fine."

"I just wanted to make sure."

Dan grinned. He turned to Goldie. "Seen Joan?"

Goldie led him away from the boy. "Was she ever juiced! She couldn't even talk."

"What's she doing now?"

"Sleeping it off on the floor."

"On the floor?"

"I heard a thump and thought maybe she had broken a leg or something. She could, you know. So I went upstairs to look, and she was fast asleep on the floor."

Dan ran up the stairs. She had been dead at least an hour. Her hands and her face were cold.

He went back outside and sat down on the steps. The drummer and his wife came up and pushed by him in annoyance. After a while he went back into the room and lifted her up and put her on the bed, and called his father and then the police.

Later, after the police had left and after the mortician had taken Joan's body, Dan remained alone with Eddie. Eddie got up and went into the bathroom and came back with a wet towel. He handed it to Dan. "Wipe your face."

Dan wiped his face. "I didn't know I was crying," he said.

Eddie lit a cigarette and looked at him. "What happened to her? Why did she do it?"

"Who the hell knows?" He passed his hand over his face.

"Who knows why they do things." He didn't know whether he was speaking about Joan or Goldie or Jesse Davis. "They don't make sense."

He was crying again and Eddie looked out of the window and said, "You ought to move out of here." Later he said, "Is this what happened with your mother?"

"I didn't know until now, but I guess so." He wiped his face again.

"Let's get the kid and buy him some dinner."

"Yes," Dan said.

"Let's go then," Eddie said.

They walked downstairs. Turk was feeling better. His temperature was gone and all that was left was a runny nose.

For the first several weeks after Joan's death Dan was easily confused. His attention wandered during classes and sometimes when he meant to drive to the store he drove home instead. He broke into tears readily and scarcely spoke to anyone.

He tried hardest to conceal his despondency from Turk and most of the time succeeded. However, on a Wednesday, a week after Joan's death, he arose and was shaving when the morning sadness seized him strongly. His heart started to pound and he broke into a sweat. It was as bad as the start of the Berkeley attack.

Turk walked into the bathroom. "I'm hungry," he said.

After a while Dan said, "All right."

"Make me some bacon."

"Go take a shower."

"I took one yesterday."

Dan didn't answer and Turk pulled off his pajamas and turned the shower on, tentatively feeling the temperature of the water. He got in and splashed about. When he got out he said, "Can I watch you shave?"

"I don't know," Dan said.

Turk started to put on the old underwear and Dan said, "There's clean stuff in your drawer."

The boy went out and came back in clean underwear and

sat down on the edge of the tub. "I always used to watch Grandpa Joe shave." When Dan did nothing he got up and went into the kitchen. "I'm hungry," he shouted from the kitchen and Dan put the razor down and went in and set some dry cereal and milk on the table. He looked at the clock. It was twenty to eight and he had only a few minutes to get the boy to school. Turk followed him into the bathroom. "I want to shave too," he said.

Dan turned away and pulled the blade down his cheek and washed it and pulled it down again. When he was finished he took the blade out and gave Turk the empty razor. Turk ran a great mound of shaving cream into his hand and smeared it on his face.

"Hurry up," Dan said, "we have to go."

He waited and he wondered if this was the way agonies ended—with the bitter realization that one can no longer afford them. If this was what Joan had failed to do. And Jesse Davis. And his mother. He put on some shaving lotion and he said, "Get dressed. Quit fooling around."

"Help me with my sweater," the boy said and he handed the sweater to Dan.

Twelve

JOAN'S AND MAX'S DEATHS had shaken Dan almost as much as the death of his mother. He went ahead and registered for the fourth year but when Noble insisted on a general admitting clinic he was reluctant. Finally, rather than work alone, he gave in, but he promptly found that his fears were well grounded. He dreaded death so badly he sweated and trembled when he spoke to a very ill patient.

On the third day of the service he walked into a cubicle and found a small boy crowing with croup. Dan lifted the blanket. The skin between the ribs was sucked in with each breath. "Just a moment," he said to the mother and went out into the hall and paced up and down trying to quiet himself. Finally he went to the cubicle where Noble was working. He sat tilted back in his chair, a pad of paper in his lap, leisurely taking a history from a stout colored woman.

"Let's trade patients," Dan said.

"I'm half done with this one. Besides it's an interesting case. Mrs. Walker's from Honduras and they have all sorts of weird diseases down there."

The fat woman smiled. "Kinds you never heard of here in the States," she said. "We got the dragging sickness and we got the elephant leg and we got the island sickness."

"Right now," Dan said. "The kid's real sick."

Noble caught the urgency in his voice. He handed Dan the pad. "I was just on the system inventory."

"In 17B," Dan said.

Noble took his stethoscope and left. The colored lady may have had some of the exotic diseases of Central America, but Dan could scarcely listen to her. After a few moments he put the pad away and went out again. He found Noble draping a sheet over the sick boy's crib. An electric steamer on the floor poured steam from the spout. "Just fixing up a croup tent until the intern gets here," he said. He inserted the spout under the sheet and the steam flowed into the crib.

"Just a minute," Dan said.

Noble followed him into the hall. "What's bugging you?"

"How's that kid?"

"He's got the croup."

"I was afraid he was going to choke to death right there, while I was watching him."

"You ought to take a sedative," Noble said.

The intern came down the hall. "What do you have?" he said.

"Croup in a kid of four," Noble said.

The intern listened to the boy's breathing. "Write him up for admission," he told Noble. "We'll keep him for tonight."

After he left Dan said, "Thanks. I think I can finish up."

Dan helped move the child to the overnight ward. There he set up a more durable croup tent. However he was miserable and frightened every moment he was with the sick child and he was relieved when the intern came back and he could escape.

It was enough. He didn't want any more of this kind of misery. He went directly to the school office and asked to be transferred to a different clinic. He studied the list of vacancies. The only service in which he would not have to deal with sick patients were surgical pathology or research. After a moment's thought he chose research.

The next morning after the lecture he took the elevator down to the basement. The research laboratories branched off one long hall. The hall smelled like a zoo. Dan peered into the rooms. Some held small wire cages in which there were guinea pigs or larger cages in which monkeys were kept. He went on to the last room, the largest on the floor. A middle-aged woman in a white laboratory apron looked up from a desk.

"I'm McDermott," he said. "I'm assigned here for a month."

"The school office called about you this morning. I'm Dr. Beaulieu's secretary." They shook hands. She looked at the clock. "He comes in about ten. I'm sure he'll want to talk over your assignment with you personally." She went back to her typing, and Dan was free to inspect the room. He stopped to examine a tall electron microscope. Some electron microscopes, he knew, cost more than a hundred thousand dollars.

A technician was injecting a milky fluid into a guinea pig's knee. Dan watched him. "What's that?" he asked.

The technician looked up. "Asbestos suspension," he said. "It causes an arthritis rather like the rheumatoid variety."

A physician in street clothes walked in. "Beaulieu," he said and held out his hand. They shook hands. Beaulieu sat down at a desk and took out a folder. "Had any experience in this field?"

"No."

"It's going to be different. No guess work. No fumbling around. You develop an idea. You test it. You prove whether it's right or wrong. Then you go on from there." He was a big middle-aged man with a gray mustache, and he had a careful and thoughtful way of talking. "On the wards sometimes you can't deal with the truth. Here all we want to know is the truth. Nothing else." He took a sheet out of the folder. "I don't want to waste you in a technical job like injecting guinea pigs or looking through microscopes. You're practically a doctor. I want you working with the effects of drugs on patients. See?"

"What kind of patients?"

Beaulieu looked up. "Patients with arthritis. That's our current project."

"That'll be all right," Dan said.

Beaulieu took a pill out of a drawer. "Looks like an aspirin, doesn't it? We call it S-14. It's been cleared by the FDA for use on human beings. We're going to use the double blind method. It's the best way of eliminating prejudice, and prejudice is our single biggest enemy." He waited a moment. "Do you know what a double blind control is?"

Dan didn't and Beaulieu explained. Dan was to dispense two types of pills, identical in appearance and identical in packaging. One of them would be a sugar pill, and one would be the drug. Neither Dan nor the patients nor the doctors in the arthritis clinic were to know which was which. He gave Dan a sheaf of blank data sheets. "Keep careful records. Later on we'll see whether this drug is any good or not. I come every morning. When you start running into problems—and you will—you simply ask me." He stood up. "I'm glad to have you along. I've checked your scholastic record and you're one of the best we've had around here for quite a while. We'll try to keep you interested."

After he left Dan took the large jar of pills of S-14 and the large jar of sugar pills and put them in vials, twenty-eight to a vial, labeling them only with the directions ONE FOUR TIMES A DAY. On one corner of the label he wrote numbers, and entered these numbers in his notebook. Only by checking his own notebook could he tell whether the vial held the sugar pill or the S-14. When he had about fifty vials, he went up to the fourth floor and found the arthritis clinic. Several doctors were already at work, and he walked in and talked to them. He was given one of the end cubicles, and the patients chosen for the test brought him slips bearing the words *Case for observation*. He gave them one or another of the vials. He abstracted the charts onto the data sheets that had been prepared for him, and in this way made up a summary on each patient so that he could tell the nature and severity of the disease merely by glancing at the sheet.

He became interested in his work. The patients were not very ill and he joked and chatted with them. The despondency that had been with him ever since Joan's death disappeared for a while and he worked right through his lunch hour. He didn't stop until the middle of the afternoon. By then all the patients were gone, and he had dispensed almost all of the vials. He returned to the research laboratory and was pleased to see that a small desk had his name on it. He was done with his day's work. He changed the white coat for his jacket and walked down the long hall. In one tiny room he saw through an open door a thin man in a plastic apron working on the head of an anesthetized cat. "Mind if I come in and watch?" he asked.

"Come right in," the research worker said. "Be done in a minute." Dan found a stool. He saw some shelves and racks on one wall and decided that the room had once been a broom closet.

The research worker was sewing the skin of the cat's head tight over some wires. When he was done he washed his gloves and gently put the cat back in the cage. He took another one out and gave it an injection.

"What are you working on?"

"An aspect of schizophrenia. My name is Duffy."

They shook hands.

"You're a technician?"

The man chuckled. "I wish I had a technician. I'm a physician and I get down here a couple of times a week and work on my six cats. I've been working on them for years. Every so often one dies of old age and I buy a new one." He grinned, and Dan liked him.

"What's your project?"

"The cause of emotional diseases."

"What?"

Duffy grinned again. "That's it."

Dan pointed to a flask of amber liquid heating over a Bunsen burner. "What's that?"

"What does it look like?"

"Urine."

"A special kind," Duffy said. "From schizophrenic patients. They put out some material that makes some cats nervous."

"Do you need any help?"

"Aren't you on Beaulieu's project?"

"I get done by three or so, and I think I'd like to keep busy."

"Can you feed my cats and clean their cages? I don't get here every day."

"What do you feed them?"

Duffy showed him the food and then showed him how to clean the cages. Then he said, "Just keep a log of your hours. I'll pay you at the end of the month."

"I'm on assignment," Dan said. "Besides I always wanted to help start a revolution."

"Then I'll add a footnote to my report. My thanks to— what's your name?"

"McDermott."

"The author wishes to express his gratitude to Mr. McDermott, who faithfully cleaned the cat shit out of the cat cages every day." He gave Dan a key to the laboratory. "Just be gentle with these cats. They're half crazy anyway from all the schizophrenic urine I've been injecting into them. Walk easy around them. Don't frighten them."

Outside it was a warm summer afternoon. Dan put the top down on the Dodge and drove to Sharon's house. Turk would likely be there and he had time to play with the boy for a while before going to work.

The baby was sprawled out in the playpen. Turk was lying on the couch reading a book. Dan came in and lifted him up and hugged him. "What are you doing? Where's Sharon?"

"I'm watching the baby," Turk said proudly.

"Who's watching you?"

"You always say things like that," Turk said. "I'm almost eight."

"What's around here to eat?"

"Shh," Turk said. "You'll wake the baby up."

Dan looked in the refrigerator and found some cheese and made himself a sandwich. "Have you eaten?"

"Sharon said she'd make dinner when she got back." He crawled over and sat on Dan's lap. "You smell funny."

"Like cats?"

Turk sniffed. "Kind of."

Sharon came in through the front door. A young man was with her. She stopped when she saw Dan. "Oh. I want you to meet a friend of my husband's. Dr. McDermott."

Dan got up and shook hands with the young man. "Not till next year," he said.

"I'm glad to meet you," the young man said. He seemed uneasy.

"You will stay for dinner?" Sharon said.

"I don't think so," he said. "I'll have to get along. I'll call you later."

Sharon waited until she heard the door close and then she flew at Dan. "What do you mean coming in here without calling? What do you think my friends think when they find a man here making himself comfortable in my kitchen?"

"I'm hungry as hell. What are you going to make for dinner?"

"I'm going out. I have a date."

Dan got a bottle of milk from the refrigerator. He put two glasses on the table and filled them. "Make yourself a cheese sandwich," he said to Turk.

"Help yourself," Sharon said. "Make yourself at home. Please do. Anything in the refrigerator."

"The kid baby-sat for you. He's entitled to some dinner."

"Don't you care if I go out?"

"Want to come to the store?" Dan said to Turk.

"What are you taking him to the store for? He should be in bed by nine o'clock."

"I'll get Goldie to put him to bed later on."

"A pervert," she screamed. "You get a pervert to take care of a seven-year-old boy!"

"He's better with kids than you are."

"That's gratitude," she screamed. "I pick him up from school. I take care of him all day, and then you tell me something like that. Get out. Go on home. All you do is upset me."

Dan poured out some more milk for himself and the boy. "Come here," he said.

She stopped shouting. "What is it?"

"Come here."

"What do you want?" She walked up to him. He reached around and patted her on the behind.

"Patting me like a dog," she shouted. "You can't get around me that way. I'm not a poodle."

"You're back to your old self," he said. "You don't know how nice it is." To Turk he said, "Finish your milk."

Turk drained his glass, wiped his mouth, and stood up.

"Where are you going?"

"I already told you. To the store."

"I'll put him to bed," she said. "Just leave him here. I don't need any help from you. Good-bye."

Work remained a welcome distraction, and Dan worked all the time either at the store or at the hospital. He kept painstaking records of the experimental arthritis patients, and when he was done he went to Duffy's laboratory and fed the cats and cleaned the small broom-closet room.

At the end of two weeks Beaulieu called him into his office. "How's it going?"

"Everything's on paper." Dan handed him the sheets of abstracts.

"Which are the placebo cases?"

"I don't know. I'd have to check the numbers on each sheet."

"Good," Beaulieu said. "That's how an honest double blind experiment should be done. That's the way you get real objectivity. I think though that it's time you started evaluating them."

After he left Dan sorted out the various abstracts of the patients' charts, marking some *Placebo* and some *Drug*. Then he compared their course in the last two weeks. When he was done he realized that there was no real difference between the two groups. The treated patients were no better than those who took the sugar pills.

The next day he showed the sheets to Beaulieu. Beaulieu studied the two groups. "We have to choose the parameters," he said finally.

"What?"

"Parameters. The right yardstick to judge improvement."

"There isn't any. The two groups are the same."

"It depends on what you use to measure them," Beaulieu said patiently. "If you use pain, then there's no improvement. You're right. If you use mobility, there's no improvement. But if you use swelling there is improvement. The joint swelling in the treated group is less than the swelling in the placebo group."

"The patients don't feel any better."

"But there was an effect on the swelling, see?" Beaulieu pushed the abstract sheets back to Dan. "I want you to go through all these and evaluate each patient on the basis of swelling alone. We can entitle this paper 'The Effect of S-14 on Swelling in Joints of Patients with Rheumatoid Arthritis.' We don't have to deal with its effect on pain or mobility. See?"

That afternoon Dan stayed and did what he was asked. He graded each patient on the decrease in swelling in two weeks, and he ignored all the other aspects of their arthritis.

Each day he saw more patients and added to the sheets. At the end of the next week the results were reversed. Patients taking S-14 had more swelling than those on sugar pills.

"Interesting," Beaulieu said. "It apparently has a substantial anti-inflammatory effect for the first two weeks, which then wears off. There's some suggestion of a rebound phenomenon. It's a promising drug. I think we can send the manufacturers an encouraging report on this."

"What do you mean?"

"Evaluation is a very difficult matter," Beaulieu said. "You just haven't had the necessary experience. Using the parameter of swelling, there is a distinct decrease at the end of two weeks, showing a clear prompt effect."

Dan was confused and he studied the sheets after Beaulieu left. Later he carried them to Duffy's laboratory and showed them to him. "What the hell is he doing?"

Duffy shrugged. "He'll send in a carefully worded, mildly favorable report to the drug company and they'll give him an extension of his grant."

"His grant?"

"Who do you think pays for his research?" After a moment he added, "If there's some trick of logic or statistics that he can use to get favorable results he'll go on with his study and read a paper on it at some medical meeting and the drug company will see that the newspapers and some of the magazines pick up his report and everybody'll be using S-14 for rheumatoid arthritis for a while. Maybe it won't be any better than aspirin, but Beaulieu will keep getting his grant and the drug company will make some money and that's the way the big ball bounces."

After a while Dan said, "I've spent three weeks down here. I think it's enough."

"You don't like research?"

"I don't even think you know what you're doing."

Duffy laughed. "That's the only way important discoveries are made. When you plan something all you do is develop what's already known. But a breakthrough has to be an accident."

"What do you expect to get out of it? The drug companies' business?"

"You're in your last year, aren't you?"

Dan nodded.

"Apply for an extension on your time down here. They'll give it to you. I'll speak to the dean. I can use you for a month. I have to find out why this schizophrenic urine is affecting the cat's electroencephalogram. If we come up with anything you'll go on the paper as a co-author. Don't forget what co-authoring a paper on insulin did for another medical student by the name of Best."

Dan shook his head. "I've wasted three weeks already. But, I'll come down and clean your cages. Maybe you've got something. I don't know."

Dan went back upstairs and took off the long white laboratory coat and put it away in his locker. He was on his way to the school office to request a transfer when he heard his name paged on the hall intercom. He picked up a phone.

"I have an outside call for you," the operator said.

A girl's voice came on. "Hello Dan?" It was low-pitched and breathless.

"Yes," he said.

"I'm Cherise. Oney's friend. He'll be so upset if he knows I called you. Please don't tell him. Perhaps bring him a book, and while you're there examine him."

"I didn't know he was sick. What's wrong?"

"He has a cough," she said, "and he's running a fever."

"He ought to get a doctor."

"He's lying in bed taking some kind of antibiotic. We have an important engagement in Brentwood tomorrow night, and I've planned it for weeks and I'm afraid he won't make it. Are all doctors like that?"

"I'll come out right away," he said.

He drove to the address she gave him. It was a new, clean apartment house on the outskirts of Beverly Hills. He parked in an underground garage and took an elevator to the second floor. Noble was lying in bed reading.

"How are you doing?"

Noble put the book down. "What brought you out here?"

Dan picked up Noble's book. "I see you've gotten to volume four."

"I'm up to the Mohammedan conquest of Spain. A few Jews are still alive."

"I hear you've been sick."

"Cherise called you," Noble said annoyed. "She has this lousy dinner party set up and she's worrying I won't go." He shrugged. "I'd rather stay home with a fever."

Dan took out a stethoscope. Noble looked at it and said, "Not again, friend."

Dan laughed. "Sit up."

"What for?"

"Maybe you have pneumonia."

"All I have is the flu," Noble said, but he sat up and pulled his shirt off. Dan examined him.

"You're right. But why are you taking antibiotics?"

"Who's taking antibiotics? She bugs me into taking something. So I'm taking aspirin and I told her it's an antibiotic. She doesn't know the difference."

"How long has this been going on?"

"With Cherise? Oh, about a year. Her father owns this apartment house."

"Yes, I see," Dan said.

"Yes you see, screw you," Noble said.

A girl came in the half-opened door. She was light tan and wore a bright short dress. She bent over the bed, legs straight, heels together, and kissed Noble.

"Dan McDermott," Noble said. "Cherise Williams."

She swept toward Dan and kissed him on the cheek. "Oney's always talking about you. You're his favorite friend."

"Also the only one."

"I'm so glad you're here. Oney's been sick and—"

"Quit it," Noble said. "I know you called him."

"How is he?"

"He'll be able to go to that affair."

"Thank you very much," Noble said.

The girl stood off and looked at Dan a moment. "Do all you boys dress like that? I threw Oney's old suits out before I would even let him take me to a show."

Dan looked at his own suit. "I'll buy another one when I graduate," he said.

She went to the closet and took out a light green silk suit. "Isn't that nice? I bought it for him on his birthday." She put it back in the closet. "It's hard civilizing him, but I love him though." She sat on the edge of the bed and took Noble's hand. "I called Silverman's and they're sending over some chicken soup and a turkey sandwich for you. How's that? Do I take good care of my little boy?"

"Oh shit," Noble said.

"He always talks that way," Cherise said. "It's terrible."

"I've got to get to the store by six," Dan said.

"I have to run along too," Cherise said. She shook a warning finger at Noble. "I want you in bed and sleeping when I call." In the hall she said to Dan, "I'm so glad I met you. Oney talks about you all the time. He is always quoting what you say."

Dan didn't know what to say.

"He has such a deep mind," she said. "He comes over to my house and talks to my father. They discuss politics and religion and all sorts of things that an old scatterbrain like me doesn't understand. He and my dad argue all the time." In the street she brushed Dan's cheek with her lips. "Bye Danny. Do please come over when Oney's feeling better. I'll make you dinner, and maybe I'll invite my daddy. You'd like him. He's a doctor too."

The next morning he stopped at the school office. The secretary looked doubtful. "This is the second change," she said. "You'll have to see Dr. Yager." She showed him into an office. The assistant dean was quite young. He looked at Dan's file for a few moments and said, "Why did you want to transfer off the wards in the first place?"

Dan wondered whether he should trust him. He decided against it and said instead, "I thought I'd be interested in research."

The dean put the file down. "I understand your wife died a little while ago. Suicide."

Someone had spoken to him, Dan realized. Possibly one of the instructors who in turn heard it from a student. "Yes," he said.

"We were sorry to hear it," the dean said. "How's it going?"

"I'd like to transfer to another service."

"Why not back to the wards?"

"I think I might be more suited for a specialty where I'm not directly taking care of patients. I'd like to find out."

The dean looked at Dan for a few moments. Then he said, "You have several years to decide that." He wrote out a slip. "The only vacancy is in surgical pathology. You can spend your next month there."

The name plate on the door of the director of surgical pathology was Dr. Hector Perkins. Perkins turned out to be a nervous plump man. He took the slip Dan handed him and said, "What brought you down here? All the good students want to be on the glamorous services?"

"I guess I'm trying to find out what I want to do."

"Maybe the first thing we ought to do is find out whether this field wants you." He got up and put a slide under the microscope. "Let's see what you know. What's that?"

Dan sat down and studied it.

"Well?"

Dan was having trouble. "It must be all tumor," he finally said. "I can't see any tissue I can recognize."

"What kind of tumor?"

"I can't tell."

"What part of the body is it from?"

"I don't know." The slide was a mixture of muscle fibers and fat, and Dan had never seen anything like it before. He heard Perkins chuckle and he looked up. The director was sitting back waiting. "At least can you identify the kind of tissue?"

"No."

"You passed the test with flying colors," Perkins said. "You're now a member of the department in good standing."

"What?"

"If you had told me this was a fibroid or a gastric sarcoma I would have sent you back upstairs with a polite note to the dean."

"What is it?"

"A piece of kosher salami."

"Salami?"

"It's a good test. It helps me get rid of the bluffers. Let's go over some real slides." Perkins spent the next several hours with Dan, showing him abnormal slides and lecturing him about the signs he should look for. Dan realized it was a great deal of time for the chief of a busy department to give to a medical student. The next day he went in early and quietly examined all the slides on Dr. Perkin's desk, and then went up to the library and studied about what he had seen. When Perkins reviewed the slides with him he understood readily what Perkins was talking about. Perkins was delighted. "I like to teach," he said. "But the students I get are all surgical or medical residents, putting in a few months to prepare for their own specialty. They have no love for this field. Why did you really choose this service? Are you seriously thinking of going into pathology?"

For reasons he didn't know himself, Dan trusted Perkins and he told him how fearful he had been with sick patients. Perkins nodded. "A lot of us feel that way. I never got over it. When I was an intern if a patient would die on me, I would suffer. Really suffer. I'd go back over everything I did and I would always find something to blame myself for. So I went into pathology. It's a lot easier on my emotional makeup."

Generally in the afternoon, when Dan finished his session with Dr. Perkins, he went across the hall to the tissue laboratory. The organs or tissues removed at surgery were brought there wrapped in wax paper. The pathology resident, a shy, soft-spoken young man, examined them, dictating into a microphone. He then cut out small pieces, which he dropped into a tiny pan. The pans ultimately were passed to a tissue technician, a gray-haired woman, who soaked them in various solutions, took out the hardened tissue, and cut off exquisitely thin slices with her microtome. She then stained the slices, mounted them on slides, and put them on the chief's desk, where Dan saw them the second day.

It was quiet and scientific and Dan liked the work at first. One afternoon, after he had been in pathology about a week, the tissue technician said, "Did you know that one of your classmates just came into the hospital?"

Dan looked up from the microscope. "Who?"

"A boy by the name of Larry O'Donnell. Do you know him?"

"We were partners in physiology. What's the matter with him?"

"Jenny in x-ray tells me he's got an ulcer."

After Dan was done feeding Duffy's cats that afternoon he visited O'Donnell in a ward set aside for sick nurses and doctors. O'Donnell was reading when Dan came in.

"McDermott! Where have you been? You dropped out of sight."

Dan sat down. "In pathology. I just heard you were in."

"If you ever get a belly ache don't tell anybody and stay away from these guys. They diagnose you to death. I've swallowed barium and I've had it pumped up my rear end. I've had so many enemas I have to sleep on my stomach." He picked up a sheet of paper. "Come here." He sketched in the outline of a stomach and drew a circle on the outer curvature. "You're a great one on books. What's the chances of having a benign ulcer in this area?"

"Is that where yours is?"

O'Donnell nodded. "They treat me like an idiot child. They don't tell me anything, but they leave my x-rays in the room while they're outside jawing over my case. So I got a pretty good look at them."

"What did you see?"

"It's an ulcer," O'Donnell said. "I saw the crater."

A plain thin girl came in and O'Donnell took the cigar stub out of his mouth and kissed her. "My wife," he said to Dan. To her he said, "Did you bring me something to eat?"

The girl shook her head. "You're on a diet."

"I'm going to have the ulcer cut out in a few days. What's the point of starving me to death before?" He lay back, holding the girl's hand. "Oakley's going to do it. Do you know him?"

"No," Dan said.

"He's a quick worker. I don't want somebody keeping me open all morning. In and do the job and out." He looked at his wife and grinned. "Isn't that the best way to do it, honey?"

The girl was putting fresh pajamas into the room locker. She shook her head.

"I've got an idea," O'Donnell said. "McDermott, watch the

door for five minutes. That's all I need. Just keep those sneaky nurses out." He reached out and started pulling the girl toward him.

She broke away. "Don't you move, McDermott," she said. "You're the only protection I have against this sex fiend."

O'Donnell roared with laughter. He picked up his cigar stub and pointed to the sheet of paper. "You didn't answer my question. What do you think about an ulcer there?"

"How old are you?"

"Twenty-nine."

"You're too young to have cancer of the stomach."

"I wish it weren't in that part of my stomach," O'Donnell said. "I'd feel better about it."

Several days later, when Dan sauntered into the pathology laboratory after lunch, the tissue technician pointed silently to a wax-paper package in a stainless-steel basin. Dan looked at it. "O'Donnell? How did it go?"

"I don't know. He's still up in surgery."

The resident came in and Dan said, "Do this one first. I know the patient."

The resident unwrapped the package and started dictating into the microphone. "The specimen consists of a portion of a stomach. On the greater curvature is a larger ulcer measuring"—he picked up the plastic rule and measured—"seven by five centimeters. The borders are rolled and hard." He stopped. "How old is this patient?"

The tissue technician got up and walked over. "It's on the slip," she said. "Twenty-nine."

"It's malignant," the resident said. He turned it over and started dictating again. "On the outer surface are a half-dozen small nodules where the malignancy has penetrated all layers of the gastric wall."

The tissue technician returned to her place against the opposite wall.

"How old did you say he was?" the resident said.

"Twenty-nine," Dan said.

"Yes," the resident said softly. He cut into the large angry ulcer and dropped several slices of tissue into one of the pans.

A middle-aged, baldheaded man walked in. "I'm Oakley," he said. "Did you see that specimen on O'Donnell yet?"

The resident upwrapped the package again. "I'm afraid your surgery was too late."

"I know," the surgeon said. "There's a few of those things in the liver too." He paused. "His wife doesn't want him to know about this. I'm going to tell him it's a benign ulcer." He looked at Dan. "This boy is a medical student. I wouldn't want any of this to get around. It would come back to him right away."

"We won't say anything," the resident said.

The surgeon nodded his immaculate bald head. "I don't know how long we can manage to keep it away from him, but if that's what she wants that's what we'll do."

"The sections will be through tomorrow."

"If they show anything I should know about call me."

"They won't," the resident said.

After Oakley left the tissue technician said, "If I ever have anything like that I hope they tell me so I can cut my throat and get it over with."

"A man believes what he wants to," the resident said. "If he wants to believe what Oakley tells him, he'll believe it."

"Maybe," she said and sliced viciously with her microtome.

About three Dr. Perkins called Dan. "I want to start some blood on O'Donnell on the fourth floor. We just got a call from the ward."

He gave Dan the slip and Dan took the two labeled bottles out of the refrigerator and carried them upstairs.

O'Donnell looked pale and sweaty. Blood was already running into one arm and Dan put the full bottle on to replace the almost empty one. "How do you feel?" Dan said.

"I'm still out in left field," he said, trying to focus his eyes. He finally recognized Dan. "Hi. How long have you been here?"

"Just came in."

"Where's my wife?"

"Sitting outside."

He squinted at Dan. "They told me it's a benign ulcer."

"So I hear," Dan said. He watched the blood drip. O'Donnell lay back and fell asleep.

Dan stopped to talk to the girl outside. "He looks good for being immediately postoperative."

"I was sitting out here," she said. "I thought he might sleep better if I wasn't in the room."

"He's sleeping fine now," Dan said. It was all he could think of to say.

O'Donnell's sections came through and were labeled and filed away so that if later a physician were doing research on cancer and wanted to examine all the slides of stomach cancer he could find them readily.

Dan was reviewing sections with Dr. Perkins when Oakley walked into the small office. He sat down. "Listen," he said. "I have a problem I'll need some help on."

Perkins looked up. "What can we do for you?"

"You remember this stomach case I did last week?"

"The medical student? Anything go wrong?"

"He's doing fine. You know, I had told him he had a benign peptic ulcer."

Perkins nodded.

"Well, he had some of his buddies bring him up some books. I wish they would keep books away from sick medical students. Anyway he's looked up the statistics on the sort of ulcer he had and he doesn't believe it's benign now."

"That's too bad," Perkins said. "He should have left well enough alone."

"I'm committed," Oakley said. "It's what the family wants. I just want to make it a good lie. I need a pathology report on that specimen saying that it is a benign ulcer. I'll show it to him."

Perkins scratched at his ear with a paper clip. After a while he said, "I'll have one dictated. We'll put it into your mailbox."

"No. On his chart."

Perkins grimaced.

"That's the only way it'll work. This kid is suspicious and knows what he's talking about. Fourth-year medical students are hell to have as patients." He looked at Dan and his long white coat. "Are you in his class?"

Dan nodded.

"We can put the false report in his chart. Do you think you might accidentally forget it in his room? I think he'd believe us then. What do you say?"

"It's up to the chief," Dan said. "He's my boss."

"He'll do it," Perkins said. After Oakley left he sat back and said, "Listen, if it works he'll have a few good months without the taste of death in his mouth all the time. That's worth lying a little for, isn't it?"

He dictated the false report and Dan waited until it was typed. He took it upstairs and took out the real report and put the other in its place. He carried the chart into O'Donnell's room. O'Donnell was pale and had lost weight. He rolled over when Dan came in. "What are you up to?"

"Checking on that transfusion I started. Did you get any reaction?"

"That was five days ago."

"So I'm slow."

"I had a little chilly feeling when it went in. That's all."

Dan made a note on the chart: *No significant transfusion reaction.*

"I have the same lousy pain I had before the operation."

"Give it some time."

"I suppose so."

"Got enough to read?"

"Watching television most of the time. How are the lectures going?"

"Same old stuff," Dan said. "Just what's in the books. See you later." He left the chart on the chair. He went outside and sat down by the desk. The ward was quiet. He found a portion of the morning newspaper and opened it to the sports section. He read for about fifteen minutes and then got up and went back into the room. The chart was on the bedside table. "I forgot the chart," he said.

O'Donnell looked at him a moment. "You're getting careless, McDermott," he said.

Two days later, in the afternoon, while Dan was studying slides alone, the phone on the worktable buzzed. He answered it.

"McDermott?"

He thought he recognized the voice. "How are you doing?"

"I'd like to take a look at that specimen of mine."

"What?"

"I'm ambulatory now. I'll be down in ten minutes."

"Wait a minute. I don't think I can find it now. It's been put away."

"Listen," O'Donnell said, "I know how the laboratory runs too. You can find that specimen and the slides, and if you can't, I can." He hung up.

Dan went across the hall to Dr. Perkins' office. The pathologist was hunched over a microscope. He looked up, blinking from the light.

"O'Donnell just called. He's coming down to see his specimen."

"Who?"

"My classmate. The one who had the cancer of the stomach."

Perkins stared at Dan for a moment. Then he opened his desk drawer and took out a mechanical telephone-number file. He ran the little button on its side down to O and pressed it, and the file jumped open. He found the number and dialed it. "Let me speak to Dr. Oakley," he said. He waited. Then he said, "You had better interrupt him." He waited a few moments longer, tapping nervously on the desk with his fingertips, and then he said, "Hello, Oakley? Your patient O'Donnell just phoned and insists on seeing his specimen. What do you want us to do?" Oakley answered and Perkins said, "There is no other specimen I can substitute. Even if I could find a stomach with a peptic ulcer in ten minutes, which I doubt, it just wouldn't be any good. The specimen and slides are all numbered and dated, and it wouldn't fool anyone who can read. It's no use." They talked a minute or two more and Perkins put down the phone.

"Show it to him," he said. "There's nothing else to do." He arose, straightening out his laboratory coat. "I've been dictating all afternoon and I'm tired. I think I'll go get some coffee." He started toward the door.

"Just a minute," Dan said. "What about O'Donnell?"

"You better take care of it," he said.

Dan went back to the laboratory. "Where's the resident?" he asked.

The tissue technician looked up. "He's off for the afternoon attending some lectures at U.C.L.A."

Dan found the specimen and put it into an enamel tray. He took the slides from the filing cabinet in Dr. Perkins' office, and laid them out. Then he sat down and waited.

In a few minutes he heard the elevator stop, and then the sound of slippered feet coming down the hall. O'Donnell came in, wearing the same robe he had had on upstairs. He was even thinner.

"Is that it?"

Dan nodded and O'Donnell picked up the formaldehyde-hardened portion of stomach and looked at it intensely. He turned it over and saw where the cancer had come through to the other side. He put it down, wiping his fingers on his robe. Then he sat down at the microscope and looked at the sections.

"He couldn't have gotten it all," he said at last. He turned off the microscope light and stood up. "Isn't that a shame," he said. Then, "Are you sure these are the right sections?"

"They're labeled," Dan said.

O'Donnell nodded. He looked vaguely around the room, the same expression of preoccupation on his face. Then he said, "I don't know why they're keeping me. There's not much point in my staying around here any longer." He turned half-

way as though to leave, and then he stopped. "Tomorrow I think
I'll buy myself a new sports jacket. I've seen some good ones
in the May Company window."

He walked out of the laboratory. Later Dan heard the grating
sound of the elevator door as it opened. He took a nail file
out of his pocket and began cleaning his fingernails. The tissue
technician began to work again.

After a while Dr. Perkins came back. He looked into the
laboratory. "Did you show it to him?"

"He just left."

"What did he say?"

"He was going to buy a new sports jacket."

Perkins looked sharply at Dan. "Why did he say that?"

"I suppose because he wanted one," the tissue technician
said.

"That's the damndest thing for a man to say." Perkins looked
puzzled and then he shrugged. He went back to his office
and in a few moments Dan heard the droning of his voice
as he dictated reports. He put the specimen back in its jar
and returned the slides to the file. When he left for the day,
the technician was sharpening her microtome.

When the week ended Dan went back to the assistant dean's
office. "I think I'd like to get back up on the wards again,"
he said.

"I just transferred you into pathology."

"I know. But I'd like to change back anyway."

"Why?"

Dan hesitated. But Dr. Yager was an assistant dean and had
the power to make arbitrary decisions. All Dan finally said
was, "I think I'd like to get back upstairs with patients now."

"All right," the dean answered. "I hope you've learned something from these secondary services." He wrote out a slip.
"You're on wards for the rest of the year. Don't bother me
again."

Dan went up to the admitting ward the next day after

lunch. Noble was examining an old man. "Are you working alone?"

"I've been waiting for you to quit this horsing around."

Dan grinned. He read over the chart and helped Noble with the examination, and later they sat in the laboratory and wrote up their findings together. The old man had leukemia, and Dan, who had had time to read in the last month, told Noble about the new discoveries which suggested that leukemia was due to a virus.

During the next weeks he found he still worried a great deal about very sick patients, but he had decided by then that, if he was ever going to be able to care for the ill, he would have to accept this particular agony. If he tried to escape from it he would become like Dr. Perkins, locked away in a laboratory.

Thirteen

DURING THE NEXT MONTH the fourth-year students were busy choosing internships. Most of them had applied to several hospitals and had received by return mail complex three- and four-page documents, which they carried around with them, showed to one another, and sooner or later filled out and mailed in. They talked frequently among themselves of the relative desirability of the various hospitals. For experience the County was best. One treated more sick people and had more responsibility there than at any of the other hospitals. But to get a start in practice and to line oneself up for future associations the private hospitals were better: Cedars, Good Sam, Queens, St. John's. The choice ultimately broke down to what specialty a man wanted to go into. For surgery County was best. For obstetrics Queens was good. For medicine, Cedars.

A boy named Fletcher carried a scratch pad about. Every morning for two weeks he went down to the doctors' garage in the basement and watched the attending physicians drive in. He listed each doctor by his specialty and under each specialty he put a check if the physician drove a new Cadillac or a new Lincoln. Dermatologists were best off—seventy-six per cent with Cadillacs or Lincolns. Close behind were the eye doctors and the orthopedists. Down at the very bottom of the list were the pediatricians. "They drive jalopies and they look so tired you don't think they're going to make it through the gate," Fletcher said.

Dan studied the list. "Where are you going?"

"The County for my internship," Fletcher said. "I'll try to get into Mayo's for my skin residency. You know a busy dermatologist can see a hundred patients a day. At ten dollars a crack that's not bad."

Dan applied only to the County Hospital. Noble wrote to a hospital in Ghana and got back an unusually elaborate form. He was delighted with it. "They pay five hundred guineas a year," he said.

"That's only a hundred dollars a month."

"The money isn't important. Do you have any idea how bad they need doctors?"

"Have you given up on Mississippi?"

Noble shrugged. "Cherise won't go for it. I did talk her into Ghana if I get accepted. Her father's pretty unhappy about it though."

Later he also applied to the County Hospital. "I won't get accepted," he explained. "My grades weren't that good. But then nobody can complain if I take the Ghana appointment."

On the wards the fourth-year students were no longer mere observers. Nor were they still overawed by the interns. Instead the students passed critical judgments on the interns. One intern they might consider good and conscientious, another dull and lacking the discretion needed for diagnosis or treatment, a third they might decide was bright enough but disorganized. They openly taunted interns who they thought were incompetent.

A big, slow boy named Holger became the object of Noble's scorn, and Noble wasted, Dan thought, a good deal of time by searching for petty faults in the orders Holger wrote. He took them word for word from a book that he always carried in one pocket of his white jacket.

"I don't miss anything this way," Holger explained to Noble. "These guys who write their orders from memory sometimes forget the most important things."

"You're been interning for six months, haven't you?" Noble said.

"It takes a lot longer than that to learn how to write orders."

"What happens if the index is wrong? Supposing you look up a case of appendicitis and they give you the wrong page and you end up with the treatment for schistomiasis?"

"Don't be such a smart ass," the intern said. "I haven't found a mistake in it yet." He pointed to the blackboard. "There's a new patient in seven. Are one of you smart asses going to go get a history like you're supposed to?"

"If you'll lend us the book," Noble said.

"I don't think I was that obnoxious when I was a medical student," Holger said and went back to writing in the chart.

Noble picked up the blood pressure machine and stethoscope. In the hall he said to Dan, "Ever seen one of those handbooks?"

"No."

"You get one for six bucks in the bookstore. It's got everything in it. Diagnosis, treatment, drugs. Even spelling. You don't have to think. All you have to do is know how to turn pages."

They went into the new patient's room. He was a heavy young man with a stubble of beard. His eyes gleamed with fever.

"How do you feel?" Dan said.

"I've got the shakes. I've been shivering for an hour. All they've given me is some aspirin."

Noble sat down and started writing in the chart.

"We'll get some orders for you as soon as we're done. How did you get sick?" Dan said.

The patient closed his eyes. "I was fine yesterday. I drove in on this run from Phoenix. Felt kind of tired when I got in, but not sick or anything. Just tired. Then I stopped off at this diner and got something to eat and threw it all up. I pulled my truck off into a side street and I got up on the platform behind my seat—"

"Platform?"

"That's where we sleep. It has a mattress on it. Then—"

"You sleep in the truck?"

"All the time. If I went to a hotel every night I wouldn't make any money on a long run."

"Go on," Noble said.

The patient did not look at Noble. He kept talking to Dan. "So in the middle of the night I get these chills. I couldn't get warm. Then my elbow started hurting. It got lumpy." He raised up his right arm. Dan felt it. Under the skin by the side of the elbow there were a number of enlarged lymph glands. The patient winced.

Noble was watching. "Some kind of lymphadenitis," he said.

"Is that bad?" the sick man asked.

"A shot of penicillin will cure you. Go on," Dan said.

"There's nothing more. I drove the truck up here, and I—"

"Where did you park it?"

"There's a school lot across the street. It had a big sign, RESERVED FOR MEDICAL STUDENTS. I parked right in the middle of it."

"I saw it this morning," Noble said. "A tractor with a big trailor all painted red."

"I have to call Phoenix," the driver said. "They have to send somebody out to pick up the truck."

"The nurses will send a telegram for you," Dan said. "What happened next?"

"I finally got to one of the benches and then I give out. I just sat there, shaking, cold, and like to die. Then a nurse comes along and asked me if I'm sick. Next thing I know I'm up here. I need something for a headache."

"Did you get a cut on your hand?"

"Just this." The patient held up his right hand and Dan looked at it. On the side there was a small reddish mark.

"It's nothing," Dan said. "You probably bumped it." He put a thermometer in the patient's mouth. When he took it out it registered 104 degrees.

He and Noble examined the patient. His pulse was rapid. His blood pressure was lower than it should have been.

"Time to call in the mastermind," Noble said.

Dan found Holger and brought him into the room. He repeated the history to Holger and the patient listened, adding a point from time to time. Holger felt the enlarged tender nodes and took the blood pressure. "Lymphadenitis of some kind," he said outside the room. "How did he get that mark on his hand?"

"I don't know," Dan said. "It doesn't look like anything."

"Probably an ascending infection. What they used to call blood poisoning."

"Do you look it up under B or P?" Noble said.

The intern shrugged, annoyed. He sat down to write the orders. He didn't use the manual. Noble read over his shoulder. "You better get a blood culture too," he said.

"I'm getting it."

"How about typhoid agglutinations?"

"I promised him something for his headache," Dan said. "How about some Darvon?"

"I'll get to it."

"We don't want you to miss anything," Noble said.

"Haven't you two got something else to do?"

Dan looked at the clock. It was five and Sharon would be irritable if he was late for dinner. "Coming?" he said.

Noble shook his head. "I'm going to stay awhile and learn how to write orders," he said.

The next day the truck driver was much worse. His cheeks were sunken in, his eyes were red with fever. He barely had the strength to roll over. He looked at Dan a few moments, trying to recognize him.

"Kind of rough?"

"Sure is," the truck driver said. "What's the matter with me? My head hurts. The medicine you gave me yesterday didn't help."

Dan felt his pulse. It was rapid and worrisome. He held the truck driver's arm up to the light and saw a number of reddish purple spots. He pulled the covers back and found the same spots on his chest and his back. He went out to the desk and sat down to write his findings in the patient's chart. Noble came down the hall. "How is he?"

"Worse," Dan said. "He has a rash now. He probably has septicemia from that infection. Did you see Holger?"

"He's down in the bookstore," Noble said. "Look." He opened his long white coat. Nestled away in an inside pocket was Holger's *Intern's Manual*.

"Where did you get that?"

"I stole it."

"From Holger?"

"Right out from under his nose."

"Why didn't you buy one?"

"I don't need it. I did it for the sake of Holger's education, and for the protection of patients."

"He'll just get another one."

"They're all out in the bookstore," Noble said. "They won't get them in for two weeks. Maybe he'll learn something about writing orders in two weeks."

"This is kid shit," Dan said. "The next thing you know he'll get sore and make a complaint." He took the book, meaning to return it to Holger, but he became interested in it. He looked up the word *Fever* in the index. It gave him a page number on which hundreds of diseases were listed, each with a separate alphabetical and numerical superscript. It took awhile to puzzle out the significance of the superscripts. They represented, he finally realized, an elaborate system of cross references. Under headache he found another list of diseases, each one also marked with superscripts.

Holger got off the elevator looking distraught.

"Here's your book," Dan said, closing it and pushing it toward him.

"Where did you find it?"

"Around here."

"Good. The bookstore's out of them." He put it into his pocket. "That truck driver has some kind of weird rash now, and his pressure has been dropping. The chief's coming up to see him. Give me a hand, will you?"

They checked the chart, being sure all the laboratory reports were in place. Noble went down to x-ray and brought up the patient's films. Finally a middle-aged man and a resident came onto the ward and Holger hurriedly showed them into the truck driver's room, Dan and Noble following silently.

"Give Dr. Johnson the history," the resident said impatiently, and Holger opened the chart and started reading from the notes. The physician, his hands in his pockets, listened intensely. "Shock from gram-negative sepsis," he said when Holger was done.

The resident nodded. "That's what we thought. We have some Isuprel going in that drip."

"The percentage of transfer to the second floor is very high in this type of shock. Over fifty per cent. I'd use plasma as well." The physician was speaking in careful jargon so that the patient wouldn't understand him. The second floor was the morgue and what he said was that more than half of the patients who developed this kind of shock had died. "Do you have a culture of the blood?"

The resident wrinkled his nose. "Nothing as of this morning. The intern started him on antibiotics before we drew the blood."

The older physician looked at Holger and Holger said quickly, "He was very toxic on admission. I didn't think we ought to wait for cultures."

"It was in the manual. Chloromycetin, half a gram every six hours," Noble whispered.

Holger flushed. "I haven't checked this afternoon yet," he said. "Maybe something's growing by now. Why don't one of you medical students go out and call?"

Dan went out to the desk and phoned the laboratory. He came back in a few moments. "Something's starting to grow, but it's growing slowly because of the antibiotic. They're not sure what it is."

"Gram negative?"

"They don't know yet."

The physician nodded. Then he felt the patient's right elbow and reached up into his armpit and felt there also.

"How am I doing?" the truck driver croaked.

"Pretty good," the physician said. "Don't let all this doctor talk upset you."

"I can't understand those words you use."

The physician smiled and patted him on the shoulder. "I'm going to come back tonight and have another look at you."

Out in the hall they gathered together. "What other plans do you have?" the physician said.

The resident shook his head. "I'm puzzled by this one."

The physician stood, hands in his pockets, thinking. "Awfully fulminating infection," he said. "Much worse than the usual septicemia. Odd kind of rash too. I don't think I've ever seen this combination before. I don't know what else you can do. Be sure and get autopsy permission if you lose him."

The resident nodded.

After the physician left Dan took the chart and sat down at the desk. "Let me borrow your book," he said to Holger.

"Where the hell is that buddy of yours? What does he mean by making a crack like that during rounds?"

"That's the way he is. He's a lot better now than he used to be. I'll give the book right back."

Holger gave it to him and hurried off to start the plasma.

Dan went through the list, checking and cross-checking. He was still working when Noble walked up. "Where were you?"

"Down in the laboratory," Noble said. "There is some organism beginning to grow from that fellow's blood. I smeared it out myself. It looks like gram-negative rods."

Dan went down the list again. "A gram-negative rod? A little one?"

"It's a lousy culture."

"Why do you think it was a rod?"

Noble shrugged. "They looked like rods. They were longer than they were round."

Dan handed him the list. "Here's what the computerized *Intern's Manual* gives for the differential diagnosis."

Noble looked at the list. "Leukemia? He has a normal blood count."

"Wait. Read a little further."

Noble read the whole list. "Well?"

"There's one here that's caused by a gram-negative rod."

Noble looked at the list again. "Plague?"

"It's on the list."

"Sure, but . . ." Noble stopped. "The plague?" He took the book from Dan and looked up plague. "What are buboes?"

"Enlarged lymph nodes in the groin."

"He hasn't got them."

"You can get them in the armpit too. Depends on where the flea bites you." He was already walking to the room. Holger was setting up the plasma drip. The patient's fever was so intense that Dan felt the warmth the moment he came into the room. "You ever do any hunting?"

"What?"

"Hunting."

"Not for a couple of years."

"There goes that theory," Noble said.

"What's this about?" Holger said.

"He's got a theory out of your book," Noble said.

"Did you handle any dead animals lately?" Dan asked.

"Oh, some squirrels."

Noble stopped at the door and turned around. "Wild ones?"

"Yes. There's a place just outside of Needles where we bed down for the night. Lots of truck drivers stop there. One of the fellows who drives for Blue Diamond always brings a .22. He got two of them that night." He was having trouble talking and he stopped between sentences to gasp. "Funny guy. He shoots them but won't touch them. I made a stew out of them. They tasted like mud."

Holger was listening. "When was this?"

The patient tried to remember. "I don't know. Maybe Tuesday. Anyhow the day I passed through Needles. I don't remember when I passed through."

"What are you thinking about?" Holger said.

"A B. pestis infection."

"Pestis? That's . . ." Holger stopped himself.

"I skinned them too," the patient said.

"Is that when you got the mark on your hand?"

"I don't know. I guess so." He looked around. "I'm sick to my stomach. I'm going to throw up."

Noble got him a pan and held him up. After a few moments the truck driver said, "Maybe it'll go away," and lay down again.

"What made you think of that?" Holger said. Dan held up the book. Holger took it from Dan and started spinning the pages.

When they were out in the hall Noble said, "Why are you putting him on? You criticize me for making fun of that dumb slob. Then you give him some cock and bull story about it's being the plague. Next thing you know he'll be writing orders for the plague."

"I'm not putting him on. It is in the book," Dan said. He went to the sink and started scrubbing his hands. After a moment Noble joined him. Holger came out of the room and sat down at the desk and put in a call for the resident. With the receiver propped between his ear and his shoulder, he opened the manual and started carefully copying orders down into the sheet.

Dan stopped at the laboratory and cleaned Duffy's cat cages. There was a scrawled pencil note on the desk. It read, *McDermott: I have a new slant. Prepare to be the co-recipient of the Nobel Prize next year. Going to Palm Springs for the weekend. Take good care of the cats—Duffy.*

On the way home he passed workmen on Wilshire Boulevard stringing gaily colored reindeer across the street. He was startled how fast the year had gone. He counted the Christmases to Joan's death and the Christmases to his mother's death, and some of the old despondency came back.

He stopped at Sharon's apartment. She was in the bedroom with the baby. Turk lay on the couch reading, a sandwich and a glass of milk beside him. He didn't look up. Dan bent over and kissed him. The boy put his finger at the place in the book. "Did you ever read this?"

Dan looked at the cover. It was *The Wonderful City of Oz.* "A few years ago."

"They've got all sorts of different colored pages," the boy said excitedly. "Green when they get into the Emerald City, blue in the Land of the Munchkins, and they even have spotted pages. It's real exciting."

"You dripped some jelly on the couch. Wipe it up before Sharon gets into a lather."

"She's always in a lather," the boy whispered and wiped the jelly away with his sleeve.

"With a wet towel," Dan said. He walked into the bedroom. "How are you doing?"

She covered the drowsy baby with a blanket. "He's just about ready to go to sleep."

He followed her into the kitchen. "Why don't you set up a Christmas tree?"

"A Christmas tree? We never had a Christmas tree in our house."

Dan laughed. "Don't be so horrified. A Christmas tree isn't going to convert you."

"What do you start with? Little things. Then little by little you're no longer a Jew."

"Where did you get this from?"

"I've been listening to you," she said. "It's what you say all the time."

Dan looked at her and thought, small stubborn women who for four thousand years had been lighting candles, preparing food in a certain way, refusing strange gods or their symbols, and keeping the tiny remnant alive and together. Probably not the men. The clever men who did well married Gentiles and dissolved in the Gentile sea. "Turk's had a tree his whole life. We can always can it a Hanukkah bush."

"A small one and no angels on it," she said. "Here." She handed him a slip. "Turk's report card. All A's."

Dan grinned. "I told you," he said and put it into his pocket.

"How long are you going to keep him?"

"His grandfather can take him back anytime he wants to."

"Is he going to?"

"Last time I talked to him he was pretty sick. I guess he thinks the boy is better off with me."

"He's getting just like you," she said. "He walks in after school and grabs himself a sandwich. He gets peanut butter and jelly all over the sink. Then he lies down with a book and a glass of milk. I don't hear anything from him for the rest of the day. He dresses like you do. He talks like you do."

"That's the way kids act. How did the store go today?"

She turned and started washing her hands in the sink. With her back still toward him she said, "Why don't you take me out? What are you waiting for?"

The question startled him. "I work late," he finally said.

"I try to do everything you want me to. I work in the store. I take good care of Turk. His mother wouldn't do any more. I take good care of the baby. I keep a clean house. But you come in, you pat me on the behind, and say 'Hello' and you sit down and eat dinner, and then you come back and take Turk. And that's all. You must have a girl. You must be sleeping with somebody, but I can't find out who. I've gone over to your apartment at night, and I've listened and all I hear is you snoring. I've even asked that queer that runs your apartment house. He says nobody comes over to see you. But you must have a girl." She waited.

"I haven't."

"Nobody?"

"No."

"Then you're frightened."

"The last time almost killed me," he finally said.

"I opened your mailbox too," she said. "I thought maybe you have somebody in San Francisco, but all you had was a bill and three Christmas cards. Here." She opened a drawer and gave them to him.

Turk came in. "I'm hungry," he said.

One of the cards was expensive and heavy. It had a New

York postmark and bore the engraved signature J. Walter Grenell. Another card was bright with pastel colors.

"Who's Gwen Kelley?" Sharon said.

"Give the kid something to eat."

"Why did she write her phone number on a Christmas card?"

"I guess she's working again. Anyway forget it. It's nothing." The third card was from Dorothy Harris. It had a snapshot of her holding her baby. Dan put the picture in his wallet.

"Who's she?"

"Just a patient."

"How did she get your number?"

"From the hospital I suppose." The bill was from Joan's psychiatrist and he crumpled it up and threw it away. "I think you're right," he said.

Sharon was stirring cereal at the stove. "It's not normal at your age," she said.

"I know," he said. "We'll go out after work tonight. We'll get Goldie to baby-sit."

"Will you take me some place I can get dressed up for?" She sounded like a delighted small girl.

He kissed her. "You're right for a change. We need some fun."

At eleven o'clock the store phone rang. It was a woman's voice. "Mr. McDermott?"

"Yes."

"Hold a moment for Dr. Oldenberg."

Dan was startled. Oldenberg was the superintendent of the hospital. He waited. A man's voice came on. "McDermott?"

"Yes?"

"I think you better get down here."

"I can't. I'm working."

"Whatever you're doing, stop it and come here immediately." Dan hesitated a moment and then said, "What's the matter?"

"I'll be in my office," Oldenberg said. "I don't want to send the sheriff's patrol to pick you up but I will if you're not here by eleven-thirty." He hung up.

Dan concealed his alarm and served the several customers in the store. Then he locked the door, and drove to the hospital. Oldenberg's small office was crowded. Noble, Holger, and the contagious disease resident sat on a leather couch. Oldenberg was talking to a small man with glasses. When Dan came in the superintendent said, "How do you feel?"

"Worried," Dan said. "I'm wondering what I did."

"You made a diagnosis of plague this afternoon."

"I wasn't sure of it."

"You suggested it to the intern, didn't you?"

"Yes," Dan said hesitantly, suddenly fearing that Holger had been thrown into such a panic that he had done something foolish.

"It didn't occur to me," Holger said.

"Me either," the resident said. "We all thought it was a case of lymphadenitis with sepsis."

"Unfortunately your diagnosis was right," Oldenberg said. "We've had the bacteriologist working on it all evening." He pushed a slip toward Dan. It was an ordinary bacteriology report. It read, *Blood culture positive for B. pestis.* Dan stared at the slip. His mouth suddenly became dry. "I didn't really think it was that."

"You're not down here to be congratulated. You're here to get shots." Oldenberg turned to the man beside him. "This is Dr. Fairley from the Board of Health. He has the authority to put every one of you in quarantine for three weeks. So you better do as he tells you."

The Board of Health physician was a small man, shabby in a baggy-kneed brown suit. "Do any of you know a Miss Connie MacPherson?" he said.

"She's a ward nurse," the resident said.

"Do you have any idea where she could be?"

No one answered and Fairley shook his head and said, "She's the one primary contact we're unable to reach. All we know is that her roommate says she drove off to Lake Tahoe by herself. My investigators have been calling every hotel and motel there."

"Take it easy, Red," Oldenberg said. "Somebody'll know where she is."

Dan looked at the Board of Health physician again. He was quite bald, with a fringe of gray hair. The name Red must have gone back many years when both he and Oldenberg were young students.

"There are over twenty hospital employees that have worked on this patient," Fairley said. "I don't want to lock you all up for three weeks. I have the women in one ward and they're being treated right now. I'm going to take charge of you four myself. We're going to spend the next twelve hours together and you're going to get streptomycin and tetracycline. You're all well and I think that will be enough. But none of you are going out of my sight until then." He turned to the superintendent. "You better get out of here, Frank. Otherwise I'll have to start giving you shots too."

The superintendent got up. "Let me know when you find that nurse."

"The first thing," Fairley said.

After the superintendent left Fairley handed out sheets of paper. "I want all of you to write the name and address of every person you've been in contact with since this plague case was admitted."

"I can't," Dan said. "I work in a store. I've talked to hundreds of people."

The Board of Health physician grimaced. Then he said, "Do the best you can."

The resident looked up from his sheet. "Just how real is the danger?"

"I don't know," Fairley said. "Every five or ten years we get a single case like this and there are no secondary cases. But twice it spread. Once down here in 1924 and thirty people died including two doctors, and once in San Francisco and a hundred people died. But we were lucky both those times. The whole country could have gotten sick."

"There's still Dr. Johnson," the resident said.

"The chief? He's locked in a bedroom at home giving himself shots."

"What happened to that truck driver?" Dan whispered to Noble.

"He died about two hours ago," Noble said. "They did the autopsy in gowns and masks. Then they scrubbed the morgue down with Lysol, and they've got a bacteriology technician checking cultures from all over the place now."

Fairley waited until the sheets were filled out. He collected them and said, "Let's get over to our ward. We'll go straight through the tunnel. I don't want any of you stopping to talk to anyone."

He led the way to a long ward in the contagious disease unit. The orderly locked them in. "I hope you aren't too uncomfortable," Fairley said. "There's a phone you can use."

He sat down and opened a chest of drugs that had been prepared. "Every one of you is going to get a gram of streptomycin every four hours." He filled a plastic syringe. Then he beckoned to the resident and the resident came up, unhooked his belt, and dropped his trousers. Fairley quickly gave him the injection and tossed the syringe away. He gave the others their shots, and then he handed around the tetracycline. Holger stared at the handful of capsules. "If the plague doesn't get you these antibiotics will," he said and swallowed all eight of them.

"I'd like to call home," Dan said. "Do we have to keep this quiet?"

Fairley was putting away the medication. "If we can't find that nurse by morning we'll be putting out a news release on it. It'll be general knowledge by then. Just don't stay on the phone too long."

"What's a pretty girl doing at Lake Tahoe by herself?" the resident said.

Dan called Sharon. "Can you keep Turk tonight?"

"I'm all dressed. I've been waiting for you."

"I'm at the hospital."

"At the hospital? Do me a favor. Go to hell!" She sounded

as though she was ready to slam the phone down and Dan said quickly, "I'm under quarantine."

"Quarantine?" She hesitated. "What for?"

"Plague."

"What's that?"

Dan thought, small women who by their devotion keep families intact and preserve the life of nations, but who, because they don't read books, know only the faces of their immediate enemies, not their ancient enemies or their potential enemies. "It's a sickness."

"Do you think I'm stupid? I know that. What kind of a sickness?"

"They quarantine you for it," he said. "Are Turk and the baby all right?"

"Is it contagious?"

"Yes."

"The baby's been coughing a little. It's nothing though."

"How do you know?"

"He coughs some every night. It's probably just a little mucus."

"How do you feel?"

"How do you think? I'm mad." Then she said, "Is it something to worry about?"

"I don't think so," he said. "Not really." He hung up. Noble and the three doctors were standing in front of an open window, talking. "I had this crazy patient up on the jail ward on the eighteenth floor," Holger said. "I caught him peeing out of the window. He was psycho anyway and I told him he'd have to go to a closed ward. Then he explained to me that he was running an experiment. He had a buddy waiting on the lawn in front of the hospital to test his theory. He figured that if he urinated out of the window it would all dry up before it hit the ground and nothing would float down but dust."

Fairley smiled politely. The resident sat down on one of the beds and started taking off his shoes.

"How do you think this truck driver picked it up?" Dan said.

"I saw your note about the squirrels," Fairley said. "It could have been that, or maybe there were rats around that place in Needles where he stayed. You know, our rats and our ground squirrels out here are infected with plague."

The phone rang and Fairley snatched it up. He listened for a few moments, and then he said, "Keep trying. Try Reno too. That's close by Tahoe. And listen, get a photo of her." He hung up and looked at the clock. "She's probably sitting in some gambling casino, playing blackjack, with a fever, and coughing on everybody that walks by."

"What percentage of our rats?" Dan said.

"Depends on the year. We always find infected ones if we look hard enough. I just don't know why we've been so lucky so long. If an epidemic ever got started, we wouldn't have enough manpower to do anything but issue bulletins and collect statistics." Fairley looked through the window at the huge town below, with its hundreds of thousands of lights, as though he expected, Dan thought, large parts of it suddenly to turn into darkness.

Dan looked at the town too. Five or six million people living together one house next to another. He had read the books and knew what had happened in the old plague epidemics. Large towns had emptied until almost nothing but dogs were left. Small towns had disappeared from the tax rolls and the history books forever.

"It's my nightmare," Fairley said. "It's my private nightmare."

"A hell of a good nightmare," the resident said.

"There wouldn't be enough drugs. There wouldn't be enough quarantine officers to enforce quarantine."

"I suppose you could give the contacts the same treatment we're getting," Noble said.

"If it really got started we'd use up all the streptomycin and antibiotics in this town in one evening. The stuff would be selling for a thousand dollars or ten thousand dollars a bottle. We'd use up everything in the United States in three or four days."

Dan picked out a bed and started undressing. The phone

rang just as he was getting ready to lie down. Fairley answered. "For you, McDermott," he said.

Dan picked up the receiver. It was Sharon. "You tell me the truth. I want to know. Are you sick?" she said.

"I've just got a pain in the ass."

"What?"

"From a shot."

"Max has a Merck's *Manual* here and I just looked up plague in it. It's a terrible sickness."

"I'm so full of antibiotics that if I spit it'll burn a hole in the floor."

"Quit joking. I've got a right to know. Are you all right?"

"Sure," he said. "We're all fine. It's just a twelve-hour quarantine."

"Really?"

"Sure."

"You're not saying that just to make me feel better?"

"All I'm going to do is take some antibiotics."

"I don't have to worry?"

"Not about me."

"I got frightened."

"I know."

"You're all right then?"

"Fine," he said again. "Go to sleep. It's late."

"You'll be home tomorrow?"

"As soon as the quarantine's lifted." He hung up.

"I've been thinking about that nurse. What did her roommate say?" the resident said.

"She left for Tahoe alone in her car this morning," Fairley said.

"I don't believe she's alone either," Dan said.

"It happens," Fairley said stiffly.

"If she's that hard to find, she's off with somebody," the resident said.

"Do you know her well?" Fairley asked.

"I've seen her on the wards."

"What kind of a girl is she?"

"Quiet. Pretty. She does her work."

"Maybe she's not the kind to spend a weekend with a man."
The resident snorted. "She's a girl, isn't she?"

Dan was worrying about Turk. "I kissed my little boy tonight," he said to Fairley. "And I visited a girl who has a baby.
Do you think we ought to give them some antibiotic too?"

Fairley shook his head. "There are a thousand or fifteen
hundred secondary contacts and by now ten or twenty thousand
tertiary contacts. If we treat that many somebody's going to
get a bad reaction to the tetracycline or streptomycin and we'll
be doing more harm than good. If you get sick, that's different.
Then we'll treat your contacts. How do you feel?"

"Worried."

"You don't know what worries are," Fairley said. "When it
comes to worries you fellows are pikers. For the last four hours
I've been worrying about a whole nation with two hundred
million people in it. I can't worry about the Czechs or the
Chinese or the Tartars. They have their own men to worry
about them. But until we find that lost nurse I have the whole
country to worry about."

"It would be an awful shame if one nurse's screwing started
off an epidemic," the resident said.

Fairley turned. "Suppose she was lying. Where would she
go?"

"Not to Tahoe. Nobody takes a girl that far. You're all tired
out from driving by the time you get to bed."

Fairley picked up the phone and dialed. Dan rolled over on
his cot. "She's with a married man," he said.

Fairley put his hand over the mouthpiece. "Why married?"

The resident sat up. "Sure. That's it. That's why it's so
hidden."

"If you were a married man," Fairley said into the phone,
"where would you take a girl?" He grinned and looked up.
"My investigator says the closest motel."

"Not for a weekend," Dan said. "More likely Palm Springs
or Laguna."

"You better find out which of the staff physicians are out of town," the resident said.

Fairley looked at him quizzically and the resident shrugged and said, "Interns and residents don't have enough money for a weekend trip."

Fairley gave his investigator more instructions and then hung up. He looked at the clock. "I better give these boys their second dose of streptomycin. You first." Dan stood up and took his shot and swallowed the pills. The phone rang and Fairley snatched it and listened and then handed it to Dan.

"I don't want to alarm you or anything"—Sharon was speaking very slowly—"but Turk's sick. He's been throwing up and he's coughing."

Dan suddenly went hollow. "When did this start?"

"He was coughing so loud he woke me up. I felt his forehead. It's hot."

Dan passed his hand over his face. "Nothing to worry about. Just a cold. Just a minute." He put the phone receiver down. "Dr. Fairley?"

Fairley had just given Noble a shot. "Yes?"

"My boy is sick."

"There's an epidemic of flu going around," Fairley said. He filled another syringe.

"He's coughing and he's got a high temperature."

"Probably a bronchitis. Why don't you prescribe some cough syrup?"

"I kissed him when I went home."

"You can't transmit it," Fairley said. "You're not sick."

After a moment Dan said, "Listen, I could have just been developing the infection. Not enough to make me sick but enough for me to be contagious. And the antibiotics would have kept me from developing symptoms." He waited.

Fairley shook his head. "I don't think so."

"He's coughing." Dan remembered the wracking cough of the truck driver. "I think we should start him on treatment too."

"Let her bring him down in the morning. We'll have one of the admitting-room physicians check him."

"By then it may be too late. It's only three o'clock."

"You're getting panicky," Fairley said. "You better calm down."

"The hell with it." Dan lifted up the phone. "Go down and open the drugstore. Get out some tetracycline." Dan spelled it. "Do it right now. Give him four."

"How old is he?" Fairley asked.

"Eight."

"Two's enough."

"No. Make that two," Dan said into the phone. After a minute he said, "How are you? How is the baby?" He listened then he said, "Good. Go get the medicine. Call me back after you've given it to Turk." After he hung up he started pacing the long room.

Fairley watched him. "I've never seen a case from a well contact and I've seen thousands of cases in Madras and Ceylon and Java."

"It could be though, couldn't it?"

"Theoretically, I suppose."

Dan started pacing again.

"Better go to sleep," Fairley said. "Stop pacing. Calm down. Stop worrying."

"I'll stop worrying when he's all right. Is tetracycline enough? Shouldn't I go out there and give him a shot of streptomycin?"

"You're under quarantine. You can't get out of this door."

Dan sat down.

Fairley gave the resident and Holger their shots. He came back and sat down by Dan. "How old is the boy?"

Dan told him again.

"They have a peculiar soft repetitive cough. What kind of cough did he have?"

"I didn't ask her." After a moment he said, "I guess it was an ordinary cough. Otherwise she would have told me about it."

"You have nothing to worry about."

"The hell I don't," Dan said. "All I've got is these three

people. Two kids and a girl. You've got a whole nation to worry about, but all I have are these three."

After a moment Fairley said, "I sometimes think if I was married and had children I wouldn't worry so much about the nation." The phone rang and he sprang up to answer it. Dan started pacing again.

When Fairley hung up the phone he said, "That's the first decent lead we've had. The roommate told my investigator this nurse used to go with a married man. My investigator called his home, and his wife said he was out of town attending a convention. We're calling every hotel and motel in Laguna, Palm Springs, and Arrowhead."

"What?"

"Never mind," Fairley said. "Call her up. Get her to bring the boy down right now. If there's any suspicion at all we'll give him streptomycin." He hesitated. "I hate to give this dosage of streptomycin to a child. It can damage the inner ear."

Dan went to the phone and called the store. There was no answer. He paced around restlessly, phoning Sharon at home every few minutes until he finally reached her. After he spoke to her he started pacing again. Fairley walked up to him. "Here," he said. Dan looked at the two red capsules in his hand.

"I don't want them."

"You should take them. You're distracting me so that I can't work."

Dan put the sedatives on the bedside table. "Maybe later," he said.

"I'll wake you up when she gets here."

"I wish to hell I could get out."

"You can't. You're under quarantine. Local and federal. I'll see the boy is taken care of by more experienced physicians than you."

Dan meant to stay awake all night, waiting for news of Turk, but sleep caught him unaware close to morning. When he awoke it was broad daylight. Fairley was tapping him on the shoulder. "You're due for your last shot."

"How's Turk? Did he get here yet?"

"He has the flu like a thousand other kids. Open your mouth." Dan opened his mouth and Fairley put a thermometer in. Dan took the thermometer out. "Are you sure?"

"The admitting-room doctors called me hours ago. He has a red throat. That's all. Now he's home in bed and your friend is giving him steam inhalations. I spoke to her ten minutes ago. Put the thermometer back in your mouth."

Dan put the thermometer back in his mouth.

"We found the nurse," Fairley said. "The man was registered in his own name. That made it easy for us. I had one investigator calling Laguna and the other calling Palm Springs and on the tenth call they found him. At the Tahquitz. She's all right. No symptoms." He smiled. "We have an embarrassed doctor though." He gave Dan the injection.

Dan sat up and groaned.

"Be thankful that's all that hurts you," Fairley said. He took the thermometer out. "All right. You're done."

Dan was too weary to attend classes. He drove home. Sharon was furious. "What's the matter with you?" she shouted as he walked into the apartment. "Making me drive that poor kid with a temperature of a hundred and three down to the hospital in the middle of the night? You crazy or something? All he had was a virus. It got worse from driving him there!"

He went in and looked at the sleeping boy. "Looks all right now." He felt his head. "His temperature is down."

"He could have caught pneumonia. It was cold last night. They all thought I was crazy. I kept telling them it was the plague." She glared at him. "Now I've caught a sore throat from all this driving around at night."

He turned around and kissed her.

"What's that for?"

"Can't you think of a reason?"

"You're crazy. Did you get any sleep last night?"

"I better take Turk out of here. The baby might catch it from him."

"You leave that boy alone," she shouted. "Driving him around in the middle of the night. Having him examined by six doctors. Scaring him to death. You just leave him alone. I'll have my mother come over and take the baby to her house."

"Sure," he said and kissed her again.

"I don't know what's the matter with you," she said more gently.

"The whole nation could have gotten sick last night."

She stared at him. "What?"

"Anything to eat?"

"I'll make you some coffee."

He followed her into the kitchen and when he was drinking his coffee she said, "All right. Tell me. What was all this about?"

"We had a case of plague at the County Hospital."

"Yes. So?"

"Nobody caught it."

"Merck's *Manual* says it's awfully contagious."

"I guess we were lucky. He had the bubonic form. When he was walking around and meeting other people he didn't have the pneumonia. The only kind that's contagious is the pneumonia."

"Pneumonia? Bubonic? I don't understand any of this."

"You don't have to," he said. "Just stay healthy."

She watched him drinking his coffee. "You ought to take something for your nerves. Your hands tremble," she said.

Fourteen

A FEW DAYS LATER Noble shyly took an envelope out of his pocket and handed it to Dan. It was heavy expensive paper and Dan's name was handwritten on the cover. "What's this?"

"Open it," Noble said. "Go ahead. Open it now."

Dan opened it. It was an engraved wedding invitation.

"I feel kind of embarrassed about that Dr. Oney Noble bit, but I didn't get them printed," Noble said.

"It's right before graduation."

"Will you come?"

"Sure."

"Do you have somebody to bring?"

"Maybe."

"I'm scared shitless," Noble said.

"Who isn't when they get married?"

"I've been thinking there's something the matter with me. When she was a girl friend it was just fine. But now that I have to live in the same house with her, eat with her, sleep in the same bed and sit on the same pot, it's different."

"You used to do that with your sister and your brother-in-law and it didn't bother you."

"I didn't sleep with them."

"Practically. All of you jammed up in that one room."

"They took care of themselves and I took care of myself. Besides I thought they were a pair of morons and they knew it." He looked at Dan as though he was seeking an answer.

"Everybody's got to do it."

"Thanks a lot, chum." After a moment he said, "There's going to be five hundred people at this wedding."

"Your father-in-law paying for it?"

"The whole damn thing is his idea," Noble said unhappily. "He's a dentist and he's going to make a business project out of it. He's inviting every patient he ever had and everybody he wants as a patient. He's going to write it off his income tax. Business promotion."

"Tell him to forget it. Go to Vegas."

Noble sighed. "How do you think I've been living for the last two years?"

"All right. I'll bring Sharon."

"You're not much consolation," Noble said. After a while he said, "You heard anything about your internship application here?"

Dan shook his head.

"I keep hoping they're going to reject me," Noble said. "I'd like to go to that new hospital in Ghana. I don't want to stay here. My father-in-law's got it all figured out. He owns a medical building and he wants me to sublease from him and start practicing. But if I get turned down, he can't say a word. After all I do have to intern somewhere."

Dan picked up the phone and called Dr. Oldenberg's office. "When will we hear about our applications for internship?" he asked the secretary.

"We won't be ready to send the telegrams for a few days," she said. "What's your name?"

He told her and she left the phone for a few moments. "I've got a note here to call you," she said when she came back. "Can you stop around today?"

He hung up. "I think she's going to tell us," he said to Noble.

On the way down in the elevator Noble said, "I barely passed that first year."

"It's the clinical years that count more."

"Besides I got suspended that time. They must have put a note on my transcript about that." He looked hopeful.

The secretary was a plump blond girl. "I shouldn't give you this information, but we have a problem. Quite a few of the interns want to leave early to go east for their residencies. You're going to be accepted. Do you think you could start early?"

"How about me?" Noble said.

She smiled. "Yes, Mr. Noble. I'm happy to tell you you've been accepted too." She looked at a calendar. "I hate to ask you this, but graduation is on the third. Do you think you two could start on the fourth?"

"I suppose," Dan said.

She smiled again, this time apologetically. "Do you think you could possibly start on the afternoon of the third? You're all done with exercises by noon." She waited.

"My father-in-law is planning a party for that night," Noble said.

She looked at Dan. "Can you?"

"Not on the third. I'll want to celebrate a little. Mark me down for the fourth."

She wrote his name down. "There's an advantage in starting early. You get first choice of rooms and roommates. Who would you like to room with?"

Dan looked at the secretary's large bosom. "Who do I have a choice of?"

The girl grinned. "If you sign up now I'll assign you your room," she said.

Noble said, "We'll room together."

"That's settled," Dan said. He started to walk out.

"Wait a minute," Noble said. "Aren't you going to help me pick out the room?"

"I've got to clean Duffy's cages. I haven't been there for a week. You go ahead and pick it out." As he left Noble was looking through the roster of rooms, trying to make up his mind. He went downstairs to the laboratory and he found Duffy giving one of his cats an injection. On the worktable were a dozen flower pots filled with peat moss out of which grew small plants. "What's all these weeds?"

The cat fell asleep in Duffy's hands. He laid it gently down. "I'm thinking of quitting," he said. "I've spent six thousand dollars this year on this project and I have nothing to show for it."

Dan picked up a flower pot. "What are these?"

"One of the schizophrenics put out a urine that calms the cat down. It took me three months and two thousand dollars to find out that whatever it is is derived from a mixture of Chinese herbs he's taking. It cost me another thousand to identify the particular herb. I'm quitting. I'm done. You want some cats?"

"Wait a minute. It seems to me you're onto something."

"I get onto something every six months," Duffy said. "It's never what I'm looking for. I should be working on a pill for baldness. A nice, red, shiny pill."

"Something upsetting you?"

Duffy snorted. "Something's wrong with a nation that is stingy with pennies to save lives but spends billions on killing people." He shook his head ferociously. "Just as soon as I'm done with this Chinese herb lead, I'm finished. I'm tired of fighting with my wife."

"How many times have you quit already?"

Duffy shot him a sharp glance. "Six or seven. I forget."

Dan finished cleaning the cages. "See you next week," he said.

The last days passed with incredible speed. The lectures became fewer, and almost all Dan's school day was spent on the wards. He was becoming familiar with patients. He found that some were angry and suspicious, but he became fond of others, admiring the dignity of one or the courage of another.

Sharon wanted to sell the store after he graduated, and in this Dan thought she was right. She couldn't run it with two full-time pharmacists and show any profit for herself. He began preparing the store for sale. He hired an accountant who went over the store books, and prepared a neat, bound summary that showed the increasing volume and increasing profits. He had the shelves repainted and new counters built to replace the old shabby ones. He was about to list it with a broker when Tompkins, the day pharmacist he had hired, spoke to him about buying it. "My son-in-law will be coming out this summer. If I buy him the store it'll give me a place to work a few months out of the year and besides, I won't have to worry about my daughter and grandchildren."

"You'll save a commission that way," Dan said. He gave Tompkins a price that would bring Sharon five hundred a month for a number of years. They spoke about it on and off for several weeks, and then after winning a few minor concessions Tompkins agreed to buy the store. Dan insisted that the transfer of the property be made before graduation. Once he and Tompkins agreed, Sharon signed the sales agreement happily.

Noble's wedding was in the home of the bride's father, a large house in Baldwin Hills. It was overflowing with people, more of them white than colored. Noble was drunk. He stood perfectly straight, his face black against the starched white front of his shirt, supporting himself against the wall. "Have a drink," he said. He stopped a waiter with a tray full of drinks and took four.

"*Lekhayim,*" Dan said.

"Here's how," Noble said and gulped his down.

"Such a lovely dress," Cherise said. "So original too. Did you make it yourself?"

"I always make my own clothes," Sharon said. "I made this from some material that my mother bought years ago. I love to sew." Her eyes were gleaming.

"So many girls can't," Cherise said. "I don't think it's beneath a girl's dignity to sew. I attended classes in sewing and my mother made all my clothes and my brothers' even though we had two maids. Just a minute. There's daddy." She hurried away and in a few moments brought back a gray-haired colored man. "Dr. Williams. Dr. McDermott."

"We're not doctors yet," Noble said.

The dentist shook Dan's hand warmly. "Heard about you from Oney. He always talks about you. Have a drink. I put in a dozen cases of whiskey for this shindig and it'll give me ulcers if I don't get it all drunk up." He stopped a waiter and emptied the tray, handing the glasses around. "I was just tickled pink when I heard Oney was accepted at the County. It's one of the best hospitals in the country."

"The way I look at it," Noble said, swaying a little, "I can do a lot more good out here. What the movement really needs is money. They need lawyers to defend themselves against those all-white juries and they need money for bail. They need money to pay for the literature that has to be distributed."

"I see you finished that history of the Jews," Dan said.

Noble looked at him and said, "What do you mean by that crack?"

"That's the thing I admire most about the Jews," the dentist said. "The way they survive. The way they hold on and live through concentration camps and pogroms and starvation. They're the greatest survivors in the world."

"That's because the only ones you know about are the survivors. There are about two or three hundred million nonsurvivors that you've never spoken to."

"Have a good time," the dentist boomed, clapping Dan on the back. "Any time you want a drink just reach out for one. The whole place is yours."

"You've got a wonderful girl," Cherise said. "Why have you been hiding her? She's so pretty." She took Sharon's hand. "I want you to meet some of my friends."

Dan was left alone with Noble. After a while Noble said, "It was a hell of a life working until two o'clock in that lousy fish place. You know I used to fall asleep in class. The worse thing was that I didn't know what was going on. If you hadn't helped me that first year I would have flunked out. I didn't feel well most of the time." He looked at Dan. "You don't believe me? You think I've sold out?"

Dan put his arm around his shoulders. "Sure. What else?" After a moment he added, "But you're probably right. You'll do more good sending them a thousand dollars every three or four months than by getting yourself shot in the ass somewhere."

Noble sighed. "It was awfully hard. I wouldn't want to do it again. Would you?"

Dan thought back, remembering Joan in the first year and the morning sadness and the other things, and he said, "Parts of it." He looked at his watch. "I've got to get back to the store. Best of luck."

Fifteen

THE GRADUATION EXERCISES were held in the morning. Dan had expected to go alone, but Sharon was determined to make a day of it. He saw her in the audience sitting between Eddie and Turk, and he was very pleased. She was wearing a white dress, her dark hair to her shoulders, and she looked a Cretan princess again. Afterward he went down and kissed her. He said, "Must be kind of a dull thing to sit through."

Eddie grimaced. "I guess I'm some use for borrowing money and funerals and graduations."

"Are you complaining?"

"I've seen you once in the last three months."

Dan took Eddie's arm. "You ought to get married. Have another baby and start all over again from the beginning. Maybe you'll do it right this time."

"You're just the one to go to for advice," Eddie said. Then he leaned over and whispered, "That's a bright kid. Are you going to keep him?"

"I think so. He's got no place else to go. His grandfather's too sick to take him. And I'd rather have him with me than in some military school."

"Don't get married because of the kid," Eddie said. "That's a mistake."

"That wasn't why I got married," Dan said.

"We're going to have a party," Sharon said. "I've invited my mother and father and Eddie and I've been cooking all morning."

"I have to check in at the hospital first. Go on home and I'll be there about one."

"Be on time," Sharon said. "I've done all this cooking. I have the table all laid out."

He walked them to Sharon's car. Then he went back to the hospital and got his room key from the superintendent's secretary. Next he went to the laundry, where he was given a large bundle of starched white trousers and shirts. On the way upstairs he stopped at the medical admitting ward to find out what time he should start in the morning. No one was at the desk and he set his stack of laundry down and started looking for the resident. Noble, wearing a dark suit and a bow tie, hurried out of one of the ward rooms. He walked over to the sink and turned on the water and put one arm, jacket sleeve and all, under the faucet. Dan stared at him.

"A patient threw up all over me," Noble said. "I gave her a hypo of Demerol and the moment I turned my back she threw up everything she's eaten for the last week." He took the jacket off and washed his arm.

"You stink too," Dan said.

Noble sniffed. "Just of vomit," he said. "You're going to have to stay and help me for a while."

"I can't. They're giving a party for me."

"Me too," Noble said angrily. "All I did was show up on the ward to ask about rounds tomorrow and the resident asked me to work up a couple of patients. They're shorthanded. You know how many a couple are? Six." He pointed to the blackboard behind the nurse's desk. "There they are."

Dan looked at the list of names. "I can put in an hour or so I guess. That's all. Sharon will kill me if I'm late."

"Don't tell me your troubles," Noble said. "Tell them to the resident if you can find him. I'm going upstairs to change clothes."

Dan took the top chart off the pile for newly admitted patients and started toward the room. Two medical students in long white coats stopped him before he got there. One was dark and tall. "Are you the intern?" he asked.

"Sort of."

"We're supposed to be assigned a case."

Dan pointed to the stack of charts on the desk. "Take any one."

The medical student frowned. "We'd like an instructive case. There's no point in working up some old crock."

"They're all sick. That's all you need." Dan went on into the room and sat down by the bedside of a small old woman. "What's the trouble?" he said, pen poised.

"Are you the doctor?"

"The only one that's around. What's the trouble?"

"That's what I came here to find out."

"What symptoms do you have?"

"Symptoms?"

"Do you have any pain?"

"Not real pain. I'm just sick."

"In what way?"

"I don't feel well."

A student nurse walked in. "Are you admitting?" she asked.

"For a little while," he said. "Why?"

"There's a red blanket on its way up. Central Admitting just called. Attempted suicide."

"You better get the resident up too. I just started ten minutes ago."

"I have a call in for him now," she said. "I'll let you know when the patient gets here."

Dan went back to his questioning. The old woman was vague in her answers. Six months before she had walked into a swarm of gnats, and they had stung her, leaving speckled spots on her body. She showed Dan a number of small discolored patches on her arms that looked like the ordinary freckles of old people.

The nurse came back into the room. "That emergency is in 14A," she said.

"Did you get the resident?"

"I have a call in for him."

He put the unfinished chart back on the desk and went to see the girl in 14A. He smelled Lysol the moment he walked into the room. She was dark and had a full angry face. A handsome man of her own age and an older woman were standing by her bedside. "What happened?" Dan said.

"She swallowed Lysol. She poisoned herself," the man said. His breath smelled of whiskey. "For God's sakes do everything you can. I don't care about the expense."

"When did she take it?"

"Get out," the girl said. "Get out both of you. I'll speak to the doctor alone."

The nurse came in the room. "I have Dr. Lothian on the phone for you." Dan followed her to the desk. "This is McDermott," he said. "I'm trying to help Noble work up the admissions. There's a girl up here who took Lysol."

"How much?"

"I don't know yet."

"How long ago?"

Dan turned to the man. "When did she drink it?"

"About half-past twelve."

Dan looked at the clock. "Three quarters of an hour ago," he said.

"Don't put down one of the big tubes. Use a small tube," the resident said. "Wash her stomach out. I'm stuck up here with a bleeder. I'll get down when I can. By the way, thanks for starting today."

"You have it wrong," Dan said angrily. "I'm not starting today. Not until tomorrow."

"You can't walk off the ward now," the resident said. "Don't worry. I'll be able to get it covered after midnight."

"Wait a minute," Dan said, but the resident had already hung up. He dialed the operator. "Let me speak to Dr. Lothian."

"He's on admitting. Is this an emergency?"

"It sure is."

"Just a minute." He waited. After a few minutes he said to the nurse, "Bring me down a stomach tray."

The operator came back on the line. "I can't reach Dr. Lothian now," she said. Dan hung up and went into the girl's room. "How much Lysol did you drink?"

The girl looked around and saw the young man and her mother in the doorway. She said, "Close the door."

Dan closed the door. "I didn't drink any," she said. "I just frightened them." Dan picked up the flashlight and a tongue blade and said, "Open your mouth."

She opened her mouth and there were burns on the underside of her lips and on her tongue.

"How did you burn your mouth?"

"I just washed my mouth out with it. Then I spit it out and screamed."

"Why?"

"He's running around with other women. I was going to teach him a lesson. You're not going to tell him what I told you?"

"I don't know," Dan said. "You sure you didn't drink any?"

She shook her head, and he started examining her. When he touched her stomach she grimaced in pain. "What's hurting you?"

"When I get upset I get a nervous stomach."

The nurse brought in the tray. The girl looked at the tube. "You're not going to wash my stomach, are you? I really didn't drink any."

"None at all?"

"Do you think I'm crazy?"

Dan returned the tray to the nurse. Then he went outside. "Did you see her drink any?" he asked the man.

He started crying. "Oh God. Oh God. Don't let her die. It's my fault. It's all my fault."

"She says she didn't drink any of it."

The man stopped crying. "What?"

"She says she didn't drink any Lysol."

"That bitch! That rotten sadistic bitch! She didn't drink any?"

"That's what she says."

The man started for the room but Dan caught him by the arm. "Wait a minute. What did you see?"

"She was having hysterics, screaming and crying. Then she locked herself in the bathroom and said she'd poisoned herself and I should leave her alone to die. Then I broke the door down and there she was with a bottle of Lysol half empty." He turned to the woman. "Did you hear that? She didn't drink any. She was just faking."

"Thank God," the woman said. She started crying too. Dan took the chart to the desk and sat down to write his note, but he stopped in the middle of it. He finally said to the nurse, "Let me have that gastric aspiration tray back."

"I returned it."

"Then get it again."

She picked up the phone.

"No, no," Dan said. "Send somebody for it."

"I'm shorthanded," the nurse said. She clicked on the receiver.

"Never mind," Dan said. He hurried to the elevator, took it up to the eighteenth floor. He brought the tray back and set it up in the room. When the girl saw the long tube she screamed, "I won't let you put that in me. I'm going to leave. I didn't come here to be tortured. I didn't drink any Lysol."

"Hold still," Dan said. She struggled so vigorously, however, that he couldn't get the tube into her nose. He went to the desk for the nurse. She was gone. In one of the side rooms he found the two medical students taking a history from an old man with a beard who looked familiar. "I need one of you," Dan said.

"We're supposed to finish this case by three o'clock," the blond student said.

"It will just take a few minutes. Come on."

Dan stopped to talk to the husband. "She doesn't want me to pass a stomach tube, but I think I ought to anyway."

"Good," the man said. "Make it a big tube and shove it down hard."

Dan and the medical student went into the room. "Hold her hands," Dan said.

"Can you pass a stomach tube without a patient's permission?" the student asked.

"I don't think so. Hold her hands," Dan said.

The medical student held her hands. Dan tried to insert the tip of the tube into her nose but she deftly avoided it by turning her head. The medical student watched. "How much did she take?" he asked.

"She says she didn't take any."

"Then why are you washing her stomach?"

The girl opened her mouth to scream and for a moment her head was still. Dan quickly slipped the tube through a nostril. She tried to turn but it was too late. He had already pushed the tube down.

The girl got one hand free and tore it out and began screaming again. The husband and the older woman came running into the room. "What are you doing to my daughter?" the woman screamed.

"Leave the doctor alone," the man said roughly. "It serves her right. They should use a garden hose."

A few drops of stomach juice were at the tip of the tube, and Dan wiped it on a towel. Almost as an afterthought he lifted the towel and sniffed at it. Then he handed the towel to the medical student. "Smell this."

The medical student smelled. "Lysol," he said.

"Hold her," Dan said. This time the student needed no urging. He held both arms firmly. Dan bent over, and the girl suddenly spat in his face. He wiped his face with the towel. Her saliva also smelled of Lysol.

"Just leave me alone," she screamed. "I want to die. Can't you understand that?" He held her head with one hand and with the other managed to get the tube in. When he put his finger over her mouth to tape the tube in place she bit him. He dropped the tape and she swung her head vigorously, trying to shake the tube loose.

"Listen," he said. "If you pull the tube out again, I'll call psychiatry and they'll commit you and put a straitjacket on you and then we'll still tube you. Which way do you want it?"

It was an empty threat. It would be several hours before the transfer and commitment could be accomplished and by that time whatever Lysol she had taken would already be in her system. However, the girl didn't know that. She stared at him and then said, "You men. You're all bastards." He taped the tube in place and started emptying the stomach. The liquid smelled strongly of Lysol.

The husband also smelled it. "Oh my God," he said. "She really drank it." He clasped his hands together. "Oh Jesus forgive me for what I've done."

"Get that whining son of a bitch out of here," the girl said nasally.

"Go on," Dan said.

"Take good care of her, please," the man said. "We can pay. We're not charity cases. Don't let her die." The dark medical student came running in. "That fellow we were examining just had a convulsion," he said breathlessly. "He rolled his eyes back and started shaking all over. I can't get a pulse."

Dan didn't want to run across the ward. Instead he broke into a rapid loping walk, suddenly remembering that this was the way he had always seen interns walk. The nurse was already in the room. "His pulse is coming back," she said. "Shall we give him some oxygen?" The blue was leaving the old man's face. He started breathing again. "He looks familiar," Dan said. "What's his name?"

The nurse glanced at the sheet at the head of the bed. "Abraham Barenholtz," she said.

Barenholtz. The prayer leader who had been too sick to lead the prayers last Yom Kippur.

"I'm getting a pretty fair pulse now," the nurse said.

The old man opened his eyes. "What are you doing with me?" he said in Yiddish.

Dan adjusted the oxygen mask. "Just lie still, grandfather," he said.

"Who can lie still with such a pain in his chest?" He looked at Dan, squinting. "I know you, don't I? Where are my eye-glasses?"

The nurse took his glasses from the bedside table and put them on his nose. He looked at Dan again. "I'm having a heart attack, no?"

"I don't know yet."

The blond medical student came back. "I figured you wanted me to keep pumping," he said. "I got out a bucket of Lysol."

"What kind of a story do you have on this man?"

The other student picked up the chart. "He's a seventy-seven-year-old retired Hebrew carpenter. He was in here last year for a stroke. This morning he had an attack of what he calls indigestion. He had chest pain and fainting." He stopped. "That's all I have. He had the convulsion when I got this far."

"Doctor," the nurse said sharply. Dan looked up. The old man was arching in another convulsion. Dan put his stethoscope on the patient's chest, but this time he heard no heart sounds at all. "The pulse is gone," the nurse said.

Dan's face and scalp were suddenly wet with sweat.

"He's tapping out right now," the medical student said.

"Get me some Xylocaine," Dan said.

"What strength?"

"Whatever you've got."

He put his hands together in the middle of the patient's chest and pushed down hard and let go and pushed down hard and let go again. To the medical student he said, "Run like hell and get a respirator."

The student looked about startled. "Where?"

"Start running right now," Dan said and the medical student sprinted down the ward, his coat flying out behind him. The blond one stayed behind feeling for a pulse. "I'm getting a pulse again," he finally said. Dan's arms were aching. He stopped and waited and then he listened to the heart. It was beating again.

"His heart is either stopping or going into some kind of ar-rhythmia," Dan said.

"I figured that," the student said.

The nurse came in with Xylocaine. She handed Dan the loaded syringe. "A one percent solution," she said.

Dan looked at the syringe. He didn't remember the dosage. It was either twenty-five milligrams or maybe a hundred, one or the other. "What's the dose of Xylocaine?" he asked. The student shook his head.

He turned to the nurse. "What dosage of Xylocaine do they use in the cardiac unit?"

"I've never worked there," she said.

If he gave the patient too little it would do no good. He didn't know what would happen if he gave him too much, but it would probably be harmful. The other student came back pushing a mechanical respirator. The nurse plugged it into the wall, and fitted the mask over the patient's face.

An orderly walked into the ward room. "Are you Dr. McDermott?"

Dan looked up. "Who?"

"Dr. McDermott."

"Oh, yes."

"There's a call for you at the desk."

"Better take a message."

The orderly nodded and left.

"Come on Lennie," the dark medical student said. "We have a four o'clock lecture." The blond one hesitated. "I'll hang around awhile," he said. "Take good notes so I can copy them."

"Thanks," Dan said.

"His pulse rate is about a hundred and eighty," the nurse said.

"I've got to find out what the dose of Xylocaine is," Dan said to the medical student. "Keep feeling his pulse. If it stops give him cardiac massage the way I did. And yell for me. Yell good and loud."

"I got you."

"What's your name?"

The student was concentrating on the pulse. "What? Oh. Evans. Bob Evans."

To the nurse he said, "Can you get me one of those monitoring electrocardiographs?"

"There's none on the ward."

"Go steal one from the intensive cardiac unit. That's where this patient belongs anyway."

The nurse left looking confused. The orderly came back. "It was Mrs. Wolfe. She wants to know what time you'll be home."

"I'll call her," Dan said.

The student counted the pulse. "About a hundred. Stronger too."

They waited and finally the nurse wheeled in the oscilloscopic electrocardiograph.

"What took so long?"

"I had to call the nursing office to get this thing released to our ward," she said, busily making the connections.

Dan flicked the switch and watched the luminescent trail on the screen. "An acute infarct," he said indignantly. "What's the matter with that admitting-room resident? Why didn't he send this patient up to the heart unit?"

"I can call the superintendent and ask him," the nurse said sweetly.

"Bring in a drip of glucose with Isuprel," Dan said.

The old man was still very close to death. He lay back unconscious, fine sweat on his face, his beard moving gently as he breathed. "I wish the hell the resident would get up here," Dan finally said.

The nurse came back with the intravenous solution. Dan put the needle in the old man's vein and set the solution flowing.

"The family would like to speak with you," the nurse said.

Dan looked up. "Send them in."

A well-dressed woman walked in followed by a short man. "I want to thank you for how much you are doing for my father-in-law," she said. "You just can't express these things in words."

Dan nodded.

"I do want you to understand though that we know how desperate his condition is. He has a very bad heart and for years now the doctors have been telling us he can go any minute. The poor dear's life hasn't been an easy one. He can't go anywhere. He can't eat his favorite foods."

The husband didn't say anything.

"I just want you to know that we understand that sometimes you doctors can't save everybody."

"Is he unconscious?" the man asked.

"Some of the time," Dan said.

"I wouldn't want him to suffer any more than he has to," the woman said.

Dan nodded again.

"We'll understand, no matter what the outcome is."

"There are some benches in the hall," Dan said. "I'll stop by and talk to you a little later."

After they went Evans scratched his nose and said, "What was that all about?"

"Seems to me she was saying it's fine with her if the old man dies."

"The hell with her," the student said.

"Yes," Dan said. He turned the ratchet a little more. The fluid flowed a little faster, and the patient's pulse seemed stronger. Dan's legs ached from standing and he went outside and sat down at the desk. He picked up the phone to call the resident when he saw Noble darting out of one room and hurrying across the hall. "Hey, wait a minute. What's the dose of Xylocaine?"

"I don't remember. Why?"

Dan frowned. "I have a patient the admitting room balled up on. They should have sent him up to the intensive cardiac care unit. I got him instead."

"Transfer him," Noble said and hurried by.

Dan called the ward that the resident said he was on. A nurse answered. "He's with an emergency. I can't call him to the phone now." He then put in a call for the cardiac resident on call. It turned out to be Rosenthal. "I can't locate him now," the operator said. "I will page him and have him call you."

"Dr. McDermott," the medical student called. Dan dropped the phone and ran into the room. "He's starting again," Evans said. "His pulse is skipping."

Dan picked up the Xylocaine, and gave a small dose slowly into the tubing, perhaps twenty-five milligrams or so. He waited, feeling the pulse. It remained irregular, waxing and waning. Dan watched the screen. After a minute he injected a little more Xylocaine. After that he thought the pulse became steadier. "Looks better," he said.

The medical student was watching too. "I guess so," he said dubiously.

"Keep your eyes on it," Dan said. He went out to the desk. He meant to find a book in which he would look up the dose of Xylocaine but the husband of the girl who had taken Lysol was waiting for him. "She's just lying there," he said angrily. "Nobody's doing anything for her." Dan started for the girl's room when an elevator opened and an orderly pushed a stretcher out quickly. He dropped a chart on the desk as he went by. Dan turned. "What's that?"

"A bleeder," the orderly said. "A red blanket."

"That's Noble's isn't it?" Dan said.

The nurse at the desk shook her head. "He just took a pneumonia case."

Dan looked at the clock. Then he said, "Get him typed and cross-matched for transfusions." He walked into the room where the girl was lying, the tube still in her nose. "How do you feel?"

"Awful sick. Did you get it all out?" She seemed frightened.

Dan didn't say anything. He filled a syringe with water and flushed it into the tube. It came back almost clear. "Whatever was in the stomach," he said.

"Am I going to be all right?"

"You changed your mind about dying?"

"It hurts so," she said.

"What are you going to do for her?" the man said.

Dan walked to the kitchen and took out a carton of milk from the icebox and brought it back. He filled a syringe and injected it slowly into the tube. The husband watched him. "What's that supposed to do?"

"It helps."

The resident put his head in the door. "Did you call me?"

"I sure did." Dan clamped the tube and walked outside. "What's the dose of Xylocaine?"

"Enough," the resident said. "Why?"

"How much is enough?"

"We generally start with twenty-five milligrams and from there on you give enough to keep the rhythm under control. Why?"

"They sent me up an acute infarct."

"Better get him transferred to the acute cardiac unit. What else do you have?"

Dan told him about the Lysol poisoning.

The resident nodded. "The big trick is getting it out of the stomach quickly. Just keep the tube in place now and aspirate it from time to time and put something bland and oily in. Olive oil or milk." He turned away.

"Are you leaving?"

"I've got four wards to cover."

The husband had followed Dan into the hall. "You think she needs a psychiatrist?" he said.

"I don't know what good that would do," Dan said. "Besides, our big problem is keeping her going for the next two or three days." He saw the misery in the man's face and he said, "I think I got almost all of it out of the stomach. That may make the difference."

He went into the ward in which the new emergency patient was lying. He was a thin young man, his skin almost as pale as his bedclothes. He was bearded and his hair was down to his shoulders.

"What happened to you?" Dan said.

The young man looked at him from a long distance, his eyes unfocused, bubbles forming between his lips.

Dan shook him. "What happened?"

The young man finally saw him. "I threw up blood. I've been throwing it up all day." He closed his eyes wearily. Dan examined the boy. His blood pressure was very low, and his pulse was fast. A hippie with a bleeding ulcer, he thought, maybe smoking marijuana, taking LSD, not eating, and then suddenly hemorrhaging. The strange despair or anger that led him to grow his hair long and go about bearded and dirty had in some way turned inward, burrowing a hole in his stomach until it reached an artery. While he was working the nurse came in with the first pint of blood and attached it.

"What do you want me to do with that Lysol case in 14A?" she said. "I just put another pint of milk into her tube."

"Put an ounce of olive oil down every hour now." He went out into the hall. For a moment it was quiet. He could see Evan's back as the boy sat watching the dancing point of light on the oscilloscope. On the screen the beats were coming regularly. His own back ached and he had to urinate badly. He thought of calling Sharon but he was too uncomfortable. He started for the washroom and was just stepping up to the toilet bowl when the door was flung open and the medical student dashed in. "He's stopped again," he cried.

Dan ran down the hall buttoning his trousers. Noble was already there, sitting astride the bed, pressing the old man's chest vigorously, his two black hands crossed. Dan stopped at the foot of the bed. The little point of light danced every time Noble compressed the chest. "I need a few minutes," Dan finally said.

Noble nodded and Dan went out to the desk. He called Rosenthal again. He was surprised when the call went through. "I've got a patient up here that should never be on this ward. He's an acute infarct. Every so often I can't get a pulse or a heartbeat."

"Have you tried Xylocaine?"

"I think you ought to take him," Dan said sharply. "He's a case for the intensive cardiac care unit."

"Haven't got a bed," Rosenthal said. "Nowhere to put him. You'll have to take care of him. I'll take a run up though."

Dan went back into Barenholtz's room. Noble was resting. "I think he's gone," he said.

"What do you mean?" He pushed Noble angrily aside and compressed the old man's chest. The luminescent point danced intricately. He kept pushing regularly. His shoulders ached. Then he stopped.

"The pulse is back," Evans said.

An attendant appeared at the ward threshold. "There's a call for you Dr. McDermott," she said.

"Take a message," Dan said.

"I guess you're in business again after all," Noble said watching the oscilloscope.

"What do you do for Lysol poisoning?" Dan said.

Noble shrugged. "Wash out the stomach. Egg white. Olive oil. How about covering me while I go to dinner?"

Dan nodded and Noble wrote out a list. "The ones with a check are in rough shape. I'll get back as soon as I can."

"I have to go too," the medical student said. "It's way after classtime."

"Sure. Thanks," Dan said.

"Mind if I come back up here again?" Evans said. "I've learned a lot following you around."

Dan thought the boy was being sarcastic, and he looked up angrily, but when he saw the student's face he realized that he meant what he said. "Anytime," he said.

The attendant came to the door again. "She's still waiting on the phone."

"Who?"

"Mrs. Wolfe."

He went to the desk but the line was dead. He put the receiver back in its cradle and went in to check on the bleeding boy. A basin by his bedside was half full of blood. The boy looked weaker. Dan attached a syringe to the bottle of blood and started pumping it rapidly into the boy's veins. When he had emptied one bottle, he went to the refrigerator and took out a second bottle of blood and attached it. He left the bottle dripping as fast as it would go and walked from one bed to another, checking his patients and those on Noble's list. He found the old woman who was his first patient of the day fast asleep, her mouth open.

He woke her up. "I'd like to finish your history," he said.

She yawned sleepily. "What time is it?"

"About eight."

"Oh yes. Well, you see, I walked across this lawn. It was up by Long Beach and they stung me all over."

"Yes," Dan said. "But what are you here for?"

"That's when I developed these spots."

"You're here about the spots?"

"No."

Dan sighed. "Anyway when did they start?"

The patient thought awhile. "Last year or maybe the year before." She looked at Dan. "Come here."

"What is it?"

"Give me your hand."

He held his hand out and she took it in both her small cold ones and said, "Oh, my dear boy, I'm so glad you're not dead too."

He took his hand away. "What?"

"I thought you were one of the dead ones."

Dan nodded. "Yes," he said.

"I'm dead," she said. "I died when the gnats stung me."

He took her blood pressure and examined her chest. He brought the chart out and put it on the desk. "This one has to be transferred to psychiatry in the morning."

"That's too bad," the nurse said. "She's the nicest patient in the ward. She helped me put the other ones to bed."

The room doors were open and Dan could see his patients. The girl who had taken the Lysol was lying quietly in bed, her husband holding her hand. An attendant was injecting oil into the tube. In the other room, blood was dripping briskly into the arm of the bearded boy. In a third room behind the desk Dan saw the old man, with the oscilloscope over his head registering each beat.

Noble got off the elevator. "If you want to get anything to eat you better be there in five minutes. They don't serve you after nine o'clock."

Dan gave him the three charts. "Here are the bad ones. Watch them for me. I want all three of them still here when I get back."

"Hurry," Noble said. "They're real independent in that cafeteria."

Dan hesitated, torn between his need to urinate and his hunger. The hunger won out and he started down the hall. The old man's son and daughter-in-law were waiting for him there. "Doctor," the man said.

He stopped.

"How is he?"

"His heart stopped a couple of times, but he's better now," Dan said. "I expect the cardiology resident will come up here and insert an internal pacemaker."

"What's that?"

"It's an electrical apparatus that we put through a vein up into the heart. It keeps the heartbeat going."

"He's an old man," the woman said. "He's been dying for years. Why don't you just let him die in peace? Why prolong it? Why torture him?"

Dan hesitated. Then he said, "I've been doing everything I can think of. In a little while the cardiology resident is coming and he'll do everything he can. And if that's not enough we'll call the chief of staff and have him come down."

The woman glared at him.

"I'll be back in a little while," Dan said. He slipped by them and ran down the six flights of steps. He got to the dining room door just as the waitress was closing the doors. Most of the tables were empty, but at one he saw Rosenthal leisurely finishing his meal. Dan strode across the room. "What the hell are you doing here? I've been sweating my balls off with this old man upstairs."

"Don't be so nervous," Rosenthal said. "Sit down." He looked up at Dan. "Sit down. You save time by telling me about him while I'm finishing my coffee."

The speaker in the corner of the dining room said, "Dr. McDermott," several times insistently and Dan said, "They're calling me. I'll be right back."

He found the booths behind the doors. "A Mr. Lechinski called you," the operator said. "He couldn't wait on the line. He'll call you back in fifteen minutes."

Dan hung up the phone. When he got out he found that Rosenthal had left and the dining room was completely empty. He sat down and waited, but no waitress came out of the kitchen. He finally went to the swinging kitchen door and put his head in. "How about some dinner?"

The waitress was unloading a tray of dishes. "Past nine," she said. "We can't serve now."

"What am I supposed to do?" he said angrily. "I haven't eaten since this morning?"

"Are you one of the new boys?"

"New and starved."

The waitress sighed. "Sit down. I'll see what I can scrounge off the cook."

He sat down and she brought him out a slice of cold roast beef and two pieces of bread. "The cook wouldn't light the broiler," she said. "This is the best I can do. Next time if you're going to be late call down and ask for a late tray."

He put the beef between the two slices of bread and the speaker again boomed his name twice. He started to put the sandwich down and the waitress said, "Eat up. I've got to lock this room."

It was probably Goldie calling him again, he thought, and he ignored the speaker and bit into the sandwich.

A phone on a nearby table rang and the waitress picked it up. "You McDermott?"

He got up chewing on his sandwich and took the receiver.

"This is 6400," a nurse said. "Dr. Noble asked you to come right up. One of your patients has gone bad." The food in his mouth dried up. He put the sandwich down and said, "Thanks," to the waitress and he broke into the loping half run of the interns. The elevator indicator pointed to the seventh floor and he had to wait. His stomach churned nervously. He looked up again and the indicator was at nine. The elevator was going in the wrong direction. He ran up the six flights and got to the ward panting.

The girl was all right, and he saw the old man lying unattended. So he was probably all right. He turned to the third room and saw Noble and the resident standing by the bed of the bleeding boy. He hurried over.

"He's shocky again. I can't get the blood in fast enough," Noble said.

"It must be a big artery that's let go," the resident said. "Have you called surgery?"

"I thought he had slowed down a while ago."

The resident walked out into the hall with Dan. "The only chance this kid has is surgery. We're not able to keep up with the bleeding. It's like pouring blood into a bottle with a hole in it. How are your other patients?"

Dan told him about the old man and the girl.

The resident nodded. "I'll be on 6800 if you need me."

Dan stood in front of the desk, uncertain what to do next. The nurse answered the phone. "There's another emergency on the way up for you," she said hanging up. "Coma of unknown origin."

"Isn't it Noble's turn yet?"

"He's got one coming up too," she said. "I took a message for you while you were downstairs." She handed him a slip. He put it in his pocket and picked up the telephone and put in a call for the surgical resident. He waited while the operator searched the wards. "McDermott on 6400," he said when the connection was finally made. "There's a bleeding ulcer here that you ought to see."

"What's the name?"

Dan read the name off the chart.

"How bad is he?"

"We can't get blood in fast enough. He's shocky now."

The voice at the other end of the phone said, "Sounds like a job for us. He'll need an emergency gastrectomy. I have a staff man here. We'll be up in ten minutes."

Dan hung up the phone. "Let's start some blood in the other arm," he said. He went back into where the pale boy lay. To Noble he said, "You better get going, Oney. You're getting a new one too."

"All this stuff I've given him is barely keeping his pressure up to eighty."

"I'll start another pint."

The nurse brought him the set and he started the new bottle of blood. He was pumping it in when a resident and a man in street clothes walked into the room.

"Is this the bleeder?" the resident said.

Dan nodded.

"I'm McCary," the resident said. "This is Dr. Angelo. Now what about this boy?"

Dan saw Rosenthal in the hall going by the desk toward Barenholtz's room. Dan then went ahead and told the surgeons about the bleeding boy, using the prescribed form that he had been taught. They examined the patient. "You're going to have to be operated on, son," the older man said.

The boy, fogged with drugs and shock, turned to look at the surgeon. "What?" he said.

"We're going to operate on you."

The boy closed his eyes without answering.

"Does he have any folks up here?"

Dan looked in the chart. "In Bakersfield."

The surgeon turned to his resident. "Set him up as an emergency. We'll do him about midnight or so." To Dan he said, "Get as much blood as you can into him." They walked into the hall. "I hate these emergency surgeries for bleeding," the surgeon said. "We lose so many of them." He looked back at the boy. "You wouldn't expect a flower-kid with a beard to have the emotional repressions that produce an ulcer, would you?"

"They're really conformists," the surgical resident said. "Maybe they get ulcers from trying to conform to the standards of their group." The surgeon grunted and the resident said, "I'll call you in about an hour or so to see how he's doing. We ought to be taking him up by eleven."

Dan nodded. To the nurse he said, "Get me up at least three more pints of blood for this boy."

"That new patient of yours is in thirteen," she said, "and here's a call for you." She handed him the phone. It was Goldie.

"What's the matter with the operators in that lousy hospital? I've been calling you for an hour. They just let you hang on the line," Goldie said.

"What's up?"

"I'm in a jam again."

Dan remembered it was Saturday night. "The Hollywood jail?"

"The University precinct jail. You know where that is?"

"It doesn't make any difference," Dan said. "I can't get there."

"What do you mean?" Goldie screamed over the phone. "Are you going to leave me here? After all I've done for you?"

The nurse tapped Dan on the shoulder. "That new patient is in coma," she said.

"Start some oxygen," Dan said. To Goldie he said, "I can't get down there. I'm working. How about Marie?"

"She won't come," Goldie said. "I've got the money. It's only a misdemeanor. All you've got to do is bring it down."

"I can get there in the morning."

"That's too late. They'll have me arraigned by then and with my record I'll never be able to straighten it out."

"Then get sick," Dan said. "They'll put you on the jail ward here and I'll see you get special privileges."

"Go to hell," Goldie screamed. "You son of a bitch. You bastard."

"I just can't leave the ward," Dan said. He hung up the phone and hurried into the old man's room. Rosenthal was listening to his heart. Dan put his stethoscope on the gray-haired chest and listened too. The heartbeats were regular and fairly strong.

"You've done a bang-up job on this one. We wouldn't have done better downstairs," Rosenthal said.

"You should have been up here hours ago."

"We don't have a bed. You'd had to have kept him until tomorrow anyway."

"No internal pacemaker?"

"That's the virtue of judicious delay. If I had come up here two hours ago when you were having this fuss I would have been doing all sorts of things to this poor fellow. Right now I'm just going to let you go on the way you've been going. It's a lot better for him." Rosenthal folded his stethoscope and put it in his pocket.

"Sam?"

"Yes?"

"I'm trying to get to the bathroom for a couple of hours. Can you watch this guy for me for just long enough?"

Rosenthal grinned. "Go ahead."

As Dan went past the desk the nurse stopped him and handed him the receiver. "There's a doctor on the line to talk to you," she said.

Dan took the receiver. "Yes?"

"I'm calling about Mr. Barenholtz," a man's voice said. "I've been his doctor for years." He told Dan his name and Dan told him about the old man. The doctor listened. Then he said, "I don't see what else you can do. The daughter-in-law called me. She was hot under the collar. She felt you were doing too much."

"I got the idea she wouldn't have minded if the old man died."

The doctor didn't say anything for a minute. Then he said, "I know. She wants to get off on a trip to Europe this summer. Her husband won't go while the old man is this sick."

"He's better. I think he might make it."

"Good," the doctor said. "Keep working. Good luck."

When Dan hung up the phone he found the daughter-in-law at his elbow. "Well," she said.

"That was your doctor."

"I know," she said and waited.

"Things are looking a little better," Dan said. "His heart is beating on its own now."

Rosenthal came out. The woman turned to him. "Are you the chief heart doctor?"

"No ma'am," Rosenthal said. "I'm just the night heart doctor."

"I would like to know what's being done for my father-in-law."

"This intern here has kept him alive," Rosenthal said. "He's the one you have to thank for still having a father-in-law."

"Let me take you home, honey," the man said. "There's no need for you to stay up."

"Your coma patient's respirations are rather poor," the nurse said.

"All right," Dan said. To Rosenthal he said, "Thanks. If there's trouble, I'll call you."

The new patient did not look good. He was middle-aged and dirty. A stubble of beard covered his chin. His breath smelled of wine, but the coma was too deep for drunkenness. Dan searched the body and found bruises on his shoulders and on his knees. With a flashlight he parted his hair on his head, and saw lice crawling among the hair roots. He found the bruise he expected. He sat down and filled out the chart and under diagnosis wrote, *Alcoholism. Probable brain injury. Recommend spinal tap.* He hesitated and then he added, *Report to Coroner's Office as possible homicide.*

The nurses were preparing the patient for the spinal tap when his breathing went bad. Dan rolled him over on his back, opened his mouth, and pushed his tongue forward with his fingers. He said urgently, "Let me have a respirator."

"There isn't one on the floor."

"Mr. Barenholtz doesn't need his any more. Hurry up." He held the patient's tongue back with one hand and with the other hand pressed on his chest, forcing air in and out. The nurse finally came with the respirator and he attached it and turned it on. "Get me my resident. He's on 6800," he said. He snatched up an ampule of stimulant from an emergency tray and gave the patient an injection. It didn't help. The man turned blue, his eyes crossed, and his heart stopped. Dan put both hands together in the middle of his chest and pushed hard. The nurse came back and Dan said, "Can you feel a pulse?"

She felt and then said, "No. Nothing."

He pushed even harder and felt ribs crack under his hands. "Now?" he said.

She shook her head.

The resident came in and tapped him on the shoulder and said, "Let me try." He let go and the resident took his place and pushed vigorously on the man's chest. After a while he stopped too. "How are your other ones doing?"

Dan was sitting down. "I don't know," he said. "I think I broke some of his ribs."

"That happens every so often with this type of resuscitation. You can't help it," the resident said.

Dan went out and sat down by the desk. The patient had been in the room at least fifteen minutes before he had seen him. Perhaps if he had seen him sooner things might have turned out differently. The resident came out and sat down next to him. He was filling out a sheet with a black border. "What are you putting as the cause of death?" Dan said.

"Cerebral hemorrhage, probably secondary to a head injury."

"Wine on his breath," Dan said.

"I saw your note," the resident said and wrote under contributing causes, *Alcoholism*. He closed the chart. "I've lost five already tonight."

"What's that supposed to show?"

"That people die. You better go take care of your other patients. Five is enough of these certificates for one night." He got up and went down the hall. After a while Dan went in to see the bleeding boy. The blood was dripping well, and the boy raised his head up when he heard Dan.

"Look at all those bottles," he said.

"How do you feel?"

"Nauseous. How am I, Doc?"

"You've been bleeding pretty badly."

Dan took his pulse and his blood pressure. They were better. He flicked on the bedside light and turned the boy's face so that he could see him clearly. Color was coming back to his cheeks.

"Some of the blood has stayed in," Dan said.

"I was kind of wiped out there for a while. What's this all from?"

"A bleeding ulcer."

"Ulcer?" The boy looked up at the ceiling, thinking about it. "That's what you get from worrying, isn't it?"

"Sometimes."

"I'm getting just like my father," the boy said. "He has an ulcer too."

"It does run in families."

He went back to the desk and called the surgical resident. "He's looking better," he said. "His pulse is good and his pressure is staying up." He told him the figures.

"Good," the resident said. "He'll take the surgery better. Hold on a minute. Let me tell my attending man about this." He came back on the phone after about a minute. The enthusiasm was gone from his voice. "Angelo wants to cancel him. He says if the kid's better he'd rather see if he'll stop on his own."

"Fine," Dan said. "I'm ahead of him now on blood and he keeps getting pinker by the minute."

"I'll take him off the schedule for now," the surgical resident said. "If he goes bad again call me."

Dan hung up. "Get me a couple more pints on that boy in thirteen," he told the nurse. He went back and looked at Barenholtz. The old man was snoring. The drip was going slowly into one arm. The oscilloscope showed a regular pulse.

While he was writing in the chart the old man woke up. "What's that? Who's this?" he said, again speaking Yiddish.

"Go back to sleep, grandfather," Dan said.

The old man squinted at him again. "I know you, no?"

"You know me," Dan said. "Go back to sleep. Tomorrow you'll be better."

"Maybe there won't be a tomorrow. How can I afford to sleep?"

"What's around here to stay awake for?"

The old man looked at the drab ward with his dim eyes. "Well said, young man," he said and closed his eyes. In a few moments he was snoring again.

Dan went down the hall and looked at the girl who had taken the Lysol.

"When are you going to take this tube out?" she said nasally. "It's killing me."

"Just as soon as I'm sure that the Lysol is out of your system."

"I didn't take that much. It's awful stuff to swallow. Maybe only a teaspoonful."

He didn't believe her. He patted her on the leg and said, "You'll be all right by tomorrow. Maybe we'll be able to take the tube out then." He went out into the hall and no new names had been added to the board. The ward was quiet, and he thought he could get to the bathroom. In the waiting room the husband of the girl who had taken the Lysol was sitting chatting with Mr. Barenholtz's son. Dan stopped. "She's a little more comfortable," he said to the husband. "The bad thing about this poison though is that it can do systematic damage." The man didn't understand and Dan said, "At first we worry about it eating its way through the stomach. It hasn't done that. Now we have to start worrying about its damaging the organs."

"Is she going to be all right?"

"We'll know in about two days."

To Mr. Barenholtz's son he said, "He seems to be making it."

"You don't know what this means to me," he said.

The doctor's bathroom was a dozen paces farther. Dan unlocked the door and was walking up to the toilet bowl when Noble rushed by, pushing him aside. Noble groaned with relief and said, "I thought I was going to split down the middle. This interning is rough on a man's bladder."

"Hurry up," Dan said.

Noble stepped back. "Your turn." He washed his hands. "Do you know it's two o'clock in the morning?"

"Two o'clock? I have to call Sharon."

Noble sat on one of the stools. "Christ, my feet hurt." He rubbed his calves.

"How did you make out?" Dan said.

"A pneumonia. Two heart failures. A cancer of the gall bladder. A diabetic in coma. Everybody's still alive."

"I lost one," Dan said.

"What was it?"

"An alcoholic with a brain contusion. Maybe a fractured skull."

Noble shook his head. Then he said, "Did you do anybody good?"

"I don't know," Dan said. "Rosenthal gave the family some bullshit about all I did on that old man. I think probably he was starting and stopping by himself." Later he said, "Maybe I got enough Lysol out of that girl to make a difference."

Noble stood up and arched his back. "We've been off call for two hours."

"What's your wife going to say?"

"I'm too tired to care."

Dan searched for a cigarette and found the slip the nurse had given him earlier. He opened it. It said, *Mrs. Wolfe called 10 P.M. and said she would wait up.* He put it back in his pocket. "Let's go back and take another look. Then we can sign out."

He returned to the ward and walked from patient to patient, worrying. He left orders for more blood for the boy. Mr. Barenholtz was still snoring comfortably, the oscilloscope showing a regular rate. The girl was in some pain and he ordered an injection for her.

He and Noble took the elevator down to the garage.

"What time do we start rounds in the morning?" Noble said.

"I guess about eight."

Noble opened the car door and slid across the front seat. He rested before turning the key. "See you tomorrow," he said.

Dan found the Dodge. It filled the garage with a blue cloud when he started the motor. The attendant opened the gate. "Good night, Doctor," he said.

"What? Oh yes. Good night." He turned down Zonal Street, driving home.